W9-BRB-059

CSI:

CRIME SCENE INVESTIGATION™

COMPANION

LEAVE BLANK   CRIMINAL

PERSON FINGERPRINTED

SOCIAL SECURITY NO.
555555555

FIRST NAME, MIDDLE NAME, SUFFIX

DATE OF BIRTH   MM   DD   YY   SEX   RACE   HEIGHT   WEIGHT   EYES   HAIR
2/15/2062 11:2   M

L INDEX

CRIME SCENE DO NOT CROSS CRIME SCENE DO NOT CROSS CRIME SCENE

CSI:
CRIME SCENE INVESTIGATION™
COMPANION

*for Barbara
from

Bob + Aleida

Christmas 2004*

Written by MIKE FLAHERTY

With case files by CORINNE MARRINAN

CSI: CRIME SCENE INVESTIGATION
created by ANTHONY E. ZUIKER

Executive Produced by
JERRY BRUCKHEIMER
CAROL MENDELSOHN
ANN DONAHUE
ANTHONY E. ZUIKER
JONATHAN LITTMAN
DANNY CANNON
CYNTHIA CHVATAL & WILLIAM PETERSEN

POCKET BOOKS
New York   London   Toronto   Sydney

POCKET BOOKS, a division of Simon & Schuster, Inc.
1230 Avenue of the Americas, New York, NY 10020

Copyright © 2004 by CBS Broadcasting Inc. and Alliance Atlantis Productions, Inc.

All rights reserved, including the right to reproduce this book or portions thereof in any form whatsoever.
For information address Pocket Books, 1230 Avenue of the Americas, New York, NY 10020

ISBN: 0-7434-6741-8

First Pocket Books trade paperback edition August 2004

10   9   8   7   6   5   4   3   2   1

POCKET and colophon are registered trademarks of Simon & Schuster, Inc.

Photos by Lorenzo Agius, Richard Berg, Tony Esparza, Bob Greene, Cliff Lipson, Michael Kubeisy, Paul Maples, Spike Nannarello, Robert Voets, Mark Wineman, and Michael Yarish

Case file photography by Ross Elmi and Image/LA

Storyboard art by Angie Robels

Glossary edited by Rich Catalani

Designed by Red Herring Design / NYC

"Alliance Atlantis" and the stylized A design are trademarks of Alliance Atlantis Communications Inc.
Used under license. All rights reserved.

CSI: Crime Scene Investigation is a trademark of CBS Broadcasting Inc.

Manufactured in the United States of America

For information regarding special discounts for bulk purchases, please contact
Simon & Schuster Special Sales at 1-800-456-6798 or business@simonandschuster.com

S VEGAS SEASON ONE: LAS VEGAS SEASON ONE: LAS VEGAS S

10

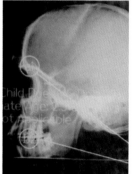

Introduction 8
Anthony E. Zuiker

Pilot 12

Cool Change 16

Crate 'n Burial 19

Pledging Mr. Johnson 24

Friends & Lovers 26

Who Are You? 29

Blood Drops 31
(If These Walls Could Talk)

Anonymous 36

Unfriendly Skies 39

Sex, Lies and Larvae 44

I-15 Murders 47

Fahrenheit 932 50

Boom 53

To Halve and to Hold 58

Table Stakes 61

Too Tough to Die 68

Face Lift 74

$35K O.B.O. 79

Gentle, Gentle 84

Sounds of Silence 90

Justice Is Served 93

Evaluation Day 96

The Strip Strangler 100

104

Burked   106

Chaos Theory   110

Overload   113

Bully for You   118

Scuba Doobie-Doo   121

Alter Boys   124

Caged   129

Slaves of Las Vegas   132

And Then There Were None   135

Ellie   137

Organ Grinder   142

You've Got Male   145

Identity Crisis   148

The Finger   152

Burden of Proof   157

Primum Non Nocere (Icings)   161

Felonius Monk   166

Chasing the Bus   169

Stalker   174

Cats in the Cradle   177

Anatomy of a Lye   180

Cross-Jurisdictions   185

The Hunger Artist   188

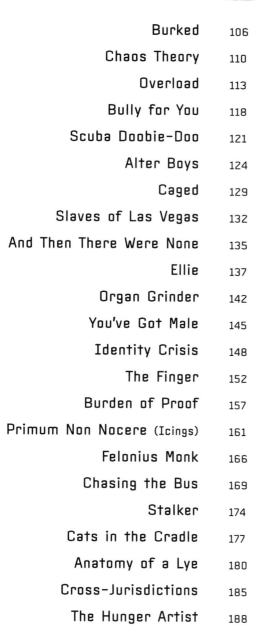

194

Revenge Is Best Served Cold   196

The Accused Is Entitled   201

Let the Seller Beware   205

A Little Murder   208

Abra Cadaver   213

The Execution of Catherine Willows   219

Fight Night   224

Snuff   229

Blood Lust   232

High and Low   235

Recipe for Murder   238

Got Murder?   241

Random Acts of Violence   246

One Hit Wonder   249

Lady Heather's Box   252

Lucky Strike   260

Crash and Burn   264

Precious Metal   268

A Night at the Movies   271

Last Laugh   277

Forever   280

Play With Fire   284

Inside the Box   290

Episode Index   298

Glossary   300

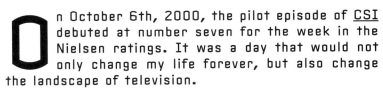

On October 6th, 2000, the pilot episode of <u>CSI</u> debuted at number seven for the week in the Nielsen ratings. It was a day that would not only change my life forever, but also change the landscape of television.

CSI marked many firsts. It was my very first television script. It was also a first for William Petersen, who made his debut in episodic television. Little did we know, at the time, that it would not only have such a profound impact on our lives, but also on so many people around the world.

What drew me to create *CSI* was a very simple statement: "The body is the perfect specimen." I began to think about the notion that blood, hair, saliva, skin, etcetera are forensically designed to tell an investigator what has happened without having any witness to a crime. I found this particularly fascinating, and I'm glad our viewers do, too. (One thing I've discovered about television is that if the audience is learning, then they are watching.)

It takes countless numbers of people to bring this combination of drama and science to the screen. The attention to detail that is paid by our writing staff, technical advisors, and researchers is second to none. I go down to the stages knowing that all of the laboratory equipment decorating our set is authentic and operable. (In actuality, we have better instrumentation on our set than most of the crime labs in America. This is an unfortunate fact that needs to change.)

I want to thank each and every fan for watching our show and for purchasing this book. I dedicate this body of work to the hundreds of crew members who don't receive the credit and recognition that they so dearly deserve. Well, here's to all the long hours and hard work. This book is truly a chronicle of your spirit. Thank you for making *CSI* part of television history.

Enjoy!

—Anthony E. Zuiker

SEASON ONE

WILLIAM PETERSEN as Gil Grissom
MARG HELGENBERGER as Catherine Willows
GARY DOURDAN as Warrick Brown
GEORGE EADS as Nick Stokes
JORJA FOX as Sara Sidle
PAUL GUILFOYLE as Capt. Jim Brass

ORIGINAL AIRDATE: 10/6/00
WRITTEN BY: Anthony E. Zuiker
DIRECTED BY: Danny Cannon

GUEST STARRING

JOHN PYPER-FERGUSON: Mr. Mandalay
HARRISON YOUNG: Judge Cohen
ALLAN RICH: Dr. Gary Klausbach
SUSAN GIBNEY: Charlotte Meridian
ERIC SZMANDA: Greg Sanders
ROYCE APPLEGATE: Mr. Laverty
BARBARA TARBUCK: Paige Harmon
NANCY FISH: Store Owner
GEDRICK TERRELL: Boe Wilson
CHANDRA WEST: Holly Gribbs

L as Vegas at night—in all its neon splendor. Bullets are being loaded into a revolver, accompanied by a chilling voiceover: "My name is Royce Harmon . . . and I'm going to kill myself . . ." A man turns into a room at the end of the hallway, and a lone shot rings out. The street is now awash with light from squad cars. In the cacophony, the arrival of Captain Jim Brass and Gil Grissom seems sedate. Inside, Harmon's body lies in the bathtub, still clasping a gun and swaddled in a sleeping bag. Grissom opens his field kit and notes the man has been dead seven days. Grissom also finds a tape recorder, and listens to the victim's suicide note.

Brass and Grissom play the tape for Royce Harmon's mother and sister. They listen in shock. His mother insists, "That's not my son's voice . . ."

At the crime lab, Holly Gribbs reports for her first night on the job. She meets Grissom, who asks for a pint of her blood. Just starting their shift are CSIs Nick Stokes and Warrick Brown. An avid gambler, Warrick suggests a friendly twenty-dollar bet that one of them will solve their one-hundredth case, thereby earning promotion to CSI 3 by shift's end. Nick confidently accepts. Catherine Willows arrives just as Brass is doling out the assignments. Nick is sent to check out a trick roll; a prostitute has ripped off an incapacitated customer (trick). Catherine joins Warrick, who's been assigned a home invasion involving forced entry and multiple gunshots.

Warrick and Catherine's home invasion has become a homicide by the time they arrive—a grungy-looking corpse lies just inside the front door. The husband explains that, after having thrown out a now-unwelcome houseguest, the drunken freeloader kept pounding on the front door, eventually kicking it in and lunging for him. He shot him in self-defense. Catherine notices that the victim's left shoe is tied differently than his right, and that the husband's got a cut on his bare left toe. She and Warrick are skeptical of his story.

Medical Examiner Doctor Gary Klausbach tells Grissom and Holly that Harmon's death was not suicide. The gore overwhelms Holly, who excuses herself, and runs into an adjoining room to vomit. The door locks behind her. In her distress, she uncovers a particularly gruesome cadaver. Grissom frees the near hysterical rookie, then drops her off at a local convenience store to process a routine robbery.

Nick finds his rolled trick, John Laverty, groggy and ashamed in his hotel room. The call girl took his wallet

Scrutinize the scene, collect the evidence, and re-create what happened without ever being there.

and his wedding ring. Laverty doesn't think his drink was drugged, but Nick notices a discoloration on his lips and takes a swab for processing. There's nothing readable on the swab.

Warrick puts a hair from the home invasion under the microscope and finds the entire pulp of its follicle attached, suggesting a struggle. When pressed, the

PILOT

We've got a killer out there who's "proficient" in forensics.

homeowner admits that there was an altercation during which he stepped on the victim's sneaker, pulling it off. He shot him in self-defense, panicked, and tied the sneaker back on. Warrick relates this explanation to Grissom, who is in the middle of blunt-force trauma experiment involving a golf club, a mannequin's head, and the pint of Holly's blood. Grissom reminds Warrick to "concentrate on what cannot lie—the evidence." This leads Warrick back to the sneaker, and to take a closer look inside, which turns up a toenail shard.

The convenience store owner rails at Holly, frustrated over departmental procedures requiring her to stay closed. She underscores her point by pulling a gun. Catherine, who has just arrived, manages to confiscate the gun. Catherine and Holly take a lunch break, where Holly admits to Catherine that she only took the job because her police officer mother pressured her.

Meanwhile, Nick gets a call to check on a young woman found passed out behind the wheel of her car. When the "working girl" comes to, he finds no suggestion of criminal activity, but he sends her to the hospital.

Believing Warrick's errant toenail a forensic reach, Brass refuses his request to ask for a warrant. Convinced that the toenail holds the key to the case, Warrick goes over Brass's head. He pays a late-night visit to Judge Cohen, who's familiar with Warrick's sports-betting habit. He agrees to issue a blank warrant in return for a tip. The judge gives Warrick five thousand dollars to place a bet for him.

Lab Tech Charlotte Meridian shows Grissom that a fingerprint on Harmon's tape recorder contains red latex flakes laced with lecithin, a common ingredient in cooking sprays. Grissom asks, "If latex rubber and cooking spray went on a blind date, how would the night end?" to which Charlotte replies, "A lot better than ours did."

A match on the latex-and-lecithin print leads to Paul Millander, a local wholesaler of Halloween novelties. He readily admits that the print could be his—he used his own hand in manufacturing his best-selling item, a rubber hand. Harmon's killer might be some-

one with a knowledge of forensics, but it could be any one of the ten thousand people who bought the gag hands.

Nick is called to the hospital by a Doctor Leever who notes that six "pros" have shown up in the last two nights—all having been knocked mysteriously unconscious, all featuring skin discoloration on their nipples. One of the most recent arrivals is the woman from the car accident. Nick offers her a choice: Tell him what the girls are using for their exotic knockout drops, and give Laverty back his belongings, and she won't be charged with attempted murder. She hands over an eyedrop bottle of scopolamine, an anti-motion sickness drug.

A young sexual-abuse victim brings Catherine to the hospital. Catherine has her look at at diagram of the human body and tell her where she'd been touched, after which the girl tells Catherine to take her doll, to make sure the same thing doesn't happen to her. Catherine is so shaken, she takes a midshift break to go home and tell her daughter, Lindsey, how much she loves her.

HALLOWEIRD

Here comes the nerd squad.

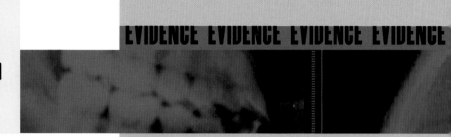

14

News of Warrick's end-run reaches Brass, who retaliates by taking him off the "toenail case" and assigning him to baby-sit Holly. Exasperated, Warrick leaves with Holly to oversee her processing of a home-robbery. At the scene, Warrick spots a patrol car and tells Holly he's got an errand to run. He heads to a sports book where he mistakenly places Judge Cohen's bet on the wrong team.

Warrant in hand, Grissom visits the home invasion scene, telling the husband he needs to give him a pedicure. When he says he's just cut his toenails and flushed the clippings down the toilet, Grissom returns with an ALS (alternative light source), which emits an ultraviolet beam capable of picking up objects and substances invisible to the naked eye. It reveals a nail fragment. Its striations—the ridged grooves left behind after the nail's severing—match those on the clipping found in the victim's sneaker.

Warrick shows up to watch the husband being led from the house in handcuffs. The husband had shot the unwanted housguest in cold blood. He then donned the victim's left sneaker and planted a few healthy kicks in the door to support the version of events he'd told the police. Grissom asks how Holly's doing, and Warrick blithely assures him that she's fine.

Holly is busy dusting the home-robbery scene when a man claiming to be a neighbor enters. He mentions that he just saw the cop car leave and asks if everything is okay. She assures him the situation is under control. But as Holly turns around to get back to work, the man reaches into his back pocket and pulls out a gun.

As the team celebrates Nick's promotion to CSI 3, Brass interrupts to tell them that Holly has been shot. He immediately puts Warrick on administrative leave pending a full investigation.

As a rule, television pilots are busy affairs, charged with the responsibility of introducing an entire cast of characters, their relationships, and the world in which they exist. In addition CSI's pilot relates three storylines—a pseudo-suicide, a trick-roll, and the murder of the drunken boarder—and plants the seeds for a number of continuing plot points—Warrick's gambling problem, Judge Cohen's blackmail scheme, Grissom's inept romancing, the investigation into Holly's shooting, Nick's relationship with Kristy Hopkins, and the ingenious Paul Millander.

"If you're going to write a pilot, you need to throw everything but the kitchen sink into it," says CSI Creator/Executive Producer Anthony Zuiker, adding that the multiple storylines was both intentional and an attempt at verisimilitude. "When I did the research for the show at the crime lab in Las Vegas, the first thing I noticed was that they will go to five or six crime scenes a night." Zuiker's determination to hit as many plot and character notes led to one of the pilot's more curious moments, Catherine's visit with her daughter.

It's like watching a sunset.

He recalls, "That beat was put there to underscore Catherine Willows as a single mother."

One tantalizing scene that never made it from script to screen portrayed Catherine and Nick as secret lovers. The scene was shot, then deemed unusable because of technical problems but mostly because it didn't feel right. "We're one scene away from not being the show we are today," observes Zuiker. "The performances were really good, but what you really have to look at in a pilot, in a series, is protecting your characters, having the audience learn along with you," says Executive Producer Carol Mendelsohn. "We didn't know Catherine or Nick well enough to suddenly understand that they were having a relationship at work." The edit, recalls Marg Helgenberger, was ". . . the right thing to do. I haven't given that scene much thought," she laughs. "Only from time to time, when George jokes about it, 'Hey guys, I made out with her in the pilot.'" For his part, Eads playfully asserts, "I'm still fighting for that to come back."

Another early excision was the character of Boe Wilson, the college intern featured in two brief scenes. Including the UNLV student, says Zuiker, was an attempt to "go young" but ultimately, he reflects, "The character just didn't feel right for the fabric of the show." "Pilot" also features the lone appearance of Doctor Gary Klausbach, the grizzled medical examiner played by Allan Rich.

If CSI's debut didn't look like anything else on television at the time, it's because of its two stylistic architects, Zuiker and Director Danny Cannon. Both were newcomers to the medium, having worked exclusively in feature films. Fortuitously, that was exactly what Executive Producer Jerry Bruckheimer was looking for. As CSI Executive Producer Jonathan Littman recalls, "It was critical that CSI aspire to big-screen values. This was a story that was going to be told visually as much as it was going to be told in words." Cannon recalls being contacted by Bruckheimer, the man behind big-screen spectacles like Top Gun, Armageddon, and Pearl Harbor. "Jerry wanted to maintain his cinematic vision on television and I'm not sure if he knew it was possible. I didn't know if it was possible. I approached the pilot as a feature film, with feature film coverage, the way we went about designing it, casting it, the attention to detail, the attention to post-production."

Cannon says, "We went the most complicated and the difficult route we could because it was always the most dynamic."

Also raising the stakes for the prospective series was its departure from conventional law enforcement drama. "This is not a cop show," Cannon says. "I didn't have macho guys chasing after each other and having all the answers." That contrast is most pronounced in the character Gil Grissom, embodied by William Petersen who was cast against his usual type.

For the show to be of a piece, Cannon says, that textual realism needed to extend all the way to the autopsy room. "I needed an attention to detail which really left me no option but to actually go inside the body." He remembers coming across a bit of Zuiker's stage direction in the pilot script which indicated: We track the bullet inside the victim. Cannon says, "I took Anthony literally and followed the path of the bullet with a camera." Zuiker points out, "We wanted to create a point of view that we'd never seen before in television—to see what a bullet looks like when it goes into a body. Danny figured out a way to use a periscope lens and bring it down into a body. He set the visual tone for the show." Thus, the CSI forensic shot was born.

"Everyone will tell you that flashbacks are a writer's lazy way of getting information across," Jonathan Littman points out, "but we determined that our flashbacks weren't that." In CSI's use of the technique, Zuiker says, "You see tiny alterations in every flashback until the final piece of evidence is put into place in Act 4, and then that flashback contains an alteration that makes you go 'Ah, that's what happened!'"

The finishing touch was Zuiker's decision to obtain the rights to use The Who's "Who Are You?" as CSI's theme song. Producer Cynthia Chvatal sent a copy of the pilot to the group's legendary songwriter and guitarist Pete Townshend. As Zuiker recalls, "He loved it."

According to Cannon, more than a few people felt that the pilot was too dark, moved too quickly, and that its dense, technical verbiage demanded too much of the average viewer. That conventional wisdom was quickly repudiated, however, after a rave pair of test screenings.

"We did not treat the audience like idiots. We actually said you're super-intelligent, you're gonna get every detail. And they did," Cannon recalls, looking back. ∎

COOL CHANGE

A bedraggled, but determined, man is pumping coins into the Hotel Monaco's Giga-Millions slot machine, believing this time he will win. He steps away and a tourist, Jamie Smith, goads her boyfriend, Ted Sallenger, into taking what turns out to be the forty-million dollar pull. Upgraded to the presidential suite, Sallenger tells Jamie to get lost. The next thing we hear is a knock on the door, "Room service." Sallenger's body lies splattered on the pavement. Grissom is immediately suspicious, noting that Sallenger was wearing glasses at the time of his death.

The fallout from Holly Gribbs's shooting rains down at the lab. Captain Brass is busted back to Homicide and Grissom is put in charge of the night shift. He announces that he's bringing in Sara Sidle, a friend from San Francisco, to handle the internal investigation into Warrick's apparent misconduct.

Doctor Jenna Williams points out shards of black glass in Sallenger's forearms are indicative of defensive wounds. Grissom and Nick found a broken champagne bottle at the hotel. Jamie is brought in for questioning and admits that she cut Ted but that he left and never returned. Her story doesn't match

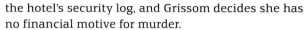

ORIGINAL AIRDATE: 10/13/00
WRITTEN BY: Anthony E. Zuiker
DIRECTED BY: Michael Watkins

GUEST STARRING

TIM DEZARN: Red Carlton
ELLEN CRAWFORD: Lt. Jane Gribbs
JOHNNY MESSNER: Ted Sallenger
HARRISON YOUNG: Judge Cohen
JUDITH SCOTT: Dr. Jenna Williams
TIMILEE ROMOLINI: Jamie Smith
CHANDRA WEST: Holly Gribbs

the hotel's security log, and Grissom decides she has no financial motive for murder.

On the Monaco's roof, Nick notices a gritty substance clinging to his pants. Grissom tells him it's Myer's Roof Dust, used to deflect the sun's rays. Grissom then conducts "Operation Norman"—named for three dummies, to determine whether Sallenger fell, jumped, or was pushed. Emerging from the crowd, Sara Sidle marvels at the old-fashioned technique. Grissom concludes, "This guy was pushed."

Taken aback by Catherine's frosty welcome, Sara suggests they work Holly's case together. Sara asks where she might find Warrick; Catherine directs her to one of his haunts on Blue Diamond Road. Grissom and Nick watch a videotape of the action around the Giga-Millions machine near the time of Sallenger's big win and discover that Red Carlton had been there for over eleven hours. Grissom finds Carlton back at the slots. Noticing roof-dust stains on his pants, he has Carlton placed under arrest for conspiracy to commit murder.

Having placed Judge Cohen's wager on the wrong team, Warrick now owes the judge ten thousand dollars and has an hour to come up with it. Fortunately, he's winning at blackjack when Sara finds him. Warrick tells her that he left to get coffee on the night of Holly's murder, unworried because there was an officer present. Sara informs him that Holly Gribbs died on the operating table twenty minutes ago.

Ballistics Tech Bobby Dawson tells Catherine that Holly was shot with her own gun. A lead emerges when a pager Catherine found at the scene rings. She manages to convice its owner that it would be worth it to meet her.

Carlton admits he had drinks with Sallenger, but he didn't kill him. After a couple hours of boozing, Carlton claims he went up to the roof alone, planning to end it all, but changed his mind.

At the Three Aces Motel, Brass and LVPD uniforms burst in on Jerrod Cooper, the pager's owner. As he's put in cuffs, Catherine notices a nasty scratch on his

> ## It's our job to know stuff nobody else knows...

cheek. She goes to the morgue to collect epithelials from under Holly's nails.

While Nick and Grissom find no roof dust on Sallenger's shoes, they do find fibers on the stem of his watch. Doctor Williams then shows Grissom a diamond-shaped contusion in Sallenger's skull; this is what killed him, then he was pushed. Nick returns to the suite and finds a brass candlestick with a large diamond shape on one side. He then applies Leuko Crystal Violet to the ground on the balcony, which reveals a large bloodstain along with prints of a hand and two knees. Jamie sits in interrogation while Grissom puts the pieces together. After leaving Carlton, Sallenger returned to the suite where Jamie hit him with the candlestick. She then dragged him toward the balcony, his watch collecting carpet fibers along the way, and heaved him over the edge. She's placed under arrest.

Greg tells Catherine and Sara that Cooper's DNA matches the epithelials beneath Holly's nails. They struggled, Cooper grabbed her weapon and shot her. But Holly, finding his pager, managed to hide it beneath the couch and leave CSI a clue.

Warrick returns to the lab to talk with Grissom, who says he'll have to let him go for violating procedures. Warrick comes clean about his whereabouts. Realizing he just can't do it, Grissom lets Warrick keep his job. "I already lost one good person today," he says, "I don't want to lose another."

18

"**Cool Change**" introduces a new character: **Sara Sidle played by Jorja Fox.** Unfortunately, Sara's addition to the team came at the price of Holly Gribbs. William Petersen recalls that although Holly's shooting had been written into the pilot the plan was for her to recover during "Cool Change." When the decision was made to recast, it put Zuiker in a strange and uncomfortable position. "I was this new television writer who was now going to kill a character . . . and also convince an actress to come in and be killed."

Fox remembers the one-paragraph description on her audition sheet: "She is a forensic scientist and a criminalist, she is driven, she is very adventurous, she is wild, she could drink anyone under the table." Most presciently, it noted that "she knows her stuff, but her social skills really aren't up to par." That personality defect suggests a kinship with Grissom, but the exact nature of his and Sara's relationship was left unexplained. "So far, we've never gone any deeper into how we knew each other," Fox notes. "The first theory was that we'd had some type of love-interest background. The second theory was that he appeared somewhere where I had studied, and we'd gotten to know each other." Petersen says he and Fox favor the latter scenario. "Our idea of a backstory is that I met her up at a convention in San Francisco—one of those two-week workshops that Grissom does periodically."

Holly's death was also responsible for a couple of other major personnel changes—Brass's transfer back to Homicide, and Grissom's subsequent promotion to supervisor. In real life, Vegas's Crime Lab is presided over by a high-ranking member of the Las Vegas Police Department. Paul Guilfoyle explains, "As an actor, I was hoping the depiction of law enforcement would be more collaborative." He felt Brass being in charge of the CSIs but not actually being one of them created two distinctive groups. Executive Producer Carol Mendelsohn agreed, "We realized, 'Where are you going to take that? Where was Brass headed?' That's why we decided to make him a detective."

With Brass's position redefined, it was then time to do something about his crotchety disposition, most evident in his scorching confrontations with Warrick and Holly in "Pilot." Petersen recalls that he and Guilfoyle were taken aback by the captain's intolerance and anger. "We were like, 'Why does he have this stick up his ass?'" As a result, a more humane Brass emerges from "Cool Change," a colleague who stands side by side with the CSIs, sharing in their defeats and victories.

A dedication appears at the end of "Cool Change" reading: "In memory of Owen Wolf, 1971–2000." He was a production assistant who was killed in the crossfire of an armored car robbery while picking up supplies for the show. ■

ORIGINAL AIRDATE: 10/20/00
WRITTEN BY: Ann Donahue
DIRECTED BY: Danny Cannon

CRATE'N BURIAL

GUEST STARRING

JOHN BEASLEY: Charles Moore
ERICH ANDERSON: Jack Garas
JOLENE BLALOCK: Laura Garas
HAMILTON VON WATTS: Chip Rundle
SAMUEL L. JONES III: James Moore
JUDITH SCOTT: Dr. Jenna Williams
JOHN LIVINGSTON: THD

Laura Garas is buried alive, screaming for help. A recorded message instructs, "Bring two million in hundreds to Charleston and Third in three hours or your wife dies. Stop me from taking the money, she still dies." At the Garas home, Brass attempts to dissuade Laura's husband, Jack, from paying the ransom, while Grissom and Nick scrutinize the message for clues. Observing a gap of utter silence and a low-frequency buzzing sound, they speculate that Laura's buried in the desert near power lines. Sara does a walk-through at the site of the apparent abduction. There are "points of disturbance" everywhere—all of which point to a struggle. When Grissom joins her, he notices dirt on the bedroom carpet. Checking outside, a sweet scent draws them to a kerchief lying on the ground, seemingly doused in halothane—a liquid anesthetic.

Catherine and Warrick are assigned a disturbing hit-and-run of a young girl, Renda Harris. Finding only a common car-paint scrape on the girl's scooter, they return to the lab, where Doctor Williams shows them on the body a partial license plate number visible in a bruise. An analysis of the dirt from the

There. Half meters below the surface.
Got to be suffocating.

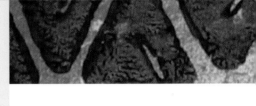

20

Garas home reveals traces of gold and cyanide. Grissom explains that miners use cyanide powder to help gold leech up to the surface. He and Sara take off in a helichopper for the three nearest sites that fit the bill.

Unable to dissuade Jack Garas from paying the ransom, Brass trails him to the drop site, where Garas heaves a gym bag into a trash can. When a young man in a baseball cap eventually retrieves it, the police converge.

Simultaneously, Grissom and Sara scour the desert with a forward-looking-infrared camera. They spot the glowing image of a writhing body underground. Frantically, they dig until Laura is unearthed.

A hit on the partial license plate number brings Catherine and Warrick to the home of Charles Moore, a gentlemanly seventy-three-year-old. Although he claims his car was stolen, a search reveals it's in the garage. Moore confesses that he was behind the wheel. He spotted Renda in the middle of the road, went to hit the brake, and instead stepped on the accelerator.

When Grissom interviews Laura Garas at the hospital, she only recalls being grabbed from behind in the hallway of her home. The last thing she remembered was something being clamped over her mouth. Laura can't remember anything about her assailant. Grissom asks for a DNA sample to check the duct tape that was used to muzzle her and to use while examining the truck belonging to the man caught at the ransom drop-off site, Chip Rundle, Jack Garas's personal trainer.

Brass informs Rundle that his prints have been found on Laura Garas's makeshift coffin. Rundle

If you want to go fast, go slow.

explains that he helped Jack move crates. Rundle is released, but Brass has recorded the interrogation for comparison with the ransom message.

Warrick and Catherine examine Moore's car. They notice the driver's seat is pushed too close for his height and the car radio is set to blast a hip-hop station. They ask Moore if anyone else drives his car, just as his grandson, James, enters. Mister Moore admits that after hitting Renda, he'd banged his head. James drove him home. Neither of the CSIs believe his story.

The AV lab has just matched Rundle's voice with that on the ransom message. Sara asks Grissom to help her reconstruct Laura's abduction after finding hair strands in the front passenger seat of Rundle's truck. She notes that fibers from the seat's sheepskin cover were found on the back of Laura's sleeves, which could only have happened if she was sitting normally. A blood test proves that Laura never ingested the halothane. Brass enters, saying Rundle now wants to make a deal, but Grissom nixes the idea. He knows what Rundle has to offer . . . Laura Garas, his accomplice.

Taking a closer look at Charles Moore's car, Catherine retrieves a small piece of a tooth embedded in the leather covering of the steering wheel. When they ask to see his teeth he plucks out an entire plate of dentures. James is arrested and Charles is freed. A sympathetic Warrick accompanies James and offers advice before he's taken into custody.

Laura strenuously denies any relationship with Rundle. Sara claims they staged the abduction as part of a plan to run away together with a chunk of Jack's fortune. To drive the case home, Nick plays three versions of the ransom recording. The final and the most damning isolates the previously inaudible sound of Laura saying, "Hurry up, Chip!" As Laura is taken away, an angry Jack Garas asks Grissom why she didn't just give Rundle up. "Self-preservation," Grissom explains. "If she rats on him, she rats on herself."

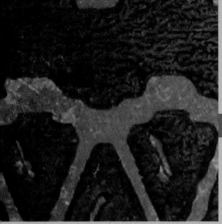

"Crate 'N Burial" is the first episode to contain a bit of whimsy right in its title—a punning sendup of the popular housewares chain, Crate and Barrel. However, "Crate 'N Burial" is most noteworthy as an early look at the interpersonal relationships of the principle characters.

One telling moment occurs when Grissom joins Nick and they discover that the voice on the ransom tape is Chip Rundle's. Grissom tells Nick he has more work to do before they can take Rundle into custody, and walks out. When Nick asks, "What'd I do wrong?" A senior tech replies, "I'm not going to spoil Grissom's fun. This is how he teaches all you guys." As Carol Mendelsohn points out, Grissom's treatment of Nick is in direct contrast to his hands-off treatment of the other CSIs. "I think Warrick is Grissom's favorite. With Nick, he really is the demanding parent. Grissom's mentor-mentee relationship with Nick is to constantly push him." William Petersen laughs at the observation. "That's pretty much how I am with George Eads. Some of this stuff is just bleedover from the way we are with each other."

That same art-imitates-life dynamic explains Warrick's and Catherine's remarkable partnership. "I feel most connected to her certainly," Gary Dourdan admits. When the truth of the Harris hit-and-run is discovered, Catherine suggests a less ethical but more humane conclusion—letting Charles Moore take the rap for his grandson. "It's Catherine who feels bad for the old man, and Warrick doesn't," Dourdan recalls. "It's those great juxtapositions—of our social lives as characters, as coworkers—those questionable places, those no-way-out situations . . . That's conflict, that's drama to me."

After Grissom and Nick excitedly display the birthday gifts they bought for Catherine's daughter, Lindsey, Sara asks innocently enough, "How long do I have to be here before I have to start kicking in for gifts?" Catherine cooly answers, "When the spirit moves you." Donahue observes "Catherine wanted to protect her lair; she was not going to make friends with her before she knew what Sara was worth." Jorja Fox is also pleased that the friction went no further. "Marg and I said very early on we didn't want to play that woman-to-woman kind of tension."

"You can't talk about *CSI* without Catherine Willows," says Carol Mendelsohn. "If Grissom's the soul of the show, she's the heart." If that heart's been hardened a bit, says Ann Donahue, it's only served to make her stronger. "Catherine knows you can't change the world, so she's decided she's going to make *her* world good, and nothing's going to break her heart," she says. "She won't allow it, because she has to be strong for her daughter." That pragmatism, Donahue explains, was crucial to the character's motivation. "It was really important that people understood that Catherine Willows was a working mom—a counterpoint to Grissom, who does this because he's a scientist. She does this because she's good at it, and it pays the bills.

"Crate 'N Burial" also contains hints of Sara's and Grissom's attraction to each other. As they work the abduction scene, Grissom counters Sara's off-hand remark about being his "star pupil" with, "That was a seminar. This is the real world." There is a subtle subtext to the entire exchange that leads the viewer to believe, that along with the crime scene, there is more here between the two than can be seen at first look. The writers assert that the flirtation was not a conscious one. However, Petersen believes that sparks were aways there. ■

Patient's Record

GIL GRISSOM
DOB
Place of Birth
Height
Weight
Eyes
Marital Status
Education

Specialization

08/17/1956
Santa Monica, CA
5'10"
180
Blue
Single
B.S. Biology, magna cum laude
Ph. D. Biology UCLA
Entomology

1972   'Unofficial' Intern Los Ang
1986   Body Farm
1987   Recruit

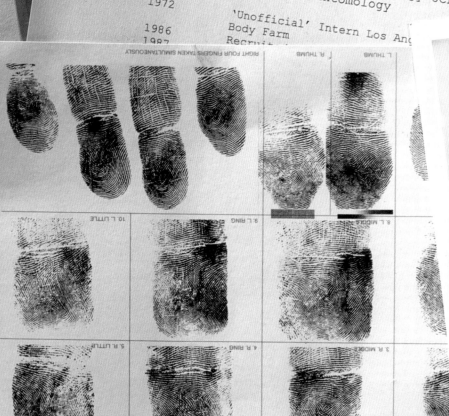

LAS VEGAS POLICE DEPARTMENT - SUPPLEMENTARY REPORT

Gil Grissom was born in Los Angeles to a strong-willed, artistic mother and a preoccupied businessman father. Grissom's mother was afflicted with ostosclerosis, a genetic condition which rendered her completely deaf shortly after the birth of her only child. The parents divorced when Grissom was five years old and his mother went to work in a local art gallery, often taking her son with her during business hours. He partially attributes this environment to his appreciation for beauty and fine things. Growing up in a deaf household, Grissom communicated with his mother using sign language. He shared his mother's love of reading, devouring every volume in their library from Ian Fleming to Shakespeare.

Grissom attended Mass with his mother every Sunday and the naturally inquisitive boy, faith without fact was a problem of logic. At an early age, he found himself questioning the scientific validity of the accounts he would read about in the Bible. He was, however, able to take away many lessons of humanity and behavior from his religious studies.

Fascinated with creatures great and small, a typical activity for the inquisitive schoolboy would be observing his ant farm or performing makeshift autopsies on roadkill. Inspired by the intricacies of nature, Grissom had an innate admiration for the complex machine that makes up animals and insects.

During Junior High, Grissom became friendly with neighborhood cops and began to hang around the local precinct after school. He met a renowned criminalist named Dr. Philip Gerard who took the boy on as an "unofficial intern" at the LA County morgue when he was sixteen. Seeing something special in him, Gerard convinced Grissom's mother to accelerate him through the remainder of high school so he could begin advanced studies at UCLA where Gerard was a professor.

An awkward teenager, he lived the same ghostlike existence at UCLA that he did in high school and put every waking moment into his studies and experiments. He often took a untraditional approach to his education, creating independent studies for himself, like going to boxing matches to examine blood spatter patterns, or mastering poker in order to finance his first body farm.

After earning his PhD in Biology from UCLA at the age of twenty-two, Grissom found he was eager to get out of the classroom and into the field. He took an entry-level position with the Las Vegas Crime lab and advanced through the steps to a CSI Level 3 only two years later. Over the next decade, the impressive success ratio of arrests to convictions by the Vegas Crime Lab won them the second highest rated crime lab in the nation. There was no question that this honor had much to do with the skill of Gil Grissom and his crack team of investigators. Grissom had gained enough leverage to battle the constant threat of budgetary cuts that would deny the lab the staff and cutting edge technology it requires.

A private man by nature, Grissom cherishes his autonomous existence. He's happy left to his books, his experiments and his thoughts. Being one of only fifteen forensic entomologists residing in the United States, he makes time for travel in order to lecture and conduct seminars. The element of perfectionism in everything he does also makes him expect much of others. He is an adamant believer that there is always more to learn.

Dr. GRISSOM, Gil
supervisor/CSI Level 3

CONFIDENTIAL

REQUESTED BY		STAR	APPROVED BY	RANK		STAR	REFER TO

	(94)ADJ. CODE	(95) BATCH NO.	(96) BATCH DATE	(97) INTERMED. NO.	(98) AMOUNT REIMBURSED	(99) DATE RECEIVED	
TI							UB-16 CHA-5 (REV 7-78)

1 COPY NO. ONE 1

.258 00.56.52 0459 0072 0

> purge{hiMem} b
echo nf pur

24

GUEST STARRING

JIM ORTLIEB: Winston Barger
VYTO RUGINIS: Phil Swelco
MARK FAMIGLIETTI: Matt Daniels
CRAIG ALLEN WOLF: Kyle Travis
HARRISON YOUNG: Judge Cohen
GRANT HESLOV: Dr. James Corbett
ERIC SZMANDA: Greg Sanders
JUDITH SCOTT: Dr. Jenna Williams
AMY COLLETT: Marti

O n Lake Mead, a pair of night fishermen make a most unwelcome catch: a human leg wearing a red high-heeled shoe. Arriving at the scene, Catherine finds Grissom already at work. He wonders what someone clad in three-inch pumps was doing here at the lake.

Nick and Sara are called to a dead body at the University of Las Vegas campus. They're greeted at a fraternity house by Matt Daniels, who leads them upstairs, where the body of a failed pledge, James Johnson, hangs from a ceiling beam but there's no sucide note.

Doctor Williams explains to Catherine that the leg was lopped off—postmortem—just as Grissom enters with a gurney bearing the body that "goes with" it. They successfully identify the victim: Wendy Barger. She had been in the water for two days, yet her husband,

So what do you think? Drowning?

Winston, had not reported her missing. A rape kit on her came back positive for semen, and there are signs of a struggle. The husband says that Wendy would take an occasional solo holiday. He claims that they hadn't been intimate in three or four months. The seminal DNA from Wendy Barger doesn't match her husband's.

When Warrick arrives at the county courthouse to testify in one of his cases, he's met by Judge Cohen. He demands Warrick tamper with a piece of evidence, compromising the chain of custody, causing the case to be dismissed. Just before Warrick is about to sign for the evidence, Grissom shows up with the news that Warrick has been promoted to CSI 3.

Doctor James Corbett tells Nick and Sara that James Johnson died of asphyxiation but he cannot verify that he hung himself. The doctor points out that's there's writing on Johnson's penis. At the frat house, Kyle Travis admits that James was behind in points. He claims he was offered a chance to catch up by going to sorority row and getting "signed." However, James was found signing himself, he was humiliated and dropped from the pledges.

A closer forensic look at Wendy Barger shows contusions with lime-green wood splinters, and that she did not drown. Wendy's stomach contents show that her last meal was fried calamari. According to Grissom, there is the only one restaurant within ten miles of the marina that serves calamari. A waitress recognizes Wendy from a photograph, saying she was in recently with a regular, Phil Swelco. They find Swelco, who admits to a relationship with Wendy. After they'd made love, she left in his outboard to return to the marina. Grissom and Catherine are confronted by the frustrated husband, who asks if Swelco was involved in Wendy's death. They assure him they will keep him informed.

The preliminary report indicates that Johnson was choked by a strip of raw calf's liver that had unidentified microscopic threads embedded in it. Travis eventually confesses that Johnson had been fed the liver as part of his initiation and had started choking. After unsuccessfully attempting the Heimlich maneuver, Daniels strung him up from the rafter to make it look like suicide. Travis is taken into custody.

Doctor Corbett quickly discredits Travis's story: if Johnson had been Heimliched, there'd likely be a

JOHNSON

ORIGINAL AIRDATE: 10/27/00
WRITTEN BY: Josh Berman & Anthony E. Zuiker
DIRECTED BY: Richard J. Lewis

broken rib or bruising, but there's nothing. He then shows them a magnification of James's "private" inscription: Jill W. and two Greek deltas. A visit to UNLV's Delta house turns up a Jill Wentworth, who admits to signing James's penis. When pressed she reveals that Kyle Travis is her boyfriend. Sara and Nick search Johnson's room, finding a piece of string with a small bloody noose at the end.

With Swelco's outboard missing, Grissom constructs an elaborate miniature reconstruction of the lake in the CSI garage. Catherine takes a different approach and walks the shoreline. Finally, Catherine spots the outboard in a tangle of reeds and phones Grissom at the lab, who's just come to the same conclusion.

Warrick sets up a meeting with Judge Cohen. He tells the judge he's skittish about proceeding with their plan. Cohen assures him, "You break the seal on the evidence box, it's over . . ." Warrick raises his thumb and Brass arrests Cohen.

Swelco is brought in for questioning. Unfortunately, Winston Barger is in the hallway, and again asks Catherine about Swelco's involvement. Reluctantly, she tells him about his wife's infidelity.

Daniels finally comes clean to Sara. James Johnson humiliated him by showing Wentworth's signature to the entire house. Johnson could still join the frat if he passed one more challenge—the "dingle dangle"—of swallowing calf's liver, which was attached to the string, and letting Travis pull it back out again. When James started choking, Travis watched as he died. Daniels walked in and saw what had happened. Travis swore him to secrecy. Travis is charged with murder.

Back in the CSI garage, Grissom asks Catherine to get into the boat and start the engine. Catherine yanks on the engine's rip cord repeatedly, failing to start it, while making her shoulder sore. Grissom explains Swelco's boat ran out of gas. Trying desperately to restart it, Wendy dislocated her shoulder, lost her balance, banged her head on the craft's edge and fell into the water, unconscious. A propeller of a passing boat severed her leg. The CSIs go to Swelco's house, finding the front door ajar. Inside they find Winston Barger who sits staring into space, a gun in his hand. Swelco lies dead. Catherine informs the grief-stricken husband that Wendy's death was an accident.

"**P**ledging Mr. Johnson" marks the debut of director Richard Lewis. "Directors have a tremendous amount of autonomy on this show," Lewis says. I think one of the reasons I landed here is that I've always made my television episodes into short films."

According to writer Josh Berman, geography was a major consideration in the plot's construction. "We wanted to center around Lake Mead, and we wanted to create a real mystery, not even knowing the identity of the victim at first," he says. "It was the first time a limb was forensically examined to determine whether the victim was alive or dead when the body part was severed."

"I'd been wanting forever to reference Sherlock Holmes," William Petersen says of his ad-lib concluding the episode's teaser sequence. "I said, He's got to look at Catherine and say, 'Well, Watson, the game's afoot.'" When objections were raised that the line may be too campy, Petersen insisted, "That's the sense of irony that the show needs."

We also learn more about the nature of Grissom's and Catherine's relationship. Catherine tells Grissom, "When Eddie was cheating on me, I sure wish somebody would've said something." When Grissom says, "You mean me?" Berman says the implication is clear, "Grissom knew about the affair but kept quiet because he's not a people person and he figured the best place for the outsider is to stay on the outside." When, against her boss's wishes, Catherine tells Barger the truth, a more heated confrontation ensues which spotlights the pair's wildly contrasting work and lifestyles. "I just think that Billy and I work really well together," explains Marg Helgenberger. "There's a good chemistry between us for a lot of reasons I can't really explain—his personality, my personality, and who the two characters are." ■

So Watson, the game's afoot.

ORIGINAL AIRDATE: 11/3/00
WRITTEN BY: Andrew Lipsitz
DIRECTED BY: Lou Antonio

26

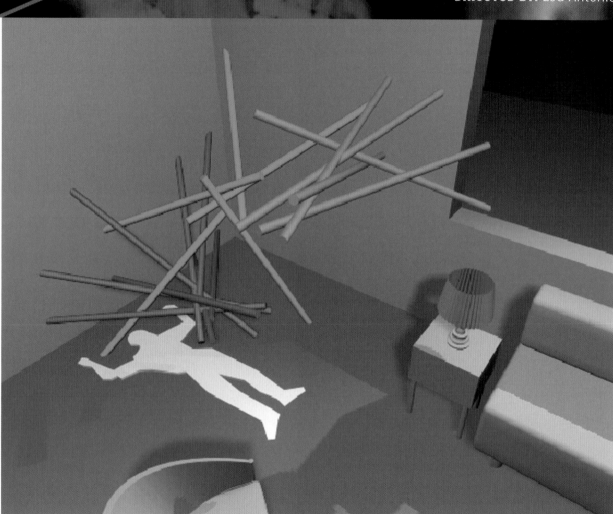

The voids mean one thing. Kate Armstrong was lying.

A naked teenage male runs frantically through the desert night; his entire being suggesting flight from an unknown terror. He's long dead now — the maggots habitating on his corpse make that clear to Grissom. Based on footprints, he was looking back as he ran. Warrick asks, "Do you want to call it?" Grissom answer, "Fear. Someone chased this kid to death."

It's Dumpster-diving time for Sara. A dead female has been found wrapped in plastic. Once the victim is removed Sara notes a strange glaze-like substance on her face. Assistant Medical Examiner David Phillips identifies the substance as biotone arterial, a chemical used by morticians. Her prints identify her as Stephanie Reyes, who was laid to rest last week.

Catherine and Nick are sent to the Verbum Dei Charter School. Its dean, Vernon Woods, is dead in his office from blunt-force trauma to his head and a stone paperweight is lying nearby. The school's founder, Kate Armstrong, has already admitted to hitting Woods — once — in self-defense. Having seen the long, arcing pattern of the blood spray, Catherine tells Nick she's lying. There were multiple impacts and a single blow wouldn't have produced any blood.

Grissom and Brass are talking with seventeen-year-old Bobby Taylor, who filed a missing persons report on Eric Berkley. He says they went to a party out at Red Rock four days ago, but Bobby says he then lost track of Eric around midnight. Taken to the morgue, he iden-

FRIENDS & LOVERS

tifies the body as Eric's. Warrick informs Grissom that an analysis of the maggots reveals jimsonweed—a highly dangerous hallucinogenic drug. Bobby admits that somebody at the rave had sold them jimsonweed tea, insisting it was not a drug and would be a "cool high." The CSIs decide to visit the next rave, hoping Bobby can point out the dealer.

Knowing Kate Armstrong's story was "heavy on b.s." Catherine and Nick "string" the office. They determine that the dean was killed exactly where they found the body, but notice a void, meaning a third party must have been present.

Sara speaks with a very jittery mortician, Randy Gesek, who says the body may have been stolen. The Reyes grave is opened and, as she suspected, it's empty. On a visit to Gesek's casket-display room, Sara's lint roller picks up different people's hair strands from a display coffin's interior.

When pressed, Kate Armstrong admits there was another person in the office, Julia Eastman, her friend and colleague. Eastman explains that Armstrong wanted her there as a witness to Woods's harassment. She says that Kate was telling the truth. He backed her against the wall, she struck him, and blood sprayed all over her blouse. Nick shows her a computer schematic, based on the stringing patterns, it shows that the fatal blow had to have occurred when Woods was on the floor.

Warrick learns Eric's system also had mentholated nose spray, patchouli, and alum in it. Grissom and he head out to the desert for the rave. Bobby eventually spots the dealer and attacks him in a rage. The cocky dealer denies selling anything. Disgusted, Grissom takes a tape lift from the interior of his car, he finds a couple of jimson seeds. He theorizes that the tea Eric drank was made from the dregs where the jimson is most toxic. They manage to retrieve two seeds from the cadaver's intestines, but they can't prove that they're the same as the seeds from the dealer's car. Plus, the seeds were not toxic enough to be fatal.

As Catherine and Nick examine Woods's bloody shirt, the shape of a hand emerges, although there's a "unique attribute" to the pinkie finger. They bring

Benihana the maggots.

GUEST STARRING

KELLY CONNELL: Randy Gesek
MILO VENTIMIGLIÁ: Bobby Taylor
AMY CARLSON: Kate Armstrong
ELENA LYONS: Julia Eastman
ERIC SZMANDA: Greg Sanders
JUDITH SCOTT: Dr. Jenna Williams
JEFF PARISE: Ethan Zalasky
TIMOTHY LANDFIELD: Alexander Woods

the women back in and ask Eastman to make a fist. She's unable to bend her pinkie down, saying she sprained it. Nick then tosses a finger splint on the table. Armstrong confesses to hitting Woods twice with the paperweight while Eastman held him down.

When Grissom informs Bobby that the jimson was not responsible for Eric's death, he notices him grasping his arm. He orders two molds taken—one of Bobby's wound, another of Eric's teeth.

Sara confronts the mortician. His fingerprints are on the plastic Stephanie Reyes was wrapped in. Defeated, he admits he's guilty of dumping the body to recycle the caskets.

Kate Armstrong's financial records suggest a payoff. Armstrong confesses that Woods was blackmailing her because of her lesbian relationship with Eastman. Woods threatened to disseminate a story about the two of them having sex on campus. As he reached for the phone to set his scheme in motion, the women attacked.

Bobby can't remember what happened after they drank the tea. Grissom fills in the blanks. Suffering from the side effects of the jimsonweed, both teens became photophobic and fled the rave. Eric experienced a rise in his body temperature and stripped. Bobby was having auditory hallucinations; he placed Eric in a headlock, his arm over his mouth to silence him. Eric bit Bobby, who, undeterred, suffocated his friend. Bobby is devastated— he knows Grissom is right.

Drained and disheartened Grissom seeks solace on a roller coaster.

28

"**I**t was very early in the series and we were still finding our way forensically," writer Andrew Lipsitz recalls. The writing team became fascinated with the process of crime-scene stringing, because of a demonstration by the show's technical consultant, Los Angeles criminalist Elizabeth Devine. "Most of us had no idea what it was, Liz came on set and did a forensic reconstruction for us," Lipsitz says. "She had strung an entire room. It was incredible—everybody got a sense of what these characters do and how they do what they do. So, we formulated a story around the technique."

Adding another layer to Catherine's character is the scene after Armstrong's and Eastman's arrest. Catherine says that the case isn't over, since they still don't know *why*. Nick reminds her, "You heard Grissom, 'The more the "why," the less the "how;" the more the "how," the less the "why."'" Catherine says, "Hey, Nick, Grissom's not always right. Do yourself a favor and think for yourself." Helgenberger enjoys Catherine's confidence, strength, and independent mind. She points out, "Catherine is Grissom's peer, and she can solve crimes as well as he can, but in a different way." Anthony Zuiker admits, "Our show works better when we don't serialize that type of business. We may have a conflict between two characters that may re-arise four of five scripts down the road, but when we try to carry the conflict over to the next episode, we seem to stumble."

Helgenberger speculates that Catherine is bothered by Grissom's limitations. "He doesn't necessarily applaud her enough. She doesn't hear, 'Hey, you did a great job on that.' But I think she's accepted the fact that that's just who he is."

Las Vegas native Zuiker clued his colleagues in on the use of the locally indigenous hallucinogenic jimson-weed. "We had no idea what it was or where it came from," remembers Lipsitz. Grissom's description "Dry as a bone, red as a beet, blind as a bat, mad as a hatter" is the mnemonic used by medical examiners to sum up the plant's unsettling symptoms. "The teaser set the tone for how we wanted to tell our stories," says Lipsitz. "You're at home and you're asking yourself, 'Why is a naked guy running across the desert?'

"Sara's investigation into the use of 'time-share' coffins, was," Lipsitz recalls, "the writers trying to cover as much of the world of the criminalists as possible. Mortuary business is an extension of that world." ■

WHO ARE YOU?

ORIGINAL AIRDATE: 11/10/00
WRITTEN BY: Carol Mendelsohn & Josh Berman
DIRECTED BY: Peter Markle

GUEST STARRING

TIMOTHY CARHART: Eddie Willows
TONY CRANE: Officer Joe Tyner
PAMELA GIDLEY: Teri Miller
ROBERT DAVID HALL: Dr. Al Robbins
K. K. DODDS: Amy Hendler
ANDY BUCKLEY: Jason Hendler
ERIC SZMANDA: Greg Sanders
ANNE E. CURRY: Mrs. Sally Green

Why would a guy speed down the Strip,
only to pull over and shoot himself?

F ar from the glitter of the Strip a plumber works through a dark crawlspace. He finds four human, skeletal fingers protruding from the house's foundation. Grissom and Nick chisel away revealing a well-dessicated corpse. The shape of the corpse's hipbones indicate that the deceased is a female, about twenty. A series of gouging, spikelike wounds on her ribs suggests she was attacked with something slightly curved, with a serrated edge.

Grissom informs Catherine that her estranged husband, Eddie, has been charged in the rape of an exotic dancer. Reluctantly, Grissom allows Catherine to handle the preliminary investigation.

At an officer-involved shooting Sara and Warrick meet Officer Joe Tyner. He tells them he responded to shots fired and pursued a speeding Jeep into a parking lot. The driver pulled out a gun and shot himself. The case gets complicated when Tyner's 9mm is found to be missing a bullet and it is the same caliber as the driver's gun. Tyner explains he doesn't "top off"—fill the gunclip—to prevent jams. Sara and Warrick point out that his less than perfect record makes it hard to take him at his word. Brass brusquely tells them to find the missing bullet.

Forensic Paleontologist Teri Miller has been called in by Grissom to "make a face for Jane Doe." Medical Examiner Doctor Albert Robbins points out that Jane Doe also suffered a hairline skull fracture, and he found traces of sand and salt in her ear. The photograph from Teri's face, shown on the local news, results in five identical identifications: Fay Green. Her grieving mother mentions that Fay had just moved in with her boyfriend, Jason Hendler, before her disappearance.

Detective Evans interviews the rape complainant, April Lewis. Catherine asks Evans to include a DNA sample from under Lewis's nails. Catherine knows if she works the case she could compromise it.

Lab Tech Greg Sanders discovers that the sand in Green's ear was man-made. Grissom and Nick then

pay a visit to Jason Hendler and his wife, Amy. Grissom notices the living-room aquarium, his curiosity is piqued when Nick steps on a squeaky floorboard. Observing that it's buckled, probably the result of water damage, Grissom removes it and finds sand beneath. The CSIs are abruptly asked to leave.

Sara and Warrick dismantle the Jeep in a desperate search for the missing bullet. Finally, Warrick finds it buried between the treads of the spare mounted on the rear of the vehicle. Ballistics tells them that it was fired from the motorist's gun.

April Lewis's rape kit indicates the presence of nonoxynol-9, polyvinyl alcohol, and glycerin — components of a contraceptive film. Since the film needs to be inserted fifteen to thirty minutes before sex, Lewis must have deliberately prepared to engage in sexual activity on the night of the alleged attack. Catherine confronts Lewis, who owns up to the bogus rape claim. Fed up with Eddie's promises of getting her into music videos, Lewis says she devised a way to make him pay.

Armed with a warrant, Nick and Grissom return to the Hendler residence where the sand between the floorboards has been removed. The penetrating ALS reveals bloody handprints on the floor. Grissom theorizes that Hendler and Fay got into a fight. He shoved her, sending her head into the aquarium, causing a deluge of water and sand. Hendler must have finished her off and dumped her body into wet foundation concrete. Hendler denies this, saying he still loves Fay. Amy backs him up, saying he was in Reno. Nevertheless, he is arrested and taken by the officers to a waiting squad car. While preparing to process the scene, Nick sees photos of the couple rock-climbing. Hendler is holding an axe — it's blade slightly curved, with a serrated edge. He turns to ask Amy about it, and finds her holding a gun on him. Amy lays out the details. Jason was in Reno, *she* visited the house to tell Fay that she and Jason would be together. It was *their* argument that led to the fatal turn of events. Nick can only stand there frozen. Then, Grissom calls her name, and Amy turns to see him holding a gun on her. Accepting defeat, she slowly lowers her weapon and is taken into custody.

The three cases—the discovery of a corpse in a foundation, head-butting with the LVPD over a shooting and a sexual-assault case—show the skill with which the writers lure the audience in. Catherine's investigation into her ex's case lets us see her at the French Palace providing a portrait of her pre-CSI life. "It's clear that she's moved on but still has a soft spot for her ex," says writer Josh Berman. "Eddie's the kind of guy who prefers get-rich schemes over hard work."

"Back then were still looking for an 'A' story coroner and a 'B' story coroner, so we'd tried out a lot of different actors," says Carol Mendelsohn. Finally, they cast Robert David Hall as Doctor Robbins. "You have to be able to say these six-syllable words like you did it every day," Hall explains. "I think I clicked right away with Bill Petersen . . . there was something going on."

Forensic Paleontologist Teri Miller, played by Pamela Gidley, immediately bonds with Grissom over their mutual entomological bent. "In 'Pledging Mr. Johnson' we put the tarantula in the cage," says Berman, "and we took it out in Episode Six. In a sense, Grissom was coming out of his cage with Teri." Clearly an admirer of more than Miller's professional expertise, Grissom says, "Teach me." Teri asks him for his hand, then places hers over his as they smooth on plaster, then knead the skull's clay surface.

"We had Grissom and Teri Miller flirt over a tarantula and then we had Catherine and Greg flirt over vaginal film," muses Berman. "It's really a different way of putting sex into an episode. 'Who Are You?' is one of my favorite episodes. It felt real because it was one of the first times that we actually used a real case for inspiration."

If it's surprising to see Nick get teary when Amy trains her gun on him, it's eerie to learn that George Eads was drawing on a real-life experience. Years ago, during a holdup at a North Dallas hamburger stand where he worked, he and a friend stood inches away from the barrel of a gun. "It was a .38. I could see the bullets. The hammer was back. I was shaking. I was praying. I had to beg the guy not to shoot me." ■

BLOOD DROPS

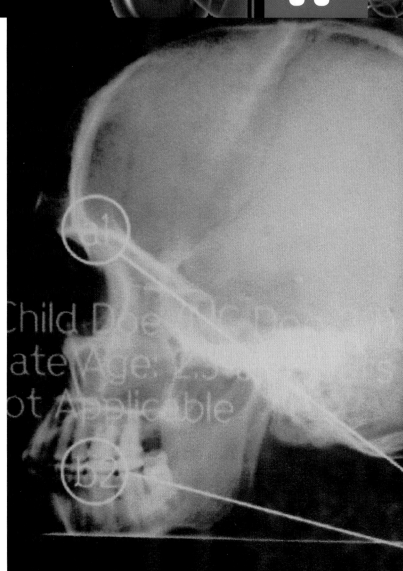

ORIGINAL AIRDATE: 11/17/01
STORY BY: Tish McCarthy
TELEPLAY BY: Ann Donahue
DIRECTED BY: Kenneth Fink

GUEST STARRING

TIMOTHY CARHART: Eddie Willows
ALLISON LANGE: Tina Collins
ROBERT DAVID HALL: Dr. Al Robbins
GLENN MORSHOWER: Sheriff Brian Mobley
MARC VANN: Conrad Ecklie

A teenage girl flings open the door of a suburban home and runs screaming into the night. Sergeant O'Riley greets an arriving Grissom with, "Four dead; mom, dad, and two teenage boys. Sisters were luckier." Grissom enters the home for a preliminary walk-through with CSI Tech Shibley. Ascending the stairs, they note the coppery scent of spilled blood. They discover the father, Shawn Collins, in the hallway. Shibley dashes outside to be sick. Sara, who's heard about the multiple homicides on her home police scanner, arrives at the scene. Continuing on, they pass a swirly design on the wall, drawn in blood. The body of Barbara Collins is in bed, there are no defense wounds, which suggests she was killed in her sleep.

Grissom continues to the sons' room where he finds fifteen-year-old Steven still under his bloody sheets. Another swirling pattern in blood is on the dresser mirror. Thirteen-year-old Brad lies on the floor beside the bed, two bloody handprints on the wall in front of him. Back downstairs, Grissom tells O'Riley to call the responding paramedics back, and orders the rest of the CSI team, and all of the lab's tools, to the house.

Four-year-old Brenda Collins sits in a squad car, gazing catatonically at the scene around her. When Grissom asks if she can help him, she stares into space, finally saying only, "The buffalo." When the rest of the team arrives, Grissom puts Catherine in charge of blood samples and mapping, Warrick and Nick are to process the perimeter of the house and a

very reluctant Sara is told to stay with Brenda. In the kitchen, Grissom notices only one open drawer, with a knife missing from the set. O'Riley astutely observes the killer probably knew the house.

Clark County Sheriff Brian Mobley presses Grissom for a status report for the press. When Grissom insists there's nothing, Mobley gripes that he should try being more like Ecklie, Grissom's more politic dayshift counterpart.

Catherine discounts the cult theory; it is only a

{hiMem} bul
riable: "file[
ianen 00
'hild

32 weak imitation. Grissom theorizes that the mother was killed first, next was her husband, who was nicked, then "finished off." Catherine counters that, if that were the case, they'd have found more of his blood. "First witness, first suspect," Grissom observes. They wonder if they should be treating Tina Collins as a suspect.

Grissom and Brass sit in interrogation with Tina, who says she was upstairs when she heard noises and unfamiliar footsteps coming from the kitchen. When asked if she has a boyfriend, she admits to hooking up with different guys, but none of them are nick-named Buffalo.

Nick finds the remnant of a small hand-rolled cigarette in the bushes, along with a discarded match. Warrick finds fresh tire tracks. They trace the tires to a 1993 Honda scooter and learn that there's one owned by a kid only four blocks away.

Studying Tina's clothes, Grissom can't find a drop of blood. He wonders why she made no attempt to help her family. Tina can't explain why she had no blood on her; she had said that she'd hugged her mom and tripped over her dad's body, *then* ran to get help from neighbors.

Catherine realizes that she's forgotten to pick up Lindsey. She rushes home to discover her ex-husband, Eddie, sitting with their daughter. She profusely thanks him.

Brass and Warrick question Oliver Kurkland, the owner of the scooter. He admits to knowing Tina, adding that a lot of guys do. He can't account for the scooter's whereabouts, as he lets three friends use it. He was in Vancouver the night of the killings.

Jesse Overton, the scooter's fourth and most obnoxious user, asks for a lawyer when pressed on the location of the scooter. As Jesse waits, he takes out a pack of cigarettes; the same brand Nick found outside the Collins's house. He has Jesse hand over the pack and the matchbook, since there is no smoking in the station. Nick aligns the spent match with its torn stub in the matchbook. The scooter—and a pair of bloody jeans—are found by Brass in a

This is a reverse Macbeth . . . Not a trace of blood on the daughter's clothes. Not a spot.

This is the only crime scene in Las Vegas tonight.

Dumpster near the Overtons' house. Overton responds truthfully during a polygraph that Tina had asked him to kill her family. Wanting to know why, Grissom looks over the family's personal belongings. He comes across a buffalo pendant belonging to Mr. Collins. He calls Sara, telling her to get ultraviolet photos of Brenda Collins so they can check for signs of sexual abuse.

While working on her blood mapping, Catherine notices something is off. Just as she is about to share her findings, Catherine is visited by a representative from Family Services. He informs her that Eddie has filed a child neglect claim and that there will be an investigation. Undeterred, she informs Grissom that the blood drops in the hallway indicate that the father was not running *to* Brenda's bedroom, but *from* it.

The photos confirm that Brenda has been sexually abused. When Grissom confronts Tina with this fact, she declares, "That was the last night he was going to touch her." When pressed about her mother's and brothers' deaths, Tina states, "They should have protected me. I was young. I learned to deal. But when he went for my daughter . . ."

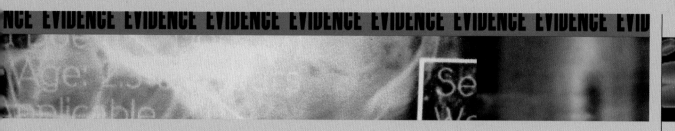

"**B**lood Drops" marks a number of firsts— the first single-plot episode, the first time all five criminalists are on one case, and the first episode directed by Kenneth Fink. Building an entire episode around one case was a risk. Writer Ann Donahue reflects, "I think it showed us that we could trust the material and go." Jonathan Littman, executive producer, adds, "I think everyone would say that 'Blood Drops' is the breakout episode. It's the one where people stood up and said, 'You know, this has all the markings of a hit show.'"

This story was inspired by the real-life experience of Technical Consultant Elizabeth Devine. Because she was still in the employ of the Los Angeles County Sheriff's Department, Devine received story credit under the pseudonym Tish McCarthy. "Liz gave the verisimilitude that I would never otherwise have gotten," recalls Donahue. "I was going to meet her to ask about how CSIs act when they're at a scene. Do they say, 'Sorry for your loss?' I didn't know. We were having lunch in Pasadena and she said, 'I'm sorry, you'll have to excuse me. I've been up five days straight on a quadruple.'"

Donahue was so impressed with Devine's experience that Ann invited her in to share it with the creative team. Carol Mendelsohn remembers, "Liz must have talked to us for about an hour and a half. She was a natural-born storyteller." After "Blood Drops" aired, Mendelsohn called Devine and offered her a full-time job.

"I told them exactly what I did the moment I got there and how I took control," Devine recalls. "I believe it is the most accurate portrayal of a crime scene so far on television."

"It was a haunted house piece," says Director Kenneth Fink. He fondly recalls how the combination of the story's rich subject matter and the series' relative youth offered boundless opportunities for his cinematic creativity, "This was only the seventh show. So that left me open."

Before Grissom has even viewed the scene, it's made clear, by the cops stumbling out of the Collins home, that something gruesome awaits inside. Similarly, Fink decided early on that the house should remain bathed in darkness during the initial walk-through. The director observes, "You don't want to see blood and gore and bodies brightly lit. It's much better to see it suggested— a flashlight swings by and the leg of a young boy is seen in the mirror. To me, that's much more terrifying and sad."

"Blood Drops" also made careful use of animal imagery. Brenda Collins's identification of "the buffalo" allows Grissom to make the case-breaking connection with the father's medallion. Subtler is a fleeting procession of rabbit images in the opening act. In the first shot, they appear as lawn ornaments. Next, Grissom and Shibley pass a figurine and a painting featuring more rabbits as they walk the crime scene. A serendipitous scouting discovery led to the show's evocative motif. "We found a house, and our people counted, like, one hundred seventy-five rabbits. So Ken thought, Let's use it," Fink recalls. "I was looking for something to contrast with the facts—that the mother would have all these gentle images, when she was incapable of protecting her own children from a monster who lived in that demented house." Donahue adds, "Here's this soft happy place, but there's evil inside."

We learn that Grissom is not the only workaholic. Sara shows up at the Collins house on her night off after hearing about the massacre on her police scanner. While despite her protests, she's assigned to keep an eye on Brenda Collins, she makes a strong connection with the traumatized child. Donahue says she liked playing against type. "Sara is a career girl—she's much more comfortable with dead bodies than with little kids; they're alien to her. When you have your characters do uncomfortable things, it makes the audience love them. I call them hero scenes." ∎

CONFIDENTIAL

Catherine was born in Las Vegas to a single mother, a hard-working cocktail waitress at the big casinos. Her mother, looking for a better place to raise her two daughters, moved around the West Coast for much of their teenage years. A whip smart young woman with a wild streak, Catherine decided to move out and make her own way after graduating high school. She landed in Seattle, attracted by its vibrant music scene. It was there she met a young rock musician named Eddie Willows. The two soon moved back to Las Vegas, where Eddie had big dreams of becoming a band manager and concert promoter.

Now reunited with her mother and her sister Nancy, Catherine felt at home in Vegas. A family friend and Casino mogul named Sam Braun found Catherine a job as a waitress at the Paradise Garden Gentlemen's Club. After working there a few months, she asked the club's manager, Ted, if she could have a tryout as one of their exotic dancers. For the next few years, she enjoyed a lucrative career as a dancer, often able to pull in a grand a night. She soon found herself supporting Eddie, who was struggling to make it in the local music industry.

Already a graduate from the proverbial school of hard knocks, Catherine found she was eager to earn a college degree and began taking night classes at Western Las Vegas University. She first turned on to a career in forensic science by the off-hours cops and criminalists who would patronize the club. They would regale her with tales of the cases they were working on, and she was fascinated by the complex puzzles they would solve. LVPD Detective Jimmy Tadero took a shine to Catherine's moxie and enthusiasm. He encouraged her to pursue Criminal Science in her studies, and became her mentor all the way through to graduation. Tadero recommended Catherine to a young CSI named Gil Grissom, who offered her an entry-level job as an assistant lab technician.

Under the tutelage of Tadero and Grissom, Catherine quickly moved up the ranks in the lab and soon found herself wanting to get out into the field as an Investigator. She had already been promoted to a CSI Level 2 by the time she became pregnant. Feeling secure in her job and relationship, she and Eddie married and bought a small house in suburban Vegas.

Being the breadwinner of the family, Catherine needed to return to work soon after the birth of her daughter Lindsay, and was ultimately promoted to CSI Level 3 in 1995. Catherine always gave her best as a wife and mother, in addition to trying to keep up with advancements in the field of forensics. Unfortunately, as her career thrived, her personal life was deteriorating. Despite an attempt at couple's therapy, with Eddie's infidelities prompted Catherine to file for divorce eight years after the birth of their daughter.

In the years that followed, Catherine has had her share of struggles as a single, working mother. She then went from a divorcee to a widow, when Eddie was murdered in 2003. The unsolved case of her ex-husband's death, in addition to the shocking revelation that Sam Braun is in fact her biological father, caused an understandable amount of distraction and has led to several professional mishaps since the tragedy. Always the fighter, Catherine has labored to get her life back in order for her daughter and for her career.

The combination of passion and business savvy she possesses has not gone unnoticed by her superiors, who believe Catherine has excellent leadership potential. She is recognized as a confident person who took the path less traveled to her career and always insists on advancing by her own merit. Catherine's is a life fully, if sometimes painfully, lived.

SIGN HERE

IVESTED BY		APPROVED BY			REFER TO
	STAR	RANK		STAR	

FAMILY SERVICES
FIELD REPORT

	SUBJECT'S NAME (Last-first-middle)		DR	00-8165
MEANS USED (Describe cal., type, etc.)	WILLOWS, LINDSEY		LV	NV 86132
CHILD NEGLECT	1216 E. FLAMINGO			
APPARENT MOTIVE	(702) 555-1369		—	
UNKNOWN AT THIS TIME				
NO. OF SUSPECTS - SEX, DESCENT				
ONE F CAUC.				
TRADEMARKS OF SUSPECT(S) (Actions or conversation)				
ACTIONS	REMOVED TO (Address)			
	36211 W. FREMO	LV NV 86141		
VEHICLE USED BY SUSPECT(S) -(Yr-make-body-col-lic. no. & I.D.)				
N/A				
CODE: R-PERSON REPORTING D-PERSON DISCOV. W-WITNESS	R- FATHER, W			
VICTIM'S OCCUPATION				
STUDENT	CLARK COUNTY			

IDENTIFY SUSPECTS
CATHERINE WI
1) RECONSTRUCT THE CIRCUMST
THE UNDER
SUBJECT'S
WILLOWS
ERINE W
MR. WILLO
11-19-00
FAILED
THE SUB
TIMES
PONDED
AND
CALLE
MR W
REPORT
THIS

LAS VEGA
POLICE DEPAR
Clark County,

POL

FORENSIC

CATHERI
PN: 5481
EYES: BLU
HAIR: BLC

POLICE
RECEIVED 5-11-03

MEMORANDUM

TO: Robert Cavallo, Assistant
FR: Gil Grissom, CSI Supervi
RE: DNA Lab Incident
DA: 05.10.03
CC: Sheriff Rory Atwater

The internal investigation into th
consequently injured several em
Catherine Willows and Warrick
resulted in the accident involved CSI Level 3 Catherine Willows
locker at 3:00am and finding it locked, left sample of unknown origin (suspected as a
chemical poison) under the fume hood in the DNA lab. Catherine Willows was not
aware that the hot plate next to the fume hood had been mistakenly left on. The hot plate
under the fume hood has been confirmed as the point of detonation. We later found that
the flammable substance was logged as a piece of evidence number 43 in case number
03-4569870. This piece of evidence was consumed in the explosion. We could not get a
positive identification of the liquid.

Attached find a complete evidence inventory, as you requested. We have discovered
most of the twenty-three active cases working at the time, evidence seems to have been
contaminated or compromised in some way on every case. LIMS has backed up every
computer on the network to minimize date lost.

I have taken it under advisement that Catherine Willows will be suspended on unpaid
leave for a total of five days without compensation. A follow up report on the damage
will be available for review within a week.

ORIGINAL AIRDATE: 11/24/00
WRITTEN BY: Eli Talbert & Anthony E. Zuiker
DIRECTED BY: Danny Cannon

CRIME SCENE DO NOT CROSS CRIME SCE

To go forward, go back.

Sleeping bag for easy clean up, open windows so the stench alerts the neighbors . . .

A man relaxes in his hotel room. He wipes the postshower steam off the bathroom mirror, then starts suddenly at the sound of his room door opening. The unfortunate guest is now lying dead in the bathtub. Taking in the scene Grissom tells Brass, "It's Royce Harmon all over again," referring to the unsolved pseudo-suicide case from three months ago. Grissom finds a tape recorder in the tub. This time the suicide note has been recorded backward, but the words are the same. The killer's back.

Nick and Warrick are assigned to investigate a reckless driver whose car went over a cliff. The vehicle is at the bottom of a ravine, and the driver is in the backseat of his car, injured but alive. Nick measures the car's skid mark and estimates that it must have been going at least seventy. A set of deep parallel grooves on the cliff's edge suggests that the vehicle seesawed before taking its plunge. There are a set of widely spaced footprints leading away from the scene, Nick thinks they're looking at an accident. The driver careened through the guardrail then ran off, leaving his ill-fated passenger to fall. Warrick spots a second set of car tracks and footprints, that are in a walking stride *toward* the cliff's edge. He thinks a crime has been committed. They decide to bet a hundred—Nick's phantom driver vs. Warrick's foul play.

Grissom and Catherine check in with Doctor

ANONYMOUS

Robbins. He tells them that Rampler's hand has a defensive bullet wound, and there's a muzzle-stamp imprint on his right temple.

Sara is at the Rampler scene dusting for prints, she comes up with none. Detective Evans shows her four outgoing pieces of mail, one has its stamp placed upside down. At the lab, Greg proves the upside-down stamp was not applied by Rampler.

The crash victim, Walter Bangler, is still unconscious, but will pull through. Nick and Warrick notice tan lines indicating a missing ring and watch. With Bangler's personal effects are a wallet with no money. In the garage, Nick uses heated super-glue fumes to print the car. He finds only Bangler's prints and traces of blue pool chalk.

Disturbed by the similarities, Grissom and Catherine visit Royce Harmon's mother to verify her original contention that it wasn't her son's voice on the suicide recording. She has a talking picture frame that he recorded "I love you" on. It's a match. The wording of the two "suicide" messages is exactly the same. After checking with an audio specialist, they conclude the two victims were reading from a script. Sara discovers that both were single men in their forties, and both had the same birthday, August 17—Harmon in 1958, Rampler in 1957. Catherine suggests the killer is sending a backward progression message.

Print Tech Mandy Webster shows Catherine and Grissom a pair of overlapping thumbprints on the Rampler tape recorder. One of the prints belongs to Paul Millander, the Halloween-novelty manufacturer who assisted them in the Harmon investigation. The other print belongs to Grissom, who concludes, "Whoever it is is telling me he's got me under his thumb." Grissom returns to Paul Millander's warehouse, and the two chat pleasantly. Explaining that he hopes to narrow the search, Grissom asks for his distribution list, Millander says he doesn't have one.

Brass tells Grissom that Stuart Rampler's bank card has been used to make some postmortem withdrawals at an ATM. Studying the machine's surveillance tape, the CSIs see a homeless man flipping a series of drawings being handed to him offscreen. First a sunburst from behind clouds, a hand, then two hands gripping a white bird, the bird dying, then the hands letting go of it, and back to the sunburst. Grissom

GUEST STARRING

BARBARA TARBUCK: Paige Harmon
MATT O'TOOLE: Paul Millander
TOM MCCLEISTER: Walter Bangler
RICKY HARRIS: Disco Placid
ERIC SZMANDA: Greg Sanders
ROBERT DAVID HALL: Dr. Al Robbins
SHEERI RAPPAPORT: Mandy Webster

37

translates, "Life, like holding a dove, Hold it too hard . . ." Catherine adds, ". . . you kill it." Grissom continues, "Hold it too soft . . ." Sara finishes, ". . . and it'll fly away." They conclude that the dove symbolizes peace of mind, and that obtaining it requires justice. Grissom sums up the killer's motive, "I'm going to keep doing this over and over again until I get justice."

The now-conscious Bangler explains that he wasn't attacked, just very drunk. He lost his money and jewelry playing pool and was hit in the head. Driving drunk, he swerved and hit the rail. He climbed into the backseat of the teetering car, belting himself in.

The homeless man is brought in. He says a man approached him, offering him a hundred dollars to flip the cards. He articulately describes a man with the same distinct features as Paul Millander.

Grissom, Catherine, Brass, and a SWAT team speed to Millander's warehouse, while Sara makes a computer search for information on their suspect. She retrieves a story; a ten-year-old Paul Millander watched from a closet as the two men muscled his dad into a bathtub and shot him. Millander is killing men who were born on the day his father was murdered.

The warehouse is empty, except for a wooden stool on top of which is an envelope addressed to Grissom. He opens it to find a blank sheet of paper. "We have nothing," he interprets.

At that moment, Millander is at CSI headquarters, he asks the receptionist to tell Grissom a friend dropped by. He then stops, smiles and waves at the surveillance camera as he leaves.

38 | "**W**e didn't want to leave the Harmon case dangling," says William Petersen. "And Paul Millander was just too interesting." Therefore "Anonymous" revealed Millander to be a criminal mastermind on a crusade to avenge his father's murder. Petersen observes, "Grissom is very similar to Millander, and that's what makes him compelling." Carol Mendelsohn adds, "The Millander-Grissom connection, much like the Moriarty-Sherlock Holmes connection, is fascinating." Their bond is demonstrated in the chat they have in Millander's bare-bones office. The scene's final shot shows the two men enjoying a cup of coffee, its silence is a sign of the men's comfort with each other.

"I thought 'Anonymous' was pretty revealing," says Gary Dourdan, pointing out that Warrick's and Nick's rapport is a reflection of the actors' off-screen friendship. "The characters' relationship is one that we've tried to develop. They've grown to be these guys that count on each other." Their boys-will-be-boys camaraderie includes a healthy dose of good-natured ridicule. Nick, feeling cocky about his theory on the Bangler case, teases, "You look tired, buddy. You want me to make you

a bottle, go night-night?" Warrick, who can always be depended on to give as good as he gets, retorts, "You want me to clock that jaw, make you go night-night?" Writer Eli Talbert reflects, "I identified with these two young guys, eager to kick ass in their profession. Confident, but very competitive."

"It was a way for Nick to connect," George Eads says of his character's needling. "With all the people on Warrick's ass all the time, about gambling, he's got this one friend who doesn't give him any shit." Gary Dourdan looks at the experience as a starting point for the characters. "We did that one scene where we're tossing the football back and forth trying to solve this case. We did it twenty times and twenty different ways," he recalls, "and that has sparked a whole slew of creative ideas." ∎

UNFRIENDLY SKIES

ORIGINAL AIRDATE: 12/8/00
TELEPLAY BY: Andrew Lipsitz AND
Carol Mendelsohn & Anthony E. Zuiker
STORY BY: Andrew Lipsitz
DIRECTED BY: Michael Shapiro

GUEST STARRING

CHRISTINE TUCCI: Kiera Behrle
JAMES AVERY: Preston Cash
DEIRDRE QUINN: Shannon
ERIC SZMANDA: Greg Sanders
GLENN MORSHOWER: Sherrif Brian Mobley
JUDITH SCOTT: Dr. Jenna Williams

We're going to make this quick and painless.

A Las Vegas Air Flight descends to McCarren International, the pilot calls to air traffic control, requesting emergency personnel. Once on the ground, Brass orders the entire craft treated like a crime scene. He and Grissom climb aboard and find a Caucasian male lying dead in the first-class aisle, surrounded by trash. Brass relates that there were ten witnesses, the victim was described as having "some kind of a panic attack" before his demise. The cockpit door features a pair of

bloody handprints and an impression of a shoe. Finding a wound on the victim's palm, Grissom suspects foul play. Sheriff Mobley informs Grissom that the FAA has jurisdiction but won't arrive until morning. CSI has twelve hours to solve the case.

The victim is an Atlanta businessman, Tony Candlewell. Grissom hands out assignments: Catherine and Warrick will go to the airport lounge and interview the first-class passengers, Nick is with the coroner, he and Sara will process the scene. The captain says Candlewell boarded without incident. The trouble began about thirty-five minutes out of Atlanta. Shannon, the first-class flight attendant, asked him to help with an angry Candlewell who was pounding on the rest-room door. Candlewell was belligerent, but didn't seem drunk.

Doctor Williams measures Candlewell's body temperature as 98.1°—unusually high for someone who's been dead for two hours. Nick reasons that Candlewell must have had a fever of 101.6° when he died. Williams also observes he has defensive injuries.

Grissom and Sara are placing orange cones with the passengers' names atop their assigned seats. In the airport lounge, Nate Metz—the passenger in front of Candlewell—tells Catherine and Brass that Candlewell repeatedly kicked the back of his seat. Metz admits he punched his seat in frustration, and

40

shows Catherine his abraded knuckles. The flight attendant recalls Candlewell complaining of a headache. She gave him two aspirin. Lou Everett—his seat was across the aisle and behind Candlewell—has a nasty cut on his face. He tells Warrick and Brass how a "psycho" Candlewell attacked him, slicing him with a CD, after he tried to calm down the situation with Metz.

Doctor Williams reports that Candlewell had intercranial bleeding, thoracic hemorrhaging, and a ruptured spleen. A broken wine bottle with dried blood visible on its jagged edge is found in Marlene Valdez's seat. She recalls Candlewell pacing up and down the aisle, elbowing Shannon out of the way. When her husband suggested that he sit down, Candlewell shoved him to the floor knocking him into the drink cart and breaking the wine bottle. In the craft's rest room the CSIs find, not blood, but semen on the sink. Catherine and Warrick speak with Vicky Mercer and Carl Finn, coworkers traveling together. Mercer admits to being in the lavatory "for a while," Finn maintains he was in his seat the whole time. Catherine is discouraged that none of the witnesses has told them anything of value.

Nick notices multiple shoe prints on the back of Candlewell's suede jacket. The prints from the jacket are compared with the passenger's footwear. They match Everett, Max Valdez, and Doctor Kiera Behrle. A surgeon, Behrle recounts going to help the fallen Candlewell, and Everett mistakenly hitting her in the face, which may have caused her to step on the victim. She claims that she performed CPR.

Catherine wonders, "What was the passenger closest to the action—Mr. Preston Cash in seat 1A— doing?" Cash is legally blind, but offers Grissom and Warrick his version of what he heard. A scuffle followed Candlewell's banging on the cockpit door, then he heard the passengers yelling, Candlewell resisting, a melee of punching and stomping, then utter silence.

Doctor Williams concludes that Candlewell was

It took five people to kill him, but it would only have taken one person to save him.

suffering from undiagnosed encephalitis. The symptoms would have been slurred speech, delirium, and loss of consciousness. With the increased air pressure and altitude, she theorizes, "Our guy was probably out of his mind." Cause of death was a combination of his pre-existing condition and the beating he took.

The CSIs regroup in the first-class cabin for a reconstruction. After a bout of turbulence, Candlewell freaked. He started hitting the call button, kicking the seat in front of him. Candlewell, now looking more crazy than ill, was dealing with a temperature and a splitting headache. The drunken Everett then swung and missed Candlewell, who slashed him with a CD. Candlewell then got up, anxiously looking out the window of the exit door. Max Valdez confronted him, he shoved him down. Marlene slashed him with a bottle. Candlewell, hand bleeding, banged on the cockpit door. Insensible, Candlewell tried opening the exit door. A free-for-all ensued. He tried to get away but was pursued and killed. Behrle rolled him over to cover up her actions. The Sheriff says that without ironclad proof of a homicide, he's letting the passengers go free.

The frustrated CSIs regroup at headquarters and debate the moral line between murder and self-defense. When Grissom points out that a lack of compassion and concern toward Candlewell led the passengers and crew to simply fear him, and, ultimately, kill him.

"**U**nfriendly Skies" presents the team with an investigatory paradox: The crime scene is crammed with eye witnesses, all of whom—except, a blind man—are unreliable. "It gave us a chance to see how our CSIs recreated events based strictly on the evidence," writer Andrew Lipsitz notes. "It's *Murder on the Orient Express* in the air."

Carol Mendelsohn was taken with the idea of "mob forensics" driving the story, "The idea is that there is anonymity in a group that you don't get when you do something individually." She explains, "If twelve of us beat the shit out of a guy and kill him, I could have kicked him and delivered the fatal blow with my foot, but unless I leave a footprint on him, you're never going to catch me. But if you hit him in the face and you leave your epithelials on his cheek, they're going to get you."

Written nearly a year before the cataclysmic terrorist attacks of September 11, 2001, "It reads very naively to me now," Lipsitz says. "It shows how much the world can change in one year."

In 2000, the crew was granted access to the tarmac of Los Angeles International Airport for the exterior shots. "We actually had an Airbus A320 that we were allowed to shoot around," Lipsitz recalls. "It was really a cargo plane that we dressed up." For the episode's onboard sequences, they redressed the mock plane interior used in the 1996 feature film *Air Force One.* "That episode was a disaster in production," Littman recollects, noting that it was designed to be an expedient, cheap hour to produce, but came in late and over budget. As a result, he says, "We figured this was going to be a disaster and nobody was going to watch it." Instead, he says, it went on to be the highest-rated episode of the first season.

"It was around that time when the writers and the actors started to gel on the set," Lipsitz

points out, a "cooperative, interactive" synergy has prevailed. "Our actors have added tremendously to the series with line suggestions or attitude suggestions. In some ways it's closer to theater than to other mediums, which comes from Billy, 'cause Billy's a theater guy."

Jorja Fox recalls Grissom's and Sara's discussion of sex on a plane, "It came up, as a lot of things on our show have, sort of spontaneously." As far as Petersen's concerned, there's nothing at all vague about the saucy banter. "There's an intentional flirt going on there, because in real life there would be," he asserts. As for a romance, Lipsitz says, "We were consciously staying away from it, at that point. But it's an example of how you can throw a little spice into an episode and it goes a long way."

Mendelsohn points out another of the show's groundbreaking achievements, the episode's jarring conclusion: "Everybody got away." The episode timed out too short, necessitating an epilogue in which the CSIs muse on what they would have done if they'd been aboard the flight, after which Grissom delivers an admonishing monologue. "Some fans have said it was a little too preachy." Mendelsohn counters, "I liked it for what it said, 'If somebody had just taken the time to just ask him what was wrong.'" ■

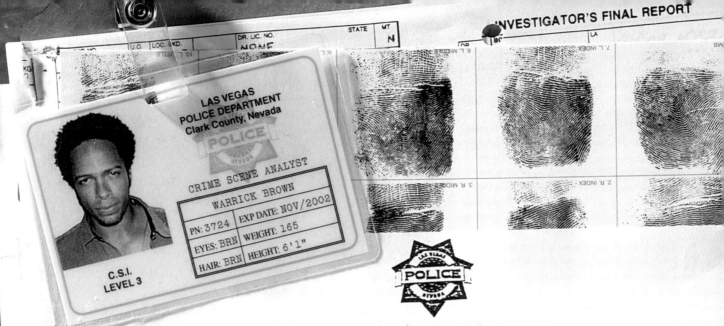

SIGN HERE

LAS VEGAS
POLICE DEPARTMENT
Clark County, Nevada

POLICE
NEVADA

CRIME SCENE ANALYST

WARRICK BROWN

PN: 3724	EXP DATE: NOV/2002
EYES: BRN	WEIGHT: 165
HAIR: BRN	HEIGHT: 6'1"

C.S.I.
LEVEL 3

POLICE
LAS VEGAS

REPORT OF INVESTIGATION

P.D. 123 Rev. 1/74

COMPLAINANT/VICTIM	Holly Gribbs, CSI Level One	DATE OF OCCURRENCE	10-
		CCN	FILE NO
TYPE OF CASE	Investigation of On-Duty Activity – CSI Brown	58787	

NARRATIVE: GIVE A SYNOPSIS OF CASE INVESTIGATION SUBSEQUENT TO THE LAST REPORT, WITH PERSONS INTERVIEWED, NEW LEADS, AND OTHER INFORMATION ON CASE PROGRESS.

On the morning of October 7, 2000, Captain James Brass instructed Warrick Brown to shadow trainee Holly Gribbs. Brown dropped Gribbs off at the crime scene, a domestic robbery at 1235 MLK. Seeing a patrol car parked outside, Brown felt that the scene was secure and allegedly went to get a cup of coffee. The dispatch log does not have any record of CSI Brown informing headquarters of his whereabouts.

While processing the crime scene, the patrol officer was called to a nearby traffic collision and left Gribbs alone at the crime scene. The officer, Lt. P. Jones, claims that he was unaware of Brown's absence and thought the two CSI^ ^^^
scene together as a team. After Lt.
perpetrator, one Jerrod Cooper (now
house and confronted Gribbs. A strug
gained control of Gribbs' firearm ai
weapon. Cooper then fled the scene.
police after hearing gunshots. Gribb
but died on the operating table sever

Brown did not return to the scene aft
met up with CSI Grissom to witness th
in a separate case. Brown then retur
wasn't until then that he was notifie
that time period of approximately a h
not check on Gribbs or call her on th

In conclusion, the evidence in this ca
violation of standard procedures and p
scene. His negligence as senior CSI 1
to the criminal attack which resulted
also strong evidence to suggest that B
gambling while on-duty. That matter i
investigation. CSI Brown remains on Ad
the full investigation of his whereabo
7th, 2000.

A

SU
NO
EXC
UNF
SUS

REC

Emp

Com

Warrick Brown was born in Las Vegas, Nevada to a young mother and absentee father. He was only seven years old when his mother died and went to live with his Grandmother and his Aunt Bertha. Warrick was a quiet, awkward child who was taunted other kids in the neighborhood because of his thick glasses and bookish nature. He spent most of his time at home with his Grandmother, who taught him the piano, at which he naturally excelled. Always reminding him of his special gifts, she called young Warrick her "work in progress".

The already unpopular boy found himself further alienated from his classmates when he tested as an exceptional student in science and math, and was placed into the advanced classes of his rough-and-tumble public school. Seeing her nephew as a target for bullies, his Aunt Bertha encouraged Warrick to spend some of his after-school hours at the local recreation center in hopes that his social skills may catch up to his intellect. There Warrick found a much needed father figure in Matt Phelps, a local who had gone on to football career and then returned to give back to the children struggling neighborhood. Thanks to Phelps, Warrick found himself to be a more confident and well-rounded teenager, balancing his studies, baseball and music practice throughout his high school years.

By graduation, Warrick was being invited to play minor league baseball in addition to having his pick of attending the best colleges in the nation. In the end, he chose to attend Western Las Vegas University so he could be close to his aging Grandmother. Not wanting to financially strain his family, Warrick paid his own way through school by holding down an assortment of odd jobs, including being a taxi driver, a bell captain at the Sahara, digging graves for the county and working as a runner for casino sports books on the Strip. It was in that position he discovered his talent at the black jack table and a knack for gambling on sports. He hit it big betting on the Giants in the 1990 Superbowl, which provided a substantial boost to his income during his college years.

Warrick graduated from Western Las Vegas University with a Bachelor's degree in Chemistry in 1993. Uninterested in the big-business research aspect of his forte, he looked into a career at the Las Vegas Crime Lab hoping to find a job both stable and stimulating. The street wise rookie was soon hired as a CSI Level One with the day shift, which allowed him to indulge in the gaming, women and music of the Las Vegas nightlife.

In 1997, Warrick was promoted to a CSI Level Two and transferred to the night shift alongside Gil Grissom, who quickly became his mentor. Grissom admired the way Warrick would fuel the fire he has for the job by constantly challenging himself, and everyone around him, to be the best they can be. Adversely, his abrasive skepticism of authority would sometimes cause friction with supervisors. On the job, he could simultaneously be up for some friendly competition with his co-workers while maintaining a professional distance which sometimes gives him a mysterious air of autonomy from the group.

In 2000, Brown was suspended from duty for breaking protocol and leaving CSI trainee Holly Gribbs alone at a crime scene, which resulted in her death. A full investigative report was filed, revealing that Brown was at a sports book at the time he should have been shadowing the rookie. Admiring Warrick's integrity in taking responsibility for his actions, and unwilling to lose one of his best CSIs over one tragic mistake, Grissom reinstated Warrick and soon after promoted him to a CSI Level Three. Since then, Warrick has vowed not to let Grissom down. Warrick faces an ongoing struggle against certain impulses that used to rule him. Having been given a second chance, he takes care to steer clear of trigger situations that could lead him back into temptation.

CONFIDENTIAL

BY		APPROVED BY		REFER TO
	STAR	RANK	STAR	

SE

44

A pair of hikers are horrified to find a blanket-ed female corpse set upon by a swarm of insects. When CSI arrives, Grissom points out to Sara, "They're our first witnesses to the crime."

Nick is assigned a missing-person case. Sheryl Applegate left for L.A., but she never showed up, her car was found at the bus station. Grissom tells Nick to treat the vehicle like a crime scene. Catherine and Warrick set out to find a Paul Sorenson, last seen at Richard Zeigler's home. Zeigler directs them to a rectangular void on his living-room wall. Sorensen is a painting. He tells the criminalists that he heard a noise and spotted the thief run-ning off. The home's security alarm had been disengaged, and

"Full of sound and fury." What does it signify, Doctor?

only his family have the code. Warrick notices an unusual image during his dusting of the wall, an earprint. They lift it for comparison.

Doctor Robbins says that the woman found in the forest was shot with a .38 caliber bullet to the head at close range. Sara says this was an intimate killing. Her facial X-rays show a series of existing fractures consistent with battered women. Grissom extracts a muscid fly from her leg—an insect found only in urban areas. Grissom hopes to establish a linear regression and thereby establish her time of death. Brass has located the victim's husband, Scott Shelton. The captain reports that the Sheltons' neighbors heard a gunshot five days ago. Scott Shelton denies killing his wife. He says he saw her five days ago before leaving for a convention in New Orleans. When he returned home, Kay was gone. He didn't alert the police because she's walked out before. Scott consents to a search of his home.

If the painting glows, it's a fake.

LIES AND LARVAE

> purge{hiMem} buffer...w
> che onfab/ unx/ sein
> tar/variance = 00010 i

GUEST STARRING

JOHN GETZ: Richard Zeigler
MARK MOSES: Scott Shelton
ROBERT DAVID HALL: Dr. Al Robbins
GLENN MORSHOWER: Sheriff Brian Mobley
MARC VANN: Conrad Ecklie
JENNIFER SOMMERFIELD: Det. Joyce Secula

At the bus station parking lot, Detective Secula tells Nick that Applegate's car has been opened and no body was found. Nick finds a few red hair strands on the trunk's carpet.

The earprint from the Zeiglers' wall matches their son, Jason. He admits to stealing the painting. Mr. Zeigler will not press charges. Jason says the painting is in his trunk. Catherine and Warrick take the painting back to the lab. She speculates that the painting could be a fake. If it is, they've got a whole new case.

On the Sheltons' couch, Grissom finds a green fiber similar to that from the blanket Kay was found wrapped in. Shelton's gun was recently cleaned and there is a bullet missing from one of his ammunition canisters. Another green blanket fiber is found by Sara on a loose nail in a hallway leading to the back door. When Luminol and the ALS are applied a large bloodstain is revealed. Sara loses it, screaming at Shelton, who snaps back, "Get your finger out of my face, bitch!" Shelton is arrested. Sara analyzes the blanket fibers and the bullets from Shelton's home. Using his "bug timeline," Grisson states that Kay Shelton has been dead only three days. Shelton uses unusual ammo that's not easily traced; Sara can't tie him to Kay's murder.

Dayshift CSI supervisor Ecklie complains to Grissom that Warrick was seen gambling at the Monaco during work hours. Disheartened, Grissom asks Sara to check on Warrick.

Concerned that he could be wrong about the time of death, Grissom sits in the CSI parking lot. He is keeping vigil over a pig carcass wrapped in a blanket. Silently, Sara joins him. She wraps him in a blanket, offers him a Thermos and her thanks.

The carpet of Sheryl Applegate's car tests positive for blood. A room at the Four Aces Motel was paid for using Sheryl's credit card, the police break the door down. She's there, willingly handcuffed to the bed. It seems that Sheryl Applegate is an unfaithful wife, not a missing person.

Having proved with ALS the painting Jason gave them is a fake, Catherine and Warrick return to the Zeigler residence with the forgery and offer a demonstration to Richard Zeigler. It seems many of his paintings are fakes. Fortunately, Warrick explains the police have recovered the originals. Jason would have art-student friends make copies of the originals. He would then replace them with the forgeries. When his father interrupted him about to switch the Sorensen, he was forced to flee. This time, Zeigler presses charges.

Grissom explains to Sheriff Mobley his new test indicates that Kay was, in fact, dead for five days. The sheriff tells him that he'll need something a jury can understand. Sara and Grissom take another look at the body. Robbins has ordered the body brought back. A pale blue discoloration is visible around the right-temple entry wound. Sara goes to Ballistics, where an examination of Shelton's ammo show they leave a powdery blue residue. Sara then finds the same blue dust—disintegrated Teflon—in Kay's hair. Shelton is arrested.

Sara hands Grissom a surveillance tape, telling him Ecklie was right, Warrick was at the Monaco.

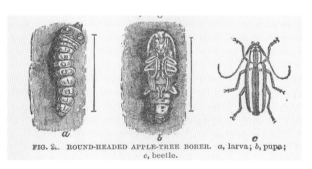

FIG. 2. ROUND-HEADED APPLE-TREE BORER. *a*, larva; *b*, pupa; *c*, beetle.

46

"**T**he larvae plot was based on a real case that forensic entomologist Lee Goff wrote about in his book *A Fly for the Prosecution,*" says Josh Berman. "He used insects to set up an entomological timeline to prove time of death. However, he miscalculated because he forgot to consider the effect of a blanket being wrapped around a corpse and how that would retard insect growth."

We see that Sara has a particular passion with cases involving victims who suffer abusers. "I love that idea for Sara," says Jorja Fox. "Although she's not really good with social skills, there really is a strong emotionality to her." When Grissom, commenting on her obsession with the case, observes, "You have empathy, Sara. That's normal." Sara counters, "You want to sleep with me?" In answer to Grissom's startled reply she explains, "That way when I wake up in a cold sweat under the blanket hearing Kay scream, you can tell me it's nothing, it's just empathy."

Thought your bugs couldn't make mistakes.

Berman explains, "My feeling is that something probably happened in Sara's past, which we may or may not ever explore, that has made her feel that way." Ann Donahue is willing to delve deeper, "Sara probably grew up with a hippie mother, and her mother was probably with some guys who didn't treat her well."

Regarding the case of the missing Sorensen, Donahue recollects, "When we started, we thought we were going to do all kinds of robberies and burglaries. What we found when we were in the writers' room was there was nothing at stake, even if somebody had something stolen that meant a lot to the victim. Drama is conflict, and murder is the ultimate conflict. It doesn't get any deeper—it is against you, it is against your person, it's against your family, it's against God. So, when you have an A–B storyline, and the A is murder and the B is a tennis bracelet, who cares?"

"The larvae storyline was really about abuse, so we wanted something a little bit lighter in tone," says Berman. "To have Nick on a case, with a wacky character who really wasn't missing, but cheating, was to add balance." It also pairs Nick up with Detective Joyce Secula, who debuts and is mildly miffed that she hasn't heard from him since their first date. There is a reason behind the revolving-door support staff, explains Donahue, "With our detectives and our techs, we try to bring new faces to the show and maybe learn more about our principal characters through them." On a more basic level, Berman says, "The reference to Nick's date illustrates that our characters do have lives outside of CSI."

The rapport between Grissom and Sara is warm enough to invite questions about their past, but not too cozy to rule out simple friendly affection. "I don't think Billy and I knew what we were playing at the time," Fox recalls. "There was some tenderness throughout that entire episode . . . moments of vulnerability that hadn't really been shown before." The scene in the parking lot "Was a turning point," says Donahue, "after which the relationship, instead of suggesting itself through chemistry, it would be consciously addressed. We could see that they had a mutual attraction and we knew that Grissom's character being distant, and her character being vulnerable, that of course they'd be drawn together." ■

ORIGINAL AIRDATE: 1/12/01
WRITTEN BY: Carol Mendelsohn
DIRECTED BY: Oz Scott

I-15 MURDERS

GUEST STARRING

TRAVIS FINE: Kenny Berlin
TONY AMENDOLA: Dr. Al Rambar
KRISTA ALLEN: Kristy Hopkins
ERIC SZMANDA: Greg Sanders
JUDITH SCOTT: Dr. Jenna Williams

A woman is pushing a cart through a supermarket. Pulling down a jar off the shelf, she drops it, mustard exploding all over floor.

That night Brass leads Grissom to an abandoned shopping cart. Missing is Margaret Shorey, her car is still in the parking lot, her purse, but not her wallet, is still in the cart. Grissom notices a yellow gob on the frame of the cart. He tastes it, grabs a jar of mustard, and drops it. "Now, where would you go?"

In the rest room Grissom notices one of the stall doors has been scrubbed clean. Using a Polilight, Grissom is able to read, "I killed 5 women. Catch me if you can?"

Having passed out the evenings assignments, Grissom confronts Warrick. He says only that he was at the casino, but he was not gambling. Sara's been assigned to the murder of Jeff Berlin. He was shot dead in the living room, a pile of his possessions are on a bedsheet on the couch. The victim's brother, Kenny, says he discovered the body and called police. Sara's curious; for a burglary there are a lot of expensive items untouched.

One of the participants of an altercation has identified herself as a friend of Nick's, so he's sent to the scene. He is taken aback to discover Kristy Hopkins, a call girl who gave him a lead on another case several months before. A hotel security guard claims she was trolling for business. She alleges he copped a feel and spit on her.

After checking Kenny for blood spatter Sara notices a small glass shard in the cuff of his pants. She has him strip, convinced he's lying. Warrick shows up, as she's sawing around the window frame to remove it, so she can do further tests at the lab.

Handwriting expert Dr. Al Rambar is called in to interpret the message from the stall door. He believes the writer is a left-handed female, with no advanced education.

Brass has discovered there are four other missing

Five stall doors. From five supermarket restrooms. Five missing women.

48

women who were last seen at supermarkets. Catherine has all the bathroom stalls from those markets sent to the lab. They all have variations of their message, and all are in the same handwriting. When Grissom rearranges the doors, in a west-to-east order, he discovers all of the abductions took place along Interstate 15.

Sara and Warrick tell Kenny Berlin that a test has shown the glass shards from his cuff are from the window. He says he crouched down by the window, and must have picked up the shard. Sara tells Warrick that a check on Kenny's finances showed he had recently suffered large losses in the stock market.

A body has been found on the roadside of the I-15. The victim is Joan Sims, she's from a San Bernardino supermarket. Doctor Williams estimates that she had been frozen until about twelve hours ago. The actual crime scene is most likely a refrigerated truck. Catherine digs up a list of refrigerated trucks that made deliveries the previous day to the supermarket. Only one had a female driver.

Warrick and Sara disprove Kenny's story. Berlin reasserts his innocence and requests a lawyer. Realizing that they'll need more evidence, they get a warrant for his computer. Inside Kenny's computer tower, Sara discovers a gun. Warrick notices a tiny piece of glass embedded in its grip. It matches the window glass.

Nick, knowing there was a large saliva stain on Kristy's blouse, arranges a friendly chat with the security guard. He tells the guard to write his side of the story down and put it in a sealed envelope. The guard readily complies, licking the envelope and giving Nick the saliva sample he needs for comparison. It proves Kristy is innocent.

Catching up with their female trucker, Catherine and Grissom ask for a writing sample. No match. She and her boyfriend are sent on her way. Grissom suggests that they look for a male driver traveling with his girlfriend, a woman he has total control over.

A delivery-truck dispatcher uses a satellite tracking system program to zero in on a suspect. Brass and several uniforms converge on the suspected trucker and his girlfriend. Grissom and Catherine climb up

You know how you're always pushing that Holy Trinity stuff? Victim, suspect, and crime scene.

into the vehicle's container, a large box freezer. In the back are three frozen female corpses. Margaret Shorey is not among them. Knowing every second counts, Brass confronts the pair and asks who wants to talk. The girlfriend directs Grissom and Catherine to the truck's cab. They find a terrified Margaret Shorey bound underneath the sleeping cabin's bed.

Waiting at CSI reception is a teenager who tells Sara he's waiting for Warrick. He has come by to thank Warrick for "busting him loose." Sara realizes that Warrick was at the casino collecting a debt that he used for the young man's bail. Chastened, she apologizes to Warrick for jumping to the wrong conclusion.

"I-15 Murders" was the third episode to be produced, but the eleventh to air. It had three subplots—Warrick's gambling problem, his conflict with Sara, and Nick's relationship with Kristy Hopkins. Anthony Zuiker recalls, "The network suggested we come out of the gate with three strong shows. After we saw 'Crate 'n Burial,' we thought that show should go third. 'I-15' ended up being a great episode, but it wasn't as strong as we felt it needed to be so we bumped it." The shuffling necessitated some reshoots and ad-libbing in order to maintain plot continuity.

The one thing that is still "off" is Sara's open contempt for Warrick. Admitting that Sara's harshness could be misinterpreted, Jorja Fox hopes, "That Sara's reaction came more from concern that Grissom was going to be let down, that somehow this man was going to disappoint him."

With the shuffle of episode orders, Fox cringes, recalling, "There's all this anger between us that didn't really have as much of a foundation anymore. The two characters had grown to be friendly, supportive colleagues." So concerned are the actors that Fox admits, "Gary and I have had a long haul trying to come back from those scenes. We're so close off-screen and I have been trying to figure out how to heighten the level of intimacy between us onscreen." ■

49

The window was broken from the *inside*.

ORIGINAL AIRDATE: 2/1/01
WRITTEN BY: Jacqueline Zambrano
DIRECTED BY: Danny Cannon

50

GUEST STARRING

STERLING MACER, JR.: Frank Damon
JARRAD PAUL: Teller #12
FRED KOEHLER: Danny Hillman
MARC VANN: Conrad Ecklie
TAMARA CLATTERBUCK: Sandra Hillman
CHAKA FORMAN: Runner 702

"I'm awaiting trial for the murder of my wife and son," says inmate Frank Damon on a videotape he's sent to Grissom. "I didn't kill my family . . . Mr. Grissom, you are my last hope. Please . . . help me." Brass knows the case. Damon is charged with arson, and the D.A. is asking for the death penalty. Grissom decides to talk to Damon. There are two hurdles: the trial is set to begin in three days, and the lead investigator was Ecklie. Brass tries to dissuade him. He points out Damon was late on his house payments, was seen running from the house with his wife and son inside, and gasoline was found in the bedroom closet.

Sergeant O'Riley meets Catherine and Nick at a parking lot, where a teenage boy is slumped behind the wheel of his car, a gunshot wound to the back of his head. It's two days before the Super Bowl, the biggest day of the year for sports bettors. Nick notices a hearing aid in the victim's ear and a blotch of condensation on the driver's-side rear window. Catherine's search of the glove compartment turns up a huge wad of cash with a betting slip taken by Teller 12. He explains it is a bet from "517" a "runner," who places bets for other people.

At the Clark County Jail, Damon tells Grissom his story. He went out to the store. Toby, their son, was asleep in their bedroom. Returning less than twenty minutes later, he found smoke billowing out from under the bedroom door. Being a volunteer fireman, he says he knew that opening it would cause a flashover explosion. He called the fire department. He admits to buying gas, but it was for his lawn mower,

and he has no idea how it got in the closet. Grissom notices a third-degree burn on his palm. Damon lies and says he can't remember how he got it. Grissom, Sara, and Warrick visit what's left of the Damons' house. The bedroom has been incinerated, its contents have been scattered all over the living room. The outside of the bedroom doorframe is charred, but the door is barely scorched. On the doorknob is an unknown substance. A narrow "V" pattern on the closet wall confirms the use of an accelerant. Melted into the discolored concrete floor are glass shards. Grissom wonders why there's no "trailing," typically an arsonist would spread the accelerant around.

Sandra Hillman identifies the dead runner as her son, Joey. She tells Catherine that his older brother, Danny, must have gotten Joey the job. They all wear earpieces so that they can communicate with their boss. Catherine and Nick consult with Warrick, who was a runner in college. He tells them to talk to Joey's fellow runners. Teller 12 points out 702. The runner knew Joey, but has no idea who killed him.

Grissom confronts Damon. He then places a doorknob in Damon's burnt right palm proving he opened the door, setting off the flashover. Damon still denies setting the fire. Among the debris, Warrick finds a charred space heater. Checking the house's circuit box, he and Grissom find there had been an overload in the bedroom. After examining the closet wall socket, Grissom discovers the wire burned from the inside out. The fire started in the wall, not on the floor. Ecklie counters that the presence of hydrocarbon on the closet floor still points to an accelerant and that is what a jury will hear.

Sandra Hillman returns with her son, Danny. He explains that he'd lost thirty thousand dollars of his customer's money. Afraid for his life, he ran, not realizing that he was putting his brother, Joey, in jeopardy. He thinks another runner is the killer. The lab has identified the condensation from the Joey's car window as nasal mucus.

Catherine and Nick track down six runners and take nasal swabs. Number 702 bets Nick that none of them is the shooter. He's right.

Do I look like a guy who skips?

FAHRENHEIT 932

Flashover; add oxygen to a fire that's reached 932 degrees, and smoke will burst into flames.

Sara points out to Grissom that hydrocarbons are present in everything from kerosene to the foam in bras, not just gasoline. Grissom, Sara, and Warrick head back to the Damon home where they find a clean-up team working on the crime scene. An enraged Grissom confronts Ecklie, who notes that it had been scheduled for months. He holds out a coffeepot and asks Grissom if he'd like a cup. Grissom swats the carafe from Ecklie's hand, sending it crashing to the floor and giving him an idea.

Grissom asks Damon how glass shards could've ended up in the closet. Damon admits that he and his wife were fighting. She was hurling things at him. One item was a glass object with a wick—a kerosene lamp.

At the casino Nick asks for Runner 702 so he can pay his bet. He notices Teller 12 is wearing an expensive watch. Nick turns to walk away, then hears a sneeze. Nick asks the teller if his new job is Joey's old route. He says wants a lawyer, Nick points to the sneezed-on glass separating them and says, "We got you."

52

"**F**ahrenheit 932" is the first episode penned by a nonstaffer. Jacqueline Zambrano is a seasoned television writer and an old friend of Carol Mendelsohn.

Its "A" storyline offers what amounts to a tutorial on a specific area of criminalistics: the procedural, physical, and chemical aspects of fire.

"I really liked that show," says director Danny Cannon of "Fahrenheit 932." "It's not a standard, linear story. It's not a dead-body-to-autopsy-to-forensic-science story. The guy Grissom is looking at is very much alive and in jail." The raging flames we see engulfing the Damon home were also very real and very dangerous. "We had three cameras rolling on a three-walled set, and we literally had a bunch of firemen stand around while we set fire to it. That was a scary place to be." As the blaze intensified, he says, "I turned to the fire department and said, 'The minute you want to put this out, just put it out, and I'll film that too.' So the cameras rolled and it burned and they looked at me and I looked at them." Finally, he recalls, "They got nervous and ran in. It was the fire department who called 'cut' on that one."

Cannon also points out that "Fahrenheit 932" is visually designed to look "down and interior and oppressive." An important part of each episode's pre-production stage is selecting a distinctive mood and color palette. "It keeps the directors interested if we keep changing the tone," Cannon says. "And I'll say to the director of photography that 'We're a little desaturated this time' or 'We're crushed,' or 'We're a little bleach-bypass this week.' "

> **I don't judge people**

Ironically, for the all of the episode's visual intensity, Cannon felt that it lacked suspense. He felt that particularly, in the fourth act, at the decisive juncture when the investigator gets the crucial clue. He decided upon a change of pace by way of an-out-of-nowhere epiphany. "There were so many times when we put things under microscopes and we explain what they are; we look things up in books or we talk to an expert. I wanted Grissom's mind to work outside the box." In fact, Cannon recalls, William Petersen had been advocating that same approach. "It was a smart way for him to look at his character." Cannon eventually came up with the pivotal visual in the break room where Grissom, finally pushed too far by the smug Ecklie, knocks the coffeepot out of his hand in a fit of anger. As it shatters on the floor, Grissom stares at the contents puddling out and realizes *that's* how the glass and the accelerant got into the closet; a moment of rage. "Grissom loses control just for a second, and an out-of-body experience occurs which gives him an idea," says Cannon. "It was something I was really proud of." ∎

ORIGINAL AIRDATE: 2/8/01
WRITTEN BY: Josh Berman AND
Ann Donahue & Anthony E. Zuiker
DIRECTED BY: Kenneth Fink

BOOM

GUEST STARRING

STEPHEN LEE: Dominic Kretzker
KRISTA ALLEN: Kristy Hopkins
MARK VALLEY: Jack Willman
MARC VANN: Conrad Ecklie
GREGORY ITZIN: Norman Stirling
TIM REDWINE: Tyler Stirling
ERIC SZMANDA: Greg Sanders
GLENN MORSHOWER: Sheriff Brian Mobley
ROBERT DAVID HALL: Dr. Al Robbins

53

I t's the end of business day in the Hansen building. Security Guard Jake Richards reminds his colleague, Dominic Kretzker, that it's time for his break. Richards sees an abandoned briefcase. He picks it up, setting off a bomb.

Grissom and Catherine survey the aftermath. Richards is the lone fatality, Brass tells them. From his wounds, Grissom can tell that Richards was directly in front of the bomb when it detonated. Catherine finds a metal fragment with the letters "FP" scratched onto it. An awed Dominic Kretzker approaches Grissom and offers to help with the investigation. Richards was one of his best friends, and he happens to know a lot about bombs. Grissom accepts his offer, however he tells a uniform cop not to let Kretzker out of his sight.

Bombs are like fingerprints. No two are exactly alike.

Don't you love the smell of sulfur in the afternoon?

At the Orpheus hotel-casino Nick sees Kristy Hopkins, a call girl he met on a previous case, struggling to free herself from a brawny companion. He gets the man to back off and offers Kristy a ride home. She tells him she's getting out of the business. Kristy asks him inside. He's hesitant, but eventually he accepts. The following morning, Nick drives by Kristy's house and is alarmed to see cop cars outside. He asks one of the officers what's happened. "Dead prostitute."

Having collected everything within a five-meter radius from the point of explosion, the CSIs look to re-create the bomb and its container. Grissom's found a balance wheel from a timing device, encrusted with a melted orange substance.

Nick tells Grissom about Kristy, and his certainty that Ecklie, the lead investigator, will find his fingerprints and DNA. Nick says that he left her house around 4 A.M., but Kristy's autopsy puts the time of death at 6 A.M. Nick overhears Ecklie telling Catherine that he's found a condom at Kristy's. Nick tells him his DNA will match. He also gives Ecklie the plate number of Kristy's harasser, Jack Willman.

Sara learns from the FBI's Bomb Data Center the most pouplar timing device is the TimeTell Snoozewell. Catherine's ascertained the explosive's container was an aluminum briefcase. They know the propellant was black gunpowder. Grissom and Sara venture out to a range to ascertain what type of metal piping housed the bomb. They discover it was galvanized steel.

A credit-card check shows that Kretzker purchased seven Snoozewell clocks in the past three months. Kretzker welcomes them to his home. He'd been listening to his police scanner and knew they were coming. Brass notices a bomb fragment on a bookcase, and Kretzker admits taking it as a souvenir from the Hansen building. Brass isn't buying it and places him under arrest.

Sara identifies the orange component as polyester. Grissom pays an unofficial visit to the holding cell where Kretzker proclaims his innocence. Brass tells Grissom of another blast ten minutes ago at a Thrift-Right Car Rental. An employee working the check-in line has been killed. Among the debris, Grissom finds a mousetrap caked in the same melted orange polyester.

Sara's eye is caught by the manager, who's wearing a Thrift-Right suit jacket made of orange polyester.

Jack Willman is interrogated by Sergeant O'Riley while Catherine and Ecklie watch. Willman claims he went to Kristy's house to apologize and witnessed her murder. According to him, Kristy and Nick argued, Nick shoved, then strangled her. Aware that Nick was connected with the police, Willman said he though it best to keep quiet. Catherine gets twelve hours from Ecklie to investigate before they charge Nick. Greg examines Nick's semen sample, he can place the sexual encounter at around 2 A.M. Catherine then examines Kristy's home. She compares one of the rope sashes on the living-room curtains with the autopsy photo of the marks on Kristy's neck. Catherine then collects skin cells from the rope and orders them checked against DNA from Willman's prior assault case. It's a match.

There is also a match between the residue on the explosives, and the Thrift-Right jacket, and their corporate headquarters are in the Hansen building. A computer search for disgruntled employees turns up Norman Stirling, a former manager. Stirling is taken into custody. Warrick has identified the implement used to scratch the "FP" onto the timing-device gear, an electric etching pen. He traces it to Summit High where Stirling's son, Tyler, is a student.

When questioned, Tyler rails against his dad's former employer, who fired him after thirty years only to hire two younger workers at half the price. He says that "FP" stands for "fair play," which his dad was owed. Tyler professes that he did it all for his father. Grissom asks him if there are any other bombs, and where.

Dominic Kretzker hears on his police scanner there's a bomb at Summit High. He dashes to the school, jimmies open Tyler's locker. He exits the building with the bomb only to find Grissom outside, pleading for him to stay still. The bomb goes off.

Later, Grissom smiles sadly as he reads "Local Hero Gives His Life: Dominic Kretzker Sacrificed His Life Today for the Students at Summit High School." He pins the piece to the bulletin board just above a tribute to fallen police officers.

"The show was new," explains writer Ann Donahue, "and so in every episode we would try to cover a new discipline of forensics." Explosives are about as spectacular—and challenging—as it gets for a film-maker. It took two days of an eight-day shoot to create the bombing in the teaser. It was done on location at an office building near *CSI*'s Santa Clarita studios. "The building had a nice graphic sense," says director Kenneth Fink. The lobby had an open feeling and a catwalk from where the devastation could be shot. "And," he adds, "it was a place that we could leave wrecked and come back to the next day." Because the building needed to stay open for business throughout the shoot, the crew had to create a set of fake scorched walls that could be removed at the end of shooting.

For the show's first fatality, Fink recalls, "We wanted to do that guy blowing up in pieces, and to examine that very last second before the bomb went off." He knew the shot of the explosion would involve "a million layers" of conventional photography and CGI (computer-generated imagery). "I knew that we should film the ratchet-pull on a stuntman, and then we let Larry do the rest in terms of the debris firing at the camera, the character firing at the camera, the character firing away from the camera, debris hitting the wall, a fireball. They were all done separately and married by Stargate. From the very beginning Larry Detweiler, who does visual effects and works at Stargate, has been able to bring to television effects that equals anything on the big screen. They are masterful."

Fink had originally advocated having the CSIs blow up a trio of cars in order to identify the bomber's material of choice. However, as he recalls, Carol Mendelsohn said, "No. Let's stay with the science of things blowing up." Ultimately, to achieve the eye candy that Fink was after, they used different colors in each suitcase. "I think it was one of the first times where we played with the pleasure that these guys get from evidence collecting and the different kinds of scientific pursuit that go into their profession."

Of the talented Stephen Lee, who played Dominic Kretzker, Donahue says, "He's such a wonderful actor. We tried to just write it and get out of his way." Fink says of the character, "He's the kind of guy who's lonely and longs to be a hero and in the midst of things. I found it rather moving." In some ways, Kreztker can also be seen as a tragicomic version of Grissom. Kretzker is naïve, a dimmer reflection of Grissom, whose outsize heart overrules his brain. The point is made obvious when, after Kretzker is placed under arrest, Grissom remarks, "I can't tell whether he's brilliant . . . or nuts." Kretzker's death is a stunning conclusion to the episode. It's also one of the show's most memorable exits.

"Boom" also contains a subtle yet significant piece of character development. It's Catherine, not Grissom, who provides most of the forensic exposition about the bomb. An earlier version of the script has her explaining that she'd taken a course with the Feds. "That was then," Donahue explains. "Because we were still new, we felt that if the audience sees this gorgeous woman discussing bombs, they're going to go, 'How does she know about bombs?' Now, if Catherine says anything about anything it's, 'Well, yeah, she'd know that.'" Although it had been implied in previous episodes that Catherine was a formidable advocate for her own investigative approach, having her drive the walk-through had the effect of substantiating her as a scientist to be reckoned with.

Catherine also takes the lead in the episode's "B" storyline, going to bat for Nick. Having established his escalating infatuation with Kristy Hopkins in "I-15 Murders," the ground was laid for a dramatic conclusion. "Nick's already on the edge, so we thought, 'What if something happened to her?'" says Donahue. "And because they had sex, we thought it was a great dramatic setup. All of his hair and fibers and some of his DNA would be there." When her murderer/pimp Jack Willman tells Nick, "She's not Julia Roberts and you're not Richard Gere," it gets to the heart of Nick's country-boy naivete. "His ideas about women seem old-fashioned," George Eads says of his character, "but they're very loving, endearing qualities." ∎

LAS VEGAS POLIC
CRIMINAL LABORATOR

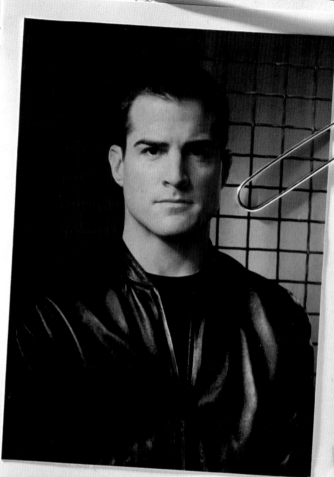

REQUESTING AGENCY: ___LVPD___

OFFENSE: __MURDER__   DATE OF OFFENSE: __

SUSPECT(S) __NICK STOKES__

VICTIM(S) __KRISTINE MARIE HOPKINS__

Investigating Officer: __LEWIS DOTY__

REPORT FI

FINGERPRINTS OF SUSPECT FOUND ON ITEI
1. WINE GLASS
2. CONDOM WRAPPER
3. BATHROOM FAUCET
4. WINE BOTTLE
5. COFFEE TABLE
6. END TABLE
7. KITHCEN DRAWER
8. WATER FAUCET (KITCHEN)

| X | RESULTS VERIFIED _____ | | 5 | 7 | 6 | 8 | 4 | 3 | 1 | 0 | 8 | 4 | | |

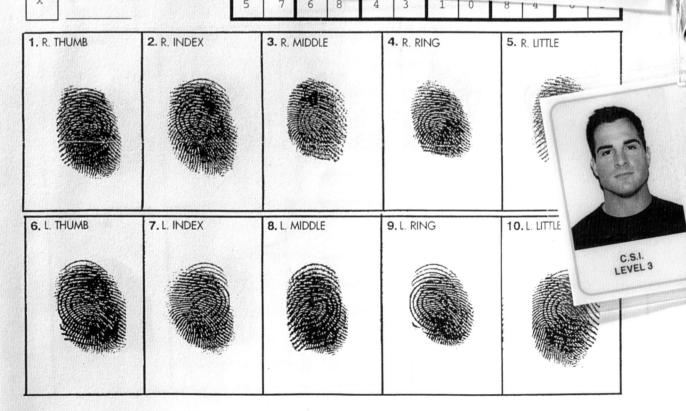

1. R. THUMB	**2.** R. INDEX	**3.** R. MIDDLE	**4.** R. RING	**5.** R. LITTLE

6. L. THUMB	**7.** L. INDEX	**8.** L. MIDDLE	**9.** L. RING	**10.** L. LITTLE

C.S.I.
LEVEL 3

SWS-4

85 37297

LAS VEGAS POLICE DEPARTMENT - SUPPLEMENTARY REPORT

Born and raised in Dallas to a family of law enforcers, Nick Stokes was destined for a future in public service. His father, a Texas Supreme Court Judge, and his mother, a Defense Attorney, both had high expectations for their son. Growing up the youngest of seven siblings, Nick was a well-rounded, straight-A student and star of his varsity football team. Accustomed to being met with more criticism than praise, he found himself always trying to please his strict and unemotional father.

The Stokes' children were taught to earn their rewards, so despite a very comfortable standard of living; Nick was not spoiled in any way. On the occasion of his sixteenth birthday, he was given an encyclopedia set rather than the car he desperately wanted. Although naturally disappointed at the time, he learned to appreciate the work ethic they instilled in him, as well as the encyclopedias, which he still uses today.

Outgoing and popular in high school, Nick was known for being a loyal friend. Always the sympathetic ear and designated driver, he was dubbed "Mr. Dependable" among his peers. He began an ambitious course load in college, majoring in pre-law at Rice University. It was there, while taking his required science classes that he became enamored with advanced chemistry. Knowing he had found his calling, he looked for a field of study that would combine his two passions: science and law. After his freshman year, he decided he wanted a change and transferred to Texas A&M to pursue a degree in Criminal Justice, while also making time for the college football team and rushing a fraternity.

Nick came into his own in college, escaping the rigidity of his family life and learning to think for himself. He did, however, retain a deeply embedded code of honor inherited from his parents which he has carried through his life. From his love of football, he has retained a respect for the value of teamwork, as well as a healthy competitive streak.

After graduating at the top of his class, Nick took a job with the Dallas Crime Lab, specializing in hair and fiber analysis. Even after three years on the job, he found it difficult to escape the imposing shadow of the Stokes family name and felt the need to work twice as hard to prove himself. Eager to make his own way, he responded to a job posting with the LVPD for entry level CSI position under supervisor Gil Grissom. As soon as Nick interviewed for the job, he knew this was where he wanted to be and Grissom was the man he wanted to learn from.

The move to Las Vegas was a culture shock for clean-cut Nick Stokes. What he lacked in street-savvy, he made up for in common sense and strength of character. Nick takes pride in speaking for the victims, but also takes great care in comforting the survivors. After four challenging years working under Grissom, Nick was promoted to a CSI Level 3. A compassionate man, Nick often feels deeply for others, but does his best to remain an objective professional.

CONFIDENTIAL

	APPROVED BY		REFER TO
STAR	RANK	STAR	

ORIGINAL AIRDATE: 2/15/01
WRITTEN BY: Andrew Lipsitz & Ann Donahue
DIRECTED BY: Lou Antonio

58

A dad and his son are playing fetch with their dog near Nevada's Mount Charleston. The dog comes bounding back, not with a stick, but a large, human bone. Grissom confirms that it's a human tibia. He leaves open the possibility it belonged to a lost hiker and was picked clean by the area's animals. Catherine is going with her gut; she thinks there's been foul play.

Warrick and Sara respond to a call at the Lucky Seven Motel where one Darren Pyne lies dead in a room festooned with streamers and balloons. There's a broken lamp and a large bruise on Pyne's forehead. The room was charged to Lynn Henry, who is checked into the Sphere Hotel. The CSIs find her having cocktails with

GUEST STARRING

EILEEN RYAN: Rose Bennett
PAMELA GIDLEY: Teri Miller
DORIE BARTON: Meg Wheeler
LISA DEAN RYAN: Lynn Henry
ERIC SZMANDA: Greg Sanders
ROBERT DAVID HALL: Dr. Al Robbins

her friends, Joyce Lanier and Meg Wheeler. Lynn says that Pyne was a male dancer hired for Wheeler's bachelorette party. After the party, he'd asked if he could stay in the room. They left him there around 3 A.M.

Looks like someone in the Dental Society database saw your posting.

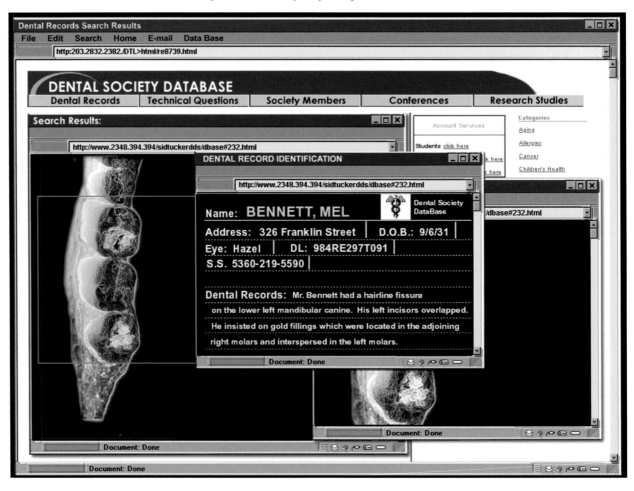

> purge{nlviem} buffer…waiting…
> echo$confab/.unx/ scim-Ruff = {3% .00$
> tar/variance = .00010. innduc/root/proc

TO HALVE AND TO HOLD

With the assistance of police cadets, the autopsy room now has a number of bones from the site. Grissom concludes their victim was an older man. Nick takes the lower jawbone so he can post it on the Dental Society website. Grissom observes jagged gashes across a number of the bones, Catherine suggesting that the man was chopped into pieces. Teri Miller enters explaining that blood in the soft tissue would indicate if the victim was alive when he was dismembered. Caught off-guard Grissom takes Catherine aside, irked that she called Teri in without asking him. A local dentist has identified the victim as sixty-nine-year-old Mel Bennett. Because grooves on the bones are coarse and uneven, Teri believes they were caused by a reciprocating saw.

Dr. Robbins's postmortem on Darren Pyne reports there were multiple blows to the head, resulting in cranial bleeding. He also had sex with someone immediately before his death, which was around midnight. Lynn Henry is asked about the bruises on her wrist. She says that Pyne came on to her. A struggle ensued. He pinned her down and raped her, but he was alive when she left.

Grissom, Catherine, and Brass go to the home of Rose Bennett, who tells them her husband, Mel, is out at the store. They bring her in for questioning. Catherine makes note of photos on the walls of their home documenting their fifty years together and maintains they looked happy. A phenolphthalein swab of the Bennetts' bathtub drain detects the presence of blood. Brass finds a reciprocating saw, which Teri confirms was the same type used in Mel Bennett's dismemberment. The cuts on the skeleton indicate its user was not adept, probably owing to a compromised musculature, maybe even arthritis. The frail Rose Bennett denies killing Mel, and says that they never even fought.

Warrick and Sara return to the motel room where they find a tiny cubic zirconia diamond. Sara receives a pager message with the results of Lynn Henry's SART exam. "She lied to us." The entire wedding party is brought in for questioning.

Grissom finds Teri packing to leave, and persuades her to take a later flight and have dinner with him. There is no blood in the vertebral tissue, Mel was carved up postmortem. Attorney Margaret Finn says her client, Rose, will admit to cutting up the body after she found him dead in the bathtub. Rose says she cut him into "manageable pieces" to transport him. Brass points out Rose has been cashing her dead husband's Social Security checks, which is both fraud and motive.

Greg performs a bioassay on Mel Bennett's skeletal muscle. He discovers high levels of digoxin, a medication used to treat congestive heart failure. Confronted with this discovery, Rose says that Mel was suffering from chronic pain and poisoned himself. He asked her to leave, and then *he* took the fatal dose. Mel had advised her to hide his body so her Social Security benefits would not be cut in half. Brass points out the evidence doesn't prove murder *or* suicide. Catherine tells Rose she will not be charged.

The wedding party, still in their gowns, is assembled in front of Sara to get "a free course in the forensics of sexual intercourse." Lynn's SART exam showed no evidence of sex in months. The bride confesses that Pyne had been flirting with her and she wanted one last fling. During the act, she had second thoughts, resisted, and bludgeoned him with the lamp. When Sara asks about her ring, she says her diamonds are real, but that Luke's ring is zirconia. One of the stones is missing from Luke's ring. He showed up, caught them in the act, and bashed Pyne's skull against the headboard in a jealous rage.

Grissom and Teri have just sat down to dinner when he receives an urgent page. He answers a call on his cell, giving instructions to the staff at the scene, hoping to buy himself some time. When he hangs up, Teri is gone.

> I'm never disappointed. And sometimes, I'm nicely surprised.

60

"That was our Valentine's episode," jokes Ann Donahue. "It turned out that it aired in February, so it looked like we planned it." The story of Rose and Mel Bennett had unromantic origins. "I found it fascinating that it's not illegal to cut up a dead body," Donahue says. "And," adds writer Andrew Lipsitz, "we were interested in how you go from one bone to figuring out who the person is and what happened to them." The writers asked Technical Consulant Elizabeth Devine how to start. She suggested the idea of recruiting police cadets for a grid search to recover the bones.

The grid search was shot in Red Rock Canyon on one of the show's first location trips to Nevada. Andrew Lipsitz considered the trip very educational. "We learned a couple of things there—for one thing, that we get more production bang for our buck by being on the Strip in Las Vegas. Whereas the topography in Santa Clarita and outside Las Vegas is very similar." Ruefully he adds, "You have to figure out what works and what doesn't work." For Marg Helgenberger, any exterior work is a treat. "I prefer being on location to any sort of soundstage just because I like being outside. I adapt really well to environments." Desert locales hold a special allure for the actress. "You've got sand, sky, and silhouettes, the silhouettes being us," she says. "It's just so stark, and just has sort of a surreal quality. I think it always adds to the ambience and texture of the filmmaking." Another example of what not to do was the scene where Catherine looks for blood traces in the Bennett's tub. "That was a real bathroom, and it was very difficult to get into." Lipsitz notes, "Now, we would build a bathroom to allow the cameras to move around and get a better look at it."

Lipsitz is proud of the Bennett storyline's unconventional conclusion; the evidence against Rose is found to be "equivocal," allowing her to go free. "There's a certain degree of audience satisfaction that derives from definitive conclusions," Lipsitz asserts. "But it only works if you occasionally mix in the times when it's not, and we try to do that to the extent that we can."

"I'd always wanted to do something about good girls from the Midwest who go to Vegas," Donahue says of the "B" storyline. "Anthony who lived in Vegas said, and I found it so fascinating, that when people get to Vegas, it's night, it's neon, anything goes, and they think that the rules don't apply. And they really think you could commit a murder in Vegas and fly back to Chicago as though it never happened." Lipsitz remarks, "The bachelorette party was an early attempt to take advantage of how sexy Las Vegas is—how to tell that, how to show that."

Love is also in the air at CSI Headquarters, though Grissom has to be dragged kicking and screaming to confront it. He resists calling Teri in to help, even though the Bennett case fairly screams out for her expertise. Grissom's and Catherine's squabble in the hallway over Catherine calling Teri in reveals the tough love and concern that's between them. "Obviously, they've known each other for a very long time," Marg Helgenberger reflects. "I don't know if she ever had a crush on him, but she's always had an enormous amount of respect for the guy."

Although William Petersen realizes the importance of viewers speculating on what kind of life a CSI can have after hours, he believes to actually place his obsessed entomologist in a relationship could lead to a dramatic quagmire. "It's kind of like cop relationships: That person's going to come home with so much baggage at the end of the day. I think Grissom knows that there's no way he can share what he does with the people in his life—it's too tedious, it's too traumatic, and it would require someone with much greater personal skills than he has." ■

TABLE STAKES

ORIGINAL AIRDATE: 2/22/01
TELEPLAY BY: Anthony E. Zuiker &
Carol Mendelsohn
STORY BY: Elizabeth Devine
DIRECTED BY: Danny Cannon

GUEST STARRING

SHAWN CHRISTIAN: Patrick Haynes
ELIZABETH LACKEY: Amanda Haynes
ERIC SZMANDA: Greg Sanders
GLENN MORSHOWER: Sheriff Brian Mobley
ROBERT DAVID HALL: Dr. Al Robbins
SHEERI RAPPAPORT: Mandy Webster

A black-tie fund-raiser is in progress at the mansion of Portia Richmond, a socialite and former showgirl. Screams ring out when a young woman is found floating facedown in the swimming pool. Grissom confers with Sheriff Mobley, one of the guests, and Brass. Grissom comments, "Come for the hors d'oeuvres, stay for the interrogation." A couple of pieces of evidence are quickly found. Catherine finds a red fingernail in the poolside grass. Warrick retrieves a turqoise-and-silver cuff link with the initials "CM" from the bottom of the pool.

The autopsy reveals the victim has had "a few upgrades": cheek implants, rhinoplasty, and silicone breast augmentation. Doctor Robbins concludes that she was strangled. Grissom orders a rape kit. Brass tells Grissom that Portia Richmond is on holiday in Europe. The party's hosts, Patrick and Amanda Haynes, say they recently met Richmond and have been house-sitting while they look for a place of their own. The victim is a stranger to them, and was not on the guest list.

61

You ever wear one of these when you were dancing?

VB VISTA BANK
Las vegas, Nevada 89114

Vista Bank

Inter
State

04
E

CRIME EVIDENCE

TOOTH   0766
Article   Exhibit No.
FEB 16 2001
Date Found, Located or Developed
PORTIA RICHMONDS BEDRM
Where This Article Was Found
G. GRISSOM
Investigation Officer

25, 24

Portia M. Richmond
6 Christopher Rd

Written Inquiries
Vista Bank
Magnolia Park Branch
PO Box 37176
San Francisco, CA 94

Las Vegas Police
53-0728-0769

Case # 53
Exhibit # 0769

TEXAS COLD CASE # 85103

CASE # 01-114A-15 'Table Stakes'

☐ **Summary of Your Business Interest Checking Account**

Annual Percentage Yield earned this pe

Beginning	
Total Depo	
Total Check Transfers,	
Interest P	
Ending B	

☐ **Impor**

Based on
charge ha

☐ Vista

Want to save on a new 401(k) plan for your smal
December 31, 2000. You will save 40% off the set-up fee if you o
401(k) plan for your smal... off the set-up fee when you open a new 401(k) plan. For more
exist... or call 1.877.261.0091.
infor...

☐

Portia M. Richmond
26 Christopher Rd.
Las Vegas, NV 89114   98

4/16   20 01   16-66

PAY TO THE ORDER OF *Cyannes Fine Stores* $2,200.18

Twenty Two Hundred and 18/100   DOLLARS

VB VISTA BANK
Las Vegas Blvd. Branch #139
Las Vegas, NV 89114

FOR   *Portia M Richmond*

⑆4500⑈1339⑆:0237⑈43432⑈41250

Portia M. Richmond
26 Christopher Rd.
Las Vegas, NV 89114   9895
                                        16-66/1220
                                        2343

4/18   2001

PAY TO THE ORDER OF *Skadden, Kruger & Rowe Auctioneers* $5,394.44

Fifty Three Hundred Ninety Four and 24/100 DOLLARS

VB VISTA BANK
Las Vegas Blvd. Branch #139
Las Vegas, NV 89114

FOR   *Portia M. Richmond*

⑆4500⑈1339⑆:0237⑈43432⑈41250

Portia M. Richmond
26 Christopher Rd.
Las Vegas, NV 89114   9895
                                        16-66/1220
                                        2343

4/18   2001

PAY TO THE ORDER OF *Skadden, Kruger & Rowe Auctioneers* $5,394.44

Fifty Three Hundred Ninety Four and 24/100 DOLLARS

VB VISTA BANK
Las Vegas Blvd. Branch #139
Las Vegas, NV 89114

FOR   *Portia M. Richmond*

⑆4500⑈1339⑆:0237⑈43432⑈41250

BULLY FOR YOU

GUEST STARRING

ERIC SZMANDA: Greg Sanders
ROBERT DAVID HALL: Dr. Al Robbins
CHRISTOPHER WIEHL: Hank Peddigrew
DUBLIN JAMES: Dennis Fram
LISA BRENNER: Kelsey Fram
JOSEPH KELL: Gary Fram
SKIP O'BRIEN: Sgt. O'Riley
ERIC STONESTREET: Ronnie Litra
JAMIE MARTZ: Barry Schickel
TESS HARPER: Julia Barrett

In a high school hallway a teenager returning from football practice spray paints an insulting slur on a locker. He then enters a nearby lavatory, where he is shot three times in the back. The boy, Barry Schickel, was an A-student, recently voted class clown, and his wallet, cash intact, is still on him. The school's principal explains that the football team is allowed in the building from the end of practice until eight o'clock. Grissom pulls a .44 slug from behind the wall mirror.

Out in the desert, Sara and Nick meet Paramedic Hank Peddigrew, who stands before a body in a gym bag. Judging by its overwhelming stench, the corpse inside has been there awhile. At the lab, Assistant Coroner David Phillips X-rays the body finding a silver dollar, a medical implant near the victim's hip, and a metal plate in his skull. Judging from the liquification of the body, David estimates that the man has been dead about two months.

Warrick joins Grissom in the bathroom to measure the distance of the shooter from the victim. Based on their calculations, the shooter was only about 5' 3" or 5' 4" tall. Catherine talks with a guidance counselor, Julia Barrett, who tells her that the spray-painted locker belongs to a Dennis Fram, a student who had regularly been bullied by Schickel. Catherine takes a fingerprint from a smear made while the paint was still tacky. Warrick plans to test the bathroom for odors with an expensive polymer sensor proboscis—an electronic nose—called the Cyranose 320. However, Grissom advocates the use of mind over machinery

and directs him to do the test old-school, with a glass tube, an air pump, and some chalk dust.

Called into Barrett's office, Dennis Fram's shirt tests positive for gunshot residue, establishing that he'd fired a gun within the last three to six hours. The boy admits that he goes to a shooting range every Monday night. His sister, Kelsey, bursts in and vouches for Dennis.

Sara and Nick reel at the wafting stench as David removes the liquified body parts from the bag. Inside, they find a gambling chip and a government-issue Army jacket with a name tag for a W. Cartsen sewn inside. Sara runs the name through the VA medical database, while Nick finds a matchbook in one of the pockets. When EMT Hank Peddigrew stops by to ask Sara to dinner, she asks for a raincheck, aware that she reeks of decomposing flesh.

Grissom returns to the school to ask Barrett about Schickel. She says that he was a bully and had a lot of enemies. Sensing a sympathy on Barrett's part for Schickel's victims, Grissom suggests that she probably knows who the killer is but gets no response from the counselor.

A digital enhancement of the matchbook reveals the name "Romanini's" which Nick identifies as a nightclub on the Strip. Sergeant O'Riley shows up to verify that their victim is William Cartsen, a Vietnam vet who was wounded in action thirty-one years earlier. He was sent home with a plate in his head and a pin in his spine. The manager of Romanini's, Aaron Targer, draws a blank on Cartsen, until he's told about the Army jacket. He knows the man as "Moses," and recalls that Cartsen, wearing a long beard, a robe, and the army jacket, would stand in front of the club scaring his customers away. The last time he saw Carsten, about two months ago, he'd given him a casino chip and asked him to move along.

Grissom studies a computer schematic of the crime scene as Brass informs him that the only suspect not checking out is Dennis Fram. Catherine reveals that the paint Schickel used contains alkyd particles that adhere and dry in thirty seconds. Dennis's prints on the locker place him at the scene and at the time of the murder. Confronted at his home, Dennis breaks down and Kelsey leads him to the bathroom, where she spoons medication into her brother's mouth.

LAS VEG

POLICE DEPARTMENT
Clark County, Nevada

Police Department
Las Vegas

ce over the last
bar attitude, prompt
thorough.
res on proficiency
d across the

FORENSTIC

LAS VEGAS
POLICE DEPARTMENT
Clark County, Nevada
POLICE

SIDLE, Sara
CSI Level 3

5. R. LITTLE

L. LITTLE

LEFT FOUR FINGERS TAKEN SIMULTANEOUSLY

CRI ME SCENE DO NOT CROSS CROSS CRIME SCENE DO NOT

ORIGINAL AIRDATE: 10/18/01
WRITTEN BY: Ann Donahue
DIRECTED BY: Thomas J. Wright

Kelsey explains to Catherine that her brother has a bleeding ulcer, acquired from the relentless taunting by Schickel. Catherine then asks Kelsey how tall she is. "Five-four, with heels." The same height as the killer.

Using the software that came with the Cyranose, Grissom and Warrick identify the scent from the lavatory as a perfume called Chanteuse. The brother and sister are confronted with the scent evidence. While she admits that she does wear Chanteuse, Kelsey claims that she was out driving around on the night of the murder.

In interrogation, Aaron Targer admits that his last confrontation with "Moses" Cartsen resulted in him driving the homeless vet out of town. Targer put the man in a duffel bag and rolled him down a hill. Targer is charged with homicide.

Dennis Fram approaches Catherine and Grissom, asking them to understand that Kelsey was only trying to protect him. He admits that he was in the school at the time of the murder. After seeing the graffiti on

his locker, he entered the bathroom, where he heard the shots fired from the stall and ran away. Although he never actually saw his sister, he smelled her perfume. Brass informs the CSIs that at the time of the murder Kelsey was at a motel with the school's football coach, Jeremy Spencer. Both of their cars had been ticketed for parking infractions. A chat with Spencer reveals that Kelsey traded him sex for his promise to intercede on Dennis's behalf with Schickel.

Grissom presents a bottle of Chanteuse to counselor Julia Barrett. He found it in her house, under a warrant, along with a .44 pistol. Barrett doesn't attempt a denial. Instead she rationalizes that her actions were better than waiting until a student is pushed over the edge and goes on a killing spree. "I did it for my kids," she says, as she's placed under arrest.

119

Our job is to think. Machinery should never matter more than our minds.

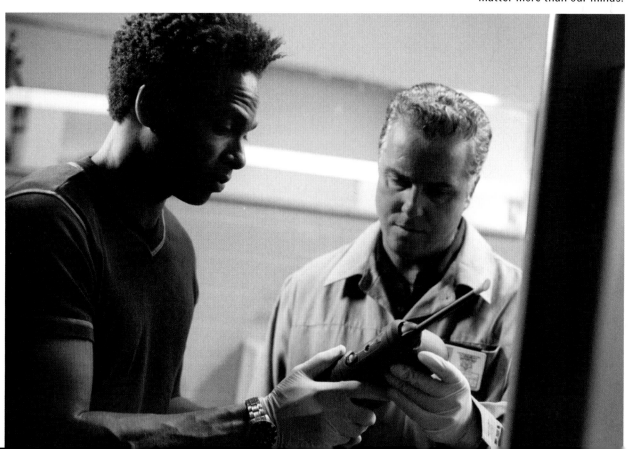

120

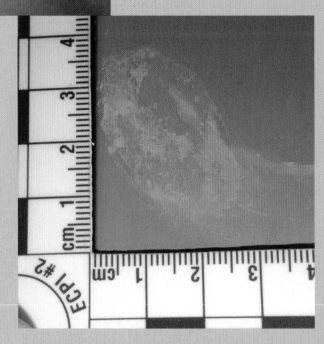

Although it was the fourth episode to air in fall of 2001, "Bully for You" was actually the first episode of Season Two to be shot. Executive Producer Ann Donahue explains, "I usually write the first script and then we film it, which gives us time to get all of the kinks out of the script for the premiere." Donahue says that she hadn't consciously intended to do an episode about post-traumatic stress. "When you sit down to write," she says, "everything comes together if you keep pushing toward shore. Suddenly, you look up and find you have a theme."

"Bully" was a backstory-rich episode as it colors in each of the criminalists personalities through a series of reminiscences about their high school years. "It took a long time to figure out that it's always best to see our characters through the prism of work," says Donahue. Thus her decision to have the colleagues casually ask one another, "What were you in high school?" as they go about working their respective cases. "The thing is, people tune in for entertainment, they want to learn about a mystery, and so you have to keep the tension tight on the mystery," she explains. "If, during that tight-wire act, you lay in character beats that are somewhat related, then we've succeeded."

"That's why I regard Ann Donahue as our strongest writer," says Gary Dourdan, alluding to her ability to enmesh the personal with the professional while keeping her scripts lean. "There's something in her writing that's really studied; she doesn't leave anything to chance," he continues. "If there's something that's not necessary, she's not afraid to just throw it out. She's very efficient."

Warrick inquires of Grissom, "What were you, a jock or a brain?" Intently focusing on the forensic task at hand, Grissom offhandedly replies, "I was a ghost." As Donahue recalls, "With every script you have maybe three lines where you think, 'Wow, that's something I'm really glad I got to say, and that was one of them.'" In response to a similar query by Catherine, Nick says of himself, "Me? I was dependable." Sara mirrors that succinctness, saying only that she was a "science nerd." And Warrick attests to a surprisingly geeky background, "I got pushed around by all the guys and never got any play from the girls." This inspires Catherine to

comment, "The girls didn't even notice your eyes? What do they know?"

Catherine and Warrick can get away with such affectionate flirting without losing their emotional grounding, Donahue says. "Grissom and Sara go up and down, depending on their most recent interaction, but Catherine and Warrick are always at the same level. They don't get their hearts broken the same way. Sara and Grissom are all intellect, while Catherine and Warrick are all viscera."

Being a science nerd, however, didn't prevent Sara's violent reaction to "liquid man," providing the episode with a bit of comic relief. "Those beats have become funny, and I've gotten to do more of them," says Jorja Fox. "As the other characters on the show have gotten to know Sara and know that she can handle it, she's been able to let more of her vulnerability show through—that these things actually do bother her." ■

SCUBA DOOBIE-DOO

ORIGINAL AIRDATE: 10/25/01
WRITTEN BY: Andrew Lipsitz
& Elizabeth Devine
DIRECTED BY: Jefrey Levy

121

SPECIAL GUEST STAR
BRAD JOHNSON: Paul Newsome

GUEST STARRING
ERIC SZMANDA: Greg Sanders
ROBERT DAVID HALL: Dr. Al Robbins
MARK TYMCHYSHYN: Stu Evans
DAVID DELUISE: Cliff Renteria
RICK PETERS: Jerry Walden
SKIP O'BRIEN: Sgt. O'Riley
ERIC STONESTREET: Ronnie Litra
JENNA GERING: Allison Scott
TERRY BOZEMAN: Brad Lewis

A landlord leads a couple to a recently vacated apartment in his building. He apologizes for showing the place before having had a chance to clean it up. What they are all shocked to see when he opens the door is the apartment's walls are covered in blood spatters. The previous tenant, Clifford Renteria, lived in the apartment with his girlfriend, explains Brass, until he left in the middle of the night. Grissom wastes no time testing the splatter—it is human blood. Sara comments that drops this small usually are indicative of a high-velocity spatter, as from a gunshot but there are no bullet holes. A luminol test shows blood all over the carpeted floor. Various blood-free voids suggest a couch, a television, and a shape that resembles an electric saw, which could explain the small, high-velocity spray. The landlord, Stu Evans, tells them that Renteria's girlfriend had moved out before he did.

Meanwhile, Catherine and Nick arrive at a Lake Mead Recreation Area. A sprawling brush fire rages around them while helicopters empty huge vats of water on the blaze. Most surprising, a body in full scuba gear is lodged in the branches of a scorched tree. As Catherine photographs the scuba tank's air-pressure gauge, Nick finds a matchbook time-delay ignition device—a lit cigarette is tucked into a matchbook.

Brass and Grissom find Cliff Renteria at his job. He says his girlfriend, Allison Scott, went to Canada to visit her parents. The bloody "mural" at his apartment was an act of revenge against the uncaring landlord. Renteria explains he has hepatitis C, which hinders clotting and gives him chronic nosebleeds. When Brass and Grissom examine Renteria's personal belongings, crammed inside the back of a delivery truck, they discover an electric saw. Renteria's possessions are brought to the lab, but there is no blood found on the power tools. Meanwhile, Greg reports that all sixteen blood samples taken from the apartment match Renteria. Grissom and Brass take Renteria up on his offer of a live demonstration. The man easily blows out a crimson spray. Renteria's demo causes Grissom to amend his original theory.

Interrupted the impulse to the heart, turning it into a bag of worms. Fibrillation.

122

Before they close the case, Greg reports that one blood sample found on Renteria's living-room lamp belongs to a female.

Robbins informs Catherine and Nick that the scuba diver didn't die in the fire, but by kymodiocordis, a cardiac concussion from a devastating blow to the chest. Greg tells Nick that the diver's pressure gauge denotes it had a full tank of air, indicating it may have exploded in the heat of the fire.

Nick finds a fissure in the bottom of the air tank, and drops acid onto it, raising a serial number. They trace the tank to the home of Jerry Walden, who says he'd lent the tank to the victim, a lifelong friend and business partner, Bruce Skeller. They were working together on a casino deal near Lake Mead. Catherine notices four marks on the floor suggesting a piece of missing furniture. Walden says they're from his coffee table, which he has sent out for refinishing. When she spots shards of wood lying nearby, she remarks, "I think it needed a little more than that."

Scott's parents said she never arrived. In the apartment, Grissom asks Sara to count the number of flies. Sara points to fly spots on the ceiling. Grissom finds traces of fresh blood in the spots, they're not feeding off of the walls. Then he notices a swarm of flies around an air vent.

In the vent grate, Grissom finds fly-egg casings, and a silphid beetle — which is known to feed on decomposing human flesh. Grissom asks Evans if he can get permission for the CSIs to break into the walls. The LVPD won't provide reimbursement, therefore Evans refuses. They return to the lab where Warrick extracts blood from the beetle; if human DNA is present they can get a warrant.

Catherine meets with District Engineer Paul Newsome. He tells her that the lakeside property was sold two weeks earlier, despite opposition from Skeller who found the plan enviromentally unsound. Catherine brings the deed to Ronnie Litra in Questionable Documents, who uses the VSC4 machine

> # I'm not mad at me, there's a body in there and that guy knows where it is.

to reveal that the inks of Walden's and Skeller's signatures came from separate pens. If the document is a forgery, it's an impressive one.

The CSIs get their warrant when the beetle tests positive for human DNA. No sooner do they finish dismantling the first wall, when Brass enters with Allison Scott. She assures them that Renteria is no murderer. Grissom takes Sara's suggestion to "think outside the box" and asks Evans if they can take a look at *his* walls.

Doctor Robbins has found wood splinters embedded in Skeller, and the wood grains are a match with Walden's coffee table. The two men argued over their co-owned land, Walden eventually punching Skeller, who fell back over the table, causing his fatal cardiac concussion.

Jerry Walden sits in interrogation with his lawyer, Catherine hypothesizes that Walden dumped Skeller's body, then set the matchbook device, believing that the fire department would think the blaze was just another hot spot. The intense heat caused Skeller's air tank to explode, propelling him up into the tree.

Grissom comments on the scented candles burning in Evans's apartment, as well as newly plastered wall. Evans offers excuses, until Brass enters with a search warrant that he obtained after learning that Evans's wife is missing. Grissom finds that the heating duct leading in the apartment is teeming with insects. They break into the wall beneath it and find a bloody blanket and more beetles, but no body. An increasingly frustrated Grissom steps outside for some air. Sara joins him to talk out the problem in a gesture of support.

Back inside the apartment, Grissom realizes there's no hot water and goes to investigate. The water pipe has been diverted to bypass the water filtration tank. Inside Grissom finds the remains of Mrs. Evans.

The case of Jerry Walden was a foray into urban legend. "We actually did a lot of research because we were arguing over whether it is possible for firefighting helicopters to scoop up divers while retrieving water from a nearby body of water, and deposit them on burning trees" explains Elizabeth Devine. "Everybody I know thinks they've heard a story where that's happened." Now all that was needed was a fire. Andrew Lipsitz recalls, "We always thought that we would CGI the fire. We just figured we would take stock footage, add some computer-generated images, and it would be fine." It turned out the summer fire season in the western United States coincided with the shoot. "We found a location that had just burned. The punishing part was that it was 105 degrees," Lipsitz says. "Marg and George were real troopers. But it was maybe the hottest I've ever been in my life."

The story of the nasal expirator, Clifford Renteria, is a classic demonstration of truth being stranger than fiction. It's derived from a case Elizabeth Devine had worked. "It was the most disgusting thing I've ever seen," she recalls of the sight that greeted investigators. "There was blood all over this apartment, and the guy's wife was missing. It just was unbelievable to me that someone had not died." So unbelievable she had to see a demonstration for herself. "I brought him back to the scene, and we actually found out that this guy took six weeks and just blew his nose all over the place." Anticipating her colleagues' incredulity, Devine showed a videotape from the real-life scene for a roomful of writers and producers. Looking back on the case, she reflects, "Every time I think I've seen everything, I come across something new. Some people just do things that you can't fathom."

Catherine's rendezvous with District Engineer Paul Newsome, "is meant to be the definitive end to that particular story," Lipsitz says. "Personally I don't think the relationship really worked that well." Marg Helgenberger agreed with the choice, "Anytime the writers have veered off into any kind of intimacy or personal life or backstory, it seems they're almost kind of afraid to go far down that particular path." Lipsitz adds, "I don't think our show will ever do an overtly emotional storyline. But that doesn't mean that you don't explore the smaller moments." For example, when Sara brushes the dust from Grissom's face, that scene was not originally in the script. "We had some problems with that episode," recalls Carol Mendelsohn. "We went into the editing room and chopped off ten minutes, and we were left with a thirty-two minute show. Ann wrote some scenes, Danny Cannon did the reshoots." The effect of that scene opened up things between the two characters. "We got the pages the night before we were supposed to shoot it," says Jorja Fox, "And we were like, 'What is this?!' " Afterward, it became a beat that had the potential to play. Although, says Lipsitz, the writers weren't thinking of the characters in romantic terms. "We were getting into the mentor-mentee relationship and all its ramifications after seeing it grow over the first season." If the meaning of the scene is inconclusive, that's as it's intended. ∎

123

He didn't exactly die in the water.

ORIGINAL AIRDATE: 11/1/01
WRITTEN BY: Ann Donahue
DIRECTED BY: Danny Cannon

124

SPECIAL GUEST STAR

DYLAN BAKER: Father Powell

GUEST STARRING

ERIC SZMANDA: Greg Sanders
ROBERT DAVID HALL: Dr. Al Robbins
CORBIN ALLRED: Ben Jennings
JEREMY RENNER: Roger Jennings
SASHA ALEXANDER: Robin Childs
SKIP O'BRIEN: Sgt. O'Riley
WAYNE WILDERSON: Paramedic
LINDSAY PRICE: Kim Marita
NICOLE DEHUFF: Tina Kolas

A Nevada park ranger spots a car on the side of the road. He ventures into the brush and stumbles upon a body—and a young man digging a grave. Nick and Grissom arrive at the scene, where the man, Ben Jennings, is in custody. Grissom deduces that the body has been moved since the time of death and orders Jennings's car impounded. The suspect stands quiet, looking almost bewildered as Sara takes his footprints and Nick lifts red fibers off his shirt.

In town, Catherine and Warrick arrive at the Mediterranean Casino's women's spa. In the locker room, Shelley Danvers lies dead on a bench. The spa's night manager, Kim Marita, says she found Danvers when she came in to check on the towels. When Catherine notices someone else tied Danvers's robe, Marita admits that she covered her naked body, and denies the suggestion that the woman had drowned in the spa's hot tub.

Grissom and Sara observe flour on the corpse, now identified as Oliver Dunn. There are also silky-looking fibers visible in his neck wound. Since he's wearing a dress shirt but no tie, they speculate that the tie may have been the instrument of strangulation. Doctor Robbins recovered three slugs, but says the cause of death was asphyxiation. Sara learns that the flour on the body is commonly used in baking pizza.

In the interrogation room, O'Riley points out that Jennings is a registered gun owner. Ben claims he lost the gun. He admits to being a delivery guy at Dante's Pizzeria, but he can't explain how flour ended up on Dunn's body. He asks, "If you know so much about these murders, what do you need me for?" Grissom, catching the slip, inquires, "Murder*s?*"

Robbins points out that there's been no serosanguinous fluid expelled from Danvers's mouth or nose; she didn't drown. However, there is bright red lividity extending the length of the body, a symptom of heatstroke. Catherine has Brass get a warrant for the spa's records.

Warrick and Catherine question Danvers's roommate, Tina Kolas, who recalls that Danvers, had made an appointment for a sauna. When Warrick finds a torn shirt among the girls' belongings, Kolas says they'd had a playful tug-of-war and it ripped. Warrick notices a blank notepad next to the phone and takes it.

A search team takes Jennings back into the desert where they discover a second body. As they recover it Grissom is approached by a priest, Father Powell. He tells Grissom that Benjamin is a member of his parish, and that the police won't let him talk with him. Nick finds a laceration on the victim's forehead. Grissom suggests he check it against the blade of Jennings's shovel. The victim's wallet identifies him as Kenny Ramirez. O'Riley announces that vehicles belonging to Oliver Dunn and Ramirez have been found at a gas station.

Nick and Sara talk with the gas station attendant, who claims to have seen nothing, having gone on a short joyride with a friend. He returned to find Dunn's and Ramirez's vehicles by the pumps. Disturbed by the blood on the ground, he cleaned it up.

Father Powell visits Grissom as he is processing Jennings's car, and tells him that Ben is a good kid. Grissom may disagree, and makes his point by showing Father Powell the backseat lit up with bloodstains from the luminol spray.

The manager insists there's no record of Danvers using the sauna. However, Warrick trains his flashlight on the notepad revealing a writing indentation: "Sauna 8:00 P.M." He points out hotel regulations mandate that an employee check the dry sauna

ALTER BOYS

every fifteen minutes but records indicate no visits after 7:30 P.M. Marita admits she found the body at 10:00 P.M. and moved Danvers's body to protect the hotel's reputation.

Sara notes the bullets pulled from both victims match and that the police found receipts proving that Ben Jennings used the gas station where the cars were found. Grissom points out their evidence proves burial, not murder. They need a gun with Ben's fingerprints on it, or the what was used to strangle Dunn. When Sara suggests that Grissom may be protecting Ben Jennings in deference to Father Powell, he agrees to send what they have to the DA.

Ben's brother, Roger, is on parole for armed robbery, breaking and entering, and assault with great bodily harm. A concerned Grissom visits Ben in his cell to ask if he was just cleaning up after his brother. Ben just stares back looking frightened, confirming Grissom's theory.

At Roger Jennings's workplace, Dante's Pizzeria, Roger claims that Ben shot Ramirez and Dunn. Grissom dismisses Roger's account saying that Dunn's murder was personal. In Roger's trailer, Sara finds a newly dry-cleaned, but still stained, pair of jeans. While checking the perimeter, Nick finds a gun buried in the ashes inside a metal burn barrel.

Unfortunately, ballistics finds that the striations from Roger's gun don't match the slugs taken from the bodies. The CSIs conclude that Roger altered the gun's barrel. There's more bad news; the bloodstains from the jeans have been too degraded by the dry cleaning chemicals for testing.

After learning that Danvers and her girlfriend were heard publicly bickering over a guy named Jeremy, Brass, Catherine, and Warrick take another run at Tina Kolas. They tell her that Danvers's stroke, while ultimately fatal, masked another malady, anaphylactic shock. Brass shows Kolas the contract they signed with their travel agent, which indicates that Danvers was

allergic to shellfish. He then recites their room service order, placed by Kolas, for two bowls of lobster bisque. Panicked, Kolas says she'd only meant to disable Danvers by way of an allergic reaction so she wouldn't be able to make her date with Jeremy. Unfortunately, says Catherine, her reaction occurred in the sauna, where Danvers's trachea, larynx, and tongue swelled, and her blood pressure plummeted, eventually killing her. As she's cuffed, Kolas breaks down, saying that she just didn't want to be left out.

Grissom meets with District Attorney Robin Childs who gives him Oliver Dunn's tie. It was sent to her by Roger Jennings. Grissom notes that will explain why Roger's epithelials will be all over it, exonerating the guilty brother. Despite Grissom's passionate contention that Ben is being set up, Childs is determined to prosecute the suspect she has. Grissom asks Ben if he has *any* evidence linking Roger to the crime. He doesn't. The indictment against Ben is certified, and he's denied bail.

Later, Catherine and Grissom are talking at police headquarters when suddenly officers rush past them. Grissom follows them to the holding-cell area and he finds Ben Jennings lying on the floor in a pool of blood. An officer says he cut his wrists with his teeth. Horrified, Grissom tries to save him. Paramedics arrive, but it's too late. He stares down at his bloody hands as Ben is pronounced dead.

> I believe
> in God.
> In science.
> In Sunday
> supper.
> I don't believe
> in rules that
> tell me how
> I should live.

ARREST – INVESTIGATION REPORT

COURT
LV. SUPERIOR
AREA

EVIDENCE EVIDENCE
CRIME EVIDENCE

AUTO CARPET 0540
Article — Exhibit No.
10-25-01
Date Found, Located or Developed
B. JENNINGS CAR
Where This Article Was Found
Investigation Officer
SIRCHIE® FINGER PRINT LABS, INC. — CAT. NO. EIL01

AUTOMOTIVE CARPET SPEC

STYLE: 0617 617/SBR
MATERIAL NAME: 12 OZ. ME

CUSTOMER: RACEMARK INT. INC.

PILE YARN:
YARN A

FIBER TYPE:	POLYPROPYLENE
SIZE:	2750/120
HEAT SET:	NO
COMMENTS:	5000 LB MIN. YARN ORDER

TUFTING:

GAUGE:	5/32" CUT (STG)
STITCH PATTERN:	ROUND CROSS SECTION
SPI (+/- .75/3):	21.5 PER 3 INCHES
T.PILE HT. (+/- 1/32):	12/32"
T.PILE WT. (+/- 1/2 OZ.):	14 OZ.
TUFTED WDT:	171.5"

DYING:

SOURCE #1:	PERMACOLOR
METHOD:	SOLUTION/PRE-DYED
TREATMENTS:	NONE
DYE MIN.:	N/A

SOURCE #2: N/A

PRIM

COMM

...TOW STEER FROM PERMACOLOR BEFORE TUFTING

CASE # 02-206A-29
'Alter Boys'

POLICE TRACE LAB
LAS VEGAS NEVADA

LAS VEGAS **POLICE**
EVI

Date Prepared	10/25
Time Prepared	

Check 1 Box Only: ☒ Recovered ☐ Evidence ☐ Found ☐ Safekeeping ☐ Seizure ☐ Other

Suspect: JENNINGS, B
Charge: HOMICIDE
Location:

Impounding Officer's Initials/P #: SS
Signature

ITEM	IMPOUNDED ITE
#	
# 1	SHIRT WITH STAIN
#	
#	
#	
#	
#	

CO-DEFENDANT ▼ — This Package

CHAIN OF CUSTODY SIGNATURE AND P # ▼

LVMPD 133 (REV. 8-97)

Search | Enter Data | POLICE DEPARTME

NAME	STATUS	PENAL CODE/CHARG
Taylor Ziegler	incarcerated	31.02. Consolidatic
Tammy Hin		
Tommy Liu		
Natalie D		
Macy Vald		
Dustin Be		
Roy Hinto		
Baron McM		
Patsy Cam		
Andrea Li		
Sally Mer		
Taylor Gr		
Dexter Pi		
James Boy		

** LVMP RECORD
CII/A053948AD048266

FELONY REC

Name: Benjamin Corey Je   Sex: M
DOB: 2/5/76
HGT: 5'9"   WGT: 165   Eye
CNT: 01
LVMP: Las Vegas

CURRENT CONVICTION
NRS 205.275 Receiving
Current Status: paroled
*DISPO: Convicted   Co
SENT: 2 yrs: Suspended.
Employment: DANTE'S PIZZA
29538 Desert Wa
Known Associates: None.
No prior criminal history.

Address: 311 Sephill Rd.
Las Vegas, NV 89

Las Vegas Police Department Forensic Laboratory

STR RESULTS- PROFILER PLUS/COFILER

| DATE: 10-25-01 | ANALYST: E. KRAUSE, DNA TECH |
| CR AMP #: 19-1672 | EVENT #: 102501-1468 |

DNA STR TYPING RESULTS

MPLE #	D3S1358	vWA	FGA	AMELO	D8S1179	D21S11	D18S51	REMARKS
SAMPLE INFO								
SWAB 1:								
NECK TIE								
MPLE #								
SAMPLE INFO								
BENJAMIN JENNINGS								
MPLE #								
SAMPLE INFO								

12

AUTOPSY REPORT

DEPARTMENT OF CORONER

No.

98-03811

Page 2

E.   Path: Skin, muscle, 7th-8th intercostal space, right lung (lower lobe), spinal column, spinal cord, left pleura, left 5th-6th intercostal space, muscle.

F.   Seque...
     right

III.   An old bull... injury).

IV.   No evidence

Evidence   Case Files

DOCKET NUM

DBase:100_0492.F
Status[online]

DBase:409_04900.D
Status[online]

DBase:69834_957.AF
Status[online]

DBase:220_95495.W
Status[online]

DBase:333_48611.C
Status[online]

DBase:690_281_84.X

sian

Blond

****
5492

FLOUR 0531
Exhibit No.
T 25 2001
ocated or Developed
'S PIZZA
icle Was Found
RISSOM
fficer
RACE COMPARISON

PHONE CALL

FOR Gil Grissom
M Robin Childs
OF District attorney's office
DATE 10/24   TIME _____ P.M.

PHONE _____ FAX _____

MESSAGE
CALL ASAP!

URGENT AND
CONFIDENTIAL

SIGNED _____

☐ TELEPHONED
☐ RETURNED YOUR CALL
☒ PLEASE CALL
☐ WILL CALL AGAIN
☐ CAME TO SEE YOU
☐ WANTS TO SEE YOU

Adams 1154

---

nty]= targeti.init.bat/.root/remote loc. = accept

Writer Ann Donahue describes the motivation behind the "Alter Boys" story, "I was trying to set up a world where somebody looked *so* guilty, and yet didn't do it." She recalls, Elizabeth Devine provided the forensic hook. "Liz said, 'Well, you can get evidence that proves burial but not murder.' I just wrapped the heart and soul of it around the mystery." The mystery became so strong that Donahue regrets having included the less powerful "B" story of death by sauna and shellfish. "I should have made it all 'A,'" Donahue says. "We could have gone deeper into those brothers and what was going on with them and what else they had done in their lives." For Donahue, the Catholic motif that runs through the "A" story was an instinctual channeling. "When you're brought up Catholic, there's no getting around it—you were brought up with theater. The Mass—and I used to think this was sacrilege—is theater, and it's all about blood. Everything's black and white, and everything's guilt-provoking. It gives you a skewed view no matter how you try to get away from it.

"Carol Mendelsohn and I always talk about evil. What's evil? Is it inherent? Is it learned? Are there people who are just good?" In this case, Ben's purity and goodness compel him to literally die for his brother's sins. However, Donahue says, "More than the brothers, the story is about Grissom. When he visits Father Powell in his church for a philosophical compare-and-contrast of their respective professions, Grissom meets his spiritual foil just as in Ben he had met his spiritual equal—a sheep who's strayed from the religious flock."

"It was very theater," says William Petersen. "It was people talking about stuff that they were dealing with in the case, but it was much more resonant."

As Donahue puts it, "Each of these men is about one hair different. Grissom finally meets someone who has the authority to judge him." Despite Grissom's protestations of faithlessness, Donahue believes that Powell's message touched a nerve. "He was saying 'You *pretend* that this is all intellect; you *pretend* that you're distant, when I know that your entire heart and soul are in this, and I know that you feel dirtied at the end of the day that you couldn't fix things—just like me,'" she says. "And that's something no one's been able to say to him because Grissom works to hard to be the distant ghost, but he's not."

For Jorja Fox, the scene is memorable not only for its powerhouse dramatics, but also for the producers' willingness to portray Grissom in a potentially alienating light. "I thought that deciding to make him sort of anti-religion was one of the bravest decisions I've ever seen," she says. "Here we are, a heartland show with a lot of viewers, and to give him that sort of take—and say it to a priest—for the audience to hear was so bold."

Grissom's showdown with Powell appears to be the

story's epilogue, but is in fact a preface to a much more disturbing climax back at headquarters when he discovers that Ben Jennings has killed himself. The episode's final image, in which Grissom crouches next to the dead youth, sums up Donahue's (and Powell's) take on the supposedly detached criminalist: "When he sleeps at night, the blood is on his hands." ■

ORIGINAL AIRDATE: 11/8/01
WRITTEN BY: Elizabeth Devine & Carol Mendelsohn
DIRECTED BY: Richard J. Lewis

CAGED

GUEST STARRING

ERIC SZMANDA: Greg Sanders
ROBERT DAVID HALL: Dr. Al Robbins
CURRIE GRAHAM: Stanley Hunter
SKIP O'BRIEN: Sgt. O'Riley
DAVID DUNARD: Train Engineer
WAYNE WILDERSON: Paramedic
JOHN DUERLER: Dean Croft
TSIANINA JOELSON: Megan Treadwell
MARIA CELEDONIO: Melanie
MICHAEL GOORJIAN: Aaron Pratt
NICOLE FREEMAN: Veronica Bradley

An SUV careens around a corner, its driver anxiously checking her rearview mirror. As she speeds down the street, her path is impeded by dropping gates at a railroad crossing. She waits for the train to pass, then suddenly rams the gates, lurching onto the tracks. An instant later, both driver and vehicle are crushed. As firemen retrieve the body of Megan Treadwell from the wreck, Grissom receives word that CSI has two hours to process the scene before the sheriff orders the tracks cleared.

Grissom leaves Catherine and Sara at the scene while he heads to the Western States Historical Society. The police found a dead body while responding to an apparent burglary in progress. The victim, Veronica Bradley, is in a gated room with reddish foam seeping from her mouth. Grissom is snapping photos when he's interrupted by a panicky young man who is concerned about the effect of the flashes on the rare books. He's Aaron Pratt, the Society librarian who set off the alarm while trying to get into the cage to help Veronica.

Pratt speaks quickly and intensely, so focused on his words that he sounds slightly mechanical. He recalls each moment in great detail, how she was sweating from her forehead and how she grabbed her stomach with both hands and called to him. Not having a key to the cage, he couldn't help her. Nick believes Pratt's unsettled body language indicates guilt, but Grissom explains that Pratt is a high-functioning autistic man with superior right-brain abilities.

As Sara and Catherine examine the train tracks, a dog scampers up to them. His tag identifies him as Maverick, from nearby Martingale Street. Megan Treadwell also lived on Martingale. The CSIs realize that the dog was her passenger. The demolished SUV is carted away, Catherine finds a piece of electrical filament, probably from a

headlight. Sara discovers *two* sets of skidmarks by the tracks, one going forward, one in reverse.

Doctor Robbins confirms that Bradley's bluish skin resulted from the blood's inability to oxygenate her tissue suggesting a blood-borne disease. Grissom suspects homicide.

Stanley Hunter, the Society's curator, explains that its special collections are kept in the vault. While Bradley's restoration work took place strictly within the downstairs cage. Sergeant O'Riley tells

The ricin made contact with the tongue . . . you're looking for a powder.

You hear that? Turbo. Probably diesel.

NOT CROSS CRIME SCENE DO NOT CROS ... S CRIME SCENE DO NOT CROS

130

Grissom that Pratt had one of the Society's prized volumes of Shakespeare in his briefcase. When Grissom asks Pratt why the book is not in the vault, Pratt says that Hunter doesn't like him, that Hunter breaks rules. He eats his lunch in his office, and apparently has been having an affair with Veronica.

The taillight filaments of Treadwell's SUV are intact—the one that Catherine found must be from a second vehicle. Her suspicion is confirmed when Catherine notices a black paint transfer on the rear fender. Inside Sara finds a bag of doggie treats, a discharged cell phone, and an engaged emergency brake.

Grissom and Nick visit Aaron Pratt's impeccably organized home. Pratt is visually agitated as Nick thumbs through his mail, and initially he ignores Grissom's question about Society books in the apartment. Pratt finally says that Veronica brought the books over, and that the two of them date. Nick finds a shrine-like array of Bradley's objects in the bedroom.

Sara and Catherine have A/V Tech Archie Johnson analyze Treadwell's last call to 911. She frantically told the operator there was a "maniac" following her. As Archie isolates the individual tracks, deleting all sounds but the car, they detect the sound of *two* engines, and identify the second engine as a turbo, most likely diesel-fueled.

Catherine and Sara try to visualize the night of Treadwell's death. They know she stopped to buy dog treats at a specialty store. The saleswomen at the coffeeshop next to the pet store remembers Treadwell having a fight with a man in the parking lot after almost accidentally backing into him. They remember the man as a regular who works nearby and note that he peeled out after Treadwell drove off.

Following Robbins's revised finding that Bradley was poisoned, Greg discovers an odd mass in her blood, which he identifies as ricin, a deadly biotoxin. The CSIs return to the book vault in biohazard suits, and bag all the items that could contain ricin.

Grissom and Greg look at an illustration in a botany book taken from Pratt's home. When Pratt is brought in for questioning he says he no longer touches the book, that "it doesn't feel right." He

recalls telling this to Hunter and Bradley. Veronica told him that sometimes books feel different after restoration. Later he saw Hunter slap Bradley, and say he was not going to let her ruin his reputation.

When Hunter is questioned, he admits that Bradley was stealing prints and replacing them with forgeries. With her dead, he didn't think it worth mentioning in his initial statement to the CSIs. Grissom returns to Pratt, asking him again for his recollection of Bradley's death. Concentrating, Pratt recalls that she pulled out a canvas bag and looked around, stared at a book, and stuck her pen in her mouth. At the Trace lab, Nick reports finding about a dozen pens at Bradley's home all chewed on, and a castor bean—the source of ricin—under her refrigerator.

When the coffeeshop regular, Dean Croft, is brought in, he claims he just sold his car. His black turbo diesel-powered SUV is soon found at a body shop with a gutted headlight and paint transfer on its front fender, indicative of prolonged contact. Catherine sees droplets of coffee on the dashboard and an empty cup on the floor along with a lipstick-stained lid. Rolling up the driver's-side window, she finds coffee splattered on the outside. They can easily fill in the rest: Croft caught up with Treadwell and exchanged words, she threw her coffee at him and raced off. When he followed her, Treadwell dialed 911. She stopped at the railroad crossing, believing she'd lost him, when with the headlights off he slammed into her, pushing her SUV onto the tracks. Rather than abandon her dog, Treadwell stayed with him, hoping to get both of them out of the car and to safety. Satisfied, they contact Brass to have him arrest Croft.

Grissom explains to Pratt that Bradley hid the altered books at his house so that, if caught, she could say he was the forger. When Hunter discovered she was a forger, Bradley tried to kill him by putting ricin in his food. However, Bradley mistakenly poisoned herself by chewing on a contaminated pen. Realizing he'd been used, Pratt sadly recites from Othello: " . . . then must you speak of one that loved not wisely . . ."

" . . . but too well," Grissom finishes.

"**C**aged" features an extremely rare pairing of Catherine and Sara. But it doesn't start out that way. Initially, it's Grissom with Catherine, who then reassigns himself to the Bradley murder. The reason? The tradition of having him recite the all-important kicker line that ends each episode's opening teaser. "That was one of the constructs of the show from the very beginning," says Carol Mendelsohn.

The cast and crew had bigger things on their minds than teaser lines during the two long, cold location nights by the railroad tracks. "We started at 5:30 or 6:00 P.M. and finished at 6:00 A.M.," director Richard Lewis recalls. The scenes required commandeering a section of an active California rail line, installing lights and cameras on a locomotive to capture the train's-eye view of the calamity, and making sure the hired conductor could take direction. The crew nearly suffered a disaster of their own when the train almost barreled into a camera and crane. Lewis recalls, "The camera cleared the train by only about half a foot. We know that because we had a B camera shooting the scene from another angle that showed the clearance exactly." Despite the close call, Lewis says. "That was a very fun sequence to shoot."

For the "B" storyline the show used the facilities at the Philosophy Library in Las Vilas, California, to represent the Western States Historical Society. Veronica Bradley's "cage" scene was done on a soundstage. The Bradley storyline made use of Elizabeth Devine's personal expertise. In creating Aaron Pratt, Devine drew upon her experience with her son, Austin, a high-functioning autistic. In the process she sought to clear up misconceptions about the condition. "I thought it would be interesting to show people how autistic people's minds work," Devine says. "They think autistic people just rock and sit in the corner and don't look at you, and that's not how it is at all. They are the best witnesses, because they can replay an entire event without any prejudice." The nature of Pratt's affliction determined the setting for the Bradley story. "I had to make this person's occupation believable," says Devine. "Restoring books or working in a library is very realistic because they're very organized, they have comfort in order, and they like things to be the same."

> ## How do you feel about murder?
> "... yet she must die else she betray more men. Put out the light. And then put out the light."

In auditioning actors for the role, Devine says, she was determined to steer clear of a Hollywood stereotype. "I did not want a *Rain Man*–type portrayal, and every actor who came in to audition did Dustin Hoffman." She explains, "Rain Man is a particular type of savant—he's less functional than a high-functioning autistic person. He could add up incredible numbers, but he couldn't be left alone in a room, and that's not an accurate portrayal of your average autistic person." Finally, when Michael Goorjian came in with a different take and got the role, Devine had him meet with Austin. "I think it was a really good experience for both of them," she says. In recognition of her son's contribution, she gave him her customary Technical Advisor credit on the episode.

Despite his initial suspicions that Pratt may be a homicidal bookworm, Grissom finds a vague kinship with the specially talented young man. "Grissom doesn't relate well with people, he has a great memory, and he's sort of a loner," says Devine.

William Petersen saw the connection with Pratt as one of several eccentric or unconventional characters with whom Grissom finds common ground. "In some ways, all of those characters possess a certain sort of brilliance, and that's really what he's fascinated by," Petersen explains. "I think Grissom truly understands that all of humanity is flawed, but he connects to that which is God-like, and for Grissom that lies in the mental capabilities of the human being. We all seek that which is closer to God—that thing that raises us up. And for Grissom, the only attempt he can make to be with humanity is on that level." ■

ORIGINAL AIRDATE: 11/15/01
WRITTEN BY: Jerry Stahl
DIRECTED BY: Peter Markle

SLAVE:

GUEST STARRING

ERIC SZMANDA: Greg Sanders
ROBERT DAVID HALL: Dr. Al Robbins
MELINDA CLARKE: Lady Heather
KELLY ROWAN: Eilene Nelson
MITCHELL WHITFIELD: Arthur Nelson
TRACY VILAR: Carla Delgado
AMAURY NOLASCO: Hector Delgado
GEOFFREY RIVAS: Det. Sam Vega
PERRY ANZILOTTI: Marvin Draffler
JOHN BENJAMIN HICKEY: Dr. Sidney Cornfeld
STACEY DASH: Amy Bonner
MANNY SUAREZ: Sante Sherna

A young couple chase each other around a playground swing. They fall into each other's arms only to discover a lifeless human face sticking up out of the sand. Grissom speculates that the park is a secondary scene, a dumping ground, not the murder site. Catherine joins him and they set to digging and sifting sand until they've created a moatlike ditch around the naked, female body.

At Sherna Check Cashing, Sara and Warrick are investigating the shooting of its proprietor, Sante Sherna. He was shot in the leg in the parking lot, while leaving to make his weekly bank run. His sister, Carla Delgado, heard a shot and ran outside to see a car driving off. Warrick notices leaflets stuck on the windshields of all the cars on the lot, while Sara finds the empty money bag. Carla seems more annoyed that she'll have to run the business alone than upset that her brother's been shot, but notes they're insured.

In the autopsy room, Grissom takes an initial look at the dead woman, not-

ing small metallic slivers near a wound to her back, glittery flakes on her skin, and burns on her wrist. She was killed two to four hours before discovery. Commenting on the scars on her back, Doctor Robbins says she's a "road map of abuse," but there's no indication of recent sexual activity. She has expensive breast implants that they recover the serial numbers of. The silvery slivers from the victim's back are aluminum-coated tempered steel and the flakes are liquid latex.

Catherine checks with the plastic surgeon, who identifies the victim as Mona Taylor and mentions that her implant operation was billed to a third party. The CSIs visit the address on the bill, where they're immediately struck by the sounds of whipping and yelping from upstairs. The hostess welcomes them to Lady Heather's Dominion. Outside, Nick and Catherine examine Mona Taylor's car but find no evidence. However, in a nearby trash can they find a piece of latex bearing the imprint of a wristwatch. Lady Heather tells Grissom and Brass that Mona's last client was around 11 P.M. and that she left around midnight. Lady Heather is puzzled to hear that fresh whip marks

I find all deviate behavior fascinating . . .

OF LAS VEGAS

were found on Taylor's back, as she is strictly "a dominant." Intrigued, Grissom asks to borrow one of her leather bondage face masks. Catherine and Nick proceed to Taylor's room in the adjacent poolhouse, a large, dungeonlike space with walls lined with various implements of domination. They find another scrap of liquid latex.

Detective Vega catches up with a possible witness. He recalls seeing two men the previous night who threatened to shove a flyer down his throat if he touched their car.

Warrick consults with Lab Tech Amy Bonner. She's tracing a tire tread left on the discarded flyer found in the parking lot, and noted an incidental mark in the tread. In Ballistics, Bobby Dawson identifies five lands and grooves on the recovered slug, indicative of a Colt. Vega notes that Sante Sherna owns a Colt.

Robbins finds that Mona Taylor died from asphyxia. He points to a small circular scar on the inside of her nose, which Grissom speculates could have been made by a drinking straw. Catherine brings in all the masks and straws from Lady Heather's. Grissom suggests that Taylor was actually a switch, dominant as well as submissive. With a DNA match, Greg uncovers the mask Taylor wore and the straws through which she breathed.

Grissom and Catherine discover the make of the watch from the impression left in the latex. This leads them to the Nelson residence, where a harried househusband, Cameron Nelson, answers the door with a baby in his arms. He denies buying a woman's $20,000 watch, even though Brass is holding the store receipt.

Sara and Vega visit Sante Sherna in the hospital, just as his sister and brother-in-law, Hector, show up. Sherna admits to owning a Colt, saying he keeps it on a shelf behind the cash register. Amy tells Warrick that Sherna's money bag was cut open with a knife that left behind red fiberglass fibers. Hector Delgado works at a fiberglass manufacturer. He hands over his knife, which bears fibers matching those found on the

money bag and admits the car belongs to a friend of his who had promised that they could rob the check-cashing service with no one getting hurt.

Grissom and Catherine pay a visit to Eilene Nelson in her corporate-law office. She admits to buying the custom-made watch but says she lost it on a business trip. They then return to the Nelson residence bearing a warrant for Eilene's watch box. She dismisses an inquisitive Cameron away as she directs the CSIs to the glove compartment of her car where they find the box—along with another scrap of latex. Grissom returns to Lady Heather with news that the DNA sample from Mona Taylor's straw belongs to a man. He shows her a photograph of the Nelson family. She recognizes Cameron.

Hector sits in interrogation, offering to give the money back to make his charges go away. After driving Carla home on Wednesday night, he'd doubled back and took Sante's gun from the register. He then showed up with the borrowed car and, wearing a ski mask, pulled a gun on Sante as he was getting into his car. Unexpectedly, his brother-in-law knocked him down, leaving him no choice but to shoot. At the check-cashing service, Sara confronts a recovered Sante with $5,000 that he'd skimmed, it was found in his jeans after the shooting. He claims he was just borrowing it but is arrested.

Grissom and Catherine take a look at the Nelson's car. They find sand and some clothes in the trunk. Eilene Nelson serves as her husband's attorney when he's brought in for interrogation. Grissom, displaying a piece of latex, explains that Cameron paid Mona Taylor to be a submissive, a stand-in for his wife. He made Mona wear his wife's watch, then painted her entire body with liquid latex, placing straws in her nostrils. Finally, his rage got the better of him, and he suffocated her. Cameron stands, ready to accept his fate. When Eilene asks where he's going, he says, "Away from you. Other than that, I really don't care."

> You spent your life uncovering what goes on beneath the surface of civility and acceptable behavior.

Lady Heather, you don't want to know what I think.

134 "The ratings had been great over the summer, and in the fall, we smashed the time period, so we said, 'Okay, now we can take some risks, we can push our stories out a little bit,'" recollects Jonathan Littman. Regarding Lady Heather's Dominion, writer Jerry Stahl admits, "Let's just say I've done some research. I've had a number of friends who happened to have a familiarity with the subject."

"The reality that many powerful men come in to get beaten and humiliated is the notion that drove the story," Stahl explains. "It also demonstrates the reverse; that those with no power in their daily lives are the ones who feel the need to dominate."

In the center of this universe stands Lady Heather, a character who in less enlightened hands could have resembled a caricature. Stahl saw her as an intellect worthy of respect. "Lady Heather knows as much about man in all his pathetic glory as anyone with a degree in psychiatry," he asserts. "In my experience, you can learn more from the gutter than the classroom, but it's harder to explain on a résumé." From her years spent dancing, Catherine is more than a little experienced. As Stahl puts it, "These two ladies understand each other because, quite simply, they understand men." Marg Helgenberger fondly recalls, "As I'm bagging zipped leather masks, we're having this conversation about our daughters! I love that scene!" The fact that Catherine started out on the seamy side of life gives her enormous insight and renders her judgment-free in encounters with someone of Lady Heather's ilk.

"And I liked 'Slaves of Las Vegas' because we learned about the characters through a subject that many people are uncomfortable talking about," Helgenberger says.

Grissom again finds common ground with an unconventional character. His heart-to-heart talk with Lady Heather follows a similar encounter with Father Powell. "The girl got to Grissom's guilt, and the priest got to his fear. And that's pretty much all we are, aren't we?" Ann Donahue says, pointing out the show's subtle mission to get inside its characters. "If characters just stand there saying what they think, no one cares. But if the audience have to ferret out the information to reveal who they are, it's more meaningful." William Petersen agrees with the oblique dramatic strategy. "The greatest thing we can do with Grissom or any of these guys is to let the audience fill in the holes for themselves. If we do all the work for them, there's nothing for them to imagine."

Of Heather's observations, Stahl says, "Grissom has always struck me as the kind of a man who has a deep secret he may not even know himself. Hence the quote, 'No man is a mystery, except to himself,' which I confess to making up and attributing to poor old Marcel Proust." As for the final soul-baring secret that Grissom is about to tell Catherine just as the curtain falls, "I believe you have to have enough respect for the audience to let them draw their conclusions," Stahl smiles. ∎

AND THEN THERE WERE NONE

ORIGINAL AIRDATE: 11/22/01
TELEPLAY BY: Eli Talbert & Carol Mendelsohn
STORY BY: Josh Berman
DIRECTED BY: John Patterson

GUEST STARRING

ERIC SZMANDA: Greg Sanders
ROBERT DAVID HALL: Dr. Al Robbins
MICHAEL CUDLITZ: Trooper Spencer
TOM O'BRIEN: Max Duncan
BRIGID BRANNAGH: Tammy Felton
LARRY HOLDEN: Darren Hanson
TOM GALLOP: Randy Paynter
SUSAN GIBNEY: Charlotte Meridien
ARCHIE KAO: Archie Johnson
JOE SABATINO: Surveillance Officer
MARC VALERA: Valet

At the Tower Club Casino, a security officer makes his scheduled cash collection—shelving black metal lockboxes onto a rolling cage. Suddenly, a blonde, a brunette, and a redhead storm the room with blazing firearms. Two of the marauders race out the door with the loot, leaving one of their team, the redhead, dead. Brass and Grissom arrive to find that five guards have been killed, three civilians wounded. They made off with $250,000. The dead robber is revealed to be a man in drag. Brass realizes that the Tower robbery is identical to a heist at a Laughlin casino a month earlier. They ask Max Duncan, a pit boss, for his version of the event, but he only recalls ducking at the sound of the chandelier crashing down.

Near the town of Calnevari, Catherine and Sara respond to a dead body at a convenience store. State Trooper Clint Spencer leaves them to their processing and returns to his patrol. Inside, they find the victim, a clerk named Dustin Bale. Raw potato pieces lie on the floor. Catherine has seen this before: "the poor man's silencer." The hanging cardboard sign on the door has been flipped to its Closed position.

Catherine lifts prints from the door sign while Sara takes an electrostatic print lifter to the counter. She gets a shoe print, it's a size six at most, suggesting they may be looking for an underage culprit.

At the casino, the witnesses provide varying accounts of the robbery. A valet tells Nick he saw a beige and battered getaway car. Nick's attention is drawn by a small puddle of burned transmission fluid left by the car. It's brown instead of the usual red.

Robbins removes a .45 hollow-point slug from the "redhead," Adam Brower, who was shot in the back at close range. Since the guards carry 9mms, Brower must have been shot by one of his partners.

As Grissom watches the surveillance tape, Warrick enlarges the image of the person nearest Brower—who they believe is Brower's killer—and they spot an Adam's apple, indicating a second male on the team. When Warrick enlarges the last person, the features are decidedly female. Warrick and Brass search Adam Brower's apartment. There's nothing there that will help identify his partners, although they do find traces of silica dust.

Sara identifies the shoeprint as a Skechers, adult size five, *female*. Catherine, meanwhile, confers with Charlotte Meridien who matches one print from the door sign to Trooper Spencer and one from the register to someone Catherine recognizes—Tammy Felton, a fugitive who along with her co-conspirator, Darren Hanson, jumped bail on a murder charge. As Catherine tells Grissom this startling news, Greg reveals the .45 casing from the casino is crusted with a foreign substance—potato. Sara shows up with another print identification, this one from the convenience store's doorknob—Darren Hanson. The slugs from Brower and Bale are identical. Brass has found the beige car abandoned off of I-93.

The CSIs rush to the site and search for tracks. Brass and Nick find a single tire tread, suggesting a motorcycle. Catherine finds Felton's body inside the car's trunk, choked to death. Silica dust is also found inside the car. Grissom notes that there's an abandoned

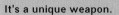

It's a unique weapon.

136

silica mine outside Calnevari. Near the mine they find Darren Hanson shot in the forehead execution-style. All of their suspects are now dead.

Warrick runs the tape from the Tower heist again and sees Pit Boss Max Duncan hit the deck just *before* Felton drew her gun to shoot the chandelier. They note that Duncan has only worked at the Tower for three weeks, before that, he was at the casino that was robbed in Laughlin. In Duncan's driveway, Catherine observes that his car is covered with silica dust. He confesses to being the team's inside man at the Tower. However, he insists that Hanson was dead when he got there to collect his share. Hanson was the only one he had spoken to, he'd "never even met the other *three*."

Attempting to identify the fourth "woman" from the Laughlin heist security tape, Sara recognizes Dustin Bale. He was Hanson's first victim, who, along with Felton, emptied out the convenience-store register to create the appearance of a robbery gone wrong. The bullet from Hanson's head is a .45 automatic, from a Heckler & Koch. The database shows that in Clark County there are only seven registered that are still in circulation; one belongs to State Trooper Spencer. Before he can deny his involvement, Catherine tells Spencer what happened: Hanson's potato only muffled the sound of the shot that killed Bale; he heard the blast and investigated, Hanson and Felton talked him into a financially appealing deal. Catherine notes the shiny dust on Spencer's shoes and Grissom follows the glowing crystals to the trooper's locker. A duffel bag stuffed with money is inside. Spencer is cuffed and led away.

"**And Then There Were None**" is an homage to Agatha Christie, even appropriating the title. Observing a mandate to leave no loose ends, the episode brings back recurring villains Tammy Felton and Darren Hanson who were last seen in "Face Lift."

"We really liked the characters," says Josh Berman. "The ones who get away always have potential for returning. I knew we weren't going to return to the characters immediately, but I was happy when the executive producers wanted to bring them back the following season." Carol Mendelsohn points out, "The idea is we're creating a world, and you want satisfaction. When Tammy Felton and Darren Hanson drive away, you want to see them again. What happened to them? In real life, they would commit another crime."

"We thought, 'Wouldn't it be interesting to do a remote crime scene?'" Berman explains, "A lot of small jurisdictions will invite a major crime lab in for something like a homicide if they don't have their own lab." Thus, Catherine and Sara go to the tiny town of Calnevari to investigate a murder." He adds, "We thought, 'This could be an opportunity to bring back our escapees from 'Face Lift.'" The last piece fell into place when Berman recalls wondering, "What if we had a bunch of suspects and then started killing them off one by one? You know, *Ten Little Indians . . .*"

This show finds the unlikely combo of Warrick and Brass amiably working together; they pay a visit to Adam Brower's apartment. The two characters have had little one-on-one contact. "I want to start to open up, to reestablish this relationship," Paul Guilfoyle says, "because Brass was much stronger with Warrick than with anybody." In the concluding scene, Grissom observes that State Trooper Spencer ". . . had his price." Catherine replies, "We all do." "I believe Catherine would do anything for her daughter," says Berman. "But it's something Grissom doesn't understand because for him the notion of committing a crime is black and white." ■

That's wonderful, Gil. If I see a gorilla, I'll arrest it.

ELLIE

ORIGINAL AIRDATE: 12/6/01
WRITTEN BY: Anthony E. Zuiker
DIRECTED BY: Charlie Correll

GUEST STARRING

137

ERIC SZMANDA: Greg Sanders
ROBERT DAVID HALL: Dr. Al Robbins
NICKI AYCOX: Ellie Brass
GEOFFREY BLAKE: Matthew Orton
NANCY EVERHARD: Cindy Orton
DANIEL DAE KIM: Agent Blackman
GEOFFREY RIVAS: Det. Sam Vega
RODNEY EASTMAN: Keith Driscoll
SANDRA THIGPEN: Attorney Grimes
ERIC STONESTREET: Ronnie Litra
JOHN FUGELSANG: Vincent Thomas Avery
MARC VANN: Conrad Ecklie

Outside a casino a tourist couple happens upon a distraught young man. He tells them he's been barred—before he could redeem the $10,000 in chips he's holding. They agree to give him two thousand dollars as collateral, and after they cash his chips, he'll give them a $1,000 thank-you. When the cage teller tells them that the chips are worthless, they run back outside. He is gone. Then, they hear a gunshot coming from the parking garage. The grifter is dead. His getaway driver apparently pulled the trigger. The hapless couple, Matt and Cindy Orton, won't be getting their cash back, it's now evidence. Back at the lab, Grissom is about to leave for an entomological convention in Duluth. He's about to place Catherine in charge when she reminds him that she'll be out of town. Heedless of Warrick's discomfort, Grissom appoints him acting supervisor. Warrick relays the news to Nick and Sara while they're snapping photos at the parking garage. They're not pleased.

Doctor Robbins determines that the victim, Vincent Thomas Avery, died from a gunshot to his left ear. Approximately fifty small coke balloons were in Avery's stomach, he was a con artist *and* a drug mule. Brass discovers that Avery has multiple arrests on his record. Greg determines that some black capsules Sara found on Avery's are activated charcoal pills, an antacid popular with drug mules. He was also carrying two plane-ticket stubs—one for him, one for an Ellie Avery. Warrick's intrigued by the discoveries, but annoyed to discover that Sara has not been keeping him informed about her progress. He tells her that he's the primary on the case and that if she doesn't like it she can clock out. Another unpleasant task follows when Warrick informs Brass that the prints on one of the airline stubs belong to his daughter Ellie Rebecca Brass. The captain replies he'll have Vega bring her in.

If I needed someone to stay up for three straight days, I'd ask Sara.

Ellie Brass is brought in for questioning, stopping only to spit on her father's badge. She claims that she barely knew Avery and went with him to Baja just for fun. A dummy casino chip falls from her cigarette pack, but she denies any knowledge of Avery being shot, saying she was home at the time. As for her car,

138

she lent it to her boyfriend, Keith Driscoll. Brass feels certain that Driscoll will turn out to be their shooter. But even when Ellie's X-rays come back clean for cocaine balloons, Warrick's not convinced that she's not involved.

In the Questionable Documents lab, Sara notes that the Averys' $100 bills are missing a line of engraved lettering on Ben Franklin's collar. Ronnie Litra reveals that all of the Averys' money is counterfeit. He advises her to notify the local Secret Service branch.

The next morning, Brass is driving his cruiser when Ellie's car peels out right in front of him. He radios it in pursuing the car. He pulls them over and finds two men inside. The terrified passenger claims to be a hitchhiker. Brass sends him on his way and angrily pulls Driscoll out. He insists that it was Ellie who got him into muling drugs. Brass pulls his gun. Squad cars arrive and Vega takes custody of their suspect.

Sara informs the Ortons that their hundreds are counterfeit. Matt doesn't seem surprised, saying he'd unsuccessfully tried to spend one earlier. Special Agent Beckman introduces himself to Warrick, mentioning the counterfeit case. Warrick replies, dumbstruck, that this is the first he's heard of it. Sara explains that she went ahead and ran with the case as she does when working with Grissom. Still angry, Warrick, who knows the case comes first, joins Nick in the garage. Ellie's tire treads match those found at the murder scene.

Sara tells Beckman that as the Ortons' bills each have different serial numbers, they must have "burned" myriad individual plates. Beckman informs Sara that the couple's real name is Duffy, and they've done time for high-end fraud. He allows Sara to tag along as he searches for the couple's minting operation.

Vega and Warrick tell Driscoll that Avery's and Ellie's plane tickets were purchased with his credit card. His attorney threatens a police-brutality case against Brass for his earlier actions and they leave. Warrick informs Brass about the tire treads, and without Driscoll, murder charges will be pressed against Ellie. Brass insists that Driscoll's their man. The captain pays Ellie's bail and offers her a place to stay. She declines, saying that she and Driscoll have their own place.

That night, Warrick receives a call about an officer-involved shooting. He rushes to an apartment complex where he discovers that Driscoll was shot in the throat. The responding officer found a woozy Brass nearby. Warrick finds that the captain's gun is missing a round. Brass tells Vega that he went to the apartment to look for Ellie. He entered and grilled Driscoll about his daughter's whereabouts. As he proceeded to the back room, Driscoll hit him with a baseball bat causing Brass to black out. Warrick finds blood on the rear of Brass's gun indicative of a slide bite, a novice shooter's injury. It tells them that Brass was not the shooter. Nevertheless, Warrick asks for his badge.

Sara, along with Special Agent Beckman, stand in a warehouse taking in the Duffys' state-of-the-art printing operation. When she asks them for the burn plates and the rest of the money, Cindy Duffy confesses that there isn't any and that the Duffys are Treasury agents. They are part of a sting where counterfeit money is put in the hands of criminals and the agents track its path back to law-enforcement officials. The agents commend Sara for her honesty in resisting the bait.

In the process of comparing Ellie's saliva from Brass's badge to the blood from Brass's gun, Greg discovers that Jim and Ellie's DNA don't share a single marker. He's not her biological father. However, neither of them shot Driscoll. Warrick checks the plane manifest for Driscoll's and Ellie's flight and notices that Driscoll had purchased a third ticket for a Marty Gilmore, the hitchhiker.

Warrick and the police rush to Gilmore's house where Warrick notices a slide bite on the man's hand. Warrick speculates that Gilmore killed Driscoll in order to take over his coke business, then implicated Brass. Gilmore claims it was Ellie who killed Avery—then doubles over and asks for a laxative. Warrick, realizing he's got a busted coke balloon inside of him, has Brass call for an ambulance.

The captain and his daughter say good-bye. Brass asks her to come back to him. She says it's too late for that, and heads home to New Jersey and her mother.

> I'm the primary... If you have a problem with that, you can clock out now.

"'**E**llie' was equal parts tremendous accomplishment and tremendous burden," says Gary Dourdan. Pressured by the network's schedule, the producers found it necessary to shoot two episodes at once.

Explains Paul Guilfoyle, "It was a double-up period which split up the cast. And Anthony and Ann wrote a very nice script for me." While Dourdan and Guilfoyle were busy with "Ellie," the rest of the cast was shooting "Caged." No matter the amount of preparation creator Anthony Zuiker (who makes a cameo in the teaser as the casino cashier who rejects the bogus chips) was concerned. "It was a very light Billy and Marg episode—the storyline would be carried mostly by Paul and Gary—and we just didn't know how that was going to track over the course of forty-five minutes." Compounding the challenge: assembling an entirely different film crew while the usual team worked elsewhere. "We shot that show almost guerrilla style," Dourdan recalls. Director of Photography Michael Barrett notes, "Many of our crew members stepped up, our best boy electric became the gaffer, our best boy grip became the key grip. We brought in an entirely new camera crew."

"It was a difficult piece of work to approach," Dourdan says. "I had to remember that Warrick has been working around Nick and Sara for years now; they're like friends—you just don't come in and get this position and start acting strange." The actors says his initial approach was to play Warrick " . . . a little out of sorts. He's trying to do his job, but he's also trying not to step on any toes. I wanted to play *that;* the conflict he's having inside." Director Charlie Correll had another strategy. "Charlie came up to me and said, 'Listen, you can't be the old Warrick, you've got to command the room.'" To get into that emotional space, Dourdan says, he took a page from William Petersen's playbook. "I started harkening back to Billy's work," he explains. "When he walks in, his voice carries—he's in theater mode. I had to try to personify that kind of authority."

Sara, not Nick, winds up resenting Warrick's newly acquired authority and, according to Dourdan, that mini-twist came at the behest of George Eads. "I think it was originally written that Nick would have issues—

that competitiveness again," Gary says. "But by that time George and I had become such buddies off the set that he looked for a different approach." Eads says, "It's like sports, Yeah, it pissed Nick off, but what's good for the team and what's good for my buddy? He needs my support to do a good job."

Jorja Fox prefaces her explanation for Sara's reaction with a showbiz rule of thumb, "You always have to defend your own character. I think that Sara was cool that Warrick was put in charge, shocked by it, but comfortable. But she perceived that he was acting like a jerk. He got defensive first."

Warrick's working with Brass was more mending of fences. "We didn't have the time for a long dramatic scene where I could tell him how guilty I feel about Holly Gribbs, and how I messed up in a leadership role," says Guilfoyle. "They all meant to say, 'I was wrong about you.'" The two actors enjoyed themselves. "We were joking on the set that this was a spinoff, *The Brass and the Black Guy Show*," laughs Dourdan.

Guilfoyle admits feeling a bit apprehensive about Ellie not being Brass's biological daughter. "Ann Donahue talked me into it," he recalls. "She told me 'You may just be reacting as the character,' which was insightful on Ann's part, and I told her so. I didn't want to be thinking that my character's wife had an affair with someone else."

The original airing of "Ellie" would be *CSI*'s first number one Nielsen ranking. Although Zuiker calls it, "The Diet Coke Number One, because it reached that touchstone with the help of reruns on the other networks." Nevertheless, he notes, "There was a lot of vindication around here." ■

**Congratulations, Brown.
You've just bounced off the
glass ceiling.**

LAS VEGAS POLICE DEPARTMENT - SUPPLEMENTARY REPORT

Greg Hojem Sanders was born in Santa Gabriel, California where he enjoyed a happy childhood living with his mother, father and Scandinavian grandparents. At an early age, his family became aware that Greg was a child with unique abilities. Ever since he picked up his toy chemistry set at age four, Greg knew he wanted to be a scientist. His parents enrolled him in school a year early, and Greg quickly advanced through grades, scoring off the charts on his standardized math and science examinations. When school administrators insisted his gifts be given special attention, Greg's parents sent him to a private school where the prodigy could be more appropriately challenged.

Greg Sanders was an active participant in his education and did his best to be accepted socially among his peers, although his aptitude was better suited for being Captain of the Chess Club rather than Captain of the Football team. He always stood out from the crowd with his wildly entertaining personality, a rarity among the serious-minded multitudes. Because Greg spent most of his teenage years around adults in mature environments, he was painfully aware that the stressful pace and highly charged competition would cause him to miss out on some of the joys of youth.

After graduating Phi Beta Kappa from Stanford on a full academic scholarship, Greg began working as a lab technician in the San Francisco Police Dept. Eager to fit into the world outside the classroom, Greg became a pop culture junkie, developing an eclectic set of tastes and interests. He in invented a hip sensibility in order to make himself appear more sophisticated and maintain a semblance of cool. While doing his best to be adventurous in his life, Greg has been known to make veiled references of many escapades that, in reality, he has probably only just read about.

After two years in San Francisco, Greg was craving a change of scenery and accepted a position as a DNA technician with the highly rated Las Vegas Crime Lab. He quickly became known for his wild dress code and irreverent humor juxtaposed with intimidating skills in the lab.

As an overachiever who is always ready for a new challenge, Greg enthusiastically expressed an interest in conducting fieldwork as a CSI. Since he has been granted his wish, the sheltered academic has found the work more grueling than he anticipated which has fostered a mutual respect between Greg and the rest of his CSI cohorts.

While his lofty IQ may sometimes make him appear overconfident, Greg is well aware that there is much more to learn. Flirtatious, audacious and sometimes a little overzealous to impress, Greg provides a much-needed levity to tense environment at the Crime Lab. Despite their playful jabs at his outlandish style and demeanor, Grissom and the other CSIs are aware that Greg Sanders may always be on the verge of greatness.

CONFIDENTIAL

LAS VEGAS
POLICE DEPARTMENT
Clark County, Nevada

POLICE

DNA ANALYST

GREG SANDERS

PN: 5412	EXP DATE: NOV/2002
EYES: BRN	WEIGHT: 155
HAIR: BRN	HEIGHT: 5'10"

LAS VEGAS POLICE DEPARTMENT
DETECTIVE DIVISION

SANDERS, Greg Hojem
DNA/Forensic Analyst

012399 - 0023

RIGHT FOUR FINGERS TAKEN SIMULTANEOUSLY

R. THUMB

L. THUMB

Las Vegas
Police Department
DNA ANALYSIS

LAS VEGAS
POLICE
NEVADA

SIGN HERE

142

ORGAN

The most important component in poisoning is patience.

A man and a woman board a hotel elevator. Their passionate embrace is abruptly broken when they see a man lying on the floor. The victim is Bob Fairmont, a well-known real estate developer. Brass notes that Fairmont is in critical condition but had no visible wounds. From the photos the captain shows him, Grissom believes the victim was dressed by someone else and posed. Brass asks Fairmont's wife, Julia, if she has any idea who might have re-dressed her spouse. She admits that he usually consorts with other women but she's in the dark about his affairs.

In Fairmont's hotel room, Sara finds a pair of used champagne glasses, a size 34C bra, and Grissom notes the scent of sexual intercourse. Nick then spots a recently used condom hanging from a light sconce above the bed. Greg's examination of Catherine's tape-lift from the elevator floor identifies white specks found as pieces of scalp skin. This suggests that whoever placed Bob Fairmont in the elevator had a dandruff problem.

Warrick tells Catherine about an investigation at the Fairmonts' house three years earlier. The man had claimed he'd accidentally shot himself, but in light of current events, Warrick decides to take another look at that case. Grissom is informed that Fairmont has died.

Robbins speculates that Fairmont was brain-dead by the time he was found in the elevator, probably the result of a stroke. The coroner notes that Fairmont was an ideal donor candidate. In fact, his wife has signed off on immediate postmortem removal of eight organs. Sara notices stripes on Fairmont's fingernails that look like Mees lines: a white striae particular to heavy-metal poisoning. They check back with Robbins for another look at the body only to learn that it's already been released to the mortuary, where Randy Gesek is already overseeing its incineration. The cremation, like the organ transplant, was approved by Julia Fairmont. Mrs. Fairmont claims that by the time he reached the hospital, her husband was "technically" dead. Her approval of his organ donations was following his wishes.

GRINDER

ORIGINAL AIRDATE: 12/13/01
WRITTEN BY: Ann Donahue & Elizabeth Devine
DIRECTED BY: Allison Liddi

Nick visits Carl Mercer, the recipient of Fairmont's kidney. He asks if he can have a sample for a biopsy, and is understanding when the ill Mercer refuses. All of the organ donors turn him down.

Fairmont's secretary, Claudia Gideon, arrives to pick up his possessions and finds they've already been promised to Catherine. She spots dandruff on Gideon's shoulder and takes a tape-lift. When Gideon is brought in for questioning, she says that Fairmont had asked her to meet him in his room at 9:00 to pick up some papers, but she found him in bed, naked and unconscious. Recalling how he'd told her to avoid scandals, she dressed and dragged him into the elevator.

Warrick admits that he may have been too willing to buy Fairmont's accidental shooting story. The bullet's point-of-origin is inconsistent with a self-inflicted wound. Gideon denies commiting the shooting, stating that she'd rushed to Fairmont's house after he'd paged her, and took him to the hospital. She can't recall where Julia was at the time. Julia Fairmont admits to having shot her husband that day, claiming she was just trying to scare him. Then as now, he didn't want the truth to come out, for fear of his reputation.

In Gideon's office at the Fairmont home, Catherine and Brass find a prescription dandruff shampoo—rich in selenium sulfide, a heavy metal poison. Gideon can't explain why it's there, then Catherine finds garlic cream cheese—an ideal substance for hiding the poison's garlicky aftertaste—in the minifridge. Sara provides some seemingly contradictory news: she's matched the prints from the champagne bottle found in the hotel room to Julia Fairmont. Julia admits that she and her husband were trying to reinvigorate their marriage, so Bob squeezed her in between meetings that day. She hadn't mentioned it because her husband was alive when she left the room.

In the CSI parking lot, Julia becomes ill. She is taken to the hospital and given a shot of hydropazine; a treatment for heavy-metal poisoning. Gideon is questioned again, and again she denies poisoning anyone. She accuses Julia of trying to frame *her* for Bob's death. Julia insists that she has nothing to

SPECIAL GUEST STARS

MARCIA CROSS: Julia Fairmont
ANNE RAMSEY: Claudia Richards/Gideon

GUEST STARRING

ERIC SZMANDA: Greg Sanders
ROBERT DAVID HALL: Dr. Al Robbins
KELLY CONNELL: Randy Gesek
JOHN F. O'DONOHUE: Carl Mercer
SPENCER GARRETT: Dr. Stockton
ERINN BARTLETT: Cindy
DAX GRIFFIN: Chuck

143

hide. Her temper rising, she angrily suggests they ask Claudia Richards about it. Julia says that she may have killed Bob when she realized she couldn't have him. An Internet search on Julia yields a ten-year-old photograph of Claudia Gideon (née Richards) with her rich husband, John Gideon. He also had died young, was also cremated, and had his organs donated. His liver was rejected by its recipient. Nick and Sara travel to an Arizona cemetery, warrant in hand, to have his body exhumed.

Nick finds 280 milligrams of sodium selenate in the small liquefied sample of the liver, most likely from livestock supplements, readily available at Gideon's dairy which was owned by her late husband. Catherine discovers that Mr. Gideon's secretary was Julia Fairmont. The two women are interrogated together. Claudia says that they'd never denied a previous acquaintance. Sara suggests that following Mr. Gideon's death, the two women spent his money and then went in search of another mark. Grissom points out the women will accuse each other, and subsequently prevent a conviction of either. The DA has decided not to mount a case. Julia and Claudia are free to go. Sara is furious. Grissom reminds her, "There's no statute of limitation on murder."

 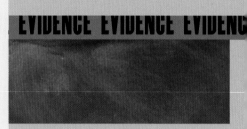
It isn't a competition. We don't win. The courts are like dice; they have no memory. What works one week doesn't work the next.

144

"**O**rgan Grinder" had its genesis in a tantalizing question posed by Carol Mendelsohn. "She said, 'What would you do if you needed to get DNA from somebody who'd had a transplant?'" recalls writer Elizabeth Devine. "I said, 'You couldn't get it. There's no way you're going to be able to get a court order to take out a section of someone's kidney.'" But what if there was a recent transplant recipient who could be persuaded to help investigators? Hence, the introduction of the good-hearted Carl Mercer. Fleshing out the story, writer Ann Donahue adds, "You're sure there's a murder, you go to get the body, and it's been harvested of its organs, so you can't tell what happened—now the organs are in eight different people and the body is being burned. For me, it doesn't get better than that. All we need is an ember of a tooth and forensics will prevail." But even the truth is useless in the face of "She said, she said" defense. Looking back, Donahue regrets not opting for a more satisfying conclusion. "If I could do it over, I would have had one of them die from taking too much poison and have the other get arrested for giving it to her."

We also learn of Greg's crush on Sara. Although on a couple of occasions he's also been smitten with Catherine, Donahue explains, "When Catherine's in a room, *everyone* has a crush on her. However, Greg has a unique crush on Sara." Eric Szmanda admits, "I went to Carol Mendelsohn's office and said, 'I really think Greg has a crush on Sara,' and it just started." He claims the brainstorm was intended to help Sara as much as Greg. "I think a lot of people see her as abrasive, just because of the way Sara's written. I wanted to see her open up a bit and let someone see inside her." ∎

Special Effects makeup artist John Goodwin prepares a victim.

YOU'VE GOT MALE

A girl riding her horse through a field finds the body of a young blond woman in a large culvert at a highway construction site. At the scene, the CSIs find a second body—a young brunette. Robbins declares that both victims died at approximately the same time, twelve hours earlier. The brunette suffered a broken neck. The blond has a nonfatal contusion to the forehead and a cut on her arm, but died due to a severed brachial artery. Observing the brunette's dyed hair and multiple tattoos and piercings, Grissom infers that she craved attention, while the blonde seems her polar opposite.

In a thickly wooded area of Spring Mountain, a park ranger escorts Catherine and Nick to a dead male slumped against a tree. He has a through-and-through gunshot wound to the midsection. He's holding a rifle, but it hasn't been fired. His driver's license identifies him as James Jasper. Although deer season had opened a week earlier, he's not wearing an orange safety vest. The ranger speculates he may have been shot by another hunter. Nick eventually finds a slug buried in a nearby tree.

Prints identify the brunette as Joan Marks, from a prior shoplifting arrest. At the Marks' residence, Sara and Grissom find a car in the garage. It's registered to Donna Marks, the other victim, and sister to Joan. The house belonged to the girls' mother, but Donna has lived in it alone since her mother's death. The primary crime scene is the back patio; it's littered with blood and glass from a sliding door that shattered from the inside out. There are numerous take-out containers in the fridge. There's a pile of mail-order catalogs near Donna's computer, overnight-delivery boxes, and an array of restaurant delivery phone numbers on her speed dial. Grissom wonders if she's agoraphobic. Sara identifies with the woman's shopping and eating habits. She ventures into the bathroom and observes the toilet seat is raised; a man had been in the house.

Greg matches the DNA from the scratches on Donna Marks's neck to the second victim, Joan. Sara reports that Joan had a temporary restraining order taken out on her boyfriend, Gavin Pallard, who also had one issued on *her*. When Pallard is brought in for questioning, he describes an on-again, off-again rela-

ORIGINAL AIRDATE: 12/20/01
WRITTEN BY: Marc Dube & Corey Miller
DIRECTED BY: Charlie Correll

145

GUEST STARRING

ERIC SZMANDA: Greg Sanders
ROBERT DAVID HALL: Dr. Al Robbins
AMANDA WYSS: Donna Marks
HOLLY FULGER: Linda Jasper
CLAYTON ROHNER: Park Ranger
ROD ROWLAND: Gavin Pallard
GEOFFREY RIVAS: Det. Sam Vega
KIRK B.R. WOLLER: Warden Mather
ROBIA LAMORTE: Joan Marks
THOMAS KOPACHE: Joe Willoughby
NICK CHINLUND: Mickey Rutledge

tionship with Joan. She'd been to his house three times in defiance of the restraining order. Pallard last saw her the day before her death when she borrowed his car. He describes the two sisters as "oil and water." Joan believed Donna owed her rent, because the house was in both of their names. Sara asks to see the bottom of his shoes, and finds them blood-stained.

Jasper's wife, Linda, tells Nick and Catherine that they had both been laid off recently, and that her husband was an experienced hunter. She can't explain why he wasn't wearing a vest. Bobby tells Catherine and Nick that the bullet they found was not the killing slug. Then Vega tells them that Linda had purchased a one million dollar insurance policy on her husband two months earlier.

While Warrick works in the layout room reconstructing Donna Marks's glass door, Sara searches Donna's computer. She finds only one name, "Apollo," on her e-mail buddy list. Curiously, Apollo appears to have sent his e-mails from seven different computers; all at the Western Nevada Correctional Facility. Grissom visits the computer room of the prison and finds inmates sitting at terminals, working as salesmen. The warden checks the user log and tells Grissom

146 | that Mickey Rutledge, aka Apollo, was released three days before.

Warrick shows Sara an unusual black fiber on Donna's clothes. It's car upholstery, perhaps from Pallard's vehicle. The blood on his shoes matches what was found on the Marks's patio. When he is reinterviewed, he admits that he went to the house and found the girls dead. He got scared and ran, adding that the restraining order dissuaded him from calling 911. Pallard appears to be telling the truth. The prints from Donna's toilet seat are a match for Rutledge, who comes in accompanied by his parole officer. Rutledge initially denies being at the house but relents when he's told of the prints. He says that Donna invited him over after his release, and that they were eating takeout when Joan showed up in a rage. He claims that he left the house when the sisters started arguing.

Sara learns that the police have found Pallard's car five miles from the site where the bodies were found. The car is brought to the garage with a cracked radiator. Whoever last filled the radiator added water, rather than coolant, which indicates either unfamiliarity with the vehicle, or desperation. When Greg detects a high sodium count in the radiator water, Grissom heads for the construction site.

Catherine and Nick realize that their investigation may have been for naught when they discover gunshot residue on Jasper's clothing. He was shot at close range. Nick says that the nature of Jasper's wound would have given him approximately ten minutes of mobility before hemorrhagic shock set in. Catherine suggests an unconventional suicide: Instead of a shot to a crucial organ, he shot himself with a second gun in such a way that he'd have time

> I call a toll-free number to place an order and I'm giving my personal credit card information to a, hello, I'm doing time life operator?

Bullet was a through and through.

to dispose of it. The nearby lake is their new search area. When Linda Jasper's signature on the body release form doesn't match the one on the insurance policy, Catherine figures it out: James forged his wife's signature on the policy, then faked his murder so he could provide for his family.

Grissom returns to the body dump site and looks at water tank, that contains sodium rich fertilizer. He then dusts the spigot for prints and takes a sample of water. Confronting Rutledge with the evidence, he surmises that Joan, enraged about the "rent," turned her venom on the ex-con. The sisters scuffled, Joan scratched Donna, and Donna fell through through the glass door. Joan then told Rutledge that he'd be blamed for it. Desperate, he strangled her, then used Pallard's car to transport the bodies to the distant site.

Sara arrives home to her sparse apartment, and discards the many take-out containers in her fridge. Then she picks up the phone and makes a call, saying "Hey, it's Sara, you want to go out somewhere?"

"We needed a 'B' story that took us outdoors because our 'A' story traveled from small room to small room and was meant to be a little claustrophobic," says writer Marc Dube, who along with Corey Miller contributed their first script to the series. "We were interested in exploring the wilderness and the sport of hunting."

The assignment, notes Corey Miller, provided the kind of mystery that writers thrive on. "The hunter's bullet disappearing into dense woods was fun to do. Based on the blood spatter, victim's position, and all those trees, how would our CSIs narrow down a workable search area? How far could the bullet have gone?" The twist was in making Jasper's death a painful, self-sacrificing ordeal. Says Miller, "The insurance storyline was developed to inject some emotion into the mystery."

Sara's identification with Donna Marks's alienated existence causes her to rethink her own. "We wanted to get a Sara story beat out of it," Anthony Zuiker points out, "her cleaning out her refrigerator . . . cleaning out her life, really resonated." As Dube puts it, "The Internet is gradually training all of us to be internal creatures. It was the perfect story to wrap around Sara's obsession with her work. The case opens her eyes to the outside world she's been turning her back on for so long."

The writers were also excited to demonstrate a fascinating forensic procedure through one of the "A" storylines. "We had some involved discussions," Dube explains, "with a glass expert about different types of glass and densities specific to each so we could forensically reassemble a shattered sliding glass door." Miller adds, "We really wanted to see Warrick working on that massive jigsaw puzzle because, in the end, that mountain of research had to be translated into something visual."

"People don't know that when you call to order stuff it could be a convict answering the phone," Zuiker says. "We felt that was cool." Dube remembers, "We had read some articles about various merchandise catalogs working in conjunction with minimum security prisons and it shocked us." Miller adds, "It was a unique and creepy way into our story about the information super-highway and its stranglehold on everything we do. The relationship between the sisters allowed us to filter in unique forensic clues—with each discovery we slowly uncover the polar-opposite lives of these women." ■

ORIGINAL AIRDATE: 1/17/02
WRITTEN BY: Anthony E. Zuiker & Ann Donahue
DIRECTED BY: Kenneth Fink

This is one of the few cases where physical evidence is secondary.

148

GUEST STARRING

ERIC SZMANDA: Greg Sanders
ROBERT DAVID HALL: Dr. Al Robbins
MATT O'TOOLE: Paul Millander
MICOLE MERCURIO: Isabelle Millander
NEIL FLYNN: Officer Yarnell
CHERYL WHITE: Mrs. Mason
ARCHIE KAO: Archie Johnson
STEVE WITTING: Pete Walker
ROB ROY FITZGERALD: Det. Champlain
JASON AZIKIWE: Court Police Officer

A motorist on a desolate stretch of highway picks up a hitchhiker. "Where you headed?" he asks. The traveler turns. "It's not where *I'm* heading . . ." he says. Several hours later, a local detective welcomes Catherine and Grissom to Good Springs. The town is out of their jurisdiction, however, Grissom has been personally requested. A dead man has been found in a bathtub inside an empty warehouse, a tape recorder holds a message for Grissom, who recognizes the voice. It's serial killer Paul Millander. In his previous two homicides, Millander preyed on men who share a birthday with the day his father was slain, August 17. This time the victim is Pete Walker of California. As before, he has been forced to record a message saying he was about to kill himself. This time, though, there's an addendum, "Happy birthday, Mister Grissom"—Gil was born August 17, 1956.

Grissom observes bluish-red stippling on one side of Walker's face and Catherine finds a single, dark, foot-long hair in the tub. Brass locates Walker's car, they speculate that Millander was hitchicking, but wonder how he could have known that he'd get picked up by a man who had the deadly birthdate? Robbins confirms one gunshot to Walker's chest killed him but can't explain the stippling on his face. Grissom recalls his last meeting with the killer at the Halloween-novelty warehouse he owned. Millander shown him his newest creation—a mask called "Good vs. Evil" on which one side of the face was normal, the other a monstrous grotesque. "He's telling me he's going to show me both sides," Grissom realizes.

Warrick and Sara find gunshot residue above the passenger seat, apparently left when Millander fired a shot through the passenger window, close enough to leave stippling on Walker's face. Greg says the bathtub hair is female, and old, suggesting Millander had been nurturing it until he was ready to plant it. As the CSIs gather evidence, Grissom states that none of it matters, since Millander is providing evidence to tell us a story.

The captain learns that Walker had no record other than a speeding ticket. Grissom has Brass check the previous victims' driving records. Each had received tickets and both had been the same written by Nevada Highway Patrol officer.

Catherine and Grissom meet the patrolman who tells them that only three judges handle traffic cases. He directs them inside the Mulberry Municipal Court building where they are shocked to see Judge Douglas Mason, a.k.a. Paul Millander. Grissom orders a court officer to arrest the judge, but Mason orders the officer to hold Grissom in contempt. That night, the judge visits Grissom in his cell. He dismisses the notion of taking a DNA test, then orders Grissom released, and invites him to his home for dinner with his family. Catherine enters as Mason leaves, and they lift the judge's prints from the cell's bars. Greg has determined that the hair from the Walker scene is from a postpubescent female. He's also detected testosterone—of the variety usually introduced via injection.

When Grissom arrives for his dinner date, Mrs. Mason tells him that they've lived there since 1992 when they adopted their son, Greg. Grissom is interrupted by a phone call from Catherine, Judge Mason's prints are a match to Paul Millander. Grissom excuses himself and goes back to the lab. Despite the prints, Grissom asks about their suspect's birth certificate. Catherine informs him that the Mulberry County records building burned down in an unsolved case of arson. Brass has more encouraging news: a current property tax account in the name of Isabelle Millander, Paul's mother.

At the home, Catherine notices a dinner table set for two. Mrs. Millander says that she always sets a place for her late husband, who started a Halloween makeup business in Hollywood in the thirties. Isabelle shows Grissom a crude plaster mold of her

IDENTITY CRISIS

> purge{hiMem} buffer...w
> unx/ sei

husband's hand, saying her child made it. Noting a curious green discoloration, Grissom asks if he can take it to the lab, promising to return it. Meanwhile Catherine looks around what seems to be a girl's bedroom, complete with photos of a young girl named Pauline. Catherine finds baseball cards in a dresser and a long dark hair on a sweater in the closet. She's interrupted by Mrs. Millander, who explains that her daughter died "a lifetime ago." But at the mention of her son, she abruptly asks them to leave.

The green discoloration from the plaster cast is alginate, a substance used by makeup artists in the 1970s. Grissom realizes that this is the source of the prints left at Millander's crime scenes. Catherine lifts a child's fingerprint from the baseball card. It matches the judge's, proving that Mason is definitely Millander. Greg Sanders then matches the hair from Pauline's closet to the one found on the bathtub. There is only one explanation: Pauline Millander took male hormone injections, most likely in preparation for a sex change.

In his chambers, Mason/Millander confesses, telling Grissom that doctors had discovered an "endocrinic ambiguity" when he was a child, and gave his parents the option to raise him as either a girl or a boy. Unable to agree, he lived outside as a boy for his father and inside as a girl for his mother. Millander says he bore this as best he could until the night of his father's murder. Feeling that if he'd been a "real" boy, he could have saved his father from his killers. He resolved to become tough enough that no one could ever hurt him—hence, sexual reassignment. Ultimately, his anger demanded revenge. As Grissom takes a DNA swab from his mouth, Millander confides that he's already chosen his next victim.

In the Clark County Courthouse, Catherine and Grissom wait for Millander's arraignment to begin. Millander, however, has already exited the building using a forged version of Grissom's ID that he has altered to include his own picture.

Grissom races to the Millander home, where he finds Isabelle at the dining-room table with a knife plunged into her heart. Then he finds Millander in the bathtub, a gunshot to his chest, and a tape recorder with its final message, "My name is Paul Millander . . . I just can't do it anymore."

"Matt O'Toole's portrayal of Paul Millander was so interesting that we just kept saying 'We've got to bring the character back,'" Carol Mendelsohn says, adding that they hammered out the story's essential structure in a mere ninety minutes. "Then the question became, 'Do we really kill him off, or do we bring him back yet again?'" Ultimately, they decided to let justice prevail. "The episode was our homage to the pilot," says Jonathan Littman. "It was a reward to our fans who'd been with us from the very beginning."

"We were all very upset that Millander was going to die," says William Petersen, "but by the same token, you don't want to create Moriarty." Of course, Petersen adds, "Matt's a wonderful guy, and didn't want to leave. He was crushed that Millander was going to die."

Ann Donahue remembers the bittersweet decision to bring closure to the Millander saga. "He was a great bête noire for Grissom, but when you twist a story the way that we twisted it, you insult your audience unless you let him go."

"The story was just unbelievable," Petersen recalls. "We sat there reading this thing and we were like, 'Anthony, what are you doing?'" Ann Donahue recalls, "None of our actors believed it. Our director didn't believe it. Everyone thought it was crazy. I had read about androgyne insufficiency, so we had a medical reality to base it on." Says Carol Mendelsohn, "It was a great hour of TV . . . so spooky." Director Ken Fink agrees, "It's a horror episode. I thought, Let's just have some fun with this one and let the audience be creeped out. I wanted the teaser to be really iconic— you know, the hitchhiker at night. I just love that moment when the audience is thinking, 'Don't go back! You'll die!'" Director of Photography Jonathan West garnered an Emmy nomination for his work on the episode.

Due to the ambivalence over losing the mind-bending villain, the show's writing team admitted to entertaining loopholes that could have allowed for another story. "We joked that Millander could rise again," says Mendelsohn. "And the fans on the Internet said that Grissom never checked his pulse, so maybe . . ." ■

5 PHYSICAL INFORMATION

PATIENT NAME

12 AUTOPS

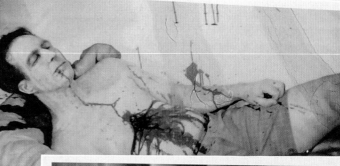

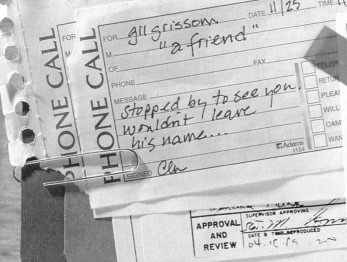

A MARAT

DAVID

ures humerus.

fracture of bone may cut the axillary

artery.

II.   Gunshot wound #2 to the chest, penetrating, fatal,

indeterminate

t lateral chest.

PHONE CALL

PHONE CALL

FOR gil grissom

OF "a friend"

DATE 11 25   TIME 1136 AM / P.M.

PHONE

FAX

☐ TELEP
☐ RETU
☐ PLEAS
☐ WILL
☐ CAM
☐ WAN

MESSAGE

stopped by to see you.
wouldn't leave
his name....

Adams
1154

SIGNED Cln

APPROVAL
AND
REVIEW

SUPERVISOR APPROVING

DATE & TIME REPRODUCED

04.15.19 2:00

Rev. 2/91

POLICE DEPARTMENT

Police Department Forensic Lab

STR RESULTS- PROFILER PLUS/CO

DATE: 01-17-02   ANALYST: G.

PCR AMP #: 19-32801   EVENT #: 2317

DNA STR TYPING RES

SAMPLE # 1	D3S1358	vWA	FGA	AMELO
SAMPLE INFO				
HAIR	16,17	17,19	20,23	
	D5S818	D13S317		
WAREHOUSE BATH TUB				

Las V

TE: 11/20/00

R AMP #: Stuart Rampler

MPLE #	D3S1358	vWA		
SAMPLE INFO				
SAMPLE	16,17	17,19		
	D5S818	D13S317		

GAS STATION
437 VALLEY BLVD.
LAS VEGAS, NV 89120
DLR# 337774426
DATE: 11/23/01

PETE WALKER
X XXXX 9031 00231

A4DG8 126788
245T659 11/23
935-08275

SELF
.89
.43

2001   **ANNUAL PROPERTY TAX INFORMATION STATEMENT**   **2001**

CITIES, COUNTY, SCHOOLS AND ALL OTHER TAXING AGENCIES IN LINCOLN COUNTY

SECURED PROPERTY TAX FOR FISCAL YEAR JULY 1, 2001 TO JUNE 30, 2002

MARK J. SALADINO, TREASURER AND TAX COLLECTOR

FOR ASSISTANCE CALL (702) 974-2111 OR (888) 807-2111

ASSESSOR'S ID. NO.   CK

DETAIL OF TAXES DUE FOR   3004 042 009 01 000 **39**

PROPERTY IDENTIFICATION

ASSESSOR'S ID.NO.: 3004 042 009 01 000
OWNER OF RECORD AS OF JANUARY 1, 2001
SAME AS BELOW

MAILING ADDRESS

MILLANDER, PAUL JOHN AND
ISABELLE MARY
13891 SAND CREEK ROAD

R 115 (Rev. 6/54) 9-922177-375M

AGENCY	AGENCY PHONE NO.	RATE	AMOUNT
GENERAL TAX LEVY ALL AGENCIES		1.000000	$ 1,750.71
VOTED INDEBTEDNESS COUNTY		.001128	$ 1.97
WATERWORKS			7.24
SPECIAL WATER			126.65
		$	50.00
			18.50
			15.00
			71.00
			319.66
			129.86
			19.88
			48.66
			4.93

DOCUMENT NO. D 779499

LINCOLN COUNTY, NEVADA

DEPARTMENT OF HEALTH
BUREAU OF VITAL RECORDS
CERTIFICATION OF BIRTH

This is a certification of name and birth facts on file in the Bureau of Vital Records, Department of Health, Lincoln County., NV.

DATE OF BIRTH   AUG 17, 1956   TIME OF BIRTH   4:55PM   CERTIFICATE NO.   156-60-144352

DATE FILED   08-20-56   DATE ISSUED   08-22-56

NAME   PAULINE MILLANDER

SEX   FEMALE

MOTHER'S NAME   ISABELLE MILLANDER

FATHER'S NAME   PAUL MILLANDER

KIRK A. SKADDEN
CITY REGISTRAR

Do not accept this transcript unless it bears the raised seal of the Department of Health. The Reproduction or alteration of this certificate is prohibited under Section 3.21 of Lincoln County, NV.

SSUMED

CASE # 01-001-108-213
The Millander Files

Approved

THE FINGER

152

Roy Logan strides into a bank just before closing with a check against his own account for one million dollars. Logan restlessly checks the clock as the manager counts out the bills, then peels out of the parking lot with the money. He's pulled over for reckless driving and the cop notices that the nervous man has blood on his hands. Catherine and Grissom are called in to process Logan, a wealthy real estate developer. Logan continues clock-watching as Catherine takes a sample of the blood on his hands. Logan's lawyer, Paul Dennison, arrives angrily protesting his client's groundless detention and escorts Logan from the building. Catherine also leaves, to attend Lindsey's nursery school recital. She notices that Logan has left his sunglasses behind and takes them out to the parking lot. He asks her to please leave as his cell phone rings. He tells her, "It's for you." Confused, Catherine takes the phone. A distorted voice orders her to put her pager, gun, and cell phone on the ground, and tells her to get behind the wheel of Logan's car and drive until they receive his next call. Otherwise, he says, Amanda is dead.

As Grissom exits the building he notices Catherine's discarded possessions. Greg tells a concerned Grissom that the blood found on Logan belongs to a female. As they they drive, Logan explains that Amanda is his mistress. He went to her condo and found "this." Logan hands Catherine a small metal box with a human finger inside. Soon after, he got a call demanding a million by day's end. Catherine suggests they go have a drink. They pull over at a restaurant, where Sara is on a date with Hank Peddigrew. Catherine breezes by, pretending not to know her, as she and Logan take a seat at the counter. They receive another call from the distorted voice, giving them one hour to reach the Horseshoe Tavern sign on Route 93. As they leave the restaurant, Catherine surreptitiously places the finger, now in a glass of ice, on Sara's table. Back in the car, she hands Logan a glow-paint stick, which she had been planning to use to decorate Lindsey's face for her recital and tells him to mark the cash.

At the Horseshoe Tavern sign, Catherine slams on the brakes, creating skidmarks, and leaves pronounced footprints as they walk through a gate. When they approach a hill, they see a gunman wearing a rabbit mask. Catherine insists that they see Amanda before handing over the ransom, the "rabbit" instructs them to drive to a pay phone on Highway 582, where he'll call them. Logan dashes up the hill and hands over the briefcase.

Brass and Nick go to question Diane Logan. She is outside her home, scolding her son for eating a peanut butter sandwich inside the car. On the advice of her lawyer, she refuses to say anything about her husband's disappearance.

Greg verifies that the blood on the finger Catherine gave Sara matches that found on Logan. Noting that Logan owns a town house under his company's name, Nick goes to check it out. Warrick reports that state troopers have spotted Logan's car coming—and going—on 582. The CSIs find the skidmarks by the Horsehoe Tavern sign. Retracing Catherine's footprints, they conclude this was the site of the ransom delivery. At the town house, Nick finds no one home, there are two lipstick-marked wineglasses and blood spatters.

A map left at the phone booth directs Catherine and Logan to a reservoir, where they find Amanda—dead at the bottom of a sewer pipe. Doctor Robbins tells Grissom that the finger was removed postmortem with a serrated blade. Catherine finally calls in to inform them the kidnapping is now a murder. Robbins notes that Amanda Freeman has been dead for forty-eight hours. "Twenty-four above water, twenty-four under." She was killed by blunt force trauma to the back of her head, the wound site containing fragments of a smooth stone. Against Catherine's advice, Logan looks at Freeman's body in the autopsy room. Distraught and unable to face his wife, Logan says he'll be at the Tangiers.

A chipped, bloodstained marble table in the town house suggests that a struggle preceded Freeman's abduction. The bathroom shower curtain liner is missing, but Warrick and Sara locate it in the sewer where Amanda's body was found. There's an oily residue on the liner, which Greg determines to be oleic acid, commonly found in peanut butter. Nick then remembers Logan's son was eating peanut butter and jelly in

ORIGINAL AIRDATE: 1/31/02
WRITTEN BY: Danny Cannon & Carol Mendelsohn
DIRECTED BY: Richard J. Lewis

SPECIAL GUEST STAR

TOM IRWIN: Roy Logan

GUEST STARRING

ERIC SZMANDA: Greg Sanders
ROBERT DAVID HALL: Dr. Al Robbins
CHRISTOPHER WIEHL: Hank Peddigrew
AL SAPIENZA: Paul Dennison
BARBARA WILLIAMS: Diane Logan
J. ROBIN MILLER: Amanda Freeman

Amanda broke the only rule.

the family minivan. Brass discovers that the last call made on Freeman's cell phone was to Diane Logan. Diane and her car are brought in. She's also accompanied by her husband's lawyer, Paul Dennison. Suspecting Diane has handled the ransom money, Catherine asks her to hold her hands out, palms up. They kill the lights and see that she's clean but *Dennison's* palms are aglow.

Dennison takes the rabbit mask from his bag. He maintains he didn't do anything illegal, he didn't know Freeman was dead. And that everything he did was at Roy Logan's behest. Dennison gives them the key to the locker where the cash is. Unfortunately, Catherine and Brass find Logan has checked out of the Tangiers and the locker is empty. Grissom speculates that Freeman, tired of being the other woman, arranged a meeting with Diane and Roy walked in on it. When Diane left, he angrily laid into Freeman, knocking her into the table and fatally fracturing her skull. He then severed Freeman's finger and wrapped her body in the shower liner, says Grissom. Logan contacted his lawyer, who could maintain confidentiality *and* help protect his assets. After intentionally making a scene at the bank, Logan drove recklessly in order to get pulled over. He puposely left his sunglasses behind, and once Catherine followed him outside, had Dennison call her from where he was watching. Logan made sure to use his wife's car to transport Freeman's body, so as to cast suspicion on a vengeful spouse. He'd assumed that the bank would mark the money and made sure that Dennison would be the one to touch it by giving it to him in a bag that was too large to fit into the locker.

It seems to have been a perfect plan. Then Catherine's cell rings, it's a state trooper on Highway 582. Surprised at having seen a speeding Lexus twice in two days, he's pulled it over and is holding Logan.

LAS VEGAS POLICE DEPARTMENT
DETECTIVE DIVISION

CLIENT #
00630-0092

TEST REQUIRED

SUITE 208

PHYSICIAN S. SCHEURICH, M.

CLARK COUNTY CORONER

DR. P. ROBBINS
NAME

3154
IDENTIFICATION NUMBER

P. Robbins
SIGNATURE

35216854321 31

FICE OF MEDICAL EXAMINER

CLARK COUNTY

CORONER'S DEPARTMENT

LAS VEGAS POLICE DEPARTMENT - SUPPLEMENTARY REPORT

Born and raised in a small town in Virginia, Albert Robbins' interest in medicine was a natural outgrowth of his upbringing. His mother, a registered nurse, would often take young Al to work with her at the local hospital. He would spend after-school hours in its corridors playing and completing homework. His years growing up in that environment left him with an intense compassion for the ill and a equally strong respect for the caretakers.

With his quick intellect and academic bent, Al was accepted into the pre-med program at the University of Virginia. He knew he wanted to become a doctor, but was still unsure as to what his specialty would be. During his college years, he took an internship with a small hospital in Lancaster, Pennsylvania and looked ahead towards higher education. He was accepted at the prestigious John Hopkins University where he concentrated his studies in Physiology for his Masters and PhD.

While completing his residency, Robbins was victim of a head-on collision with a drunk driver and emerged from the incident with serious injuries. He spent the better part of the next year in the role of the patient, recovering from the physical trauma which resulted in the amputation of both his legs.

Trying to look at his situation as an extension of his education, he was able to learn much from the physicians, nurses and technicians who cared for him. With a remarkable survivor's disposition, he took advantage of the slow process of recovery by teaching himself how to play guitar, as well as pouring over everything from anatomy textbooks to classic literature in order to keep his mind sharp and focused.

When he was finally able to complete his medical training, Robbins decided he wanted his talent and energy to be applied to benefit the less fortunate population. He opted out of higher paying positions in order to start up his own clinic in Baltimore. It was there that he met his wife and married.

After twenty years as a General Physician, the encroachment of the HMO industry and escalating malpractice insurance costs forced him to close the doors of his clinic. Disenchanted with the business of medicine, Robbins decided he needed a change of pace and accepted the position of Assistant Coroner for the Arlington, Virginia Police Department. He found the job very fulfilling. As soon as he had helped solve his first crime, he knew that he had found his true calling.

After a few years working as Coroner in Arlington, Robbins moved his wife and children to Las Vegas, where he has served as Chief Medical Examiner since 1995. Now a fixture with the LVPD, he enjoys his work and loves the freedom his job affords him. He is now able to spend more time with his family, as well as pursuing outside interests, such as playing lead guitar in a rock band he started with his day-shift counterpart. In short, he loves his work without letting it define him.

CONFIDENTIAL

Dr. ROBBINS, Albert David
Medical Examiner

ED BY		APPROVED BY		REFER TO
	STAR	RANK	STAR	

A severed finger. A million bucks. And Catherine's not allowed to talk to anyone.

156

"**A** guy walks into a bank," according to Carol Mendelsohn, was the opening of Danny Cannon's pitch for this episode. "It was a departure for us," observes Jonathan Littman. "Departures are fine as long as they have a great story and a great ride. And 'The Finger' was a great ride."

The episode's less-is-more forensics parallel the sparse, desolate landscapes in which the story takes place. Marg Helgenberger observes, "It was different, it was a noir thriller." And, she adds, "It was really fun for me, because I was literally and metaphorically driving it. I remember Carol saying, 'I think you're really going to like this episode.' And she was right."

"The Finger" also took Director Richard Lewis to some new places. "It was a director's dream," he says. "I think Danny had wanted to direct it himself, but he was too busy. It was a compliment for him to give it to me." Lewis admits to being very partial to the reservoir scene, where Catherine and Logan discover Amanda's body, thanks to Location Manager Paul Wilson's exquisite

location choice. And he has another great memory of the episode, "Marg utters my favorite line of all time, 'Give me the finger.'"

On a character note, Sara and Hank are shown dating. Jorja Fox was happy to see her character reaching out, though a little surprised by her choice. "Here's this woman who's so not cool in the regular world and who's lucky enough to have all these guys at work who are crazy about her. So it's kind of funny that she'd be looking outside that world to find someone." For Ann Donahue, Sara's decision to hook up with Hank represents an acknowledgment of the futility of her crush on Grissom. "It's like, 'Okay, I'm going to make a life for myself.'"

The groundbreaking hour offered real-world satisfaction for Marg Helgenberger. "I got a call from Billy Petersen when we finished, she says. "He said, 'Honey, that episode is amazing. It just shows where our show can go, and you're fantastic.'" Her most important review, however, happened well off-set, "As my husband said, 'Honey, you're really cool.'" ∎

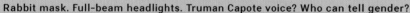

Rabbit mask. Full-beam headlights. Truman Capote voice? Who can tell gender?

BURDEN OF PROOF

ORIGINAL AIRDATE: 2/7/02
WRITTEN BY: Ann Donahue
DIRECTED BY: Kenneth Fink

157

GUEST STARRING

ERIC SZMANDA: Greg Sanders
ROBERT DAVID HALL: Dr. Al Robbins
JANET GUNN: Jane Bradley
SARA PAXTON: Jody Bradley
DAN BYRD: Jake Bradley
TERRY BOZEMAN: Brad Lewis
NANCY VALEN: Neighbor
MONNAE MICHAELL: Doctor
JASON BEGHE: Russ Bradley

Let's get this body out of here. We've got cross-contamination.

G rissom walks through the woods where a macabre collection of corpses lies rotting in the open air. Searching with flashlight, he finds a specimen that interests him. "That one's not ours," Edward Cormier tells him. Cormier's in charge of Vegas's body farm, a facility where research on situational decomposition is conducted. To the unknown killer, it must have seemed the perfect place to hide a body.

In the autopsy room, Robbins searches the chest cavity unsuccessfully for bullet fragments. Grissom is puzzled to come across *Genus Hypaderma*, a large maggot normally found in a cow's intestinal tract. Catherine identifies the man as Mike Kimble, but when the CSIs arrive at his home, they find it

engulfed in flames. After excising the area around the entry wound, Robbins finds a pinlike titanium fragment, possibly a medical implant.

After the fire is out, Nick and Warrick observe the burn pattern by the ceiling is indicative of a downward-moving fire. They speculate that it was "chasing" an accelerant. There is also a bloody patch of carpet among the debris. Having learned Kimble was engaged, the team goes to the home of his fiancée, Jane Bradley. Shocked by the news, Jane tells Catherine they were going to be married next week. Her children, Jody and Jake, loved Mike and she wonders how she will tell them. Just then her ex-husband, Russ, drops by for his scheduled visitation. Catherine asks to examine his hands. There is no gun shot residue on them. He tells Brass if they need to speak to him he's always available at any one of his four grocery stores.

Nick uses an ion detector in the scorched upstairs bedroom to search for accelerant, which is identified as nail polish remover. Meanwhile Grissom proceeds to Kimble's studio, where he finds a framed photograph of the deceased with Jane, Jake, and Jody. He then notices a couple of photos wedged behind it. They feature provocative shots of twelve-year-old Jody. When asked about the photos, Jody says, "I loved Mike. And he loved me." When Catherine

158 | suggests that Jody has fallen into the "protect-the-abuser trap," Brass has the girl undergo a physical exam.

In the A/V lab, Warrick examines the snapshots and notices a partial finger obscuring a portion of the frame, an amateurish mistake; Kimble was a professional photographer. Warrick attempts to digitally glean a print from the photographed finger. After conducting an experiment with some rotting beef, Grissom tells Sara that the meat found in the wound was not imported by the flies; it must have been there already. He decides to talk to Russ Bradley and rises to leave, dismissing Sara's inquiry of his progress by instructing her to photograph and dispose of the rotting beef experiment. "I'm a vegetarian," she says, refusing to handle the meat. He curtly tells her to have Nick do it instead. Bradley tells Brass he never liked the way Kimble looked at his daughter. Grissom examines Bradley's gun, noting it's been recently cleaned.

While disassembling a bullet, Grissom takes a sip of soda, then gets an idea when he notices the ice is melting. He gets a package of raw ground beef, molds some "meat popsicles," and places them in the freezer. Catherine tells him that Jody's exam has detected symptoms of chronic sexual abuse, as well as a burn on her wrist. She may be their arsonist. He tells her to recheck the evidence recovered from Kimble and dismisses her as he'd done with Sara.

At the Bradley home Nick finds one of Jody's nightgowns has semen on it. Greg tests DNA

I need to see that gun.

> ## What I think and what the evidence proves are possibly two different things.

samples of all the men who spent time with Jody and establishes that her brother, Jake, was the depositor on the nightgown. Jake comes in for questioning, accompanied by a lawyer. He admits that he has a set of keys to Kimble's house but denies taking the photos or planting them there. Nick, playing a hunch, asks if he can have a word alone with the adolescent. He conjectures, correctly, that Jake used Jody's nightgown from the laundry hamper to clean up an embarrassing emission. He then asks about Kimble's behavior around Jody. Jake remembers nothing unusual, but does mention Jody's enthusiasm whenever he came over.

When Grissom's ground beef is sufficiently frozen, he carves a "meat bullet," which he loads into a gun and fires. Such a projectile would wound like any other bullet, then disintegrate inside the body and disperse among the soft tissue. Grissom and Brass confront Russ Bradley with that discovery, and tell him they're also found traces of beef in his pistol's reloader. As a grocer, Bradley had made regular meat deliveries to the body farm for experiments. He thought he had the perfect dump site for Kimble's corpse. When Brass suggests that he then doused Kimble's bed with nail polish remover and torched his house, Bradley makes a formal confession. He says he killed Kimble because he was abusing his daughter. Grissom reminds Brass that the arson investigation is not finished and that they should restrict their prosecution of Bradley to the murder.

Grissom is puzzled when Sara suddenly requests a leave of absence. She says she needs to work in an environment of communication and respect.

Meanwhile, Warrick shows Nick what he has recovered from the photograph—a reflection in Jody's eye of what appears to be a porthole. Mike Kimble didn't own a boat but Russ does. Warrick promptly finds the vessel; the interior matches the photo. Catherine sits with Jody and Jane Bradley, she suggests that her father took pictures of her on his boat. He then planted them at Kimble's apartment. Jody says her dad threatened to kill her if she ever talked about the abuse. She told Kimble, who promised to "fix things." Warrick enters with a brown paper bag, showing only Catherine its contents.

Body farm. Creepy.

Russ Bradley and his lawyer return to the interrogation room. Grissom shows them a photo of a vaginal- and semen-stained sleeping bag found on his boat. Finally at a loss for words, Bradley beseeches his attorney to cut a deal. The lawyer can't. Sex with a minor under fourteen carries a mandatory life sentence with no chance of parole.

Later, Catherine and Grissom share an after work drink at his apartment. She's heard about Sara's complaint and advises him that a supervisor needs to be more personally engaged with his staff. He picks up the phone, calls a florist, and orders a plant for Sara as an apology.

160

However hard to believe, there are people who keep dead bodies and check on them from time to time. As Ann Donahue points out, there are at least two body farms currently in operation, one at the University of Tennessee, another in British Columbia. "More and more, CSIs are using them because of what they can learn," she says. "As always, we needed a story, and Anthony came in with his research on a body farm. He was out of his mind with excitement and said, 'That's it! You've got to do something on that!'" What followed was a sad look at a contemporary American family. "We're all kind of a nation of Brady Bunches—everybody's part of a blended family," Donahue says. "So I thought we'd look at what happens when you get divorced and you have to let your kids go with someone who you don't even like. The twist was, the new husband ain't the problem; it's the old husband." As for the murder weapon, "I was fascinated by the meat bullet idea because I had read about it in my research," Donahue recalls. "I thought, How smart is that? It's like stabbing someone with an icicle—you can't find it!"

For the destruction of Mike Kimble's home, the production crew used an existing, intact house and built an extension on top of it. They then set the extension ablaze. "That wasn't CGI, that was real," director Ken Fink says, adding that he intentionally didn't prepare the actors for the magnitude of the explosion that erupts from the second story. "It startled everybody," he says. "If you look closely, the camera actually does a little bit of a reaction." Special Effects Coordinator Mark Byers remembers it. "We basically filled in a corner on the second floor and created a façade that we could put our pyrotechnics behind and it would blow out and appear that there was a room behind it." The scenes at the ersatz Kimble residence were doubly tricky because the home was being shot both inside and out. "We were limited to where we could work," he says. "The company would be shooting in one room while we were working on the exterior."

A more personal moment has Nick chatting with Jake Bradley, whose DNA has been found on his sister's nightgown. "I was a drama school teacher with seventh graders for years," George Eads says. "So I'd told the writers that I'd wanted to do something with children." To prepare his young costar, Dan Byrd, he says, "Dan and I went out to the trailers and rehearsed the dialogue." That impromptu coaching, says Fink, made his job a bit easier. "It's nice to have scenes where you can sit back with the camera quietly and let the writing and acting carry the day."

As for Sara's threatening to quit because of Grissom's lack of awareness of her, Donahue points out, "We've done a season and a half of Sara having a kind of hero worship for him. She has her pride. He's given her mixed signals, so she's not going to take that anymore." As Jorja Fox describes the scene in the lab, "I propelled Sara to think, 'This is insane. I'm totally fixated on this guy and he doesn't know the most basic thing about me?'" Donahue asserts. "It *isn't* about the ground beef. Sometimes the only power you have is to say no, so she's exercising it. It's the only way Sara can tell Grissom she needs more."

"It's that Grissom has a marionette-ish control that he uses on Sara in a way he doesn't use with anyone else," William Petersen explains. "There's a personal thing with Sara that makes it harder for her and more interesting for him." By the same token, however, Sara is uniquely skilled in getting under his skin. "Grissom can't be hurt by Warrick, or even by Catherine. He can be hurt by Sara," Petersen says.

With a rift opened up between the two characters, Grissom receives counsel from Catherine in the episode's epilogue. "I find it a very interesting scene," says Fink. "I like its sense of the sadness that exists underneath Grissom's life, the loneliness." Of course, Catherine's completely aware of Grissom's pained obsession with Sara and his inability to get past his own fear.

His way of following her advice is to call the florist and send Sara a peace offering. He sends not flowers, but a plant; and not to her home, but to the office. Donahue comments, "When the woman on the phone says, 'What's the sentiment?' the very word *sentiment* just baffles him. And he could say a million things—'Take care,' 'I love you'—but he just says 'Grissom.'" ■

PRIMUM NON NOCERE

ORIGINAL AIRDATE: 2/28/02
WRITTEN BY: Andrew Lipsitz
DIRECTED BY: Danny Cannon

SPECIAL GUEST STAR

NICOLE ARI PARKER: Lillie Ivers

GUEST STARRING

ERIC SZMANDA: Greg Sanders
ROBERT DAVID HALL: Dr. Al Robbins
JEREMY RATCHFORD: Tommy Sconzo
ABBY BRAMMELL: Jane Gallagher
PETER MACKENZIE: Dr. Ron Stockwell
DAVID ANDRIOLE: Terry Rivers
JEFFREY D. SAMS: Det. Lockwood

Inside a local ice rink, Terry Rivers, a weekend skater for an amateur hockey team, takes a hit that sends him flying into the boards. While the ref calls a penalty on the opposing team, the facility's on-site doctor, Ron Stockwell, stiches Terry up, gives him some pills, and urges him to sit out the rest of the game. Rivers, however, pops the pills and skates back onto the ice. Not long after, he trips over the opposing team's goalie and winds up on the bottom of a frenzied pileup. Rivers's body lies on a rinkside bench. Doctor Stockwell tells the CSIs that Rivers was cognizant enough to be helped off the ice, but died minutes later. A gruesome throat slash apparently ended his life. Sara and Grissom slowly traverse the length of the rink, gathering evidence, while Catherine interviews Stockwell, who relates his unsuccessful attempt at CPR. Grissom and Sara speculate that the rink's Zamboni machine may have picked up evidence from the ice. They melt and search the snow reservoir, and find a piece of a tooth.

At a nightclub in the Aladdin Hotel, Warrick and Nick arrive as singer Lillie Ivers winds up her set. They're met by Detective Lockwood, who leads them

Means I got the night off and didn't feel like going home.

backstage to the body of saxophonist Stan Greevey. It looks like a heroin overdose but none of the usual paraphernalia is present. Warrick lifts some white powder from a nearby table and notes there are two coasters but only one glass. He also finds a lone contact lens.

A tox screen on Terry Rivers turns up quinine. Doctor Robbins believes that Rivers was playing through a lot of pain, noting several recent injuries. He can't be sure about a cause of death, but the cut on the neck that nicked his carotid artery was from a clean, double-edged blade, possibly a skate. There's also serious damage to his basilar artery and blood in the intimal space, which could have caused loss of consciousness. Brass and Catherine collect both teams' equipment as evidence. Catherine reads the rival team's roster then catches up with Jane Gallagher, the team's lone female player. Although Catherine suspects bad blood from Rivers's opponents, Gallagher says it was Rivers's own teammates who really hated him.

Catherine and Grissom visit Terry Rivers's sparse bachelor pad. The profusion of stains on his mattress suggests he was a player in more ways than one. Sara has tested the jerseys and skates. One pair is especially bloodstained, its blades well-sharpened. They belong to Jane Gallagher.

Greg breaks down the white powder found in the

James Brass was born and raised in Newark, New Jersey to a blue-collar family in a working class neighborhood. Jim was a street smart kid who did well in school, but got mixed up with a tough crowd as a teenager and got into some minor trouble with the local law enforcement. These misdemeanors resulted in some eye-opening time performing community service in the inner city. The lessons he learned from the experience set him on a straight and narrow path towards living a productive, goal-oriented life.

After receiving a Bachelor's degree in History at Seaton Hall University in 1973, Jim was eager to settle down and start his life. In the same year, he married his college sweetheart and decided to join the police force in his hometown. Brass spent the years following working his way up the ranks in Newark's busy Homicide Division. As violent as the streets could be, he found the corrupt politics inside the precinct to be even more atrocious and unjust. He eventually became a Serpico-like figure in the department and was snubbed by many after putting away crooked cops who, even after incarceration, were still woven into the fabric of the community.

The hard headed zeal with which he approached his work took its toll on his life, both personally and professionally. Brass' family life suffered from his distraction and the never ending demands of his job. When his wife filed for divorce in 1994, Brass decided he needed a change. After twenty years with the Newark Police, he took a position with the Las Vegas Police, reluctantly leaving behind his wife and eight year old daughter, Ellie.

In Vegas, Brass was welcomed by the department and admired for his tenacity. He once again wholly immersed himself in his job. For two years, he worked as a Captain in homicide until 1996 when Brass was involved in the accidental shooting of a suspect. The incident was investigated, and although Brass was exonerated by Internal Affairs, he was subsequently transferred to the Crime Lab, where he made the adjustment to his new career as night shift Supervisor. Organized and politically savvy, Brass proved to be a good administrator with excellent delegation skills. Having never been formally trained in forensic science, he left the more hands-on work to his team of experienced CSIs, including Gil Grissom and Catherine Willows.

When the department was rocked by the on-duty death of rookie Holly Gribbs, Brass took the political fall and was transferred back to homicide while Gil Grissom assumed the position of Supervisor. After being relieved of the managerial duties that he had been growing weary of, Brass made a smooth transition back into his element working as a homicide detective.

Despite a few bumps in his career, Brass is respected among his peers, looked upon as a consummate realist with a wry sense of humor. His broad range of experiences has built an excellent understanding of law, politics and forensics. This valuable combination of skills makes Jim Brass an ideal compliment to Grissom and his team.

CONFIDENTIAL

SIGN HERE

RUESTED BY		APPROVED BY		REFER TO
.IK	STAR	RANK	STAR	

Las Vegas Police Department Forensic Laboratory

Plots - Kaz-Homicide-PP-TAW(demo)   2:22:00 PM
Las Vegas Police dept.   Genotyper® 2.1

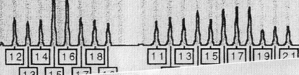

120	140	160	180	200	220	240	260
D3S1358		vWA			FGA		

• Sample 1 Detective Brass Badge #410

| 12 | 14 | 16 | 18 | 11 | 13 | 15 | 17 | 19 | 21 |
| 13 | 15 | 17 | | | | | | | |

Las Vegas Police Department Forensic Laboratory

STR RESULTS- PROFILER PLUS/COFILER

ANALYST: SANDERS, G. -

EVENT #: 3217 - 121201 - 7

DATE: 12-13-01

PCR AMP #: 19-1672

DNA STR TYPING RESULTS

SAMPLE # SAMPLE INFO	D3S1358	vWA	FGA	AMELO	D8S1179	D21S11	D1
SAMPLE #1: DET. BRASS BADGE #410	16,17	17,19	20,23	X,X	13,13	30,32.2	
	D5S818	D13S317	D7S820	D16S539	THO1	TPOX	CSF1PO
	11,11	11,13	12,13	9,12	7,9.3	8,9	10,10

2ND READER _____

REMARKS

SAMPLE # SAMPLE INFO	D3S1358	vWA	FGA	AMELO
SAMPLE #2: BLOOD JAMES BRASS	8,10	10.1,22	17,1	X,Y
	D5S818	D13S317	D7S820	D16S539
	0,21	3,22	4,15.2	8,41

SAMPLE # SAMPLE INFO	D3S1358	vWA	FGA	AMELO
SAMPLE #3: GUN BLOOD SAMPLE	7,19	10.1,22	17,1	X,Y
	D5S818	D13S317	D7S820	D16S539
	5,21	3,6	7,14	8,41

SAMPLE # SAMPLE INFO	D3S1358	vWA	FGA	AMEL
SAMPLE #4: DNA KEITH DRISCOLL	15,16	17,16	20,23	X,Y
	D5S818	D13S317	D7S820	D16S
	10,18	13,21	15,12	16,

* DENOTES LESSER PEAK HEIGHT, INC.= INCONCLUSIVE RESULT.

	RFU	NOTES:
COLOR		
BLUE		

BRASS, James

LAS VEGAS METROPOLITAN POLICE DEPARTMENT
Clark County, Nevada

POLICE

CAPTAIN

JIM BRASS

PN-8750   EXP DATE: NOV/2003
EYES: BRN   WEIGHT: 170
HAIR: BRN   HEIGHT: 6'1"

C.S.I. LEVEL 3

164 | cabaret's dressing room: It's China White heroin which is usually around 75 percent pure. This sample clocks in at 91. Warrick and Nick search the Aladdin's trash bins. Mentioning that Greevey was from L.A., Warrick maintains it's unlikely Lillie Ivers had met him before the previous night. They discover a syringe wrapped in a black scarf. Ivers admits the scarf is hers but says anyone could have taken it from the dressing room.

A search of Rivers's computer reveals that he had handled stock market investments for his entire team. Gallagher, a former team member, denies that she had recently switched teams because Rivers's investment advice had cost her $10,000. Suddenly, Jane vomits, and then claims she had eaten some bad shrimp. When she excuses herself, Grissom collects a sample, which tests negative for shellfish but positive for blood. Greg notes that is common in early pregnancy. Further testing confirms she is pregnant. Wondering if Rivers might be the father, Grissom and Sara decide to search Gallagher's apartment. At the lab, Grissom and Sara examine Gallagher's bedsheets, and find a toenail. It's from a male. Greg matches it, not to Rivers, but to the tooth found during their Zamboni search.

Nick and Warrick question Bill Baker, whose prints were found on the syringe. He says that he'd attempted to get rid of the overdose evidence out of consideration for the Greeveys' eight-year-old son. When asked, he informs the CSIs that he doesn't wear contacts.

That night, Ivers and Warrick warm up to each other over a cocktail at the Aladdin. As she walks away, Warrick turns to notice their bartender handling coasters and surreptitiously pocketing some cash.

Tommy Sconzo shows Catherine and Grissom the temporary tooth he's had put in. When asked about his relationship with Gallagher, he asserts, "I treated Jane better than that mutt Rivers ever did." He denies having orchestrated the deadly attack but is pleased to hear of Gallagher's pregnancy, assuming that he's the father. Robbins tells Grissom that Rivers suffered from Wolff-Parkinson-White syndrome, an unusual coronary condition that impedes the heart's electrical system. Quinine is lethal to anyone with the syndrome.

We still don't know how or why he died. We know how he lived. Good start.

Warrick tells Nick that the coasters from the dressing room have tested positive for heroin. The bartender at the Aladdin is the likely dealer who conceals the heroin between two coasters and passes the drug to his customers. This explains the one-glass-two-coasters conundrum from the dressing room. Nick recalls that Lillie was using two coasters when they asked her about the scarf, but Warrick doesn't want to hear about it.

Grissom asks Gallagher about Rivers's condition, and she recalls a recent lovemaking session during which he had passed out. To keep it from Sconzo, she had Doctor Stockwell take Rivers to the emergency room. Catherine reports finding no quinine at Rivers's house. Whoever killed him had to be familiar with his medical condition. Grissom, Sara, and Brass confront Doctor Stockwell at his office with a prescription for quinine he had written the previous month. Grissom notices a framed picture of Stockwell and Jane Gallagher. The doctor finally admits giving Rivers the quinine pills after he'd stitched him up, but claims ignorance of his heart condition. Sara points out Stockwell learned of it the night he took Rivers to the ER. When Stockwell learned Gallagher was pregnant, he arranged for Rivers's death thinking she would turn to him. "You killed the wrong guy," Grissom says, pointing out that Sconzo is the father. Stockwell is arrested.

Nick asks the bartender for one of his contact lenses predicting it will match the one found near Greevey's body. He admits selling the deadly heroin, and Lockwood arrests him. Then Warrick tells Nick that he's going to meet Ivers, ignoring Nick's advice to steer clear. Warrick and Ivers chat on a balcony at the Aladdin, but their conversation is cut short when Warrick spots track marks on her arm. Knowing there's no future with a junkie, he apologizes, and leaves. Despondent, he sits down at a gaming table and is about to indulge in his own vice when Nick sits down next to him, providing some unspoken support.

All this anger over money and a little stick work?

The title, "Primum Non Nocere," writer Andrew Lipsitz says, "was meant to be a clue for those viewers who speak Latin. It references the Hippocratic Oath— 'First do no harm,' so it hints that the doctor is the killer." The story's genesis, Lipsitz says, came when "Carol Mendelsohn said, 'We wanna do something a little bit different.'" Being both a fan and a hockey player Lipsitz reasoned that nothing could be more different than a story set on ice—in Vegas. Besides, he adds, "I love Zambonis."

"There's a great rise in female hockey now," Lipsitz says. "That allowed us to put a woman into the episode, which made it much more interesting. Jane Gallagher helped the writers explore how all the energy from male testosterone goes into hockey, and how this female character impacts that world."

When Grissom and Sara sit in the stands at the rink, Grissom comments on hockey's brutality and winds up talking about beauty and Sara. William Petersen recalls, "Originally my line was some nonfunctional response, maybe about bugs or something. And right before we shot, I went over to Danny and I said, 'Listen, I've got an ad-lib here, and I'll let it go by like I didn't even say it.'" Mendelsohn remembers, "I actually heard those lines about beauty in the dailies and thought, did we just go too far? I was afraid we'd jumped ahead in the relationship, that it was too revealing. But it came out of who those characters are, who they had evolved into." Ann Donahue says of moments like that, "We call them *CSI* sex scenes, because that's as deep as we'll go. We want to see everything through the prism of work. We don't want to see the messiness of the weekend at home." Petersen adds, "There are two things happening: There's the truth of it, and there's 'Why did he say it?' We had to go down and process the ice, and we wanted that to carry over to the montage."

To visually match the sequence, Danny Cannon "locked down" a camera at one end of the rink, handed the scene over to Petersen and Fox, and then stepped away. He recalls his instructions to Billy, "I wanted them to be working together but always far apart. So if he was close to the camera, she had to be far away. If she was standing up, he had to be down." The Director of Photography Michael Barrett adds, "You are very aware of their proximity as they work the same crime scene. You feel the awkwardness. Should they shout across the ice to talk to each other? That scene ushered in a new way to cover a processing montage."

Of course, the pair immediately loosen up when they analyze the mound of ice deposited by the Zamboni. "The place where they're really confident is in evidence collection," Lipsitz says. "Once you step away from that they become much more awkward. It was a nice character beat."

A friendly chat between Lipsitz and Gary Dourdan inspired its "B" storyline in which Warrick plays piano. During the conversation Lipsitz learned of the actor's real life musical background. The next thing Dourdan knew, "Danny comes up to me with this idea that Warrick used to play in some bars, and while he's working on this case, he's tooling around on this piano." In fact, the tune he plays is an original Dourdan composition. "I didn't want to do it for just some pop element," Dourdan says. "It scared me a little bit, to tell the truth, because I didn't want to cheese it out. I thought, 'Is this a characteristic of Warrick's?' I was really confused as to whether I wanted to go there, so it took me a minute to fall into place with it."

Warrick and Lillie's relationship provided an opportunity to reintroduce Warrick's gambling habit. "It's a different level of addiction that tripped something in him that wasn't on the notes," Zuiker says. "Getting emotionally involved with this girl, then realizing she was a user *and* a liar flicks the gambling light on in him." Although Zuiker thinks the coda "worked beautifully" in the context of the episode, he's frustrated by its larger implication. "Nick sits down with his friend, and they play. It was all warm and fuzzy and Warrick, the compulsive gambler, has been miraculously cured. He never talks about it." Zuiker adds, "But don't worry. We'll get there sometime." ∎

ORIGINAL AIRDATE: 3/7/02
WRITTEN BY: Jerry Stahl
DIRECTED BY: Kenneth Fink

SPECIAL GUEST STAR

BRUCE MCGILL: Jimmy Tadero

STARRING

ERIC SZMANDA: Greg Sanders
ROBERT DAVID HALL: Dr. Al Robbins
MARSHALL BELL: Pete Hutchins Sr.
AARON PAUL: Pete Hutchins Jr.
NICHOLAS SADLER: Mark Kelso
SKIP O'BRIEN: Sgt. O'Riley
MARC VANN: Conrad Ecklie
RANDY THOMPSON: Major Irv Phillips
MARK DACASCOS: Ananda

Four Buddhist monks kneel in prayer in a candlelit temple. One glances up to find a rifle pointed at him. When Grissom, Sara, and Nick arrive at the temple, they find all the monks dead, shot execution style. Sara observes the temple's gold statues and well-decorated money tree by the altar. Grissom concludes that they're looking at a hit, not a robbery, and points to the *placa* scrawled on one of the walls. It's the tag of the Snakebacks, a local gang. In the temple's garden, Grissom's search turns up a rifle. Sergeant O'Riley is interviewing one of the surviving monks, Ananda, who says he was out making a bank deposit into the temple's school fund at the time of the murders.

Catherine is at a bar chatting with a soon-to-retire Detective Jimmy Tadero, her old friend and mentor. They discuss the deathbed confession of Mark Kelso, whom Tadero nabbed fifteen years earlier for the slaying of Stephanie Watson, Catherine's best friend and coworker. Kelso has admitted to murdering a man but maintains his innocence in Watson's stabbing. When Catherine wonders if Kelso might be telling the truth, Tadero reminds her to believe the evidence.

The temple's part-time cook, David Suddahara, remembers seeing gang graffiti on a wall a couple of months earlier and that Ananda discouraged him from reporting it to the police. In the temple, Sara finds a shell casing, a smudged partial print on one

of the Buddha statues, and a wad of chewing gum on another.

A test-firing of the rifle matches it to the casings found at the temple. Ananda's prints are on the weapon. The monk explains that he found the gun on his desk and went into the prayer room to ask about it. Seeing the carnage, he removed the rifle from the holy place and put it in the rock garden.

Aware that the Watson file will be destroyed once Kelso dies, Catherine has Greg retest the bloodstains from the murder weapon. It verifies the original results—the blood on the blade was Watson's; the blood on the handle Kelso's. A closer look by Trace reveals a faint third blood sample between the handle and the blade. The bloody glove that was supposedly at the scene is no longer in the evidence box. The log indicates it was deposited by Tadero—two days after the murder.

Sara reports that Ananda's fingerprints are on the rifle's stock, not its trigger. He held it but didn't fire it. Then the police reports the Snakebacks have been out of business for nearly a year. Grissom theorizes that the grafitti is not authentic.

Following September 11, the Air Force's satellites have been keeping constant surveillance on U.S. military bases and the surrounding areas. The temple is less than two miles from a base, Grissom asks to see satellite's photos from the time of the murders. He zeros in on a license plate reading "PROUDUS." Finding the truck bearing that plate parked outside a coffeeshop, Nick and Grissom talk to the drivers, Peter Hutchins Sr. and Jr. The elder gripes that his coffeeshop's business has dropped since the monks' arrival and he is not surprised to hear about the killings. Sara searches the truck and recovers a string of prayer beads.

Catherine and Tadero return to the alley where Watson was murdered. She mentions the glove that was not logged in for two days. Tadero says that he found it in the alley the day after Kelso's arrest. When she questions Tadero's ethics, he walks away.

Peter Hutchins Sr.'s alibi checks out, so the CSIs turn their attention to his son. Since the material smudged on the temple statue is paintball paint, they visit the Paint 'N' Shoot Battle Ground, where they find Pete Hutchins Jr. His footprints are a match

FELONIUS MONK

for ones that were lifted from the temple. Pete admits that he and some friends had been in the temple and one of his friends stole a statue. He went back later to return the statue and, as he was preparing to remove his boots to walk inside, Pete saw the bodies and ran. Grissom asks how he knew to remove his boots. Pete admits that he'd spent time there and his father leaves in disgust.

Warrick pages Catherine with news on the glove: An amylase test found Kelso's saliva *and* blood. Catherine reasons that saliva plus blood usually adds up to a mouth injury, not a cut. That could mean the glove was planted.

Tadero admits he "helped the evidence along" by stuffing the glove into Kelso's mouth after pummeling him, then pocketing it. Catherine asks him for a blood sample to compare with the third stain on the knife. The test results exclude him as a match, but Catherine turns Tadero in for evidentiary malfeasance because while he was framing Kelso, Watson's killer got away.

Bank records show that the monks had raised $13,000 for the school fund, but Ananda deposited only $12,000 on the day of the murders. After finding traces of curry in the cash box, Grissom asks about David Suddahara. When Ananda says that the cook has moved on, Grissom surmises that he'd been caught stealing. Ananda confirms his suspicion. Suddahara sits in Interrogation, chewing gum, as Grissom announces that his DNA was a match to the gum left behind in the temple. Thinking that Ananda would report him for taking the money, Suddahara decided to eliminate his accuser. He returned to the temple with his rifle, but Ananda wasn't there. Furious, he killed the other monks.

Grissom returns to the temple that night and sees Ananda and Pete Hutchins Jr. peacefully praying together. Meanwhile, Catherine writes "Do Not Destroy; Case Unsolved" on Stephanie Watson's evidence box.

The past is the past. True. But sometimes it leaves its fingerprints on the future.

How do you get one vic, let alone four, to sit still while you put a bullet between their eyes?

168

"I'm no stranger to Buddhism," says writer Jerry Stahl. "My sister lives in the foothills of the Himalayas and practices the philosophy." The story was inspired by an actual temple robbery, and the *CSI* location shoot was in an actual temple in North Hollywood, California. "The temple has a beautiful façade and a beautiful pitched roof," recalls director Ken Fink. "We were supposed to shoot inside too, but at the last second they said, 'We can't have a depiction of death in the temple.' So Richard Berg built the breezeway and circular prayer area on a soundstage."

A bigger challenge, says Fink, was weaving the episode's two plotlines into a coherent a whole. "When I read the script I thought, This will balance interestingly," he recollects. "But it was tough to contrast the energy of the Buddhists with that of the corrupt cop. When you cut between those two kinds of energies, it can be very jarring."

"Felonious Monk"'s "B" storyline is another solo story for Catherine. Marg Helgenberger says, "I was thinking about Catherine's past, and the path that took her from exotic dancing to the world of forensic science. So I pitched an idea of a detective who used to come to the club, and, over a beer or two, Catherine would ask him about the cases he was working on. Then I would tell him my thoughts about them." Eventually, the detective became a mentor for the brainy stripper. The producers knew they needed a powerful performer who could hold his own when Helgenberger squares off against his character. They chose well-known character actor Bruce McGill. "Good actors bring it out in each other. It's like a tennis game," Fink says, "I don't know anybody else who could express rage so believably. When you get actors like that you wish they had more scenes." Stahl confesses, "I've always been attracted to gorgeous, strong, high-IQ, street-smart women in real life. Catherine embodies all those things. So writing her character is always a kind of love letter to her gender." ∎

Why shoot four people, then leave the murder weapon behind the temple where even a blind man can find it?

I CROSS CRIME SCENE DO NOT CROSS DO NOT CROSS CRIME SCENE DO NOT CROSS DO NOT CRO

CHASING THE BUS

ORIGINAL AIRDATE: 3/28/02
WRITTEN BY: Eli Talbert
DIRECTED BY: Richard J. Lewis

GUEST STARRING

ERIC SZMANDA: Greg Sanders
ROBERT DAVID HALL: Dr. Al Robbins
DENIS ARNDT: Larry Maddox
JOSEPH D. REITMAN: Sean Nolan
CARA BUONO: Tracy Logan
SCOTT PLANK: Chris
EDDIE JEMISON: Vincent Doyle
KEVIN WILL: Martin Draper
ERIC MATHENY: Dr. Hawkins
LAUREN HODGES: Jill
KRIS IYER: Dr. Leever

The passengers chat animatedly, excited about going to Vegas while an inebriated man offers the bus driver a swig from his brown paper bag. He refuses, saying, "I know my limits." Then he's depressing the gas pedal until the bus is doing 80. Suddenly, the chassis starts to lurch, tossing everyone around, until the bus disastrously careens off the road.

The commercial passenger bus lies on its side, wrecked at the bottom of a hill off Interstate 15. Grissom and the entire CSI team wait their turn as gurneys with the injured are wheeled from the crash site. Grissom has Warrick call the entire staff, including police cadets, to help process the sprawling, horrific scene. Greg arrives to assist, although due to his lack of field experience, he's restricted to taking notes for Nick. Larry Maddox, owner of the Mohave Express bus line, gives Brass the passenger manifest. In addition to the driver, Martin Draper, there were twenty-three on board, one of them a parolee. Warrick and Sara join the others to search the stretch of highway leading up to the crash.

Catherine and Grissom find that the front right tire had blown. He tracks the dysfunction from the tire to a severed radius rod, which is designed to keep the axle secured to the chassis. The broken rod, Grissom deduces, caused the driver to pull the bus to the left, causing the right tire to blow, and send the bus off the road. Compounding the disaster, the bus landed atop a Camaro. The driver is extracted and rushed to the hospital.

Amazingly, Draper, the bus driver, is still alive but highly disoriented. Nick suspects he may have been drinking and administers a Breathalyzer test. Draper inhales deeply, spits up blood and then passes out. Nick yells at Greg to get help, but the tech just stands there frozen. Greg is apologetic for his inaction, but Nick reminds him that without field training, he is simply not qualified to work crime scenes.

Warrick snaps photos of skid marks along the highway's retaining wall. He notes an elongated impression in the road surface, speculating it was made by the bus's dangling radius rod. He also comes across a large sheared bolt which he takes back to the lab for a Rockwell Hardness Test. Doctor Robbins reports that there was no alcohol in Martin Draper's

They do their job. Then we do ours.

system and suggests that hunger may have been responsible for his wooziness. The overweight forty-year-old had type II diabetes, and crash-dieting may have led to a fatal hypoglycemic reaction which would have produced symptoms similar to drunken-

DESERT PALMS
HOSPITAL

Form K 747 Revised 5/94

IDENTIFICATION SUMMARY

MOJAVE EXPRESS BUS ACCIDENT
CASE # 022602-7684

CASE # 02-218A-41
"Chasing The Bus"

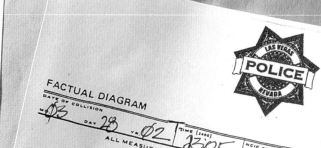

POLICE
LAS VEGAS NEVADA

FACTUAL DIAGRAM

DATE OF COLLISION
MO. 03 DAY 28 YR. 02 TIME (2400) 2305 NCIC NUMBER 073200653 OFFICER I.D. NV381528 NUMBER MOJA

ALL MEASUREMENTS ARE APPROXIMATE AND NOT TO SCALE UNLESS STATED (SCALE

Martin Draper
(Driver)

                A B   C D
Gwen Murray   1   ☒   Calvin McBride
                                        VACANT
John Smith   2   ☒   ← bottle fou

                ☒   3   Jane Brown

Jack   4   Ryan Hyde

                ☒ ☒   5   Mr. Parker
                                        Mrs. Parker
PJ   6   ◯

                ☒   7

Sabrina Wright

                ◯   8   Diane Cooper
Tracy Logan   Walt Cooper
                ◯   9   ☒

                        10   Michael Goodman

                ☒   11

Jill
Matthew   12   Lavatory

DRAWN BY
D. Smith
CHP 555—Page 4 (Rev 11-85) OPI-042

I.D. NUMBER 128   MO. 06 DAY 03 YR. 02   REVIEWER'S NAME GNGOTSOM   MO. DAY YR.

ulky Exhibit - Inventory ⬛⬛⬛ Evidence
D-192 (Rev. 7-18-85)

itle and Character of Case

MOJAVE EXP⬛

BUS SALES, INC.

DATE

01

UN

☐ EMPLOYEE M

A. INTERIC

1. State inspec
2. Entry doors
3. Temperatur
4. Neutral sa
5. Horn,

13.
14.
15.
16.
17.
18
19
2

TOUR BUS TRAGEDY
CLAIMS SEVEN LIVES

Jean, NV - A Mojave Express tour bus crashed on the northbound I-15 late last night killing seven passengers, critically injuring four and injuring at least fifteen others. The accident was called in by a passing trucker who spotted the twisted wreck of the tour bus lying on its side off the interstate, about forty miles outside of Las Vegas. When a rescue operation arrived on the scene, they found another vehicle had been totaled by the collision. The driver of that vehicle was unresponsive rushed to the hospital to undergo emergency surgical treatment. Fire Chief Walker was on the scene, creating a bucket brigade to take the victims from the mangled bus and to safety said "This is a horrible tragedy, and I know our guys are doing all they can to salvage as many lives as possible."

Lester Maddox, owner of Mojave Express, stated "Our safety record is excellent. Accidents are inevitable on any mode of transportation, but I have a family and sometimes they ride my buses. I won't take a chance with their lives or anybody else's. We screen all my drivers. Zero tolerance for drugs or alcohol. We keep strict maintenance records. Vehicles are inspected every forty-five days, as required by law. I'm as eager as anyone to figure out what happened."

Investigators on scene still trying to determine what caused the fatal crash.

Date
MAR 28 2002

84

0-218A-040

45 days or 3000 miles

"A" (CERTIFIED INSPECTION)

CUSTOMER NAME
MOJAVE EXPRESS INC.
MILEAGE 62,386

00711

DISCREPANCIES ON FOLLOW UP FORM.

	OK	REP. REQ'D.

PARTMENT

	OK	REP. REQ'D.

ss & leaks
arm
mounting
t springs, bushings and U-bolts
7. Engine leaks, lines, filters, hoses-mounts
8. Starter mounting and connections

PPS6

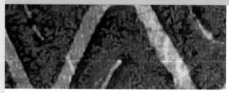

Reckless disregard for safety and human life. Mitigated by bad bolts. Mitigated by greed.

172

ness. Grissom concludes that it was a vehicle malfunction, not its operator, that caused the accident.

Larry Maddox claims that the bus was serviced the previous week and found to be in perfect working order. Grissom isn't convinced, Warrick has discovered that the sheared bolt matches those used in the bus's suspension system. It's marked as a Grade 8—the hardest, most durable rating—but the Rockwell test has identified it as a Grade 5. After finding another 5 among the salvaged parts, the CSIs conclude that the company was using bogus bolts that could have caused the suspension to fail. If the bolt snapped halfway through the skid, Grissom wonders why Draper hit the brakes in the first place. The body count rises as the Camaro's driver, Eric Kevlin, dies on the operating table.

Warrick and Grissom visit Larry Maddox at the bus garage. He staunchly defends the company's safety record, and is incredulous to learn that one of his bolts has sheared. He admits that he recently switched to a new, less expensive spare-parts supplier, and grounds the fleet for an immediate inspection.

Catherine and Nick return to the crash scene for another look at the Camaro. Nick finds a photo of Eric and a girlfriend he was apparently hoping to surprise in Vegas. Nick recognizes her as Tracy Logan, one of the survivors pulled from the bus. Logan relates that Kevlin surprised her at a Barstow truck stop, but it was an unwanted intrusion, as she was on an all girls' weekend. When he tried to convince her to come back to L.A. with him, she told him to leave her alone, and watched him drive off.

Sara, who's been busy analyzing what's left of the right front tire, receives a printout and concludes: "Sabotage." Grissom's discovered that the bus's blown right front tire was the accident's "first action." Sara reveals that the blown tire was no accident: It was injected with chloroform, which broke down the elasticity of the rubber. Grissom asks Warrick to have Maddox send over one of his buses for some "exercise."

Catherine and Grissom look at a passenger list, wondering if the sabotage was committed with a specific victim in mind. Grissom wonders about Tracy Logan, pointing out that, as a doctor, her boyfriend would have had access to chloroform.

Sara dusts the rim from bus's blown tire, while Grissom starts a tire test by placing a bus on a huge treadmill. Sara finds a print on the suspected rim: Sean Nolan, a former bus driver at Mohave Express. The tire being experimented on blows just as Sara enters the warehouse. The time frame points to Barstow as the sabotage site. Catherine reports that her scan of Kevlin's car and clothing revealed no traces of chloroform. At Mojave headquarters, Maddox tells Warrick that he fired Nolan two months earlier after finding marijuana in his locker.

Warrick calls to report that three Mojave buses have had blowouts since Nolan started working at the service station in Barstow. Nolan denies having handled chloroform recently, but is contradicted when Catherine gives him a once-over with the ion detector. He confesses to the sabotage. Being fired branded him a junkie and prevented him from getting another job driving. In retaliation, he decided to give Maddox and Mojave "some problems," but hadn't meant for anyone to die. Brass places him under arrest.

Exercise a bus.

"'Chasing the Bus' was probably the biggest episode we did that season," says director Richard Lewis. "The producers seem to like to give me the huge ones. I'm the guy who does the bus wrecks and the train wrecks." Carol Mendelsohn points out, "Richard always thinks 'epic.' He's not confined by the TV screen. He's always jumping up and down saying, 'Look at this shot!' There's no way you're going to be able to do it on television. But he manages to do it." Lewis gives credit to the skill of Director of Photography Michael Barrett. "We used miniatures for the crash, and were smart about simulating the interiors. Michael knew how to make it look huge." Specifically, Lewis points out, "We decided to do two things technically, that I think were smart moves: First, we put these work lights down there around the bus, and second, we decided to use a documentary technique. We had hand-held shots and juxtaposed them with static shots."

A huge first came for Eric Szmanda, as Greg made his first appearance at a crime scene in the episode. "There was some great stuff for me in 'Chasing the Bus,'" he recalls. "I represented the audience experiencing the gravity of the situation as a newbie." Of course, Greg completely choked in his stint as an auxiliary CSI. "Initially my overblown ego wasn't too happy with that."

For the record, says Elizabeth Devine, in real life it's highly unlikely that a team's DNA analyst would have any desire to get his hands quite that dirty. "They sort of play it like Greg's trying to be a CSI, and I've tried to talk them out of it. It makes it more interesting for the story, but in fact, the DNA expert has the most education, the most specific science background and training, and makes more money. They tend not to go out in the field at all." That's small consolation to Szmanda, who jokes, "I'd like to see sunlight sometime." ∎

ORIGINAL AIRDATE: 4/4/02
WRITTEN BY: Anthony E. Zuiker &
Danny Cannon
DIRECTED BY: Peter Markle

SPECIAL GUEST STAR

DOUG HUTCHISON: Nigel Crane

GUEST STARRING

ERIC SZMANDA: Greg Sanders
ROBERT DAVID HALL: Dr. Al Robbins
BRYAN KIRKWOOD: Adam Piorrio
ARCHIE KAO: Archie Johnson
SHELLEY ROBERTSON: Doctor
LELAND ORSER: Maurice Pearson

A young woman sits trembling on the floor by her phone as threatening messages come in on her answering machine. "Didn't I tell you not to bite your nails?" the last one rails, Jane *is* bitting her nails. Terrified, she runs down the hall and hides inside her bedroom closet. It's a fatal mistake; a pair of leather-gloved hands grab her from behind. Catherine and Grissom find Jane Galloway's body posed over her toilet as though she was vomiting, her hair wet with red dye. Their walk-through reveals no sign of forced entry or even a way for the killer to exit. The doors are triple-locked, windows nailed shut, shades are drawn, and a state-of-the-art alarm system's engaged. In the bathroom, Nick is strangely riveted by the sight of the posed corpse. Catherine locates an unusually thick hair on the bed. Underneath, they find a plastic grocery bag with a red smudge on it.

Nick returns to the lab, where he's irritated to find a copy of his "Crimestopper" profile from the department newsletter posted on the bulletin board. He rips it from the wall and gets back to business. He gives Warrick the hair and tells Sara to research the victim's phone records.

There are no signs of sexual assault, and Catherine wonders what kind of murderer poses his victim but doesn't rob or rape her. Greg tests the blond "hair" and discover it's fiberglass. He's then summoned by Nick, who's fuming the plastic bag from under Galloway's bed. Nick stresses to Greg that he didn't ask for the "Crimestopper" article, and he doesn't

want the attention. Greg asks him if his victim died of suffocation. Nick turns to see that the imprint of Jane's screaming face is on the plastic bag.

Galloway had a restraining order against her boyfriend, Adam Piorrio. Nevertheless, he called her thirteen times on the day of her murder. At his house, Brass and Sara find him passed out over the steering wheel of his car and covered with blood. In Interrogation Piorrio recalls that Jane suddenly started "acting weird" a few weeks earlier. She stopped returning his phone calls. As for the thirteen phone calls, Piorrio says he was heartbroken and on Ecstasy. Catherine reports that the blood on Piorrio belongs to a Ricco Manzo, with whom he fought the night before. With that alibi, Piorro's released.

Nick arrives home from work, passing a cable installer on the sidewalk. He finds an e-mail from his high school prom date, it has an old photo of her hunched over the toilet, exactly as Jane Galloway was. Nick concludes that someone must have accessed his e-mail somehow.

Brass tells Grissom about Maurice Pearson, a clairvoyant, who had a vision of Galloway's murder before it happened and knows details of the case that weren't reported. Sara learns that Galloway took a leave of absence from her job, and that she'd been prescribed sedatives. A day after returning from leave, she quit her job and checked into the Monaco Hotel for two nights. Brass discovers that Pearson was at the Monaco in the room adjoining Galloway's. She'd also stocked up on locks and alarms; got a phone screener; changed her phone number; and canceled all but one of her credit cards. Her phone records show an abundance of her incoming calls coming from *inside* her house.

The captain and Grissom accompany Pearson to the hotel, where he says he'd called to warn her of negative energy emanating from her room. Picking up on Grissom's extreme disbelief, he rattles off a few more visions about Galloway: "Three locks . . . Hanging ghosts . . . A-frames. Wooden beams . . . Church dark." At Galloway's home, Pearson says that in his vision he was looking down on everything. He professes a similar recollection of her closet, where Grissom finds a hatch in the ceiling that leads to the attic.

STALKER

Grissom ascends, and finds there are holes drilled through the ceiling of each room. He notes the fiberglass insulation, a telephone handset used by repairmen, and extensive digital recording equipment.

Sara, Catherine, and Grissom interview various utility personnel on Jane's block. Nick and Warrick visit the home of Nigel Crane, who installed Jane's cable TV. Once inside, Warrick gets a call on his cell and steps out for better reception. Nick spots some red droplets on the kitchen floor and finds a red-stained latex glove. Just then a pair of boots silently descends from behind him. Warrick's conversation is dramatically interrupted when he sees Nick come crashing out of the second-story window. Nick lies in a hospital bed with a concussion, cracked ribs, and a sprained wrist. Grissom orders Warrick to stay with him, as he and Catherine return to Crane's house. The house is empty except for a chair and a computer. Grissom investigates the attic—it contains an entire audiovisual studio.

Back at the lab, Grissom and Catherine begin screening Crane's tapes. One of them shows a busy Vegas street scene; shot in night-vision. In another, the camera idly records the interior of his hideout, and Catherine sees Nick's "Crimestopper" article on the wall with his photo circled.

Why would he do that? Why Nick?

Nick is resting at home when Pearson shows up saying he's had visions of his house. Nick gets a call from Grissom, who tells him that Crane has been in his house, and backup is on the way. Nick grabs his

He looks down on the world, separating himself from others. It's fascinating, really.

He tells Nick to consider her death a gift. Crane turns serious as he alleges that Nick has snubbed him by passing him by on the sidewalk a few mornings ago. He wants to make sure Nick remembers his name, and places the gun under his chin. Nick lunges to stop him as the the cops bust through the door.

gun and looks for Pearson, who left the room when the phone rang. The stillness is broken by the crashing sound of Pearson's dead body falling through the ceiling to the floor and Crane bounding down after him. The gun is knocked from Nick's hand and Crane scoops it up. He tells Nick that they met when he installed his cable and that they talked. "It's like I knew you my entire life," he says. Galloway, his previous obsession, "would have totally gotten between us."

The CSIs watch from the viewing room as an incoherent Crane is interrogated. Grissom speculates that Crane's obsession wasn't really about Nick or Jane but Maslow's Hierarchy of Needs, which offers that social beings crave belonging. For Crane, Grissom explains, Galloway was someone he could control, but Nick was someone he wanted to become.

176

"Stalker"'s predominant tone is meant to convey nerve-wracking claustrophobia. To that end, it contains few exterior shots. It focuses on Galloway's self-imposed imprisonment, Crane's video-surveillance lair, and Nick's beseiged apartment.** Says writer Anthony Zuiker, "We had Nick being stalked, and it's, like, 'C'mon—I'm not sure if that's the right way to go.' Our show is most interesting when it personally affects a character, but when they *fall victim* to it is when we cross the line and get ourselves in trouble." To help steer clear of cliché, Zuiker wanted the stalker's victim to be a male. George Eads volunteered. "Carol Mendelsohn told me, 'We're going to do an episode where this guy comes to you and say 'I'm being stalked,' but *he's* going to be the stalker," Eads remembers. "And I said, 'You know, why don't you have him stalking me?'" Somewhere between conception and execution, however, Eads soured on the idea. "How could a guy as smart as Nick not know that there's someone in his attic?"

Initially, Eads admits, his irritation seeped into his performance. "The first day on set, the first thing we shot, is me ripping that Crimestopper thing off the bulletin board really pissed off," he recalls, "and I really *was* pissed off." An on-set chat with Gary Dourdan and Jorja Fox, however, calmed him down. "They talked me out of it, and I decided to run with it." Casting Doug Hutchison as Nigel Crane, he recalls, was another encouraging sign. "Doug and I had done a pilot together a few years before, so when they got him, I knew we were going to be all right."

"That was a very turbulent time," Zuiker recollects. "I made the mistake of writing that Nick drinks Red Bull and plays Max Payne, and George pointed out that that's what *he* does. It was a little weird." In the end, however, the cast and crew felt they'd made a great episode. "People still talk about how scary it is," Zuiker says. ■

CATS IN THE CRADLE

ORIGINAL AIRDATE: 4/25/02
WRITTEN BY: Kris Dobkin
DIRECTED BY: Richard J. Lewis

GUEST STARRING

ERIC SZMANDA: Greg Sanders
ROBERT DAVID HALL: Dr. Al Robbins
ED LAUTER: Barclay Tobin
DIANE FARR: Marcie Tobin
TUC WATKINS: Marcus Remnick
MEGAN GALLAGHER: Janet Trent
STEVE HYTNER: Johnny Claddon
ELLEN GEER: Ruth Elliot
FRANK MILITARY: Tyler Elliot
SKIP O'BRIEN: Sgt. O'Riley
LARISSA LASKIN: Debbie Stein
COURTNEY JINES: Jessica Trent

You want to tell me why I swabbed their cat?

On a surburban street, a neighborhood cat walks up the driveway of a run-down house. Inside, there are even more cats, it seems they are everywhere, including on top of an old woman's corpse which they are feeding on. Grissom and Catherine learn the victim was Ruth Elliot. Assistant Coroner David Philips says she has been dead for three or four days. Grissom zeroes in on one deep stab wound among the chewed-out gashes, and announces, "I guess the cats are off the hook." Catherine manages to lift a shoeprint, perhaps from a high heel. In the bedroom closet, Warrick dusts an empty, unlocked wall safe, and pulls a few prints from the door.

Outside a body shop, Nick and Sara meet Brass. A brand-new luxury sedan, belonging to Marcie Tobin,

sits incinerated. The only eyewitnesses are Tobin and the mechanic, Marcus Remnick. Tobin says she was on her way to her father's office when the car started making strange noises. She brought it to Remnick's shop. He opened the hood and, seeing a bomb, grabbed her and ran only seconds before it detonated.

Doctor Robbins finds that the bite marks on Elliot were made post-mortem. The cause of death was cardiac trauma caused by a stab wound. He can't identify the weapon, but notes that the wound tract is slick with a foreign substance. The victim also had a severe staph infection. Grissom and Catherine visit one of Elliot's neighbors, Janet Trent. Her young daughters, Jackie and Jessica, recall seeing another neighbor, Mrs. Stein, enter Elliot's house. The girls heard the two women yelling, then saw Stein leave in anger.

Nick searches through the debris from the car, and finds an end cap from a pipe bomb. The cap has distinct marks from a vise grip on it. Johnny Claddon, Tobin's husband and the only other person

According to Mark Twain, the most striking difference between a cat and a lie is that a cat only has nine lives.

178 | with access to the car, is a junior foreman at her father's demolition company, C & D Incorporated. Claddon says that he knows how to make a bomb, as do all of his coworkers, but denies involvement in the bombing. His father-in-law, Clay Tobin, tells the CSIs that he believes Claddon is unfaithful and gave him a job only because he married his daughter. He offers to provide them with whatever they need. Greg identifies the explosive as nitroglycerin mixed with sawdust—dynamite. Sara finds a print on the end cap, a match to Claddon who says that as foreman, his prints are on everything. He recently logged out a case of dynamite for a job, and when the job fell through, one stick was missing. He mentions that Marcie has made enemies by shorting employees on their overtime hours but only at her father's insistence.

Catherine and Warrick speak with Stein, who says Elliot's odorous house made it a blight on the block. She visited the woman six days earlier, trying to persuade her to find homes for the cats since she's legally allowed to own only three. Elliot angrily vowed not to allow anyone to take her "children" away. Stein says she was in L.A. on the day of Elliot's death. A print taken from Elliot's wall safe matches her son, Tyler. When interrogated, he says his mother had forgotten the safe's combination and called for his help when a cat got locked inside. He says she had no money to steal, she even willed the house to a cat sanctuary.

Sara visits with Claddon and Marcie Tobin and asks about Claddon's alleged infidelity. He becomes enraged, Marcie downplays her father's accusations. When neither C & D's vise grips nor one from the Tobin-Claddon home are a match to the marks on the end cap, Sara and Nick decide to look at the car again. The bomb was on a timer, therefore it would detonate shortly after being triggered, but by what? The hood latch has been blown apart. Remnick lied when he said the hood was open, it was closed.

Greg finds that the substance in Ruth Elliot's wound is mineral oil that is sometimes used to treat knives. The CSIs return to Elliot's house and find no potential weapons but come across a new lead when they follow a lone cat exiting the house and crossing the street to the Trent house, where the girls are playing outside. Grissom notices a wound on the cat. They

reluctantly allow Catherine to take a swab. Grissom tells Catherine that the cat's wound, may indicate a staph infection, gotten from Elliot since it is communicable from species to species.

Sara and Nick ask Remnick why his prints were not found on the car's hood. He says he was wearing gloves, and allows them to take a look around. They find a vise grip and take on impression. It matches the one on the end cap, but Remnick's prints don't match those on the tool. Sara has better luck in the C & D employee database, the prints are Marcie Tobin's.

Marcie owns 25 percent of C & D, but would lose half of that if she got divorced. However, if Claddon were to be convicted for the blast, he would be out of the picture, monetarily and otherwise. Using the dynamite Marcie stole from the case in Claddon's SUV, and an end cap from C & D's inventory, she and Remnick built the bomb in his garage. A $50,000 payment to Remnick from her and her father's credit cards, ostensibly to repair a car, is uncovered, obviously payment for his help in framing Claddon.

The cat tests positive for staph, but Janet Trent and her children are healthy. The cat may have originally belonged to Elliot, but somehow the Trents adopted it. Using the ALS in the girl's bedroom. Catherine detects the presence of blood on a "floaty" pen that contains mineral oil in its shaft. Jessica and Jackie sit in interrogation with Catherine, while Janet watches from the viewing room with Grissom. They first blame the murder on their mother. When Catherine explains that the fingerprints on the pen belong to a child, Jessica admits that when Elliot refused to give them the cat, Jessica handed the cat to Jackie and told her to run. When Elliot threatened to tell their mother, Jessica stabbed her with the pen from her knapsack. Grissom asks Janet if she knew what had happened. She says that she'd promised the girls they could have a cat only if Elliot gave them one, knowing that she never would.

"**C**ats in the Cradle"'s teaser features no live humans. It's also told through the eyes of a feline. A shot accomplished, says director Richard Lewis, by mounting a camera on the front of a golf cart. Depicting Ruth Elliot's demise was not easy for actress Ellen Geer. "She was such a trooper. Incredible," says Lewis. "She just said, 'Okay, put the cat food on me, I'll lay down and have the cats lick me.'" Conversely, Lewis recalls that working with the team of cats was difficult. Unlike actors, he says, "You get one take, and that's it."

When Grissom and Catherine go for a consultation with Greg they find the DNA analyst rocking out to Marilyn Manson's "Fight Song" while wearing a mask. "The producers gave me the choice of what I wanted, and I picked 'Fight Song' because the lyrics are very fitting to the show and also, Manson's a friend of mine," Eric Szmanda recalls. "Then I asked Danny how far I could go with it, because by this point I don't even know anymore." Cannon was glad to assist. "He actually came to the set and helped me make the mask I wore," Szmanda laughs. "That was another vibe that I sort of brought—letting Greg ham it up and try to invent scenes," Lewis says. "Greg can get away with all this stuff." There's a reason for that, says Carol Mendelsohn. "It's really not humor for humor's sake; it comes out of character. There's a roteness to what he does at work, but there's more to the guy. His humor is a way to work off that energy."

Outside the Trent house Grissom remarks, regarding the impertinent girls, "One thing about my mother: Even though she was deaf, she was always the boss." William Petersen observes, "I like the idea of it being an unusual way into knowing Grissom. We dole it out in little bits and pieces so that we go, 'What was the deal with him and his mother and that growing-up thing?'" Grissom, having had a deaf mother, Petersen speculates "is also why he's so well-read." Petersen points out a striking omission, "He doesn't mention his father. I think if we ever talk about him, he's probably going to turn out to be somebody who didn't influence Grissom's life in a positive way." Anthony Zuiker says of the family dynamic that produced Gil Grissom, "It also makes sense as to why he was a self-educated loner who didn't fit in. He wasn't on the football team. He didn't date. He was the kid who got calls from a police precinct saying, 'Come pick up this dead possum, this dead dog, this dead cat.' He would bring it to his basement and dissect it." ∎

ORIGINAL AIRDATE: 5/2/02
WRITTEN BY: Josh Berman & Andrew Lipsitz
DIRECTED BY: Kenneth Fink

A young boy playing in the park falls, and stumbles to the ground. He gets up crying, "Mom! Mom! The dirt burned my hands!" A Hazmat team discovers a corpse beneath the corrosive soil. The victim's clothing has dissolved into shreds, his skin all but burned off. The killer covered his prey with lye. Sara and Grissom find the remains of the man's wallet, which identifies him as a Bob Martin. They're intrigued by a small metallic flake near the victim's body. Doctor Robbins estimates he died twenty-four hours earlier. Fractures on both of Martin's legs indicate contact with a car. There were several other injuries, but the absence of arterial lacerations and vessel damage suggest Martin survived the original impact and slowly bled to death over approximately forty-eight hours.

In the middle of a field located in the wilds of Diablo Canyon, Nick examines the body of Stacy Warner. There are no tire treads or footprints near the body, how did it get here? Nick retrieves a down feather from her mouth, and a maggot from her ear.

Brass and Sara meet with Martin's roommate, Reed Collins. He took Martin in six months ago — after the man's wife kicked him out. Collins last saw him the previous Monday when they drove in to work together. He wasn't worried by his absence since on Mondays Martin took a bus home

Sometimes I'm glad I only deal with dead people.

Ashes to ashes, dust to dust—without the wait.

from the university and sometimes his wife would take him back. Grissom stands outside the university's photography building, where Martin was logged into a darkroom from 10:00 to 11:00 P.M. on Monday. In the middle of the street, Grissom and Sara notice the same silvery flecks they found by Martin's body, and a piece of a plastic headlight cover.

The insignia from the shard identifies it as coming from a luxury sedan. Greg has narrowed the search, the composition of the metallic flecks were used only on rare '99 models, only five of which were sold in Nevada. One of the cars belongs to Ben Weston. Grissom and Sara speak with Weston in his office at a prestigious law firm. Weston says the car was stolen on Monday night and he reported the theft. He agrees to hand over the clothes he wore on the day his

car disappeared. He just picked up them from the dry cleaner. Sara suggests that the burn holes in shirt were caused by lye and asks Weston to remove the shirt he's presently wearing. For that, the lawyer says, they'll need a warrant.

Nick is stunned when the assistant coroner, David Phillips, tells him that Stacy Warner has drowned in the middle of the desert. Nick and Detective Lockwood question Warner's fiancé, Matt Hudson. He says he didn't file a missing person report because he knew that she was on a solo hike, and he was at a triathlon in Montana all week.

Brass, Grissom, and Sara find Weston's car at Sullivan's Junkyard, where Mitchell Sullivan says an anonymous caller offered him a great deal on it. He didn't ask any questions. When he tells them it's already been dismantled, Grissom says that they'll

ANATOMY OF A LYE

GUEST STARRING

ERIC SZMANDA: Greg Sanders
ROBERT DAVID HALL: Dr. Al Robbins
GABRIEL OLDS: Ben Weston
ANTHONY STARKE: Matt Hudson
ZACHARY QUINTO: Mitchell Sullivan
ERIC STONESTREET: Ronnie Litra
ADAM NELSON: Derick Moore
PAUL SCHACKMAN: Bob Martin
JEFFREY D. SAMS: Det. Lockwood

need every part. Luminol applied to the parts reveals that the seat and dashboard are covered with blood.

Nick has taken water from Hudson's pool and tap, Lake Mead, and Clark County reservoir, but none of them match the water found in Warner's stomach. Warrick identifies some small rocks found under Warner's body as basalt, which is found at altitudes upward of 4,000 feet. Warner was found at 1,500 feet.

As expected, the blood from inside Weston's car is Martin's. Grissom also finds spatter on the underside of the passenger seat, which must have splashed up from a puddle on the floor. The ignition lock hasn't been punched causing Grissom to conjecture that there wasn't a theft. Weston claims that he left keys in the ignition while he ran into a take-out restaurant, and that he didn't tell the police to avoid being accused of negligence by his insurance company. Confronted with a warrant, Weston removes his shirt, which reveals a seat belt bruise on his chest. Weston explains it by saying he hit something, then got out of the car but saw nothing. Brass places him under arrest.

While retracing Warner's steps up the mountain canyon, Nick and Lockwood find a man's down jacket with down protruding from a tear and a map to Diablo Canyon with Matt Hudson's name on it is in one of its pockets. In interrogation, Hudson says he gave Warner his jacket. When he seems overly concerned about getting his trail map back, Nick decides to examine it more closely.

Brass, Grissom, and Sara show up at Weston's house with a warrant and find a large bleach stain on his garage floor.

Robbins notes that Martin's "dicing" glass wounds are indicative of a head-on impact. Sara suggests that Martin would have been hurled through the passenger-side windshield, his blood dripping onto the dash and interior. Although he bled out for two days, Grissom points out that Martin could have remained conscious until he'd lost one third of his circulating blood volume, and hypothesizes that Martin could have spent that time in Weston's garage. When Sullivan again insists he doesn't know who he got the car from, Brass notes that he attended the same high school as Ben Weston. When they threaten to charge him as an accomplice after the fact, Sullivan admits that Weston offered him the lucrative salvage job.

Grissom tells Nick that the maggot from Warner's ear belongs to a family of Sarcophagids, its growth stunted by exposure to below-freezing temperatures. Greg points out that Nevada is a basin-and-rain state: Near-zero rainfall in the desert, but forty inches a year in the mountains. The Vegas weather the previous week was warm with steady pressure, it rained in Diablo. The result was a flash flood. Warner drowned while clinging on to the canyon's side, then got swept downhill to low ground, which later dried rapidly in the desert heat. Nick confronts Hudson with his report: Hudson tampered with the map to put Warner off course. Hudson insists he just wanted to make her hike more challenging so that she wouldn't beat his time. Nick concludes, "What you did isn't a crime . . . but it *is* criminal."

Sara plays Weston a tape of a 911 call made from his cell phone by Bob Martin. Laying wedged in the windshield of Weston's car inside the garage, Martin struggled and reached the cell phone. Unfortunately, he passed out before he could provide the necessary details. Grissom alleges that Weston was drunk and decided to sober up before calling in the accident. But he hadn't counted on Martin coming to, and reporting it would have exposed his heartless neglect. They explain to Weston that he might have faced a homicide charge, but Martin had written a suicide letter to his wife. Sara explains, "You were off the hook." Then Grisson adds, "Until you let him die."

Las Vegas Police Department Forensic Lab...

STR RESULTS- PROFILER PLUS/COFILER

DATE: 4/28/02

ANALYST: G. SANDERS, DNA TECH

PCR AMP #: 198456722

EVENT #: 2877623987-899

DNA STR TYPING RESULTS

SAMPLE # 1	D3S1358	vWA	FGA	AMELO	D3S1179	D21S11	D18S51	REMARKS
SAMPLE INFO								
BLOOD NEAR POOL	15,16	18,20	21,24	X,X	11,11	31,33	12,12	
	D5S818	D13S317	D7S820	D16S539	THO1	TPOX		

EVIDENCE EVIDENCE EVIDENCE EVIDENCE

CVLA95-57...

CASE # 02-221B-44
'Anatomy Of A Lye'

LAS VEGAS
LAB REPOR...

File : C: ...
Operator

POLICE

1"=4,000'

2-18-95

Las...
POLICE

Cathedral
Rock

7500

7200

CANYON

GOLDEN

2.0mi
3.2km

1.8mi
2.9km

Peak

Peak Trail

8564ft
2610m

Peak

7850

3.4mi
5.5km

7200

River

HOLE

7200

Las Vegas Police Department Forensic Laboratory
POLICE

FILED

SUPERIOR COURT
CLARK COUNTY NEVADA

STATE OF NEVADA }
COUNTY OF CLARK } ss.

MARRIAGE LICENSE

No. C 02

THIS LICENSE WILL AUTHORIZE ANY LICENSED OR ORDAINED MINISTER OF ANY RELIGIOUS SOCIETY OR CONGREGATION WITHIN THIS STATE, OR ANY JUDGE OF THE DISTRICT COURT, OR ANY JUSTICE OF THE PEACE IN THEIR TOWNSHIP WHEREIN THEY ARE PERMITTED TO SOLEMNIZE MARRIAGES, OR ANY COMMISSIONER OF CIVIL MARRIAGES, OR ANY JUSTICE OF THE SU

EXPIRES 1 YEAR AFTER ISSUANCE

GROOM - NAME

WARNER, STACY
CASE#013776-2978

	DR 08534-94
... DEPARTMENT	TYPE (Mur-Stat, Rape-Batt., etc.)
...OMPLAINT OR	1. MATT HUDSON	DOM. DIST.
...PORT	2. STACY WARNER	REPORTING DIST. 38
	LOCATION OF OCCURRENCE
...cal, type, etc.)	12688 OWENSMOUTH AVE, LV, NV
	DATE AND TIME OCCURRED	DATE AND TIME REPORTED TO P.D.
...TURBANCE	23 APRIL 02 19:04	APRIL 23, 02
...E 1-FEMALE	TYPE OF PREMISES
...or conversation)	RESIDENTAL
	INVESTIGATIVE DIVISION(S) OR UNIT(S) NOTIFIED AND PERSON(S) CONTACTED	VICTIM'S COND. (HBD, NORMAL, ETC.)
...make-body-col.-lic. no. & I.D.)	LIST ANY CONNECTING RPT(S). BY TYPE AND DR NO.	NORMAL

...REPORTING CRIME W-WITNESS	CODE	RESIDENCE ADDRESS (Bus. add. if firm)	CITY	RES. PHONE	X BUS. PHONE X
				(702)555-0159	(702)555-0187
...CENT - DATE OF BIRTH	V	12688 OWENSMOUTH AVE		(702)555-0159	(702)555-0185
...UDSON	V	12688 OWENSMOUTH AVE		(702)555-0166	(702)555-0173
...WARNER	R	12683 OWENSMOUTH AVE			

...NO. (Name-address-sex-descent-age-bt.-wt-hair-eyes-complexion-clothing-identifying characteristics. If arrested, include bkg. no. & charge.)

...HUDSON 1268 OWENSMOUTH AVE L.V. BRN HAIR, BLUE EYES

...WARNER 1268 OWENSMOUTH AVE L.V. BLUE EYES

...SUSPECT(S). (2) RECONSTRUCT THE CRIME. (3) DESCRIBE PHYSICAL EVIDENCE, LOCATION FOUND, AND GIVE DISPOSITION. (4) SUMMARIZE OTHER
...CRIME. (5) TIME AND LOCATION WHERE VICTIM/WITNESSES CAN BE CONTACTED BY DAY INVESTIGATORS IF NO AVAILABLE PHONE NUMBERS.

...RESPONSE TO DOMESTIC DISTURBANCE CALL AT 19:04
...ANSWERED BY SUSPECT 1. AFTER REPEATED KNOCKS
...NT DOOR OF DWELLING. SUSPECT APPEARED AGITATED
...NG OUT. WHEN ASKED HE SAID HE HAD BEEN
...TED DISCUSSION OR ARGUMENT WITHIN HIS
...HE STATED HE KNEW NOTHING OF
...GIRLFRIEND WHILE WORKING OUT. HE HAD SPOKEN LOUD
...NOT CLASSIFY THIS AS AN ARGUMENT
...R HE DID NOT STRIKE OR PHYSICALLY
...ECT 2. SUSPECT 2 CLAIMS S
...NOT KNOW OF ANY REASON F
...MESTIC DISTURBANCE CALL, SHE CL
...S RESPONDED LOUDLY TO HER B
...SPECT 1. WHEN SHE RAISED

...ME CLEARED BY ARREST ☐ YES ☒ NO	If additional space is required, use SER. NO. - DIV. - DETL.	INTERVIEWING OFFICER(S) - SER. NO.
...VISOR APPROVING		C. DERMOTT R9191
	R9187	F. COMPTON R9357
...3 APRIL, 02	...E & TIME REPRODUCED - DIVISION - CLERK	MISCELLANEOUS COMPLAINT OR CRIM...
...3.10 (Rev. Dec. 1967)		

IMPORTANT MESSAGE

FOR NICK STOKES
DATE 04.29.02 TIME 632 A.M./P.M.
M RONNIE LITRA
OF QD
PHONE/MOBILE X 3246

TELEPHONED	X	PLEASE CALL	
CAME TO SEE YOU		WILL CALL AGAIN	
WANTS TO SEE YOU		RUSH	
RETURNED YOUR CALL		SPECIAL ATTENTION	

MESSAGE

HAS FOUND AN
INCONSISTENCY ON
THE DIABLO TRAIL
MAP - STACY
WARNER CASE

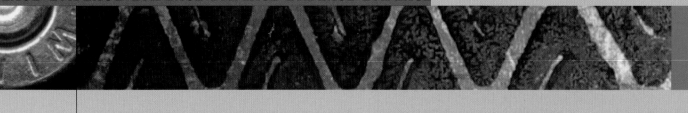

184

A nurse's aide hit a homeless man with her car. The impact wedged the man's upper torso through the passenger side of the windshield, where he remained—alive, immobilized, and pleading for help to no avail. The woman parked the car in her garage where the man died after several days of suffering. "We were just so moved by the event and we had to do it as an episode," says writer Josh Berman. The nurse's lawyer claimed that rather than murder, she should have been charged only with reckless disregard for human life. Berman recalls, "We made sure our case was about a murder. It was man's inhumanity to man, sunk to a new low."

In re-creating the stranger-than-fiction tale of cruelty, Berman says, "It's one thing to hear about it; it's another thing to see it like we showed it. It was pretty graphic." Nowhere more so than in the flashback re-creating the point of impact between Weston's car and Martin's knees. "Yeah, that was a good one," says director Ken Fink, speaking strictly cinematically, of course. "We used a very, very long lens and the compression I thought worked perfectly. I sort of duck when I watch it." The scene in which suicide-turned-homicide victim Bob Martin is shown struggling to make a 911 call is difficult to watch, but it was downright torturous for guest star Paul Schackman. "We put something under his body," Fink says. "Unfortunately, when your head is on that down angle for so long, that can be really painful. So we got him out periodically and he would walk around with the glass sticking out of his head and blood all over the place and have his lunch with everybody else."

The "B" storyline of Stacy Warner's demise is aided by man but carried out by the cold, indifferent earth. "By that point we were late in the second season and trying to really branch out," writer Andrew Lipsitz says. The Warner plotline brought meteorology into the show's forensic domain. "We wanted to explore how weather can tell a story, and to explain the difference between Las Vegas and the rest of Nevada. The city

sits down in a basin but there are mountains all around it. In this case the evidence was the weather itself."

In order to portray Warner's death director Ken Fink recalls, "We built a huge water tank above that a rock ledge. Although we had a stunt person there to do the fall, that water was really hitting her, so the images were pretty powerful."

This show represents a landmark for Nick. A year after he'd griped to Grissom about never being allowed to work a dead body solo, he finally did in the Warner case. This is the second appearance of Jeffrey D. Sams as Detective Lockwood, allowing him to join Geoffrey Rivas's Sam Vega in an elite *CSI* club: The recurring detectives. "The show is about the CSIs, not cops," Berman says. "In reality, our CSIs would be working with many different cops on different cases." ■

> Aristotle said, "The whole is more than the sum of its parts," but then again, he'd never been to a chop shop.

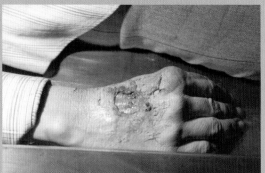

CROSS-JURISDICTIONS

ORIGINAL AIRDATE: 5/9/02
WRITTEN BY: Anthony E. Zuiker,
Ann Donahue, Carol Mendelsohn
DIRECTED BY: Danny Cannon

SPECIAL GUEST STARS

DAVID CARUSO: Horatio Caine
EMILY PROCTER: Calleigh Duquesne
ADAM RODRIGUEZ: Eric Delko
KHANDI ALEXANDER: Alexx Woods
RORY COCHRANE: Tim Speedle

GUEST STARRING

ERIC SZMANDA: Greg Sanders
ROBERT DAVID HALL: Dr. Al Robbins
DAVID ALAN BASCHE: Adam van der Welk
JEFFREY D. SAMS: Det. Lockwood
KARI WUHRER: Tiffany Langer
JOHN KAPELOS: Chief Rittle
JENNA BOYD: Sasha Rittle
DARLENE VOGEL: Mina Rittle

185

A Seven Hills mansion is alive with the sights and sounds of a glitzy bash. A little girl peeks out of her room to see three people ducking into a room across the hall. She returns to bed, only to be awakened by the sound of gunshots. Terrified, she calls out "Daddy," but is visited instead by a shadowy stranger. It's two days later, the housekeeper arrives for work and summons the police. The investigators find the host dead, hands cuffed behind his back, an apple crammed in his mouth. It's the former Chief of Detectives Rittle, who left the department to become a very successful security consultant. There's no sign of the chief's wife, Mina, his daughter, Sasha, nor his car.

Catherine finds a lone 9mm casing, standard issue for the LVPD, and a search discovers that the chief's 9mm handgun is missing. She wonders if Mrs. Rittle might be in on the slaying, but Grissom is skeptical. Detective Lockwood says the security guard saw Rittle, wearing sunglasses and a baseball cap, leaving in his car with his wife and child, sitting in the back. However, he never actually saw the chief's face clearly. Brass calls to say the car's been located in a parking garage.

A body and Rittle's baseball cap are in the trunk. Brass gets a report from the Florida Highway Patrol. A girl, matching Sasha's description, has been spotted wandering along an access road. Grissom dispatches Catherine and Warrick to the scene.

The FHP search for Sasha Rittle on a remote Miami access road. CSI Horatio Caine discovers the scared little girl sitting among the palm fronds. Catherine and Warrick arrive, asserting their right to process the girl. Caine genially agrees. Catherine talks with Sasha and finds a bullet casing clenched in the girl's fist. She says that her mother urged her to run away during a roadside stop. The abductor fired several shots at her. Ballistics Expert Calleigh

He was coming home to Miami.

186

Duquesne points out that the shell is probably from a Baretta knockoff called a Taurus 9 manufactured in Brazil and popular in Florida. Caine deducts the killer is local.

Sara and Nick get a hit on a print found on a glass from the party. It belongs to an Orpheus showgirl named Tiffany Langer. She reveals that her date was not a regular, and she knew him for only five days. Langer says his name was Adam van der Welk, when pressed for more description she says that he wore a sickly sweet cologne.

On the access road, Warrick finds a diazepam tablet. Duquesne suggests that Mina may have been sedated. Caine wonders why the abductor stopped the car, putting it together he finds footprints into the brush, and traces of urine.

Grissom gives Catherine a heads-up about van der Welk's strange fragrance. She, along with the Miami CSIs, are waiting to meet with federal agents. The Feds believe the Rittle case fits into a case of theirs involving a serial killer who targets wealthy couples at play.

The CSIs join their colleague Eric Delko at a canal where tire tracks lead into the water. Delko dives in and locates the car and Mina's body. Medical Examiner Alexx Woods observes that Mina's genital area has been wrapped in plastic and all of her body orifices are filled with honey. Delko retrieves the water-logged Taurus 9. Caine and Catherine visit a night-club named Hives. Inside, a woman clad in a cello-phane bikini lies on the bar as bartenders pour honey over her. Caine takes a sample.

In Vegas, Robbins and Grissom pore over medical books looking for conditions that produce odd body odors. Finally, Robbins suggests diabetic ketoacidosis, in which the body converts its excess glucose to ketone, which is excreted through the pores.

Speedle identifies the swab of honey as rare Tupelo honey and match it to the honey found on Mina Rittle. The CSIs sort through the club's receipts for a recent purchase of the $500-a-bottle delicacy. Duquesne finds one from two nights earlier and the doorman remember a big-tipping limo driver named Gordon. Apparently, he was working for some high-rollers in from Vegas. Gordon Daimler is stopped on his way to the airport. He

Grissom rarely says anything, until he's good and ready.

says his client paid cash for the ride, so he never got a name and that now he's picking up a couple named Corwin. Inside the limo, a sickly sweet smell wafts out when Caine switches on the air conditioning.

Grissom tells Catherine they're looking for a diabetic who uses Novalin insulin. She and Caine examine blood that was in the urine sample. The test shows traces of synthetic insulin. A pharmacy data-base reveals that the limo driver, Daimler, purchased Novalin. Caine deduces that he must have taken it before they stopped him, explaining why he didn't smell at the time.

They rush to the Coconut Grove residence of Dylan and Sissy Corwin, the couple that Daimler was en route to pick up when they spoke to him. Warrick spots a blood trail leading to the garage. Catherine finds shreds of plastic wrap on the bed. Duquesne finds a 9mm slug in the garage wall, and a piece of scalp. Caine finds honey on the shower wall. Speedle points out that the Corwins' yacht is missing from their dock. They alert the Coast Guard.

The CSIs find the Corwins' boat in a marina. Special Agent Sackheim explains that the Coast Guard has been unable to establish radio contact. Speedle trains an infrared heat-sensor on the vessel and pick up two life signs—one pink and one red. The FBI agent orders the sniper to take out the "red" suspect. However, Duquesne says the figure's body language doesn't seem to be threatening the other. Caine remembers a photo from the Corwins' house, featuring their personal jet. He concludes that Daimler's probably air-bound and simply left the couple on the boat to die. He gets the FBI agents to abort the operation. Caine has Speedle instruct the FAA to ground the Corwins' plane, then boards the yacht with Catherine. They find a devastated Corwin below with his dying wife.

At the airport they find Daimler—aka van der Welk—on board the jet, sipping champagne in preparation for a flight to Monaco. Daimler shrugs, saying, "Rich men don't go to jail," but Caine reminds the deluded killer that he's not rich. As they escort him off the plane in cuffs, Catherine promises, "I'll have my DA call your DA."

Little girl saw a monster. Showgirl saw a husband.

"**W**e had a great deal of concern," recollects Jonathan Littman. "We worried the *CSI* actors might feel we were turning our backs on them and moving to the next thing; *CSI: Miami*."

Director Danny Cannon recalls, "Anthony had a great way of putting it. He said, 'That show shouldn't be called 'Cross Jurisdictions,' it should be called 'Miracle.'" The first challenge, Cannon remembers, was trying to find actors of the appropriate stature and chemistry to inhabit this new world. "Casting people that you hope are going to stay on for an entire season is an unbelievable pressure," Cannon says. "Anthony Zuiker, Carol Mendelsohn, and Ann Donahue were writing while I was in Miami scouting locations. While I was casting they were still writing. While I was *shooting,* they were still writing."

By the time he returned to Vegas, Cannon says the story's essential premise was in place. "If you've got a killer and he skips town, do you just give him up to another jurisdiction?" Not if you're Catherine Willows. "What I liked about that was, she gets on a plane, she gets on a chopper, and she goes after her man."

"Everybody was really cool," Marg Helgenberger recalls. "Nonetheless, it was hard—physically, psychologically, emotionally. The writers had to keep in mind, 'Who are these new characters,' and 'How can we show off Miami?' And they kinda of rolled the plot around those two issues." She and Gary Dourdan, the two actors sent to the distant location, worried that it would seem they were just down there to go "Yeah?" and "Uh-huh." As Zuiker recollects, "It was touchy. I thought that maybe none of our actors would want to go." But, he says, after some "microsurgery" on the script, "It was a pretty good deal."

Donahue recalls, "We opened the sliding glass doors out onto this gorgeous Floridian Atlantic and screamed, 'I love this job!'" At the end of the day, she says, "It was one of the hardest times in my life, but one of the best."

Zuiker sums up the drama surrounding the episode with an anecdote, "We had a big discussion about the ending. We thought that the ending may be Caine sitting with the girl. But could we really button on that character in a *CSI* episode?' Finally Danny reeled off what he thought the final scene should be, and I took a stab at it. And that was the ending—Catherine comes back and sees Grissom, 'Nice tan.' 'Nice suit.' 'I'm going to the funeral.' 'I missed you.' and she walks out. And we're back at CSI and all is well." ■

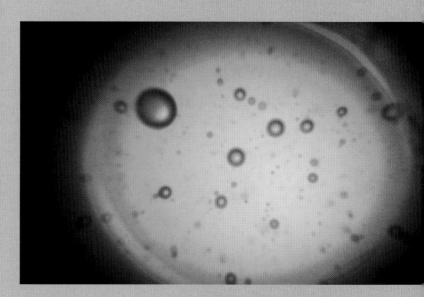

THE HUNGER

Inside a sumptuous bathroom, a young woman prepares for her bath. She clamps her hair back and unrolls an array of grooming items. The bath water rises over the rim, and washes over the floor.

Grissom receives a call in a doctor's waiting area, he informs the receptionist that he'll have to reschedule. Under a freeway overpass they find a lifeless woman, wrapped in a blanket and placed inside a shopping cart. When he and Brass lean in for a closer look, a rat squeezes out from between her teeth. Grissom finds hypodermic syringes inside the victim's handbag. Her tox screen comes up negative except for botulin. The small puncture wounds in her forehead suggest repeated use of Botox. She also has myriad facial scars, old and new, and gouged-out craters in her cheeks caused by an unknown weapon.

The CSIs discover what seems to be the remnants of her life in the shopping cart. Sara works to decipher the arcane notations in the pages of the victim's calendar. Warrick wonders why a homeless woman would even have a three-hundred-dollar handbag and a day planner. Catherine works with Tech Dusty Green on

I'm not sure of anything.

a facial reconstruction. When they finish, Dusty is convinced she's looking at a familiar face. Greg confirms it's the cover girl, Ashleigh James.

At James's loft, glamorous portraits of her adorn every wall. Grissom finds a minty-smelling white powder on a table, while Catherine discovers a man's toiletries bag. They proceed to the bathroom, where

there's blood on the sink, boxes of enemas, and plastic Baggies filled with excrement. The fridge contains only spring water and a carton of Botox bottles. In the closet, Catherine finds a dirty woolen coat that is out of place in a model's designer wardrobe. Outside, Warrick and Nick examine the interior of James's car. It is awash in candy and fast-food wrappers, and

ARTIST

ORIGINAL AIRDATE: 5/16/02
WRITTEN BY: Jerry Stahl
DIRECTED BY: Richard J. Lewis

GUEST STARRING

189

ERIC SZMANDA: Greg Sanders
ROBERT DAVID HALL: Dr. Al Robbins
SUSAN MISNER: Cassie James
BILL SAGE: Frank McBride
MARK A. SHEPPARD: Rod Darling
TRICIA HELFER: Ashleigh James
CATHERINE MACNEAL: Doctor
JIMMIE F. SKAGGS: Homeless Guy
BONNIE BURROUGHS: Dusty Green

there's a note that reads, "Babe, he's not good enough for you. . . . I know you'll live to regret this decision."

As Grissom exits the building, oblivious to Nick and Warrick's calls, he walks the alleys and the streets until he's at the underpass where the body was found. Sara's there too, she points to a billboard with James's face staring down at them. They wonder how and why she was placed here.

The author of the note is traced to a low-rent bungalow. He's not home, but Nick and Warrick look in his garbage can and find a ripped-up photo of James. Catherine and Brass interrupt modeling agent Rod Darling at a fashion shoot as he berates one of his models for overeating. He tells them that James is no longer one of his clients. Suddenly, a man emerges from the crowd of onlookers wielding a knife, rushing Darling and screaming, "He killed her!" Brass subdues him. The attacker, Frank McBride, is the man behind the note and the torn photo. He says Darling made James completely dependent on him. McBride destroyed the picture in disgust because James was throwing her life away. Darling denies an amorous relationship with James, claiming she only was an "asset" that needed protecting.

Sara finds pubic lice and crabs in the jacket from James's closet. Sara surmises that one of her homeless neighbors had been in the apartment, and Grissom adds that the owner of the jacket is most likely the owner of the cart. He revisits the underpass, where he notices one of the vagrants is wearing an expensive scarf with a red stain on it. Grissom trades his jacket for the scarf just as a young homeless woman

approaches, claiming she gave it to the man. Grissom assures her that he acquired it in a trade. An expensive ring she's wearing catches his eye. He trades her his flashlight for it.

The blood on the scarf matches James's, while Nick has determined that the blood on McBride's knife matches only Darling who had been nicked in the aborted attack. There's also blood traces all over the tools in James's manicure kit. Epithelials taken from the homeless woman's ring are a familial DNA match to Ashleigh James. She's Ashleigh's sister, Cassie. Catherine and Grissom pay a visit to Darling at his agency. He admits that he gave up on Cassie. He shows them a three-year-old magazine cover with a stunning picture of Cassie. Her decline began, he recalls, when she got into drugs.

Grissom finds Sara still trying to decipher the code in the day planner. She's also learned that Ashleigh stopped working two months earlier, but

Las Vegas Police

53-0728-0766

Case # 53

Exhibit # 0766

12

AUT

Page 1

JAMES, ASHLEIGH

CAUSE OF DEATH:
Kidney Failure

One malnourished adu
long from the heel.
as Ashleigh James.

Preliminary Tox Scre
bot
inc
ins
tro

Fac
wo
ta
ma
un
in

Bl
te
fi
bu

La
an

E

B
T
r

T
n
r

CASE # 02-223A-46
'The Hunger Artist'

98 03810

He's not good enough for

doesn't have the history that

mean the world to me. I k

live to regret this decision.

spa fashion
September 2001

Can you have
an
rel

ough

02-223A-
JAMES, A

U.S. $2.79 Can $3.79

77757574875

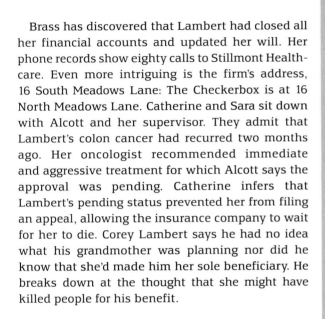

Brass has discovered that Lambert had closed all her financial accounts and updated her will. Her phone records show eighty calls to Stillmont Healthcare. Even more intriguing is the firm's address, 16 South Meadows Lane: The Checkerbox is at 16 North Meadows Lane. Catherine and Sara sit down with Alcott and her supervisor. They admit that Lambert's colon cancer had recurred two months ago. Her oncologist recommended immediate and aggressive treatment for which Alcott says the approval was pending. Catherine infers that Lambert's pending status prevented her from filing an appeal, allowing the insurance company to wait for her to die. Corey Lambert says he had no idea what his grandmother was planning nor did he know that she'd made him her sole beneficiary. He breaks down at the thought that she might have killed people for his benefit.

osh Berman, the writer of the episode, recalls the incident that inspired the "A" storyline, "There was a true case where a driver crashed into a bunch of street cleaners, killing some of them. She wasn't drunk or high; she was just exhausted." The accident sparked speculation among CSI's writers. "Wouldn't it be interesting if she did it on purpose?" Berman then asked, "'Why would an old woman purposefully crash into a building?' We then peel the onion to find out she had a real mission, and a statement." The crash sequence required a building situated at the top of a T-shaped intersection. "It took us a long time to find it," says director Richard Lewis. "And there were so many variables that needed to be there—like a curb where we could knock a newspaper box away, and a place where we could have tables close to the window, but not too close." Eventually, they found a warehouse in Pasadena that was both ideally positioned and that could be made to look like a restaurant. "Michael Barrett, the director of photography, and I were trying to give it an immediacy and a kind of a vibrate-y little feel." Lewis adds, "I enjoyed that a lot."

"Crash and Burn" marks the end of Sara and Hank's relationship. "There were very few scenes, over the seasons, where he got to be doing something really cool," eulogizes Jorja Fox. "He was kind of this bumbling, golden-retriever type character. The assumption is that he's probably a hot-shot paramedic, but he really never got to play that except for his final show." Berman asserts, "Even if Sara had not found Hank cheating on her, I think the relationship would have eventually ended anyway. Hank came in at a time when Sara really needed him, and left at a time when Sara was evolving as a character." ∎

ORIGINAL AIRDATE: 4/3/03
WRITTEN BY: Naren Shankar & Andrew Lipsitz
DIRECTED BY: Deran Sarafian

268

T wo off-roaders are navigating a stretch of Nevada desert. One of the riders takes a tumble onto an overturned industrial drum labelled: "Hazardous Waste" and "Poison." Grissom and Catherine are called out, the drum is holding a corpse in an advanced state of decay. Back at the lab, Robbins strains the liquified contents of the drum, catching a ring.

Having cleaned the remains, Robbins explains to Catherine that the victim was killed by a severe downward blow to the temporal bone. His foot was sheared off with a power tool of some kind. DNA from the bone marrow is a match to Christian Cutler, an army sergeant honorably discharged three years earlier. Sara studies the ring found in the barrel. She determines that the Omega Zeta Alpha on the ring is from a mechanical engineering society. Nick pulls a serial number from the drum. It belongs to a defunct chemical company. The CSIs and Brass pay a visit to the chemical company warehouse where a "robot rumble" is in progress. Small remote-controlled fighting machines battle within a Plexiglass-enclosed ring. Ginger Davis, the event's announcer and promoter, says that she's been holding the competitions since her father left her the warehouses. She last saw Cutler about six weeks ago, when his prized 'bot, Smash-N-Burn, destroyed several opponents.

A "misplaced" body gets Grissom and Warrick's attention. Ten days ago a man thought homeless was brought in. He's been identified as Keith Mercer. There was a laceration on the left side of his face. Among his few possessions were his clothes. His belt has yellow particles attached to it. Cheryl last saw her husband, Keith, when he left to go mountain climbing. She went to her sister's house in New Mexico, returning home ten days later to find him missing. She tells Grissom and Dectective Vega that no one would pay attention to her. At the Mercer home, Warrick finds Keith's climbing gear and an empty keepsake box but no sleeping bag. A Luminol spray reveals a large blood patch and a trail of bloody footprints leading to the mantel. Warrick sprays the mantel and gets a glowing hit on the base of a small stone statue.

You have a gaming license?

> ## Metal weapons, money, competition, testosterone . . . We got a room full of murder suspects.

PRECIOUS METAL

Nick and Sara dismantle and test the innards of Cutler's opposing 'bots. Parts from all three come up positive for Cutler's blood residue. But when Nick experiments with the 'bots' weaponry on suspended pig legs, he finds that none match Cutler's wounds. Nick and Brass follow up with Cutler's business partner, Brian Kelso. The two men trafficked in 'bot parts and as such Kelso says he wouldn't have wanted Cutler dead. Kelso explains that Cutler often took off for weeks doing special-effects work for a rock band.

A raid at a 'bot machine shop gives the criminalists new evidence. Nick spots a rust stain on the floor, which matches the dimensions of the drum Cutler was found in. He and Catherine also find blood spatter on some metal mesh.

Cheryl is visibly upset when Grissom shows her a photo of an empty keepsake box. It contained a valuable coin collection they'd inherited. Greg tells Grissom that he's identified the yellow particles from Mercer's belt as sulfur. He mentions that some coin dealers use it to polish coins. Mercer used his cell phone to make two calls to Jones Collectibles. Because of his knowledge about coins, Greg is sent to the dealer. He offers to trade the proprietor one of his rare pennies for a 1916 "D" dime. Jones sizes him up, then retrieves a case from a locked drawer with the piece inside.

The Omega Zeta Alpha website shows no listing for Christian Cutler, however Brian Kelso is a member. Brass and Nick confront him with the ring found with Cutler's body. He confesses that Cutler's death was an accident. After they'd made some changes in Smash-N-Burn's program, the 'bot suddenly went into overdrive and attacked Cutler. First it nearly severed his foot, then, after he'd fallen to the ground, it attacked his skull. Believing he'd be held responsible for the accident, Kelso cleaned up, dismantled the 'bot, and disposed of the body. Testing Kelso's story, Sara and Nick reassemble the 'bot, when Nick tries working one of the remotes, he finds the 'bot unresponsive. He then realizes that the bot's transmitter module, on the remote and receiver, is tuned to a different frequency. Kelso wasn't in control of the 'bot when it killed Cutler.

GUEST STARRING

269

KATHERINE LANASA: Ginger Davis
MATT WINSTON: Brian Kelso
GEOFFREY RIVAS: Detective Vega
GARRET DILLAHUNT: Luke
MATT DECARO: Rocky Jones
BLAKE ADAMS: Willy Reddington
SARAH LANCASTER: Cheryl Mercer

Nick and Catherine return to the machine shop, where she notices an upstairs office that would provide an ideal spot for someone to secretly operate Smash-N-Burn. A work station belonging to a 'bot designer, Luke, reveals a plastic container with compartments holding the receivers and transmitter modules. The one that matches Smash-N-Burn's receiver—04—is missing. Luke comes in for questioning. He gripes about how Kelso and Cutler destroyed his 'bot. Nick shows him the transmitter from Smash-N-Burn with his DNA on it. Luke was working the 'bot when it killed Cutler. Believing he was responsible, a panicked Kelso asked Luke to keep the accident a secret.

Greg revisits Jones, this time with Grissom and the police. Jones claims a man came in a couple weeks ago looking to sell his coins. Grissom asks for a transaction record for the fifty-thousand-dollar-plus collection. When Jones can't locate it, Vega helps him look in his car. The trunk is found littered with sulfur dust as well as a small bloodstain. Mercer had called Jones to arrange for the sale, and mentioned that he and wife would be out of town for the weekend. When Mercer came home early, he saw the coin dealer robbing him, Jones bludgeoned him to death with the statue.

270

"'**P**recious Metal' was, to a certain extent, demographically driven," says writer Naren Shankar. "We talked about getting into some subject material that might appeal to a younger audience, because we had done so many episodes that were domestically oriented." An idea had been tossed around early in the season to create a storyline around a demolition derby, but the notion proved too unwieldy from a production standpoint. So *CSI* decided to go big by going smaller. "The kind of physical force these 'bots can actually put out is incredible," Shankar explains. "They're little tanks." The show's writing staff took a field trip to a 'bot rumble. "It was pretty impressive," Shankar remembers. "We ended up actually using some of the equipment from it." However, the experience reinforced the advantages of creating living, breathing murderers. "It was hard to get personalities out of the 'bots," Shankar recollects. "When you have a machine doing the killing, it's more difficult to become emotionally invested."

"We wanted a preview of what's to come," says writer Andrew Lipsitz of Greg getting to do field work. "It's very difficult for a lot of our characters, who in the 'real world' work in one particular setting and do the same thing over and over again," Lipsitz observes, "so they look to expand, and I agree with them." Eric Szmanda couldn't be happier, "It's kind of a dream come true. Not only being on the show in the first place, then becoming a regular, and now being able to work my way up to a more equal status with the rest of the cast. I understood that my character has to sometimes fall on his face in order to rise up again and learn something." He adds, "It's hard as an actor to see your character let people down, because you think that's going to somehow cause you to lose

the respect of the audience, but I actually found it had the opposite effect. People are able to relate to you."

William Petersen maintains that Grissom has come to take Greg more seriously, although he notes that the pivotal transition point was left on the cutting room floor during the second season. "There was a scene where he really berates me," Petersen remembers. "We're in the lab and I've given him a hard time and he says, 'Look, I don't understand. What is it that you don't like about me? That I'm weird? *You're* weird!' We cut it because it was a little cloying, but it was a pretty major scene, and it established a certain amount of respect on Grissom's part." ■

You didn't lose. You got destroyed.

A NIGHT AT THE MOVIES

ORIGINAL AIRDATE: 4/10/03
TELEPLAY BY: Danny Cannon &
Anthony E. Zuiker
STORY BY: Carol Mendelsohn
DIRECTED BY: Matt Earl Beesley

GUEST STARRING

CHARLIE HOFHEIMER: Kevin McCallum
CYIA BATTEN: Kelly Goodson
MEGAN WARD: Audrey Hilden
FINN CARTER: Maude McCallum
PETER DOBSON: Anthony Haines
SKIP O'BRIEN: Detective O'Riley
WALLACE LANGHAM: David Hodges
ROMY ROSEMONT: Jacqui Franco
ARCHIE KAO: Archie Johnson
KEVIN CHRISTY: Erik Barry
TODD GIEBENHAIN: Usher

Looks like I wasn't the only person who dropped something tonight.

At the Wonderland Art House theater, the audience is disturbed by a ringing cell phone. In the rear, the man with the phone sits slumped in his seat. When an usher taps him on the shoulder, his head drops forward, a stream of blood dribbling into his popcorn. The victim is Gus Sugarman, a dentist from Henderson. He's got a single puncture wound to the base of his skull where the murder weapon penetrated right down to the brain stem. Grissom speculates that the pinkish impression around Sugarman's neck was left when the killer yanked a chain off of him. Catherine drops her flashlight, which rolls down the floor leading her to the murder weapon—a screwdriver. Out in the lobby, Brass and Grissom question an audience member who recalls a tall redheaded woman left her seat right after the best, and loudest, part of the film; the gunfight. At the lab, Greg and Jacqui process the screwdriver for blood and prints. Sugarman's cell phone records show that his last outgoing call, before the film's 10:40 start time, was only twenty-

six seconds long. Grissom notices that Sugarman received call-backs from the same number at 11:26, 11:27, and 11:28. He was already dead.

At an abandoned warehouse, Nick, Sara, and Warrick process the body of Timmy McCallum. Around the teenager are beer bottles and shell casings. Nick inserts trajectory rods into the bulletholes on the wall, some of which are fifteen feet high. The horizontal trajectories lead to questions on the shooter's vantage point. Warrick pours out the beer

272

into specimen jars, while Sara photographs tire tracks and muddy shoeprints, and then finds a makeshift ladder angled against the building. She returns with a long bamboo pole from atop the roof. Warrick also locates some clear glass shards and pieces of black plastic. There are a hundred and nine bulletholes, the same number as the casings.

Grissom and Catherine visit the home of Sugarman's caller, Audrey Hilden, a redhead. She says that Sugarman is her dentist and he'd asked her to go to the movies. She'd agreed, then backed out. She felt bad about standing him up and called him back three times to apologize. Grissom notices a schedule from the movie theater in her kitchen. The captain reports that Audrey Hilden filed a sexual malpractice suit against

Thursday night is Noir Night.

Sugarman. The dentist hired a high power attorney for a countersuit, Hilden then dropped hers. Brass also reports an usher saw a redhead make a phone call in the lobby halfway through the movie and throw something in the trash. The CSIs revisit the theater. One of the cleaners is wearing black leather gloves that she found in the trash.

McCallum had two fractured ribs and deep contusions of the chest wall that could have been caused by a high-velocity impact. Doctor Robbins puts the cause of death to a single long-range gunshot to the chest. The downward 25-degree angle Warrick observes was too too low for a rooftop, and too high for a person of normal height. The photos from the warehouse show a nonspecific tire treads and they suggest that five people walked in, but only four walked out. Greg confirms the number when he detects five different DNA donors on the beer bottles. Two of them are related. Maude McCallum, a single mother, is accompanied to the police station by her other son, Kevin. When questioned, he claims that he bought a twelve-pack for his little brother and kept a bottle for himself.

Warrick and Sara check the twenty-foot bamboo pole for gunshot residue. Hodges shows Sara a series of spiral gouges extending the length of the bamboo. He also determines that the glass shards came from an optical lens of a videocamera.

The gloves match prints on the murder weapon and the lobby phone, but any DNA has been compromised by ammonia on the cleaning woman's hands. Brass says the phone call from the lobby, to Hilden's house, occurred at 11:25, ruling her out, since she called Sugarman from home at 11:26. They decide to call on her again. A knock at Hilden's door that night gets no answer. Brass leads as Grissom and Catherine follow. They find Audrey Hilden hanging, dead, from an extension cord tied to her second-floor railing, at her feet is a gold necklace. Grissom notices another set of horizontal lines on Hilden's neck as well as postmortem bruising, leading him to suspect that she was strangled, then hanged. The theater schedule is gone. He remembers that it had a handwritten note on it. Grissom

Notice anything else about her?

Backstage at the Sphere, Grissom, Brass and Catherine speak with Anthony Haines, who doesn't know Hilden but admits that E4117 is his parking space. Grissom sees a Wonderland schedule on the mirror at the dressing station of Kelly Goodson, Haines describes the dancer as a "royal pain in the ass." She enters to find Grissom looking in her locker, he's found a card for the law firm of Langly & Langly, and a unique cream Kelly uses for her sore muscles. Back at the lab, Catherine discovers that Kelly Goodson filed a sexual harassment suit against Haines, and she and Hilden had the same lawyers. Grissom believes that the gloves may have evidence, there may be transfer on the outside.

McCallum's three friends are brought in. All have the same superficial injuries. One of them turns over the warehouse videotape. Kevin is seen introducing a stunt called "speedway surfing." Kevin tells them that Timmy was crazy about those "don't try this at home" reality stunt shows. The friends decided to create their own stunts. The final one was "Bamboo Russian roulette," a pole was lowered through the hole in the warehouse roof, a semiautomatic on fire was thread on the pole and spun, it spiraled down the pole. The boys scattered to evade the bullets. On the last time, a bullet struck Timmy in the chest. The boys panicked and fled.

notices water on the bathroom floor and uses a plunger to retrieve the schedule from the clogged toilet.

The tire treads from the McCallums' van match those from the warehouse. Inside the van, Warrick sees the twelve-pack box and blood on the interior of the driver's door. Sergeant O'Riley grills Kevin McCallum, who denies being there. Nick enters to ask about a bandage on Kevin's elbow, it's covering a large abrasive wound. The teen takes off his shirt, his chest has round bruises identical to Timmy's. A computer program, based on the bullet trajectory data, displays the projectiles coming from a tall vertical line in the center of the warehouse. Nick has the liquor store's surveillance tape, it shows Kevin McCallum with four other boys, including Timmy.

The water-damaged movie schedule has a scrawled note that reads: Sphere, E4117. It is written above the show time for Alfred Hitchcock's *Strangers on a Train*. The film is about two men who meet and arrange to kill people in each others' lives, the idea being that with no known link between them and the victim, they won't get caught. If Grissom is correct, there is another victim waiting to be discovered.

In the backstage area, Catherine suggests to Goodson that she and Hilden met and complained about the men in their lives. They struck their *Strangers on a Train* bargain, Goodson did her deed, but Hilden wouldn't hold up her end of the deal. Goodson killed her, leaving Sugarman's necklace behind. Goodson is unmoved until Grissom produces the evidence; her unique skin ointment was found on the gloves and extension cord.

POLICE
LAS VEGAS
NEVADA

120   140
D3S1358

SAMF

VB VIS
Las vegas

☐ Checks Paid

03-319A-
SUGARMAN, G

ONDERLAND

ORT HOUSE
LAS VEGAS
(702) 555-1842

Saturday

Amount
70.80
18.86
210.18
500.00
108.25
600.00
90.84
162.00
11.88
1,637.48

ed Hitchcock presents

ROPE

NO
NOR

rtigo

THE
RCIST.
RECTOR'S CUT

ST

UU
CE ODYS

Sphere
EA-117

Alfred Hitchc

.70
.88
.00

I was getting myself a soda. You know, we're allowed to do
that. Tall redhead came out of the theater, made a phone
call from over there. Yeah, she was wearing (gloves)
actually. I thought it was weird. It's like seventy
degrees in here. She threw something into the trash and
headed out. Cleaning crew's in the theater now. They got
a late start because of you guys.

05-6505

3 of 3

REVIEWED BY

Interior of abandoned warehouse. Day. The cement floor is littered with a multitude of bullet casings. The walls riddled with bullet holes.

"I just wanted to kill someone in a movie theater," Danny Cannon offers. "The story came from that, and from the idea of a theater being a perfect dark place to kill someone." When he raised the notion of two people striking a homicidal pact, Mendelsohn immediately cited Alfred Hitchcock's *Strangers on a Train.* A way of putting a twist on the show's recurring old-versus-new Vegas theme, Catherine and Grissom were paired for the old-fashioned cinema-inspired murder.

"I thought it would be nice to have them hunting someone down clue by clue," Cannon recalls.

"I kind of joked about it," Helgenberger says of the comfortable rapport between their characters. "It was our *Thin Man* or *Hart to Hart* kind of episode." Teaming up the two more experienced CSIs is a reflection on the other members of the cast coming into their own. Ann Donahue remembers, "When we were first starting out, we kind of kept the powers-that-be in separate stories, so that they could lift each one." The fact that George Eads, Gary Dourdan, and Jorja Fox have made their characters' their own has given the show's writers the leeway to pair Petersen and Helgenberger. "It's funny," says Donahue, likening it to the new flexibility of parents whose children have grown up, "it's like, 'Now we can go back and hang out together!'"

As for the "B" storyline, Anthony Zuiker says, "I personally sat down and said, 'I'm writing *Jackass*,' the MTV series where thrill seekers attempted an assortment of stunts." The fictional tale attracted as many accusations of irresponsibility as the real thing. Zuiker recalls, "The script went to the network and they had to decide if showing on *CSI* a Mac 10 spinning around a bamboo pole would inspire someone to do it."

"That was one of my favorites," Jorja Fox says. "I loved how the writers tied in the two stories—video and film. It was one where the mysteries unraveled beautifully." She's particularly pleased with the experience of working with Dourdan and Eads. "We got to work on those relationships a lot this year. Some really lovely intimacy has developed between Warrick and Nick and Sara." ■

LAST LAUGH

ORIGINAL AIRDATE: 4/24/03
TELEPLAY BY: Bob Harris & Anthony E. Zuiker
STORY BY: Bob Harris & Carol Mendelsohn
DIRECTED BY: Richard J. Lewis

277

Michael Borland takes the stage at Vegas's Comedy Hole to a smattering of applause. This crowd has come for shock comic Dougie Max and has little interest in Borland's act. Then Max takes the stage and he starts by taking a gulp of water and spitting it at a couple of guys. "Hey, kid, it's a cruel world . . ." The crowd finishes, ". . . ain't it great!" Brass leads Catherine and Grissom onstage, Max died in the middle of his set. The club's owner, Alan Sobel, explains that tonight's appearance was the successful comic's annual return to his roots. As for potential suspects, Sobel points to a photo-covered wall of comics. Catherine works the club's green room. A food platter sits on the coffee table alongside cocaine. Onstage, Grissom notices six bottles of Innoko water, three partially drunk, three unopened.

Robbins states Max's cause of death as myocardial necrosis, which is consistent with a heart attack, except there was no coronary blockage. The tox screen comes back positive for cocaine, but not enough to kill him. The true culprit was Naratriptamine, a new migraine medication, that was ingested at twelve times the normal dosage. Greg determines it wasn't food from the green room, but a bottle of Max's Innoko water that was spiked with the drug.

Brass asks Nick for his help in reinvestigating an old case. A woman, Shelly Stark, slipped in her bathtub, cracked her skull, and drowned. Her husband, George, was devastated. Brass ruled it was an accident. However he just saw the widower out with a young blonde and driving a Ferrari, and the husband called the insurance company on the morning of his wife's death demanding the $750,000 benefit. Reviewing the scene photos, Nick and Sara imagine that Shelley had lost her footing while getting out of the tub and grabbed the towel bar, it gave way, causing her head to slam against the tub. Her autopsy was abbreviated, the cause of death drowning, her head wound was nonfatal. Nick looks at the Starks' bathroom. It's been painted, and the towel bar's been removed. Stark claims he's preparing to sell the

GUEST STARRING

BOB GOLDTHWAIT: Michael Borland
JEFFREY ROSS: Dougie Max
GILBERT GOTTFRIED: Kenchy
BRYAN CALLEN: Barry Yoder
ALAN BLUMENFELD: Alan Sobel
JEFF PERRY: George Stark
TOM GALLOP: Randy Paynter
WALLACE LANGHAM: David Hodges
SANDRA PURPURO: Cindy
MAGGIE WHEELER: Comedienne
LESLIE BEGA: Leah Hanson
LARRY THOMAS: Manager
MOLLY WEBER: Cindy's Lawyer

When was the last time a comedian died of natural causes?

[path] remote : end Usr ID 1002
urge{hiMem} buffer...waiting...
echo$confab/ unx/ seim-Buff =

I've been a detective half my life. And I can count on one hand the surviving spouses who used the past tense, "was."

278

house. Nick suggests to Sara they look at the model home since the bathroom would be identical to Stark's.

In the model home's bathtub, Sara reenacts Shelley's slip, she grabs the towel bar. It doesn't budge. Nick yanks it repeatedly, finally it detaches from the wall. Shelley's death is looking less than accidental.

At the Comedy Hole's open-mike night, Grissom watches as Sobel flicks a light switch behind the bar. A red light flashes, signaling the performer to end the set. Yoder, the bartender, recalls placing the water bottles on stage before Max's set. Grissom confiscates all of the Innoko water, Catherine learns that Yoder has a prescription for Naratriptamine. Meanwhile, Warrick is sent to investigate a teenage boy lying dead at a convenience store. The kid had opened an Innoko water and began drinking it before dying. Catherine immediately orders a total recall of Innoko water from the Vegas area.

Greg finds the levels of Naratriptamine in the water from the club and the convenience store are identical. The store bottle has no discernable leaks. Catherine finds tiny white granules in the threads of its cap. The killer most likely dripped the Naratriptamine solution into the threads, capillary action pulled it inside and it dried into white crystals. With every sip the deadly solution flowed into the bottle. By comparing the lot numbers on the Innoko bottles from the club to the convenience store ones, Grissom determines that both tainted bottles were from the club. It's likely the killer planted one at the store to create the impression of tampering.

Robbins defends his original assessment of Shelley Stark's death, balking at the idea of an exhumation.

This place is a riot. You find anything?

When Brass stresses the potential risk of not catching a murderer, the doctor finally agrees to reexamine the body. Robbins and David Phillps discover a large bruise on Shelley's back. Robbins explains embalming can accentuate bruises that were barely noticeable at the time of death. More bruises appear when they remove her makeup. George Stark comes in for questioning. Nick displays for him the photos of the newly revealed bruises. Brass alleges that George entered the bathroom and smashed his wife's head against the back of the tub, then drowned her. He ripped the towel bar from the wall, to give the impression it was an accident. Stark's lawyer dismisses the accusation and escorts his client from the building. Outside, Stark sees his Ferarri being towed. The captain explains that Shelley's insurance company has sufficient grounds to mount civil charges against him.

The Naratriptamine would have to be ground up before it was dissolved. The coffee grinder from the club's green room tests positive for the drug. Greg reports that the coffee grind traces were from a variety called Kopi Luwas, the world's most expensive coffee. Find the connoisseur, he says, and you've found the killer. Michael Borland is on stage, drinking coffee and working an indifferent crowd. His patience tried, he starts making snide comments about Dougie Max's act, which meets with unexpected laughs. Grissom motions to Sobel to hit the red light, and Borland announces that he's getting the hook. He then silences the audience by admitting he's responsible for Max's death.

Oh China.

This isn't about the public, the press, your office, you or me. This is about Shelley Stark.

"Last Laugh" allowed the writers a chance to get a long-simmering idea onto the screen. "We always wanted to do something about product tampering," remembers Eli Talbert. "We'd been pitching that idea around since season one, but we just could never get it to work." As the staff was working to weave a tale around a comedy club, says Talbert, "Somebody yelled out, 'This could be our tampering story!'" Expanding a lone murder in a comedy club to a would-be citywide catastrophe, then returning to the club's stage made for an interesting plot structure. Anthony Zuiker says, "We wanted to make it bigger and then bring it back to where it came from."

The "B" storyline, about the bathtub murder of Shelley Stark, came from Carol Mendelsohn. "We needed a little 'runner' story," Talbert recalls, "and we thought, 'You know, Brass works on all these other cases. What if he saw somebody and he just got a gut feeling?'" Nick and Sara are carrying the case, but it's Brass who uses his experience to enable the team to discover the truth. The story's high point is Brass's heated showdown in the coroner's office with Robbins, who takes Brass's request that Shelley Stark's corpse be exhumed as an impugning of his professional credibility. "That's something that we want to do more of," Zuiker says. "To go into Robbins's backyard and start calling him on his stuff is dramatic. Robbins is always the nice guy with the cane who walks around giving out information." Zuiker observes, "You think you know somebody, then you say something and they snap at you, and it's like, 'Whoa, this guy can kick some ass!' That's cool and that's interesting." ■

ORIGINAL AIRDATE: 5/1/03
WRITTEN BY: Sarah Goldfinger
DIRECTED BY: David Grossman

280

GUEST STARRING

LEE GARLINGTON: Mrs. Frommer
PATRICK FABIAN: Rhone Confer
ELAINE HENDRIX: Harper Fitzgerald
SUSAN WALTERS: Meredith Michaels
JONATHAN SLAVIN: Jason Banks
MICHAEL MANTELL: Dr. Stevens
OLIVIA FRIEDMAN: Alyssa Jamison
NIGEL GIBBS: Pilot
LISA WILHOIT: Girl #3
ARIELLE KEBBEL: Girl #2
JEFFREY D. SAMS: Detective Lockwood

The cabin of a private jet is alive with socialites on their way to Vegas. In the plane's cargo hold is an agitated horse and a woman lying dead at its feet. Grissom and Catherine learn that the victim is Lori Hutchins, the animal's trainer. The plane's crew says that Hutchins was a dedicated pro who always traveled with the horse, High Folly. Inside the horse container, Grissom finds a small, bloodstained pair of scissors, a spent tranquilizer dart, and a rifle. Catherine finds another dart, stuck in the insulation on the cargo hold's ceiling, some nondescript brown shavings, and unused tranquilizer syringes. Nick then discovers a shoeprint in a clump of manure matching a designer driving loafer.

At the USDA holding center, High Folly will sit out her mandatory forty-eight-hour quarantine. The horse's owner, Meredith Michaels, insists that she be allowed entry. While the CSIs confer with a veterinarian, Doctor Stevens, Grissom notices sutures on the horse's hindquarters. Stevens explains that High Folly is a "dirty mare," and the stitches prevent uterine infections. The vet notes that tranquilizer guns are not supposed to be used on horses, as the shock and resulting adrenaline surge can result in the opposite effect.

> So that's how and why. We're still looking for who.

Sara and Warrick venture to the Hell's Gate section of Death Valley, where a young man in a suit lies dead on a blanket. Sara swabs a chalky white stain from the blanket while Warrick finds a wallet indicating the victim is Toby Wellstone, who's only fifteen. He is wearing a transdermal patch on his left palm with the painkiller Fentanyl. Warrick learns that Wellstone had been in seven foster homes before Child Services lost track of him. Robbins states that he found a post-op narcotic among the stomach contents. The tox report identifies the drug as Cisapride, a kinetic agent that hastens the body's absorption of painkillers. A second victim, a teenage girl, is found nearby. She also has a Fentanyl patch. Sara notices that the handmade prom dress she is wearing is too big.

Doctor Robbins examines Lori Hutchins, noting perimortem bruising and scraping on her right forearm, consistent with trampling. Her pinpoint pupils were caused by the powerful tranquilizer Etorphine, and a puncture wound confirms she was shot by the tranquilizer gun. The shoeprint is matched to the plane's owner, Harper Fitzgerald. She says she visited the cargo hold to woo Hutchins away from Meredith— her current employer— with a salary increase, but Hutchins declined. The handrail leading down to the hold yields prints for Fitzgerald, a steward, and Rhone Confer, a passenger. Catherine identifies the brown shavings as tobacco from illegally imported Cuban cigars. Confer admits he procured cigars on occasion, but had no contact with Hutchins. He went into the hold to look at High Folly, the horse grabbed a cigar from his breast pocket. He then noticed Hutchins's lifeless body, not wanting to put a damper on the party, he kept this discovery to himself.

Warrick mentions that the girl's stomach contents and tox results matches Wellstone's. Their prints were also on each other's Fentanyl patches. The CSIs wonder why the girl left the scene. Detective Lockwood informs them that the girl was Jill Frommer. Her mother says that Wellstone lived with them as a foster child five years ago, but he was difficult, so she sent him back. Jill brought him home

FOREVER

about a year ago and begged her to let him stay. Sara suggests that someone assisted with their suicides, and asks for a list of their friends. Mrs. Frommer says she has no idea who Jill's friends were.

Catherine and Grissom discover High Folly is dead. Stevens says he opened the stiching and administered antibiotics but he was too late. Recalling the suture scissors, Grissom speculates that Hutchins had known of the ailment and tried to treat it. Forensic wildlife expert Jessie Menken performs equine necropsy and detects an extremely high white blood cell count, indicative of infection. She removes the uterus, finding a small sack containing uncut diamonds and red lentils inside.

At McKinley High, students tell Sara and Warrick that Jill hasn't been at school all year. The dress belongs to Alyssa Jamison, who works as a volunteer at the hospital. The CSIs find Jamison behind the counter at the hospital's pharmacy. She says Jill asked if she could wear the dress for a "special occasion." Jamison recalls that Jill had been depressed but insists that she couldn't have given her any drugs, pointing to the surveillance camera.

A search of Doctor Steven's office turns up traces of diamond dust and red lentils, used to prevent the diamonds from chipping during transit. Grissom speculates that Stevens, who's suddenly left town, grabbed what he could from the animal's uterus. But

So, Romeo had a Juliet. Who fell out of bed and landed a half-mile away?

282

he must have had a partner on the plane who killed Hutchins. Comparing the weight of lentils to the diamonds, the CSIs determine that there are four sacks missing.

Only in Vegas.

Greg tells Sara and Warrick that hospitals haven't dispensed Cisapride in three years. He's also identified the white film on the blanket as denatured milk proteins. It's baby spittle and DNA confirms it's from Jill's and Wellstone's baby. A search finds Cisapride and Fentanyl in the Frommer kitchen cupboard. Mrs. Frommer explains that it was to treat the symptoms of her late husband's chemotherapy, and her back pain. Warrick and Sara hear the sound of a baby from inside the refrigerator. There they find a baby monitor, leading them to an infant in the master bedroom. Mrs. Frommer says she's the baby's only chance, and that in Nevada it's not illegal to watch a suicide. Certain that Frommer did more than passively watch, Sara threatens her with a murder charge and a

child services investigation. As Lockwood cuffs her, Frommer maintains that, as a blood relative, she'll get the baby back.

Grissom turns up trace evidence of carrots from the recovered stones, which implies that Hutchins packed the diamonds after feeding High Folly. Doctor Stevens had not one but two accomplices. The CSIs check the backgrounds of Fitzgerald's entourage, finding information on a Rhone *Kinsey*-Confer.

At Kinsey Diamonds' cutting room, Brass presents a search-and-seizure warrant to its proprietor— who happens to be Confer's mother—for its raw stones.

When Rhone Confer is brought back in, Brass presents a warrant requiring him to remove his shirt. He does, displaying a large red bruise on his sternum. Hutchins must have struggled with Confer to prevent him from using the tranquilizer gun on High Folly. Confer fired the first dart into the ceiling, but fired again, hitting Hutchins in the neck. She fell into High Folly's pen, where the frenzied horse unwittingly stomped her trainer to death.

Where to start? First witness. First suspect. The horse. Of course.

"'**E**llie' had dealt with drug muling, so we didn't want to do that again. We needed something that wasn't detectable by X-ray. So diamonds became the next best thing," explains writer **Sarah Goldfinger.** In deciding on how to move the contraband, Goldfinger recalls, "We thought, 'A horse is huge.' You could hide anything in it—either by feeding it to it, or the way that we went. They get quarantined, but then they're free to go." Elizabeth Ruffenacht, an assistant to editor Tom McQuade, trains and travels all over the world to retrieve horses for clients. "We asked her how she transports them," Goldfinger says. "When she said that they fly on airplanes, we said, 'Are you kidding?'" The next piece for the story came from a news clipping about an incident aboard a jet in which a frenzied horse kicked out an electrical panel and forced an emergency landing. Wrapping a social setting around the death of Lori Hutchins was the easy part. After all, it isn't just anyone who can afford champion horses, let alone have the means to transport them in style. "Dealing with the lifestyles of the rich and famous allows you to have a little fun," Goldfinger points out, "and take your audience into a world that they'd might not otherwise get to see."

If the "B" storyline of Toby Wellstone and Jill Frommer seems stranger than fiction, it is. "For all the twisted things we do on *CSI,* there always seems to be an even more twisted real-life parallel," says Carol Mendelsohn. "Thankfully, it's real hard for writers to come up with horrible, horrible things that don't exist," explains Josh Berman, who offered a newspaper article for inspiration. "The truth is," he says of the show's inspired by real-life stories, "if we're sitting around talking about them, then we know people will be sitting around talking about the episodes."

When "Forever" was in the works, the writers became aware of Warrick's streak of getting murdered young people. They included a line in Act 2 where a demoralized Warrick accepts Catherine's offer to handle Robbins's preliminary solo, saying, "I'm not ready to deal with another murdered kid." Mendelsohn recalls, "I didn't realize that we'd done it again and again during the season." Acknowledging Warrick's fatigue provided an opportunity to depict an important self-preservation skill. "When you're a CSI and you're in it for the long haul, you develop an instinct for when you cannot put yourself into certain situations." Gary Dourdan can only guess as to why his character was singled out. "I think the writers know that I have children, so they figured that I would be able to personify a guy who deals with these crimes." ■

283

Open on desolate exterior of Hell's Gate in Death Valley. Day. Wrinkles undulate through the red earth.

ORIGINAL AIRDATE: 5/8/03
WRITTEN BY: Naren Shankar & Andrew Lipsitz
DIRECTED BY: Kenneth Fink

284

SPECIAL GUEST STAR

BOB GUNTON: Robert Cavallo

GUEST STARRING

MAX MARTINI: Jason Kent
LUIS ANTONIO RAMOS: Jesus Cardenas
REBECCA MCFARLAND: Kimberly March
WALLACE LANGHAM: David Hodges
ROMY ROSEMONT: Jacqui Franco
ARCHIE KAO: Archie Johnson
OLIVIA ROSEWOOD: Alison Carpenter
RAYMOND CRUZ: Miguel Durado

Two teens hurry out from under the bleachers to the announcer's booth at the top of the stands. The moment is spoiled when they open the door to find a dead woman inside. Nebraska resident Alison Carpenter's murder was not a robbery gone wrong, Grissom and Nick decide, since her possessions are untouched. Petechial hemorhaging and pronounced lividity indicate that she was strangled in the booth, a wound on the inside of her calf suggests that the body was moved

postmortem. Her liver temperature is 98.1 — she was killed recently, the CSIs hurry to collect latent prints that will be lost during the corpse's cooling process. Nick manages to find a partial on the victim's ankle.

At the lab, Catherine and Warrick conclude another day, there's no one in the evidence vault. As is customary, Catherine leaves their evidence, a green glass jar containing an unidentified liquid, under the fume hood in the DNA lab until it can be logged in the morning.

Sara and Nick process Carpenter's rental car. They find ripped panties and semen stains in the backseat, and a blister pill pack along with a tiny white ceramic fragment in the front. In Carpenter's motel room, Nick finds a tape recorder in her suitcase. Her cause of death was asphyxiation via strangling. Robbins points out the bruising on the left side of her neck indicates a right-handed killer. Although her other wounds are consistent with rape, Robbins determines that it was rough but consensual sex.

David Hodges tells Grissom that the blister pack contains 40 mg methadone pills, used by recovering heroin addicts. The white fragment, he continues, is from a dental crown. Jacqui Franco narrows the partial ankle print to nineteen possible matches. She will now hand examine the prints to get the match. Greg announces that the semen from Carpenter's car

PLAY WITH FIRE

matches Jason Kent. Known as the "Circle Killer," Kent's just completed a fifteen-year sentence. As he is arrested, Grissom notices a wound on his lip and asks to see his hands. His nails have been recently cut, but Grissom finds a tiny nail shard stuck in his clippers.

Following several thwarted efforts to have a personal conversation with Grissom, Sara heads back to the break room. On her way, she glances over at Greg, who's standing over the fume hood. Suddenly, the DNA lab erupts in a ball of fire, the blast propelling Greg through the lab's window into the corridor. The concussion knocks Sara senseless.

Paramedics wheel a semi-conscious Greg out on a gurney, Grissom sees Sara sitting on the curb, a nasty-looking gash on her palm, and directs a paramedic to stitch her up. Robert Cavallo, the lab's assistant director, orders a complete inventory of lost, contaminated, and salvageable evidence. Grissom places Catherine in charge of the investigation.

At Brass's request for an odontological sample, Kent tosses a mouthful of bridgework on the table. One of his crowns is chipped. From the hours of audiotape Carpenter recorded during her visit, Nick and Archie Johnson uncover a recording with Kent getting into her car with a busted lip and a broken tooth. Carpenter then asks if the injury had anything to do with a Jesus Cardenas. A computer search turns up Cardenas's conviction for possession and sale of heroin, and manslaughter. He's currently serving twenty-five years at Kent's former prison. The CSIs discover that Carpenter visited Kent thirteen times in the last eighteen months, and during her last two trips, she also visited Cardenas. Nick and Grissom watch a visitors' room surveillance tape showing Kent concluding a visit with Carpenter. She then moved to an alcove obscured from the camera's view where Cardenas joined her for about five minutes. Archie enhances the image, it shows Carpenter having sex with Cardenas. Nick and Sara visit Cardenas, who says Carpenter's sexually servicing him was payment-in-kind for the debt Kent owed him.

In the decimated DNA lab, Catherine and Warrick start gathering evidence. No crater means that they're looking for a combustible liquid. Catherine discovers that the hot plate under the fume hood was left on and Warrick finds a piece of melted plastic from the developer pan.

Franco matches the partial from Carpenter's ankle to Miguel Durado, a fellow gang member of Cardenas's. Grissom speculates that Durado was assigned to collect the debt. He followed Kent and Carpenter to the announcer's booth, slugged Kent, and strangled Carpenter.

What did you do to my lab, Grissom?

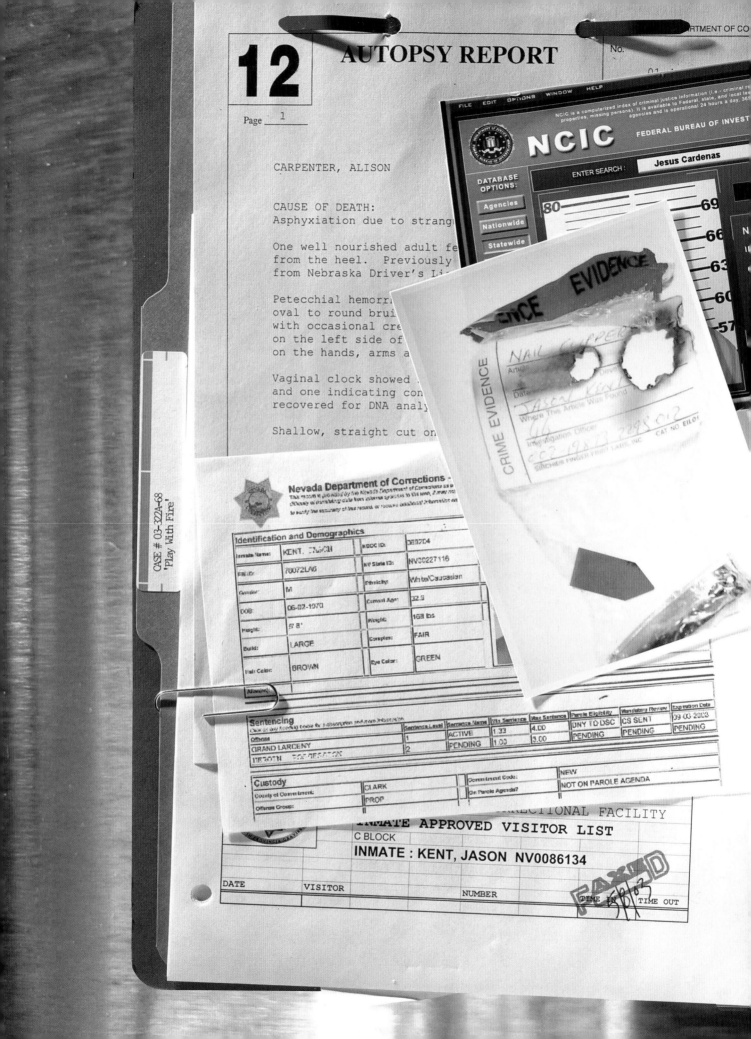

OPERATOR'S LICENSE

Nebraska

ALTSON CARPENTER
1987 OAK STREET
OMAHA, NE 68103
Number 1199908768

NEBRASKA

Expires 7/15/06   07/01/77

Las Vegas Po

SCIENTIFIC
FIELD INVES

POLICE

LAS VEGAS METRO POLICE DEPARTMENT

FINGERPRINT RECORD

ARREST – INVESTIGATION REPORT

SUBJ. NO.	DATE OF	☐ ARREST	COURT LV. SUPREME	FILE NUMBER 112799-620-
			AREA	

6

USE SCALE TO DESCRIBE
INTENSITY OF RIGOR MORTIS
AND LIVOR MORTIS. USE
SHADING ON DIAGRAMS TO
ILLUSTRATE LOCATION OF
LIVOR MORTIS. DESCRIBE
INTENSITY OF COLORATION
AND WHETHER LIVOR MORTIS
IS PERMANENT OR BLACHES
UNDER PRESSURE.

SCALE
0=Absent/Negative
1 +
2 +
3 +
4 +=Extreme Degree

CLARK COUNTY
CORONER'S OFFICE

CORONER

Name: CARPENTER, A

Case No.: 03322A-68

RIGOR MORTIS

NECK:

Anterior Flexion	2+
Posterior flexion	1+
Right lateral flexion	0
Left lateral flexion	3+

JAW: 2+
SHOULDER: 4+
ELBOW: 3+
WRIST: 2+

LIVOR MORTIS:

TEMPERATURE:

ENVIRONMENT TEMPERATURE: 85 °F

LIVER TEMPERATURE= 98.1 °F

WHERE TAKEN

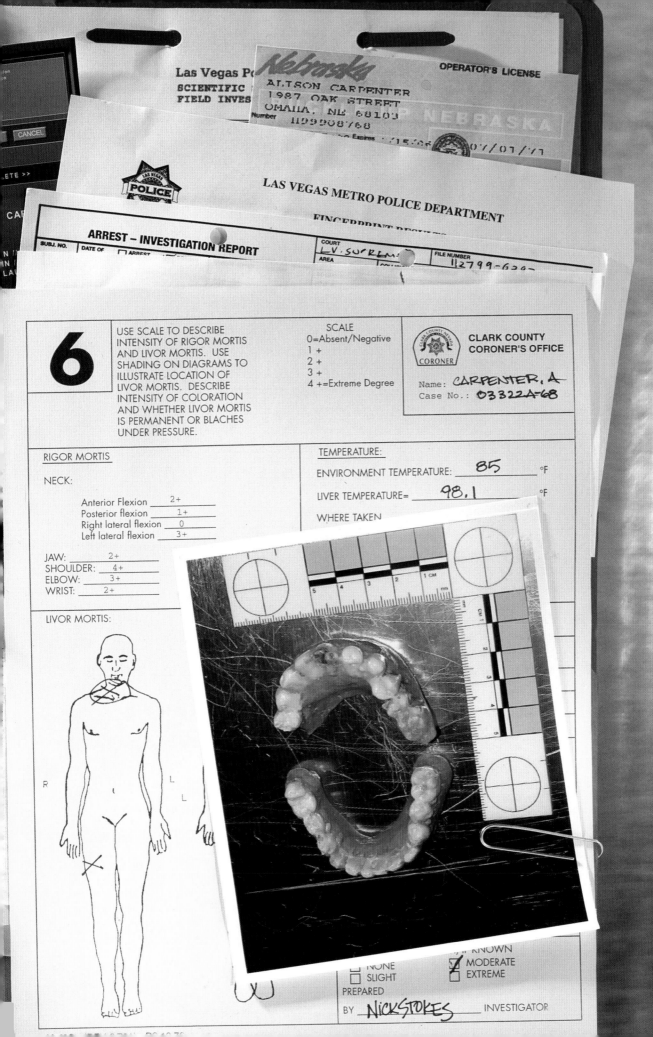

R   L

L

☐ UNKNOWN
☐ NONE   ☑ MODERATE
☐ SLIGHT   ☐ EXTREME
PREPARED
BY NICK STOKES   INVESTIGATOR

Catherine scrutinizes a schematic she's created of the decimated lab, placing markers on a plastic overlay. She identifies a jar as the primary fragment. "Then who blew up the lab?" Warrick asks. Catherine answers, "I did." Grissom and Catherine are in Cavallo's office, she explains that the liquid in the bottle was a possibly poisonous substance that she placed under the hood. She wasn't aware the hot plate had been left on. Grissom attests that unlogged evidence is routinely placed under the hood. Reminding them that DNA evidence in thirteen cases has been tainted or destroyed, Cavallo suspends Catherine for five unpaid days.

Sara follows Brass and some officers as they burst into Durado's apartment, guns drawn. On her own, Sara kicks open the bathroom door, where Durado is trying to climb out the window. Brass is furious at Sara's violation of procedure. Nick joins Sara at the apartment and identifies the wound on Durado as a human bite mark. Durado admits that he was there but insists that Kent is the killer.

Brought back for interrogation, Grissom and Brass allege that Kent had sex with Carpenter in her car, then took her up to the announcer's booth where he planned to pay off Durado by having Carpenter prostitute herself. When Carpenter balked, Kent strangled her. Durado hit the fallen Carpenter's leg with the door, then moved it aside. Grissom traces an outline of Kent's hand, confirming it is the same size as the killer's, based on the bruises on Carpenter's neck. Kent is led away in cuffs. Grissom admits to Brass that, without the evidence destroyed in the blast, he'll likely go free at trial.

Sara is standing in Grissom's doorway, she proposes that they should go out to dinner and "see what happens." Grissom is taken aback, then declines her offer. "I don't know what to do about this," he says, pointing between the two of them. "I do." Sara adds, "By the time you figure it out, it could be too late."

In "Play with Fire," as in "Accused," the entire night shift is put on trial, this time in the form of Assistant Director Robert Cavallo. "It wasn't meant as a plot thread," explains writer Andrew Lipsitz. "We were interested in seeing the real side of the lab—we wanted to make it a little bit more human." Carol Mendelsohn recalls the writers were hoping to regain an element of tension. "The best decision we ever made was making Brass a homicide detective again," she says. "But we missed the conflict that was there in the pilot. So we basically said, 'How do we get that again?' We asked Liz Devine and Technical Consultant Rich Catalani, 'What are the politics of the lab?'"

Cavallo makes reference to Catherine's sloppy work on a case file that Grissom had to kick back to her. This set the stage for her error of not checking the hot plate, which in led to the explosion. Marg Helgenberger, while accepting the dramatic premise involved, can't resist defending her character. "If there's nobody in the evidence vault, they always put it under the fume hood," she protests. "It wasn't just me! Some idiot left the hot plate on, but I took the rap."

Setting up the lab blast, director Ken Fink created a curious calm before a calamitous storm. "I asked the writers to do a bait and switch. You think you're with Sara following Grissom, that you know that she has some affection for, so that takes everyones' attention off what might happen next." Shooting the scene was a precarious, day-long process that required everyone to be on their toes. They were using *CSI*'s actual set, which needed to be intact for the season finale and beyond. Fink remembers, "We were very concerned that if we did too big an explosion inside the lab, we would break glass all throughout the place. And it was very difficult to find the right camera speeds—you don't want to slow things down so much that you start seeing the elements of debris flying at you and you start to wonder what it is. But you don't want to go so fast that the whole thing is over in an eighth of a second. I think we hit it."

Jorja Fox recalls, "They had two or three cameras going at the same time—the stunt double for Eric Szmanda went crashing through the window, and my double hit the wall." She and Szmanda watched closely,

It's not your job to protect your people; it's to protect the integrity of this lab. Without the people, there is no lab.

they had to mimic the stuntpeople's actions for the close-up shots. "Eric was really excited about it," she says. "I'd rather sit in the lab and play with hair fibers. I was like, 'Why are they blowing *us* up?'" According to Carol Mendelsohn, "Greg's fear as a newbie field CSI is that the danger is outside, and we were saying 'Nuh-uh, the danger is *inside*.'" Deciding on who else, she adds, "It was really process of elimination. We just thought it would relate so much to who Sara is—you know, 'I can tough it out. I just get up, dust myself off, and I'm okay.' So it really gave us a great story to play."

Noticing a gash on Sara's palm, Grissom says, "This doesn't look good" and directs a paramedic to get her stitched up. That's the way it was originally scripted, but when the camera started rolling, William Petersen added an ad lib. Grissom was now saying, "Honey, this doesn't look good." Naren Shankar, one of the writers, couldn't believe his ears. "I was, like, 'Um, Billy, did you just say *honey?*'" The actor was insistent that the term of endearment was entirely reasonable under the circumstances, even for the closed-off Grissom. Petersen recalls, "They said, 'He can't call her "Honey." But that's *exactly* what would happen.' He's afraid for her, he's afraid for everybody." Petersen then adds, "But it *is* specifically for Sara. He knows the stress she's been under with him. With her shock, she doesn't even know until later on that he called her honey. *He* doesn't know that he called her honey. Only the audience knows."

The explosion has damaged more than Sara's palm. On her way out to meet Nick, and resume the Carpenter investigation, Sara finds herself averting her head from imaginary glass shards flying at her as she passes the DNA lab. Later Sara recklessly draws her gun and enters the suspected killer's apartment before it is cleared. Fink says, "The idea was that the explosion puts her into this state of mind that makes Sara willing to approach Grissom in a way that she's never done before. Fox observes, "The relationship between Grissom and Sara seemed a little strained for some part of the year. As long as they could talk exclusively about the work, then everything would flow, but with anything outside of that, there was an air of discomfort." Sara's accident gave her what she needed "The idea that she could've died before she would've been able to say what she wanted to say, thrust her into that room at the end."

Petersen and Fox were opposed to the script's original indication that Grissom would turn her down decisively and for good. "I said, 'You can't do that. We have chemistry together,'" Petersen recollects. "We have so little interaction between the characters as it is." Grissom gently turns her down but not without expressing some ambivalence, both in his words and his actions; he stands outside his office, pauses, and then appears to walk in her direction. Shankar agrees with Fox's and Petersen's take on the situation, "When you work with somebody and you have feelings for them, you can't just end it; it's not possible. It was really about bad timing. Grissom is sitting there worried that he's going to go deaf, and she's coming here and saying, 'Hey, let's get together,' and he's kind of saying, 'I can't deal with this right now.' There is some value in keeping that door open just a little bit." ■

ORIGINAL AIRDATE: 5/15/03
WRITTEN BY: Carol Mendelsohn & Anthony E. Zuiker
DIRECTED BY: Danny Cannon

290

Inside the First Monument Bank, four armed men in ski masks line up the customers— including Detective Lockwood— while one of them forces the manager downstairs. There, he detonates explosive charges on a wall of safe-deposit boxes. Upstairs, a young mother with her son panics and tries to make a run for it. When one of the gunmen takes aim, Lockwood tries to inconspicuously pull his gun. He is shot, just as the thief from downstairs emerges. Outside, an LVPD squad car is disabled with a few carefully placed shots, enabling the robbers to escape. The scene is swarming with police personnel, media, and onlookers as Grissom and Catherine arrive. Brass stands over Lockwood's body, reporting that the robbers were pros who had no interest in cash.

Grissom notes the placement of the charges were focused on a specific safe-deposit box. An electric blasting cap and a brown "leg" wire feeding into a grommet indicate a military construction. Brass announces that the getaway vehicle's been found with its driver dead inside.

Whatever they were after was more important than all the money in the world.

Grissom, Warrick, and Archie Johnson watch one of the gunmen rub a black substance over the surveillance camera lens. David Hodges reports the substance is camouflage cream, and he found an eyelash in it. The getaway driver is Larry Whiting. Being that he was a convicted criminal, they are surprised to learn that Whiting had a non-gaming card to work at the Rampart Casino. The casino is owned by Catherine's friend, Sam Braun. The casino magnate tells Catherine the name doesn't ring a bell. While they talk, Catherine mentions the still-unsolved murder of one of his cocktail waitresses, Vivian Verona, last year.

Warrick and Brass check out Whiting's apartment. They find a couple of Rampart's five thousand wrappers. The bullets from Lockwood's back and the radio car were 308s, Bobby Dawson tells Grissom most likely from an M-1A. Those guns are only registered to their initial purchaser, and their serial numbers are not recorded. However, the ability to take out Lockwood and a moving car at long range suggests a highly skilled marksman.

Sara's reconstruction of the charred, mangled deposit boxes shows box number 729 is missing. The box is registered to Benny Murdock, a long time employee of Sam Braun. Grissom and Catherine question Braun about Murdock, who died a couple weeks ago. Braun says they had a falling-out six months ago, but they had made their peace before Murdock's death.

Grissom is able to get a thumbprint off the battery of the explosive's detonator. Print Tech Jacqui Franco gets a hit: Robert Rubio. A security expert, he also works at the Rampart. The SWAT team bursts into Rubio's home. Empty. A burning smell from the patio leads Brass, Catherine, and Grissom to a barbecue, they find the remains of a burned black coat, and box 729. Inside the box is a shred of silky multicolored fabric. Grissom swabs a bloodstain from the box.

The desert holds the bodies of three men, their gunshot wounds were inflicted at close range. All of

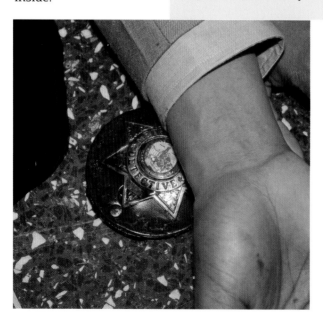

INSIDE THE BOX

the victims were carrying undrawn guns, it's clear they knew their attacker. In the distance, a piece of fabric hanging from some brush catches Grissom's eye. It's a match for the piece found in box 729, even to the bloodstains. Greg gets a hit on one of the blood samples from the box. One sample is from Vivian Verona, the murdered cocktail waitress. Her autopsy report indicated the unrecovered murder weapons were a pair of knives. The second blood sample comes back unknown.

Grissom looks over the photos from the Verona investigation. The shot of the victim shows her wearing the scarf from the safe-deposit box. Seeing Warrick cut open the scarf's evidence bag, Grissom realizes that the weapon used in the waitress's murder was a pair of scissors. He concludes that the murder weapon was then wrapped in her scarf. Sara reports that Verona was murdered in a Pike's penthouse suite the

SPECIAL GUEST STAR

291

SCOTT WILSON: Sam Braun

GUEST STARRING

MICHAEL SHAMUS WILES: Rob Rubio
ROMY ROSEMONT: Jacqui Franco
GERALD MCCULLOUCH: Bobby Dawson
DAVID SELBURG: Bank Manager
EMILIO RIVERA: Bank Robber #4
CHRISTIE LYNN SMITH: Mother
JEFFREY D. SAMS: Detective Lockwood

Where's he going?

AUTOPSY REPORT

12

Page 1

No.

DEPARTMENT OF COR...

Las Vegas Police
53-0728-0791
Case # 53
Exhibit # 0791

EVIDENCE EVIDENCE EVIDE...

EVIDENCE

High Roller Gives $50,000.00 Tip

Cocktail waitress Vivian Verona of Pike's Gambling Hall
Receives $50,000.00 tip from Asian High Roller

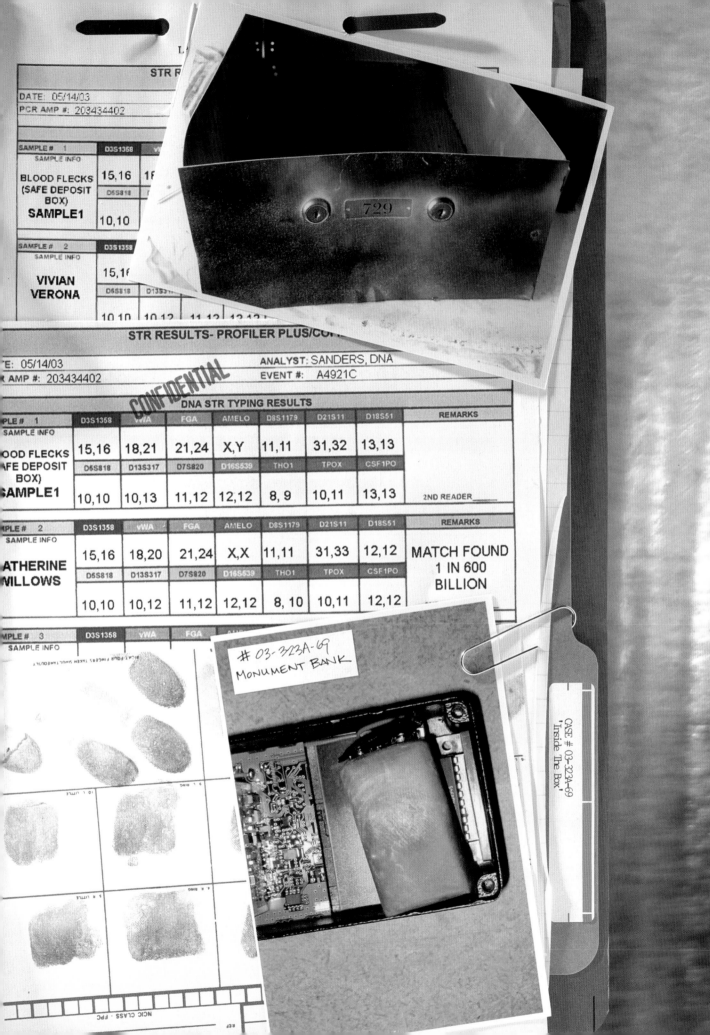

STR R...

DATE: 05/14/03
PCR AMP #: 203434402

SAMPLE # 1 SAMPLE INFO	D3S1358	vW...
BLOOD FLECKS (SAFE DEPOSIT BOX) SAMPLE1	15,16	18
	D5S818	
	10,10	

SAMPLE # 2 SAMPLE INFO	D3S1358	
VIVIAN VERONA	15,16	
	D6S818	D13S31
	10,10	10,12	11,12	13,12

STR RESULTS- PROFILER PLUS/CO...

DATE: 05/14/03
R AMP #: 203434402

ANALYST: SANDERS, DNA
EVENT #: A4921C

CONFIDENTIAL

DNA STR TYPING RESULTS

PLE # 1 SAMPLE INFO	D3S1358	vWA	FGA	AMELO	D8S1179	D21S11	D18S51	REMARKS
OOD FLECKS AFE DEPOSIT BOX) AMPLE1	15,16	18,21	21,24	X,Y	11,11	31,32	13,13	
	D5S818	D13S317	D7S820	D16S539	THO1	TPOX	CSF1PO	
	10,10	10,13	11,12	12,12	8, 9	10,11	13,13	2ND READER____

PLE # 2 SAMPLE INFO	D3S1358	vWA	FGA	AMELO	D8S1179	D21S11	D18S51	REMARKS
ATHERINE WILLOWS	15,16	18,20	21,24	X,X	11,11	31,33	12,12	MATCH FOUND 1 IN 600 BILLION
	D5S818	D13S317	D7S820	D16S539	THO1	TPOX	CSF1PO	
	10,10	10,12	11,12	12,12	8, 10	10,11	12,12	

PLE # 3 SAMPLE INFO	D3S1358	vWA	FGA	A...

03-323A-69
MONUMENT BANK

CASE # 03-323A-69
"Inside The Box"

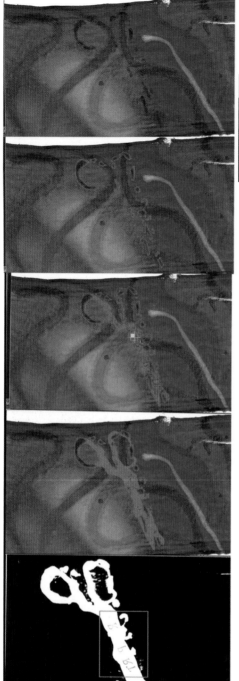

Look familiar?

night before it was imploded. Nick speculates that it was an attempt at making the waitress "disappear." Catherine suggests they pay a personal visit to Braun, however, Grissom tells her he can't go because he's on his way to have surgery. She asks if there's anything she can do. "Just take care of the case," he says.

Rubio is apprehended, but he tells Brass that he's not interested in making a deal, and he has nothing to say about anything Sam Braun might have done. Catherine goes to Braun's office, where she takes in the framed photos on his wall celebrating the openings of his properties. All of them feature a mounted pair of oversized ribbon-cutting scissors, except for the

Rampart's. Braun admits that Benny Murdock killed Verona, after he caught her cheating on him with Braun. He claims that Murdock admitted to the murder on his deathbed, telling Braun the scissors were in the safe-deposit box. Catherine can't believe that Braun hired a team to rob a bank just to retrieve a pair of scissors. Braun replies that he would go down with Murdock if the scissors were ever found. Catherine tells him that she's had her DNA tested against the second unknown blood sample from the box. The results indicated seven alleles in common, meaning that the killer is a biological relation of hers. Not only is Braun her father, but it was he who killed Verona, and had Murdock cover it up for *him*.

Grissom sits prepped for surgery, when he spots Catherine standing at the door. She's come by to wish him good luck.

Showdowns are boring, Sam.
I need the truth.

" **I just love the way vaults and safes look, and it was so much more interesting to me that, instead of robbing the bank and taking money, they go for a safe-deposit box," director Danny Cannon says.** "The writers got together and we thought really hard about what's in the box. How can we tie it to Sam Braun?" Josh Berman suggested that it should contain *CSI*'s raison d'être—evidence. "You know how someone will say something and it just stops everything?" Cannon muses. "That's when you strike gold." That presented the episode's biggest challenge. "The great mystery was, 'Who goes into a bank and blows it up and doesn't take a dollar, but takes something from a safe deposit box?'" recalls writer Anthony Zuiker. "We were hoping that mystery would track." Jonathan Littman expressed some skepticism, "There was a lot of concern. It's a very elaborate crime, and you want the payoff to be worthy of it. Then you look at it and you go, 'All of this just for a pair of scissors?'"

In an episode full of notable moments, the most startling is Catherine's discovery that Sam Braun is her father. Marg Helgenberger speculates, "I think they wanted to explore Catherine's ties to old Vegas, and then decided, 'Hey, he's sleeping with her mother, so what if . . . ? '" For Zuiker, the fatherly demeanor evident in Braun's interaction with Catherine provided a realistic basis for the revelation. "We wanted to have this thing link back to something we'd already learned. We were writing the scene with Catherine and Braun, and Carol Mendelsohn just typed in 'Because I'm your father.' and I was like 'Huh?' Then we all stopped and said, 'That's great! Let's do that!'" Littman was not so sure, "Was this one step too far? Were we overreaching? Carol passionately believed that in the world of Vegas, it was credible. And, you start to understand Catherine's journey a little bit more."

Grissom's coming clean about his medical condition to Robbins and Catherine was not quite the denouement that the show's writers had planned. "When we initially

started it, I had hoped to play it out over many seasons," Mendelsohn recalls. "I thought if Grissom ever rides off into the sunset, it would be because he couldn't hear." Unfortunately, she notes, the disengagement that the affliction caused was painting Grissom into a corner. Another reason for ending the subplot was the malady didn't justify all the drama. "We'd met too many people who'd had that operation," Cannon says, "and it wasn't the end of the world." Zuiker recalls William Petersen's resolve to keep the scene as light as possible. "Billy was like, 'Catherine comes down to see me off, she says good luck, and I walk away and my smock is open, and she sees my ass.'" A vote taken in the writers' room broke down strictly along gender lines, with its seven men in favor of it and its three women opposed. To hedge the show's bets, Cannon shot the scene with and without. Ultimately, the episode aired without the image. Mendelsohn observes, "Maybe it was the safer choice, but I don't know if there was a right or wrong decision to be had there . . . beside, it gives us something to show on the DVD." ∎

TITLE	EPISODE NUMBER	PAGE
$35K O.B.O.	118	79
A LITTLE MURDER	304	208
A NIGHT AT THE MOVIES	319	271
ABRA CADAVER	305	213
ACCUSED IS ENTITLED, THE	302	201
ALTER BOYS	206	124
ANATOMY OF A LYE	221	180
AND THEN THERE WERE NONE	209	135
ANONYMOUS	108	36
BLOOD DROPS	107	31
BLOOD LUST	309	232
BOOM	113	53
BULLY FOR YOU	204	118
BURDEN OF PROOF	215	157
BURKED	201	106
CAGED	207	129
CATS IN THE CRADLE	220	177
CHAOS THEORY	202	110
CHASING THE BUS	218	169
COOL CHANGE	102	16
CRASH AND BURN	317	264
CRATE 'N BURIAL	103	19
CROSS-JURISDICTIONS	222	185
ELLIE	210	137
EVALUATION DAY	122	96
EXECUTION OF CATHERINE WILLOWS, THE	306	219
FACE LIFT	117	74
FAHRENHEIT 932	112	50
FELONIUS MONK	217	166
FIGHT NIGHT	307	224
FINGER, THE	214	152
FOREVER	321	280
FRIENDS & LOVERS	105	26
GENTLE, GENTLE	119	84

PLEASE NOTE THAT THE FIRST NUMBER OF
THE EPISODE REFLECTS THE SEASON IN WHICH IT AIRED.

TITLE	EPISODE NUMBER	PAGE
GOT MURDER?	312	241
HIGH AND LOW	310	235
HUNGER ARTIST, THE	223	188
I-15 MURDERS	111	47
IDENTITY CRISIS	213	148
INSIDE THE BOX	323	290
JUSTICE IS SERVED	121	93
LADY HEATHER'S BOX	315	252
LAST LAUGH	320	277
LET THE SELLER BEWARE	303	205
LUCKY STRIKE	316	260
ONE HIT WONDER	314	249
ORGAN GRINDER	211	142
OVERLOAD	203	113
PILOT	101	12
PLAY WITH FIRE	322	284
PLEDGING MR. JOHNSON	104	24
PRECIOUS METAL	318	268
PRIMUM NON NOCERE	216	161
RANDOM ACTS OF VIOLENCE	313	246
RECIPE FOR MURDER	311	238
REVENGE IS BEST SERVED COLD	301	196
SCUBA DOOBIE-DOO	205	121
SEX, LIES AND LARVAE	110	44
SLAVES OF LAS VEGAS	208	132
SNUFF	308	229
SOUNDS OF SILENCE	120	90
STALKER	219	174
STRIP STRANGLER, THE	123	100
TABLE STAKES	115	61
TO HALVE AND TO HOLD	114	58
TOO TOUGH TO DIE	116	68
UNFRIENDLY SKIES	109	39
WHO ARE YOU?	106	29
YOU'VE GOT MALE	212	145

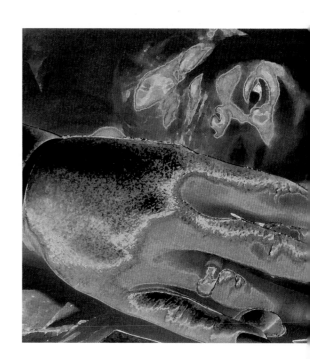

accelerant a substance used to ignite and spread a fire.

acid etching the process by which impressions in a metallic surface are restored with the use of a corrosive agent.

AFIS Automated Fingerprint Identification System; a computer database for fingerprint comparison.

ALS alternate light source; a high-intensity (usually ultraviolet) illumination capable of detecting body fluids, fingerprints, and trace materials.

amido black a stain used to enhance latent impressions and prints that have been contaminated by blood.

APB all-points bulletin.

bindle a small envelope used to contain trace evidence.

blood spatter the dispersal pattern of blood resulting from a violent trauma.

buccal swab a tissue sample rich in DNA taken from inside of the cheek.

bullet batching tracking a bullet by comparing its particular markings to other bullets manufactured in the same lot.

bunter a device that impresses the head stamp onto a cartridge case.

casting the preservation of an impression using a plaster or another malleable substance to create a durable relief of physical evidence such as bite marks or tire treads.

cast-off blood spatter from the directional motion of a weapon.

centrifuge a machine that employs a high velocity circular momentum in order to separate substances by densities.

chromatography the technique of separating and analyzing the components parts of a mixture of liquids and gases by selective adsorption based on their affinity for a stationary and mobile phase. (ie GC Mass Spec)

CODIS Combined DNA Index System; an FBI database of DNA records from convicted offenders and crime scenes. ·

Cofiler and Profiler Plus trade-names of DNA-analysis programs.

DB dead body.

DNA deoxyribonucleic acid; molecules found in every cell that are comprised of chromosomes; the typing of which is unique to every individual on earth.

electrostatic print lifter a device which deploys a static charge on a collecting film, which in turn attracts fine particles, such as dust, to visualize a latent print.

electrothermal atomizer a device which can detect the presence of various metals in paint or other substances.

epithelials skin cells.

erythema an atypical redness of the skin caused by congestion of the capillaries; inflammation.

exsanguination the draining of blood from a body.

FLIR forward-looking infra-red; an electro-thermal camera that can be used to detect the presence of living beings by sensing body heat.

fluoroscope a device that combines an X-ray machine and a fluorescent monitor to allow a view of the internal components in the body; utilized in searching for any foreign objects inside a corpse.

follicular tag the bulb containing the pulp of a hair's root sheath cells, the presence of which can signify a struggle.

FTIR Fourier Transform Infra Red; a device used to identify the range of chemical composition in trace evidence samples of such materials as paint flakes and fibers.

fuming a method of raising latent prints from a surface by exposing it to the gas of acrylic resin; cyanoacrylate (super glue).

glass sink-float test a procedure by which the density of a piece of glass is determined by immersing it in a variety of liquids and matching it to an exemplar sample.

grid search a demarcated area is divided into a checkerboard pattern and a line of searchers examine the surface on each axis looking for evidence, thus ensuring the area is covered twice and checked by two different searchers.

GSR gunshot residue

Haeckel marks stress marks at the edge of radical fractures in glass which can indicate direction of impact.

ion detector an instrument used at fire scenes that detects the presence of hydrocarbons, a chemical by-product of accelerants.

lands and grooves the raised and recessed areas that are broached or pressed inside the barrel of a firearm in a spiral pattern designed to give the bullet a spin which stabilizes it in flight.

ligature a device used to bind or tie, commonly referred to as an instrument of strangulation.

linear regression a method of determining a timeline of death based on the age of the various insect species found on a corpse.

lividity a discoloration of the skin caused by the gravitational settling of blood at the time of death.

luminol a chemiluminescent compound which generates electromagnetic radiation (light) by the release of energy from a chemical reaction. Used to detect latent bloodstains by reacting with the hemoglobin in blood, causing the stain to glow.

mapping the sketching of a precisely measured ground plan, or overhead view, of a crime scene.

marbling a stage of bodily putrefaction in which the decomposition of blood causes the skin to take on a mottled bluish hue.

micromike cylindrical instrument used to measure the diameter of blood drops.

muzzle stamp an abrasive impression inflicted on skin indicating a gun was held directly against the victim when fired.

NCIC National Crime Information Center, the FBI's database of crimes and criminals.

necropsy autopsy

ninhydrin a liquid or crystal substance that raises latent prints on paper and other porous surfaces by reacting with amino-acid residue in fingerprints.

off the board a term used by CSIs to describe a case that is not on the daily assignment list.

OIS officer-involved shooting.

one-to-ones photos taken at a crime scene utilizing a scale (a ruler) placed in the frame so that the prints can be enlarged to a full 1:1 scale for comparison purposes.

otosclerosis a condition of soft bone growth in the inner ear that obscures the oval opening, thus progressively limiting hearing.

PAL parolee-at-large.

peri-mortem around the time of, or during, death.

perivascular tissue cellular matter surrounding blood vessels.

ph a measurement of hydrogen ions in a solution; a neutral chemical solution has a pH of 7.0; a lower figure indicates increased acidity, a higher figure increased alkalinity.

phenolphthalein or Kastle-Meyer color test; a chemical agent which, when mixed with hydrogen peroxide, detects the presence of blood by eliciting a pinkish-red reaction.

pipette a narrow tube into which fluid can be drawn by suction for measurement and/or dispensing.

projectile trajectory analysis determining the path of an object through space using rods, strings or lasers.

propellant the component which rapidly burns when ignited, provides accelerating pressure, such as gunpowder.

ridge details the basic elements of a fingerprint (whorls, loops, and arches) which contribute to a unique pattern.

rigor or rigor mortis; the stiffening of a corpse, directionally from the head to the feet, starting at two to six hours after death.

SART sexual assault response team; typically nurses who collect a sexual assault evidence kit from a rap victim. The kit includes fluid samples, hair combings, fingernail scrapings, trace evidence and photodocumentation of wounds.

sodium rhodizonate chemical substance used to detect the presence of lead found in gunshot residue.

spalling the discoloration of concrete, cement, or stone caused by a high-temperature fire.

striations or stria; microscopic scratches left by a tool on an item that it comes in contact with. (ie. a bullet is marked as it passes through a gun's barrel.)

stippling or tattooing; pinpoint hemorrhaging in the skin caused by the close impact of unburned or partially burned gunpowder particles that come from the muzzle of a gun.

stringing a blood spatter analysis technique utilizing string or lasers to determine the origin of a blood droplet from the point of impact.

swab sterile cotton fibers attached to the end of a wooden stick. An essential collection tool used to absorb trace fluid or dried stains for analysis.

tape lift the retrieval of evidence by use of a sterile adhesive tape.

through-and-through a gunshot that passes through the body, creating both an entrance and exit wound.

trailing visual evidence of an arsonist's having spread an accelerant.

Tread Assistance a computer reference program which contains over 11,000 tire-tread patterns.

TRO temporary restraining order.

UVLS ultraviolet light source.

VICAP Violent Criminal Apprehension Program; a FBI database used to investigate homicides and missing persons cases.

walk-through the initial preliminary examination and evaluation of a crime scene.

Y incision the initiating cut in an autopsy that extends from both shoulders, meets at the sternum, and continues downward over the abdomen to the pelvis.